"A MAGNIFICENT
ACHIEVEMENT
IN STORYTELLING,
THIS MESMERIZING
TALE CHALLENGES
THE IMAGINATION AND
BEWITCHES THE HEART."
—*ROMANTIC TIMES*

W9-ADM-517

Dear Reader,

You are holding the book I dreamed of writing for ten years. Within its pages, you will meet Renard and Aveline, destined enemies made lovers by a twist of fate.

He is a warrior yearning for peace who is about to discover that what he had believed in all his life is a lie and that the only woman who can heal him is the one woman he is forbidden to love.

Aveline is that woman, a woman of mystery and power, the possessor of a terrible secret that can destroy her and all she holds precious. Theirs is the world of torchlight and harpsong, where the clang of steel and the whisper of treachery are ever present. A world in which love is the ultimate danger and the greatest mystery.

I hope you will join me there.

Maura Seger

"AVELINE,"
HE MURMURED, "SWEETLING,
SO BEAUTIFUL . . ."

Renard's voice was low and rough, the words only semicoherent. Passion raged through him. It had been so long, so very long, since he had known a woman and even then, he had never felt what he was feeling now.

He was alive in a way he had not hoped to be again. After so many years, so much blood and death, so much struggle and despair, magical Aveline on a summer day woke him to wholeness again.

"A tender love story, a tantalizing mystery, danger and excitement—delightful reading."
—Roberta Gellis

"Richly detailed . . . romantic and suspenseful . . . this tale of star-crossed lovers with divided loyalties unfolds at a brisk pace, leaving the reader enthralled to the very last page. An absorbing read."
—Ellen Jones, author of
The Fatal Crown

Also by Maura Seger

Beloved Enemy

Available from
HarperPaperbacks

Harper
Monogram

Tapestry

MAURA SEGER

HarperPaperbacks
A Division of HarperCollinsPublishers

HarperPaperbacks   *A Division of* HarperCollins*Publishers*
10 East 53rd Street, New York, N.Y. 10022

Copyright © 1993 by Maura Seger
All rights reserved. No part of this book may be used or reproduced in any manner whatsoever without written permission of the publisher, except in the case of brief quotations embodied in critical articles and reviews. For information address HarperCollins*Publishers,*
10 East 53rd Street, New York, N.Y. 10022.

Cover illustration by Morgan Kane

First printing: April 1993

Printed in the United States of America

HarperPaperbacks, HarperMonogram, and colophon are trademarks of HarperCollins*Publishers*

❖ 10 9 8 7 6 5 4 3 2 1

Heartfelt thanks to all the many people who offered encouragement and advice for this book. And to my husband, Michael, and my children, Katie and Matthew. You're my inspiration.

Prologue

The watchman was drunk. He stumbled against a stone trough set low in the ground and cursed. Above him a painted badger creaked on leather hinges. In the shadows of the second story a shutter opened.

"Git on, ye lazy scum." A shower of rank liquid rained down inches in front of him. He jumped back as the lantern attached to his pole swung wildly.

Clutching the pole with both hands, he turned once, twice, first on one foot, then the other in a limbs-akimbo jig that failed to locate his bearings. Sober, he could walk the street in darkness as easily as in full daylight. Drunk on sour ale and mash, he couldn't quite remember who he was or what he was supposed to be doing.

Up ahead, two streets converged. In the center where they crossed was an old stone well, the gathering place for uncounted generations of women. Some said the well had been dug in the days of the Romans back when the place was called Londinium. Others said it was older even than that, its stones having been laid in the shadow time when the great monument builders ruled.

Their flocks of sacred white cows were believed to have drunk from the underground stream that supplied the well.

One of them seemed to be slaking its thirst now. Or so it appeared to the watchman, who straightened up abruptly, eyes fear wide, and gazed at the white shape huddled over the well. Something moved beyond it, a ripple in the veil of the moonless night, gone in an instant, as though swallowed by time. But not before steel flashed, dappling the lantern light bloodred.

"Jesu Marie, save me. . . ." Tangled in the wide skirt of his rough spun tunic, one sleeve caught on the lantern stem, the watchman babbled half-remembered prayers. The sodden contentedness of the alcohol turned abruptly to sour sobriety. His stomach heaved. He bent double, shoulders hunched, and vomited against the nearest wall.

When he was done, he straightened up again and peered warily at the shape. It had not moved. A dry breeze rippled down the narrow street. Riding on it, above the smells of the river and surrounding buildings, came the iron tang of carnage. Or sacrifice. The difference was often obscure.

The lantern bobbed. Its dancing light cast a widening circle as the watchman approached. He stopped when his foot slipped. Glancing down, he saw the thick, spreading stain darkening the ground.

His scream punctured dreams. A flock of blackbirds rousted from their roost in the drooping eaves rose frantically into the sky. The beat of their wings was as the murmur of many voices in a great, empty place—whispering of vengeance and eternity.

1

Fourteenth Day in the Month of April,
Anno Domino 1077
City of London

A crack in the darkness, the opening of a door, and a line of supplicants filed out of the low, stone building that is Thorney cloister. Shrouded in cloaks of fine black wool, they wound like a mourning ribbon through the dying night, past the bramble bushes and low-hanging apple trees to the nearby abbey of the Westminister.

The abbey rises like a great shadowed mountain set at the center of this island, where the river divides. It dominates the surrounding city, reminding all of the absolute supremacy of God and the constant nearness of His eternity.

Not that the supplicants needed any such reminder. They walked with their heads bent, hands clasped reverently in prayer. Their steps were measured but not slow, God's business not permitting of delay. The soft scuffing of their wooden pattens and the rustling of their cloaks should be the only sounds.

And would be were this a tale told by a poet for the diversion of his noble audience. But it is not, it is my tale, and I will tell it truthfully. The supplicants heard the blackbirds shriek. A few more daring than the rest looked up in time to see the frantic birds wheeling like so many stricken spirits against the sky.

I know because I was there.

I am Aveline of Canterbury. Not that my name will mean anything to you, whoever you may be. I see my own words, black against the dun-hued vellum (I cannot afford white) and I wonder how I have the audacity to do this thing. Books are for God and of God. Father Andrew, who hears our confession at St. Margaret's, would say I am guilty of the sin of pride.

But truly it is not that; at least, I pray it is not. Last sennight, I began my twentieth year. By rights I should be married with a profusion of children gathered at my skirts, or sworn to holy vows, or dead. I am none of those things.

Yet I am for the most part oddly content, ten times oddly when you know the truth of me and how at odds with truth that contentedness must be.

Since my early youth, I have been privileged to live in a great abbey—as great as Westminster will ever be— ruled over by a woman of strength and spirit. In this place, I learned to read. Say equally that I learned to live, for to me the two are the same.

Later, when I showed myself to have some talent for it, I was also trained in letters. I might have become a copier of books except that St. Margaret's is renowned for its needlework and it was to that I was drawn. But for some tasks linen and wool are not enough.

I digress; it is a habit of mine. To return to the matter at hand, it is spring in the year of our Lord 1077, although most of us alive at this time will tell you that God seems very little present, at least in England. Eleven years after the Normans came raging over the water, our poor land still bleeds with the sorrow of our defeat.

And yet the sun still rises in glory each morning. The seasons still turn, children are born, there is laughter and even happiness, however fragile. I want to understand how this can be. How can joy so stubbornly persist in a world that seems ruled by sorrow? I have asked God about it.

"Work it out for yourself, Aveline," He said.

God never speaks this way in Holy Writ but that is how He sounds to me. Which is how I justify this book. I can give it little except truth, but that seems to be what God cares about most.

On that still, gray morning of murmured prayers and fluttering blackbirds, I cared most about keeping my place in line and not disgracing Mother Eldgythe, she who is reverend abbess of St. Margaret's, Canterbury, that is home to me.

I walked directly behind her in the line of suppliants. From my position, I could not help but notice that her hem was frayed and her pattens needed to be replaced, so worn were they at the heels.

Irrelevant—and irreverent—details have always been my undoing. I can never seem to escape them. Mother Eldgythe says that is part of being an artist, but Mother Eldgythe loves me.

I knelt beside her during the service, which was mercifully brief, and followed her to the altar for communion. Father Percy, who said the Mass, is an old, tired priest whose few remaining duties are no more than a sinecure. He performs them by rote, uninspired by any god and oblivious to the rest of us. Which, all things considered, may be just as well.

It came my turn to receive the Host. I opened my mouth and closed my eyes, the better not to notice the dirt on Father Percy's fingers.

The bread was a dry lump adhering to my tongue as though it had grown there. I could not swallow for my life. Father Percy moved on down the line of supplicants. Around me heads were once again bent in prayer, hands reverently clasped, blessedly oblivious to my trouble.

The muscles of my throat convulsed, the bread slid down, and my stomach received it with a surge of relief. Saved—for the moment. And only just in time. The Mass was over, the others were rising, heads still bent, eyes downcast, to file out of the small chapel.

"That's done, then," Mother Eldgythe said as we left the chapel. Already night was fleeing. In the soft gray light, I could see her work-worn hands in the moment before she folded them within the long sleeves of her gown.

She regarded me briskly. "You'll eat a proper breakfast, I hope. If you get much thinner, a good breeze'll blow you away."

So now you know that I am thin. Know also that my hair is red, the legacy, Mother Eldgythe said, of my mother, although on her I suspect it managed to look beautiful.

In my dreams, I remember my mother vividly, but in the stark light of day, long-dead Edythe is little more than a phantom dancing behind the blue veil of my eyes. They are mine from my father, though no one has ever said so.

No one ever speaks of him, not even Mother Eldgythe, who dares a great deal.

"I do eat," I said, taking shelter in the literal truth. It would hardly do to admit that lately I have been denying myself small things as penance for the fecklessness of my nature.

Mother Eldgythe muttered under her breath and turned down the gravel path connecting the small chapel to the abbey proper. I followed. Little puffs of dust rose beneath my feet. In this season of drought, the ground of England, so bloodied and coveted, is blowing away day by day.

"'Tis no wonder," Mother Eldgythe said when we were seated before trenchers of stale bread moistened with a few spoonfuls of yesterday's stew. Under her breath, the abbess added, "We all know who's to blame."

On either side of us, milk-faced sisters of Thorney Abbey pretended not to hear. They are well accustomed to Mother Eldgythe, since we visit frequently. There are things she can say by virtue of her particular status, which others are wise not even to hear, much less comment upon.

A novice came around with a large tun of porridge. I accepted a portion and went so far as to add a dollop of honey to make it palatable. I excused the indulgence by reminding myself what we had shortly to face.

From the head of the table, a stout woman robed in ebony silk called to us. "You are to see the bishop, I hear."

Mother Eldgythe stiffened. She glanced toward the abbess of what had been her own mother house, and frowned. "Information travels swiftly, sister. Or is it merely that there are so many idle ears to receive it?"

Mother Ursuline drew back, affronted. She was a Norman lady of good family, as she never failed to remind us. The call to serve God in England was her cross to bear.

That it had also made her richer and more influential than she could otherwise have hoped to be was never mentioned, at least not by those wishing to keep her favor.

Mother Eldgythe felt no such restraint. I leaned nearer and reminded her, "Wulfgarth will be waiting."

She relented with obvious reluctance. We completed our breakfast in silence. Outside, in the shade of the columns beyond the hall, she said, "The Lord must truly enjoy fools, he suffers so many of them to live."

"She is always good to us," I said, trying to be fair. "Her hospitality is always there for the asking."

Mother Eldgythe smoothed the snug black cowl about her head and looked at me in mock reproach. "Surely you aren't suggesting that Normans are ignorant of courtesy's very rudiments?" More softly, she added, "I was a girl in this house. This is where I took my vows. To turn me away would be unthinkable."

But undoubtedly tempting, I thought as we left the sheltered courtyard and moved through the narrow, dark passage that ended in a small plank door. On the other side of it was the street and along that the guest house for male visitors to the abbey.

Wulfgarth had already breakfasted. He stepped around a fat pink hog snuffling for scraps and greeted us. "Good morrow to you, Lady Eldgythe, Mistress Aveline. I trust ye're well?"

"Passingly," the abbess said. She eyed the burly giant with stern affection. Wulfgarth had been born with Mars in the constellation of Taurus. That might account for his appearance, at least in part, and for the savagery of his temper when aroused.

Life had left him scarred in many ways; not the least was the loss of one eye. Yet he saw more from the remaining one that many whole folk and we knew him as a wise friend.

Smiling, Eldgythe added, "Aveline has been counseling me to behave myself." She ignored my protest and continued. "I do the same for you. Let us finish this business as quickly and easily as we can."

"*If* we can," Wulfgarth muttered. He fingered the hilt of the knife strapped across his chest and smiled. "Odo always gave out that he liked a tussle. Mayhap I could oblige him."

"There'll be none of that," I said. "We'll hear him and be on our way. This isn't the time or place to provoke an argument."

Beside me, in the shadow of my young conviction, the older two glanced at one another. I had the uneasy sense that something passed between them, just beyond the reach of my understanding. Best then to ignore it. The bright day beckoned, undimmed even by our unsavory chore.

No, that is not true. The day was bright enough but like the blackbirds' flutterings, intimations of violence haunted me. I did not know whether to fear or welcome them. Although, please God, I would constrain such thoughts for the length of time it took to meet with Odo, Bishop of Bayeux, and possibly the most dangerous man in England.

The stone of the bishop's keep is freshly hewn, still scarred by the white flecks of the masons' hammers. Set on a low rise near where the river turns, it commands a view of flatlands and marsh grass. Ducks wade among the reeds. Pigs amble nearby, snorting and snuffling over their finds.

A wide road runs past the keep and another cuts away to the north. If London ever grows sufficiently, Odo will have neighbors. For the moment he lives in princely isolation.

Some speak admiringly of Odo's keep, but then

some will do anything to curry favor. I think it ugly, as all such places are. They lack the grace of the vast timber halls my people built. And so plain, with no ornament to relieve the endless stretches of dull, cold stone.

In the great halls where the bards sang, the walls were painted with coiling serpentine designs, reminders of the hidden world beyond human knowledge in which there is no beginning and no end. When the oak-scented smoke curled to the sky and the walls rang with the laughter of fellowship, the designs came alive, turning and revolving upon themselves as they knit together the seen and unseen, the real and the unreal in the immutable bonds of eternity.

All lost and for what? Cold stone walls and cold stone people. I have not cried since my childhood, but such thoughts can tempt me to it. Rather than give in, I lifted my skirts and stepped swiftly from the carrack that had brought us.

Many were coming and going around us, their presence testifying to the importance in which Odo is held. His kinship to the Conqueror places him close to the center of power. His own ambition keeps him there.

A Norman brushed past us, a tall, black-haired man, heavily muscled with the look of a warrior. I met his eyes for a moment and saw—what? I have no name for it, only that I was suddenly more aware of myself than I want to be.

Wulfgarth's hand went to his sword. For a moment I feared the worst, but the Norman appeared distracted and passed on. We climbed the steps to the keep, where a steward met us. He looked nervously at Wulfgarth, inclined his head fractionally to Mother Eldgythe, and ignored me.

We were directed to one side of the hall, where a crowd of hangers-on and suppliants awaited the bishop's notice. Wulfgarth cleared a bench for us by the simple expedient of telling the men occupying it to move. The Normans grumbled, but not too loudly. There is a keen, howling edge to Wulfgarth, a sense of a man whose loyalties lie in the shadow world of the dead.

Mother Eldgythe and I sat down to wait. I kept my eyes lowered, striving for the appearance of calm. The minutes dragged by. I tried to follow Mother Eldgythe's example and engage in silent prayer, but that proved elusive. Finally I drew a folded fragment of linen from my pouch and settled down to work despite the poor light.

Beneath my needle, held taut by a small wooden frame, an eagle soared on currents of gold and azure. The piece is meant as an inset for an altar cloth. The Bastard's wife, gentle-spoken Matilda, personally commissioned it. Such notice is an honor many envy. It is one I could do without, particularly since it seems to have led me directly here to Odo's keep.

Time passed. The intricacy of my work kept my attention diverted. Not so my companions. Wulfgarth stirred restively as his scowl deepened. Mother Eldgythe remained impervious, hands folded, features composed, until without warning she stood up and gathered her robes around her.

"We have waited long enough," she told the steward. "Tell the bishop we will see him at another time."

A startled murmur ran through the hall. Mother Eldgythe ignored it. She swept toward the door with Wulfgarth and me following hurriedly.

The steward lurched in our trail, barely managing to impose himself between us and the rectangle of light that was the door. "You cannot leave. The bishop summoned you."

"For an hour and more ago," Mother Eldgythe said. "He has obviously forgotten and we obviously cannot wait here all day. Stand aside."

So unprepared was he for such defiance that he almost obeyed her. Only an instinct for self-preservation stopped him.

"Don't let them leave," he told a startled guard, and dashed off.

The stream of people coming and going centered on a curtained-off portion at the far end of the hall. Shapes moved behind the dark red partition, illuminated by grudging sheaves of light slipping through windows that were little more than clefts cut in the stone.

The steward reappeared from behind the partition and motioned to us.

Odo sat in state on a high-backed chair that resembled but just missed being a throne. He is a tall, fleshy man customarily robed in scarlet. The weight of his body has settled around his hips, giving him an almost feminine look. The face, too, is soft, except for the small, flashing eyes perched above a sharply tapered nose. His hands are unexpectedly slender, the fingers slim and pale as a girl's. One tapped rhythmically on the table before him.

He made no effort to rise as we entered, despite the reverence and courtesy due the abbess of St. Margaret's. Nor did Mother Eldgythe make any effort to acknowledge his authority. They stood, eyeing each other, as around them uneasy silence grew.

Abruptly Odo cleared his throat. "If you are as skilled as you are ill mannered, we have something to discuss. Otherwise you may as well leave now. Be warned I will have only the best."

"Undoubtedly there are many others who would suit you well beyond our poor capacity," Mother Eldgythe said. She turned to go.

"Enough," Odo exclaimed. "I had heard that you were the most arrogant woman in England. God only knows how you have survived this long, but you have and I must deal with that." Grudgingly he said, "Our beloved queen speaks highly of you."

Mother Eldgythe said nothing. If the favor of the Conqueror's wife meant anything to her, it was not evident.

"I have a commission in mind," Odo said as though that was not already evident. When there was still no response, he turned his attention to me.

"Who is this?"

"My ward."

"Does she have a name?" Odo said, letting his exasperation show. "Or a tongue?"

That was enough. No care or caution could persuade me to keep silent any longer. I straightened my head and let him glimpse what lay within my soul.

"My name is Aveline. If it is altar cloths you want, we can make them for you, but there will be a long wait. We have promised many others already."

"Is it you who decides such things?" Odo asked.

"Aveline's gift is great," Mother Eldgythe interposed. "It is only right that she have a say in what is done."

Her praise was greatly overdone. My talent is meager. What gift I have is for persistence. That trait was commonplace in my family. It was the foundation upon which our fortunes were built, and upon which they fell in ruins.

Odo looked disposed to argue further, but thought better of it. Instead he said, "It isn't altar cloths I want. This is something else, something far more important." He frowned at the others crowded into the small chamber and beckoned the steward. "We will discuss it privately."

When we were alone, Odo pressed his fingers together and looked at us over them, waiting until he judged the time was right.

Finally he said, "I wish to commission a memorial honoring our king. It is to be a very special work commemorating the great events that restored this land to its rightful ruler. I have chosen St. Margaret's to create it because the medium of needlework is well suited to what I envision. The work must be detailed, exact, easily understood, and—this is key—portable. I want something that can be moved around without difficulty and set up to be viewed by large crowds of people. Do you understand?"

"Too well, my lord," Mother Eldgythe said. She had paled and her mouth was narrowed to a thin, white line. "St. Margaret's is not worthy of the honor. We are, after all, an English abbey."

"I am fully aware of that," the bishop said. "You will do the work because you are the most skilled needlewomen I can find and I will have nothing other than the best. And should you consider giving less than that, I remind you that St. Margaret's has enjoyed unusual favor, which can be removed at any moment. Do I make myself clear?"

"Perfectly," I said, for I did not trust Mother Eldgythe to speak again. From the corner of my eye, I saw Wulfgarth stir.

Odo saw him, too. "Hold, savage," he said, "or the women die."

"Truly," Mother Eldgythe murmured, "you are William's brother."

"And proud of it, madam. My hall teems with those sensible enough to seek my favor. Think of that, then come back on the morrow. We will discuss my requirements further."

"We had not planned to stay on in London," I said.

"Change your plans," Odo replied, and turned away, dismissing us.

Later, in the boat going downriver, I sat in icy fury, struggling to control myself as I have rarely had to struggle before. Beside me, Mother Eldgythe looked worn and tired. Wulfgarth's face was blank, but behind it thunder gathered.

"He cannot dare," I said, protesting like a child who rails against the inevitable. "No Norman, no matter how arrogant, could think that we would—"

"He is William's brother," Mother Eldgythe replied, "and he aspires to more. He will do anything he likes."

"We should have told him no and been done with it," Wulfgarth said.

"You heard him," I replied, "St. Margaret's has enjoyed unusual favor, but that doesn't have to last."

"He does not have the authority—" Wulfgarth began.

"Perhaps not," Mother Eldgythe said, "but he does have the power, and that is worse."

She was right, of course. With William gone so much from England and his heirs in disarray, more and more power rested in Odo's pudgy hands. He did not hesitate to use it.

Somehow I must keep faith with God and with myself without bringing Odo's wrath down on those I love. There must be a way and I must find it, although just now as I sit in the fading light I have no idea where even to look.

God give me the strength to do this thing and also to find mercy in my heart, for I have been reminded yet again that it is sorely lacking. I know now what shocked the blackbirds into flight. A Norman merchant is dead, killed not far from where we prayed this morning.

Upon hearing the news, my first thought was to hope that the killer escaped. I still hope so, but I am trying not to.

And so, ink-stained, to bed.

2

Earlier the same day and not very far away . . .

A hand shook Renard's shoulder. Without opening his eyes, he made to brush it off.

"Sir." The voice was unrelenting. "You are needed."

Renard groaned. He lay on his stomach, his head buried in a plump feather pillow, his long, lean body uncovered except for a sheet of finely woven linen. The bed itself was substantial, carved of oak and set on a low dais. Its hangings were pulled back to admit the grudging breath of air from the river.

The room around it spoke of privilege and power. Neither, however, encouraged a good night's sleep.

"What's wrong?" Renard demanded, still without opening his eyes. He refused to do that until he was convinced sleep was truly lost.

It was his own fault, of course. He had sat up too late with the Venetian traders drinking their fine muscadine, the rare wine they made by aging not in wooden casks but in clay amphorae, as the ancients had done.

It was said that until the Venetians recovered the process, no such wine had been tasted in more than a thousand years. Considering the throbbing in his head, he wasn't certain that was to be regretted.

"There's been a killing," the young clerk said. He stood back from the bed and held out a tunic of finely bleached wool. Doing so, Burgess averted his eyes from the nakedness of his master, who, ignoring such sensibilities, tossed back the sheet.

He was a large, solidly built man with the heavy muscles of one trained for the twin goals of brute stamina and the lightning strike. In his midtwenties, he bore scars an older man would have envied, testifying as they did to the courage and eventfulness of his life.

His mother had named him for the fox to which he bore no resemblance at all. The ancients far to the north, who understood such things, would have said his spirit animal was the wolf, and not without cause.

His hair was thick, black, and unruly; his eyes gray, deep set, and unabashedly intelligent. A night's growth of beard obscured his jaw. He scratched it absently as the young monk continued.

"A watchman found the body. He set off a hue and cry in the neighborhood, with the result that the guard had to be sent in. The worst of the clamor is over, but I thought you'd want to see what happened for yourself."

Renard squinted at him discouragingly. "You did, did you? And why would I want to do that? One dead body is much as another. It's not as though we had a lack of them."

Burgess shrugged. Strands of flaxen hair framed his stolid features. Pale Saxon eyes revealed nothing. "This one is Norman."

Renard sighed. The last hovering thought of sleep

flew out the window and sailed away down the murky river. "Bloody hell."

He went first to the barber's. The body had been laid out on a wooden slab in the back room. Lamps were lit against the darkness. They smelled of rank oil.

The barber and his assistant hovered nearby. They would drink for a week on the details of this visit—what manner of man d'Agounville seemed, how he spoke and dressed, what he said and did.

He was but newly appointed high sheriff in London, yet his reputation had preceded him. He was said to have fought a day and a night at Hastings (although all admitted the battle there had lasted a bare six hours) and to have personally saved the Conqueror's life a dozen times; to have laid scourge single-handedly to villages from the white cliffs to the Weald, so that not a man or beast was left alive in any of them; to have killed a hundred men of York with his bare hands and then drunk their blood.

Even more startling were the rumors that he could read, but few were credulous enough to believe that.

Renard ignored his audience and stared at the corpse. He flexed his broad shoulders surreptitiously as he repressed a yawn. The dead imposed such restraint, whoever they might be.

"What do you make of it?" he asked.

Burgess scanned the body dispassionately. "As you said, one more dead man."

"But Norman." Renard looked closer. The man's lineage was unmistakable. His head, turned to the side, showed the shaven back of the scalp that in the past had been almost the clan mark of the Conqueror and his warriors. The true brotherhood, those who had been there from the beginning, were abandoning the fashion as the latecomers made it their own. The rest of the hair was cut short as though a bowl had been placed on top of it. A fringe obscured the forehead. With the eyes closed, the face was shuttered and ungiving, in no way remarkable. The throat was, if only for the large jagged cut that severed it.

"His windpipe was cut," Burgess offered helpfully. "He wouldn't have been able to cry out."

"How long would you think it took him to die?" Renard asked. Burgess had studied healing at one time and still took an interest in the various means used to dispatch human beings into eternity.

The young clerk considered. "That depends on several factors—whether he was a fast bleeder or slow, whether he moved or remained still, whether he was struck anywhere else."

"There don't appear to be any other injuries."

"A moment or two, I would think, if he bled fairly quickly. Not long."

"Long enough for him," Renard murmured. He looked at the man again. He was about forty, sturdily built and well dressed if one discounted the large bloodstain across the front of his tunic. His hands were large, the nails blunt but clean, the palms and fingertips uncallused.

"A merchant," Renard said. "One anxious to proclaim his Normanness."

"Why not?" Burgess asked. "Isn't being Norman the surest path to prosperity, if not actual divinity?"

Renard made a rude sound and walked away. He stood with his back to the room, looking out over the tiny courtyard heaped with the assorted wastes of people and animals.

"Where did it happen?" he asked.

"Near the One-Eyed Badger in Cheapside," Burgess provided. With a hint of relish, he added, "He was draped over the well. It's a Norman street. His neighbors may not be so anxious to draw water for a few days."

Renard turned. He regarded his young clerk tolerantly. "Whereas had he been a Saxon, they would rush to drink whatever was left of his blood?"

Burgess looked discomfited. "I didn't say that . . . exactly."

"I can't think how you restrained yourself," Renard said testily. He was tired and out of sorts. There were times when it seemed as though he'd spent most of life looking at dead bodies, and being responsible for them one way or another.

The younger man flushed. "Am I really that tiresome?"

"Sometimes."

"I'm—sorry. Actually you've been very good to me."

Renard made a low sound of dismay. "Jesu save us, don't turn soft now. If I didn't have you to goad me, I don't know how I'd manage." Briskly he added, "Let's see the place."

In the predawn light, the street was silent and motionless. Nothing stirred save for a lone mongrel dog making its way around a corner. It ignored the men standing beside the well and continued on out of sight.

Renard glanced at the thatch-roofed buildings pressing close on every side, their windows shuttered despite the hour and the early warmth. Eyes bored from behind them, observing their every move.

At the base of the well the ground looked swollen, dark, and clotted. He bent down on his haunches and touched it. Particles stuck to his fingers. He regarded them as he said, "The merchant was killed here."

"Apparently," Burgess agreed, "since no trace of blood extends beyond this area."

"That doesn't strike you as odd?"

"You mean because no one admits to having heard or seen it happen? But they wouldn't anyway."

"Not that," Renard said. "The watchman found him—when?"

"In the hour after matins."

Renard glanced up at the sky. The sun was near to rising. He judged four hours had passed since the discovery. "Had he passed near the well before then?"

Burgess hesitated. "Normally he would have, but I gather he was indisposed last night."

Renard straightened up and looked at him narrowly. "What do you mean, indisposed?"

"Drunk."

Thick black brows rose. "Was that usual for him?"

"It couldn't have been," Burgess said with some asperity, "or he would hardly have held on to his job, would he?"

"A watch post isn't the kind of thing a man would throw away carelessly," Renard mused. He did not add, though the thought was clearly there, that a Saxon would be particularly foolish to do so. Good positions were few and far between for the vanquished race.

"I gather he found the drink when he came on post," Burgess said reluctantly. "He's a sound man normally, but it was more than he could resist." Softly he added, "His youngest daughter has become leman to a mill owner."

Renard grimaced. Burgess's few words spelled out a common enough reality. The watchman was Saxon, while all mills were owned these days by Normans, most of whom could well afford to keep a mistress. A father's despair was due respect even if the timing couldn't have been worse.

"All right then," Renard said, gathering his thoughts. "Up until sunset, the body would surely have been seen. Therefore he must have come here between compline and matins, or shortly afterward. In other words, after dark. He was a prosperous man, but there's no sign of any escort. For that matter, he didn't even carry a torch."

"How do you know that?" Burgess asked, interested despite himself. The realization that the man had come alone—except for his murderer—at a time when the bravest shunned London's streets cast a new light on the matter.

"There were no traces of soot or pitch on his hands," Renard said.

"He could have carried a lamp," Burgess pointed out. "Or the killer might have had a light and taken it away with him."

Renard nodded. "Possibly, but why come here at that hour? Why not meet indoors?"

"There must have been a reason. Is it really so important?"

"I don't know," Renard admitted. "But it might give us a better chance of catching whoever did this."

Burgess looked at him chidingly. "How many murders were there in London last year—two hundred, three? And how many of the killers were caught? Not more than a handful, to be sure. Norman or not, the odds are heavy that this fellow will go to his grave unavenged."

"It's not vengeance I seek," Renard said softly. He passed a hand over his face, feeling the weathered skin stretched taut over strong bones. He still had a warrior's body, though it was several years since he'd taken up the sword on King William's behalf.

These days the only war he waged was against the sordidness he saw all around him. It was an odd occupation for one who had killed and ravaged with the best of them, but it seemed to suit him.

A high, sweet sound pierced the stillness. Above the thatched roofs of the surrounding houses, floating against the lighting sky, a bell rang out. First one and then another and another. Until from Barking Abbey in the east to the nearby abbey of the Westminster came the call to morning prayer.

"Lauds," Burgess said unnecessarily. "The bishop expects you in two hours. Before then, you are supposed to break fast with the tanners who sent you that petition. And you have letters to dictate."

"My conscience," Renard grumbled. His instinct was to linger by the well, or better yet to go into the low, shuttered buildings and question the residents until someone yielded up some nugget of information. But he knew that Burgess was right, the chances of solving this particular killing among all the others were infinitesimal. His attention would be better spent elsewhere.

Still, his gaze drifted over the old well and the dark stain being rapidly absorbed into the dry earth. Only reluctantly did he turn away.

The solitude of Odo's keep added to the sense of its unsteadiness. It and its master both gave the impression of having been imposed on ground neither ready nor willing to receive them. By comparison, William's tower a mile downriver seemed solidly rooted, an immutable part of its surroundings, for all that it had stood a scant decade.

Perhaps it was merely the difference between the brothers, Renard thought as he left the shallow carrack that had brought him upriver and climbed the steep steps to the center hall. Half brothers, more correctly. William and Odo shared a mother, the ever-resourceful Herleva, who had risen from tanner's daughter to mistress of a duke and, after his death, wife to an ambitious Norman willing to help her bastard son claim his patrimony.

William had succeeded because God favored his cause. Every right-thinking man knew that. Still, it hadn't hurt that his character was as strong as the great stones that made up his tower.

If William was rock, Odo was water. Quick, glib, bright, shaping itself to its surroundings. And able, given sufficient time, to steathily reshape them to its own needs.

Renard sighed. The breakfast of mutton and ale that he had shared with the tanners—shades again of Herleva— sat poorly on his stomach. He was tired and finding it difficult to muster patience. Worse yet, the killing itched at him. He had a sense of having missed something important, but he had no idea what that could be.

He paused just within the entrance to the keep, allowing his eyes to adjust to the relative dimness. A low ceiling supported by thick pillars cast long shadows across the deep space. It reminded Renard of a cave he had seen near Ponthieu. The place had been filled with bats and smelled of their excrement. He refused to draw the obvious parallels.

From his thronelike chair, Odo greeted him. "D'Agounville, at last. You're late."

The man who had been interrupted, a merchant come to solicite Odo's help on some matter, cast Renard a glance in which fear and pleasure mingled equally. Fear that the bishop had been roused to ire, pleasure that the merchant himself was not the target of it.

Renard felt only a continuation of the irritation that had plagued him since his too-early wakening.

He gestured at the hourglass set in the center of the table. "Some say you count every grain. Is it true?"

The bishop's laugh was shallow. He rocked back and forth in the great chair, wheezing softly, as he expended his ration of good humor. "I had forgotten why I liked you."

Renard smiled coldly. He was not misled by Odo's joviality. The man was pleasant to him for one reason only. Eleven years before, on the blood-soaked battlefield at Hastings, a fifteen-year-old boy had deflected an ax blow meant for the man fate had designated Conqueror.

William had been suitably grateful. More to the point, the occasion had led him to discover that Renard could reason as well as fight. Such men were useful.

The same could not necessarily be said for ambitious half brothers.

"You wanted to see me," Renard reminded him.

"Yes, of course." Odo waved a hand. The merchant vanished along with two attendant scribes, a servant, and several others of unknown purpose.

The bishop pressed his palms on the sides of his chair and stood. The scarlet silk of his canonical robes fluttered about him. He smelled of cinnamon, to which rumor said he was addicted.

"The day beckons," he said, smiling at the childishness of the notion. "More to the point, I would like to escape these fools for some small measure."

The flattery was implicit—and pointed. But then Renard had never considered himself a fool and needed no such confirmation that he was not. He took the comment for what it was and did not reply.

They walked beside the river. The tide was low. Bits of flotsam were scattered along the shingled bank. The air smelled of the slick green slime that lapped the shore as soon as the days grew hot. Renard noted in passing that the level of the water was low. There had been no rain in several weeks.

Odo moved slowly, his shoulders hunched in the attitude of a far older man. He was in his early forties so far as Renard knew, yet he might have been an ancient graybeard for the way he held himself. Was he ill?

The idea was tempting but unlikely. Odo had the constitution of a horse. It was more plausible that he thought the suggestion of weakness would be disarming. Renard's guard, already high, rose yet further.

"I have a favor to ask," the bishop murmured. He coughed into his hand, making a show of it so that boatmen passing on the river raised their heads to look at him.

In his scarlet garb, he was unmistakable. That night in the taverns of Southwark and elsewhere, the word would spread—Odo is dying. People would muse over it, Normans trying not to look too pleased, English hoisting a mug.

Lies, all of it, Renard thought. Cynicism curled around the edges of his soul, making him think of how steathily paper burned in the moments before it exploded in conflagration.

Damn Burgess. He wished he'd never let the young Saxon monk teach him to read. How much better off he'd been when that dream had been safely elusive. Once made real, it had assumed nightmare proportions. He was forced—will he, nill he—to think.

"What would that be?" he asked. He stood, hands clasped behind his back, looking out over the river. The linen of his tunic brushed his bare knees. He had left off chausses because of the heat and wore only sandals held by crossed thongs reaching up his calves.

Nothing signified his rank except the band of fine embroidery around the tunic's collar and hem. That and the chased gold hilt of the sword strapped around his narrow waist. The black hair that had gone uncut for several months was brushed back from his high forehead. Rarely had he looked less like a Norman—or felt more keenly the weight of that heritage.

On the opposite bank, houses clustered close to the water's edge. He saw a woman bent over the hoe in her garden, a man pausing to test the edge of his ax, a child carrying a basket almost as large as itself.

The fragments of ordinary life heightened his own sense of isolation, driving him further into himself. Whatever Odo wanted, he was tempted to refuse it and the consequences be damned.

"Someone is stealing from me," the bishop said. He sounded genuinely aggrieved, as though such ordinary circumstances shocked him.

Renard smiled. "This is London. Everyone steals."

Odo drew himself up. The small, dark eyes—so incongruously like his brother's—looked shocked. "Not from me."

"You haven't been here very much," Renard pointed out reasonably. "Most of your time is spent in Normandy. Are people so different there now?"

"They are—respectful."

Renard laughed. He was beginning to be glad after all that he had come. Relief was found in the most unexpected quarters. "Not here," he said. "Disrespect is a point of honor among the English." More soberly he added, "It is the only rebellion left them."

"Then they have been left too much." The bishop spoke with the cold edge of certainty. When it came to matters of how much power the English should have, there was no room for argument. The only acceptable answer was none.

Renard's silence spoke for him. Odo frowned. "Surely you agree?"

Did he? Renard was sure of very little these days, but one thing he knew with certainty, nothing was as simple as it had been when he was fifteen years old and tremulously glad to be overlooked by death.

"I agree," he said in measured tones, "that William is king. He rules here. It is only right that the English obey him. For the most part they do. The rest . . . we deal with."

"I am surprised," Odo said, sounding for all the world as though he was truly that. "I thought you were made of sterner stuff."

"Why?" Renard asked, knowing the question was perverse, he would not like the answer, but asking anyway because the too-bright day seemed to demand it. The sky was a steel helmet reflecting the glare of the sere earth. Not a cloud could be seen from one horizon to another. Beneath such unrelenting clarity, nothing could be hidden or denied.

"You fought," Odo said. "At Hastings and again at York. You killed with the best of them. But now you have become a—" He paused, his lip curling. "A clerk."

Had he said that Renard's manhood had been removed from him, the slur could not have been more cutting. But the response it drew fell short of the mark.

"Do not," Renard said gently, "believe that the battle is any less for all that it is waged without visible weapons. Never in my life have I confronted such foes.

Incompetence is the least of them. Corruption, venality, and the apparent desire of every human being to injure every other are what I confront daily."

For good measure he added, "As a churchman, you must know all that."

Lost in this maze of unpalatable truth, Odo responded as best he could. "You sound like a churchman yourself. I would never have thought you had such concerns." Recovering somewhat, he tried again. "Perhaps it is that handsome Saxon monk you keep so close who has influenced you."

Deep within Renard, beneath the cold, ash-strewn fires of the man he had been, anger stirred, but briefly. In his youth, such an aspersion would have brought the ring of steel. Now he felt only hollow amusement.

"Burgess flagellates himself," he said. "He thinks it cools desire and enables him to look upon all women as a brother would."

"Does it?" Odo inquired. He knew those who had tried the technique, though he had never been tempted to it himself.

Renard shook his head. "I doubt it."

"But you don't know."

"My back is unscarred, if that is what you mean."

"Dear boy, I would never dream of asking. Your preferences are your own. My concerns are far more mundane. If we might return to the question of theft . . ."

Two sides of beef, seven shanks of ham, a cask of Rhenish wine, three bushels of flour, a good wool cloak and two less fine, four blankets of plain spun, fifty count of arrows with two short bows, and lastly a dagger of Turkish manufacture with an inlaid silver blade.

The bishop's list was substantial and precise. All the thefts had occurred within the last fortnight. No member of the household admitted knowledge of them. Nonetheless the bishop had his own explanation.

"It's the English, of course. I should never have let them be hired. One tries to be charitable, to help those less fortunate, but how often such impulses turn upon us."

"Most of your household is Norman, is it not?" Renard asked.

"Of course, but there is no reason to think that any of them are responsible. All are well paid and delighted with their positions."

Delighted, certainly, to be working for a wealthy, powerful prelate who visited rarely but would want only the best on display all the same. How much of that best worked its way through the wily hands of well-placed servants?

"I'll find out whatever I can," Renard said. He was resigned to having at least to make an effort, that on top of everything else demanding his attention. There were times when he wondered if William had truly meant to reward him with his present position.

"On another matter," Odo began.

Renard steeled himself. He had thought all along that the bishop's reason for summoning him was suspect. Odo had some other purpose in mind, doubtlessly far less ordinary.

"Have you seen Rufus recently?" the bishop asked.

"No."

Moments passed before Odo accepted that further comment would not be forthcoming, at least not without more effort on his part. "We spoke yesterday. Such an . . . energetic young man, so unlike his brother."

"Which one?" Renard asked. "Do you mean Curthose, who seeks to take Normandy while his father still lives, or Henry, who might as well still be in swaddling clothes, or perhaps Richard, so conveniently dead these past two years. It is an energetic family, for scheming at least."

He stopped, knowing he had said more than he'd intended, but unable to regret it.

Odo looked pleased. "So refreshing to encounter someone who speaks his mind. For myself, I hold my royal brother's welfare above all else."

That blatant falsehood did not merit a reply. Renard waited until the bishop felt compelled to add, "It has always been so since we were boys together. I would cut off my right arm"—he held the limb out as though in offering—"before I would see William suffer the least inconvenience."

"His eldest son is in outright rebellion against him in Normandy, the best of his seed is dead, and Rufus—when he isn't drunk or in bed with some boy—is plotting heaven knows what. You do not consider that inconvenient?"

Odo flushed. His heavy cheeks mottled as soft, rosebud lips grew taut. "Nothing I could have done would have prevented any of that. I serve my brother best by serving God."

Renard was willing to give odds that God would be hard-pressed to recognize Odo, so fleeting was their acquaintance, but he resisted the impulse to say so. Nothing could be accomplished by baiting the bishop further.

"We all serve William as best we can," Renard said quietly. "Nothing else will keep the peace. Rufus may be as energetic as he likes so long as he remembers that."

"Peace," Odo repeated, as though the word was not overly familiar to him. "I wouldn't have thought you so attached to the notion."

"It is better," Renard said succinctly, "than war."

Odo looked doubtful but undisposed to argue the point. "If you say so. At any rate, I return to Normandy shortly and I would like to know that someone here will be keeping an eye on Rufus."

Lest there be any misunderstanding, he added, "Merely to ensure that the lad doesn't inadvertently harm himself in his enthusiasm. His father has more than enough to occupy his attention at the moment and shouldn't be troubled further. However, I would appreciate being kept informed."

"I would make a poor nursemaid," Renard said flatly. "And I am a worse correspondent. You will have to find someone else."

"I don't think you quite understand what I am—"

"I understand perfectly. You want me to spy on Rufus and inform you—not the king—of his activities. That I will not do. My loyalty is to William."

"Very commendatory, but hardly realistic. A man does well to do as our Lord advised and cast his bread upon the waters that it might return to him a hundred times."

"I shall remember that," Renard said grimly, "when I break bread tonight. The bread from the king's granaries in this, the king's city, eaten by the king's high sheriff, who serves at his favor."

He had not meant to suggest it was fear of losing that favor that stopped him from helping Odo, but the bishop chose to interpret Renard's words that way. He yielded grudgingly.

They walked back together to the keep and parted there. Another of the swift little carracks was depositing its passengers on the nearby wharf. A tall, shaggy Englishman stepped onto the dock and extended his hand to a small, plump woman in the dark robes and taut white cowl of a religious.

Next to alight was a girl, straight and slim with pale skin and hair that appeared torn from the fiery heart of the sun. The look in her eyes was mutinous.

Neither of the women did more than glance at Renard, but the shaggy giant shot him an ugly look. A thick white scar ran down the left side of his face through the hollow socket where his eye should have been.

Hatred rolled off the man in great shimmering waves. He fingered the dagger at his belt, clearly relishing the thought of digging steel into Norman flesh.

Renard did not oblige him. He turned away and stepped into the carrack. Moments later he was heading downriver. The bishop was forgotten as he turned to the far more straightforward subject of murder.

3

Of all the duties attendant upon his rank, Renard decided that he disliked petition listening the most. Since he could almost never do what the petitioner asked, the exercise seemed pointless. If it achieved anything at all, it was to give him yet another glimpse into the pettiness of the human soul, something he would willingly have done without.

"And so, honored lord," a small, saturnine man intoned, "as can clearly be seen, the wrong is my neighbor's—that scum upon creation—and redress should be mine. I ask only that you give to me—"

"Enough," Renard said. He drummed his fingers on the arm of his chair and furrowed his brows over glittering gray eyes in a look that made most men hear the wings of the death raven bearing down on them. The effect was usually enough to discourage even the most stubborn petitioner.

"But, lord—"

Usually, not always.

"Enough, I said. I will consider your claim." This was

a lie; it was already clear to him that the small man was to blame for his own loss. Anyone who let his cow wander in the streets of London had to expect to end up cowless.

Burgess ushered the fellow out with an encouraging shove to the small of his back. Flecking a spot of dust from his robe, he said, "The anteroom is full. Everyone and his uncle seems to need a word with you."

Renard stifled a groan. "I'll be here all day." No matter how hard he tried, he could never become accustomed to being cooped up inside when a bright sun and a freshening breeze beckoned. That was fine for the pasty-faced clerks who served William with such energy, but it did not sit well with him.

Burgess sighed. "Just in passing, and only because I am mindful of how much I owe you, the dead Norman has a name."

Renard's spirit lifted. Perhaps there was hope for the day after all. "What?"

"Bertrand Lagounier, a merchant, as you surmised, long settled in London." Swiftly the Saxon added, "But with that crowd out there, you'll never get as far as the front door."

"All the more reason to use the back," Renard said, and sprang to his feet.

"We should take an escort," Burgess complained when they set off alone.

Renard laughed and did not slacken his pace. "Fine idea that. Announce our coming with men-at-arms clanking, banners flying, hangers-on doing whatever it is they do. Any chance we'd have to find a scrap of evidence would be well and truly gone."

"You should pay more heed to your consequence," the monk insisted. Under his breath he added, "Not to mention our comforts."

He had a pebble in his sandal, but there was no chance to stop and remove it, not with Renard unfettered, launched into the day with a smile on his lips for the first time since rising and the light of discovery in his eyes.

Not that there was much to feast them upon. Lagounier's shop was in a low, timbered building set back a little distance from the road about three minutes' walk from the well where his body had been found. There was a small plot of grass in front where a goat stood tethered. It looked at the men idly as it chewed.

"The door's bolted," Burgess said.

"From within," Renard said softly. "Who so thoughtfully locked the door behind him?"

"His wife," the monk said promptly. "It always turns out that way. A randy young bride, a dried-up old husband, and a ruttish lover eager to take his place in the saddle. It's a surefire recipe for murder."

"He wasn't that old," Renard said, still studying the door. "There must be a way in at the back." He glanced along the street. Two houses down, a narrow alleyway ran off into shadows.

Rats scurried as the pair made their way along. Burgess wrinkled his nose. "Cistern needs cleaning."

"Don't they all? There now, what did I say?" Ahead was a small sunken door less grand than the one fronting the street, but leading to the same destination. It gave easily beneath Renard's touch.

Within was hot, stale air and little else. No smells of cooking, no scent of rushes, no sense of the myriad small traces left by daily living.

"There's no wife," Renard said, glad to be certain of something at least. Glad also to deflate Burgess, who was always in need of it.

Thin shafts of light shone through the shutters, illuminating deep shelves piled from floor to ceiling with bolts of cloth. Renard cracked the shutters open, flooding the small space with the bright day.

His dark brows, slashes across the rough-hewn face, shot up. For an instant he felt as though he had stepped into a sultan's den, so rich was the sudden rush of color and texture. Lush brocades embroidered with golden thread were heaped next to silks dyed almost every color of the rainbow.

Burgess sucked in his breath. "So perish the wicked who cherish worldly display and do not go humbly before the Lord."

"It's the merchant who's dead," Renard reminded him. "Not his customers."

There was a lamp and tinder on a small shelf beside the front door, ready for use should they be needed. The merchant had gone out into the night without them, to his death.

In a nearby alcove a rumpled bed stood. The disarranged covers made it appear as though the occupant had risen suddenly. A small table was nearby with silver candlesticks set out on it. Pewter dishes could be seen in a cupboard against one wall.

Lagounier had lived well for his class. The place was clean, without dust or cobwebs, and with fresh rushes laid. Either the merchant had a talent for keeping house or he paid someone to do so. That might be worth looking into.

"The backdoor also has a sturdy bolt," Renard said. "Whoever was with the merchant must have been freely admitted. That likely means the dead man knew his killer."

"Oh, I see," Burgess said. "Find out everyone the

dead man knew, find out which of them had a reason to do away with him, and you'll have your killer. Of course, you've got time for all that what with half the population of this godforsaken town at the throats of the other half. Not to mention his lordship the bishop carping about his missing hams."

"I want to take another look at the well," Renard said.

The other shops along the street were open and doing a brisk business. But the crossroads where the well was located was empty except for a wagon rumbling past.

Renard bent down again where he had been earlier and examined the ground. The stain was all but gone, soaked into the parched earth. He braced his hand against the rough stone base. Like a blind man seeking his way, he felt the design before he recognized it.

Slowly, he moved back. The carving was blurred by time and weather, but still decipherable. Buried within the stone, looking out with ancient eyes, a horned god smiled.

A cloud moved before the sun. Renard straightened in its shadow, his face thoughtful. He raised his head, looking around again at the busy shops.

They were all, like Lagounier's, involved in one way or another with the cloth trade. Not far away was another street where every manner of jewelry could be found. Nearby was another the scribes went to, and there were more for tanners, sword makers, horse mongers, sellers of every imaginable food and so on, all sensibly separated into their own part of the increasingly sprawling city.

But none of the stores looked to have so large or opulent a selection as he had seen in the dead man's shop.

Surely Lagounier would have been envied. Had one of his colleagues in the trade lured him to his death?

He was still mulling that over when out of the corner of his eye he caught a flash of red. He turned in time to see a girl, slender, plainly garbed, vanishing into one of the shops.

A giant of a man lumbered after her. He looked vaguely familiar. Renard frowned. What was the death-eyed Englisher from the baron's keep doing here, so close to where a Norman had lately died?

Coincidence, he supposed. For an instant he considered following the girl, but thought better of it. He would succeed only in embarrassing her and provoking her protector. That he could do without.

"Stay here," he told Burgess. "Ask around if Lagounier had a woman, even someone who cleaned for him. If the shopkeepers don't know, try the tavern. See if you can get a name."

"Where will you be?" the monk inquired.

Renard grimaced. "At the bishop's, hunting for hams."

The young Saxon smiled. He disliked his assignment, having no truck with women, but Renard's was worse. He was welcome to it.

"After that, find the watchman and bring him to see me. I want to hear firsthand what he saw."

"I have the correspondence with the tanners to finish, the merchants from Rouen have requested an audience, and there's the small matter of the accounts. Unless you want to end up like the bishop, they have to be balanced."

"I like to think you keep me from Odo's fate," Renard said. "As for the rest, it can wait."

Burgess tossed his flaxen hair, long but for the tonsure, and said, "Perhaps, but why should it? This is a fool's errand. What does one more death matter, even a Norman's? The world reeks of death. Life is but a miserable passage to the inevitable end. We exist in a charnel house that—"

"Enough," Renard said, "I know it all, I just don't have time for it. Find whoever knew Lagounier and locate the watchman. One Norman death may count for nothing, but I want to make sure it will stay that way."

"Stay how?" Burgess asked, sufficiently curious to forget for the moment how pointless life was.

"Stay at one," Renard said as he walked away.

He went to the river, where he flagged down a boatman for the trip upstream to Odo's. There, the usual crowd was hanging about in the hope that favors might drip from the bishop's table or contenting themselves merely to be seen in such illustrious circumstances.

Renard sought out the steward to say he would require an exact listing of all those in the bishop's employ with the length of their service. The man stuttered in his eagerness to assure the illustrious high sheriff that he lived merely to assist him in his inquiries.

That done, he toured the kitchens, stern of demeanor, nodding occasionally as though some private thought had been confirmed, and generally frightening the staff by his presence. Few heads would rest easily that night under Odo's roof.

For good measure, he dropped by the stables, the true cause being a fine roan stallion he had heard Odo had lately acquired. The bishop rode surprisingly well given his girth, but Renard doubted he would be able to handle the spirited animal. Most likely the stallion would languish, exercised only by terrorized stable boys.

He was preparing to leave when a servant ran to summon him. The bishop, hearing of his presence, wished to speak with him. Renard denied the urge to plead a pressing engagement and went.

Odo was where he always seemed to be, in the alcove off the great hall. He was not alone. The red-haired girl was there. Renard started when he saw her.

He believed in fate no more than the next man, which was to say quite a lot, but for his path to cross hers twice in a single day suggested they were meant to meet, her guardian notwithstanding. He was there, too, glowering off in a corner while the plump, older woman stood nearby, hands folded in her sleeves, surveying all with stern-eyed disapproval.

"Ah, Renard," the bishop chirruped. He held out a hand, sausage fingers beringed, and summoned him closer. "So good of you to attend personally to my little matter. I shan't forget your diligence. But then it's what I would expect of you, a hero of Hastings and all."

The girl stiffened. There was no mistaking it. Color fled from her heart-shaped face. She turned her head away and stared at the wall.

"I've been trying to tell them what it was like," Odo went on, "but don't you know, memory fails. The shouts, the tumult, the very sky cleaving at such a moment of glory, it all fades with time. Too much has happened since for my poor mind to recapture the truth of it."

"Actually," Renard said, "you weren't there."

The bishop waved a hand, dismissing that small fact. "In spirit I was, sir, most definitely in spirit. That's what I've been trying to explain, how magnificent it all was, this happy group of men chosen by God for the great work of reclaiming what He had always intended to be ours."

A low growl came from the direction of the wall. The girl flicked an eye toward her large friend and, almost imperceptibly, shook her head. He subsided, if reluctantly.

Renard was impressed. To control such unbridled hate was no mean feat. Clearly there was more to the lass than mere dazzling beauty.

He looked at her again, more closely, and saw the intelligence gleaming in the light blue eyes and, too, the barely suppressed rage simmering within her woman's body.

Rage, he thought, more suited to a man, yet seeming well at home in her. Did Odo know what he played with?

The other woman was less revealing of her soul, but no less formidable. She turned flinty eyes on the bishop as he said, "You know our high sheriff, Renard d'Agounville." He waved a hand, encompassing both the women. "Lady Eldgythe, abbess of St. Margaret's in Canterbury, and her ward, Aveline."

"Mesdames," Renard said with a slight inclination of his head. The burly gentleman apparently merited no introduction.

"St. Margaret's is renowned for the fineness of its needlework," Odo went on. "No less an authority than our beloved queen, my sister-in-law, has assured me of this." He paused and leaned forward confidingly. "I am arranging a small gift for my esteemed brother, a commemoration of the great events eleven years ago."

"Indeed," Renard said, mainly because he could think of nothing else. That Odo intended to give the king a gift was no surprise; he had given many such, always hoping against hope that they would influence his brother's thinking on matters dear to the bishop's heart, chief among them being the bishop himself.

There was no evidence that this had ever been the case, but Odo refused to give up. He remained convinced that someday, in some way, he would find the key to overriding William's better judgment. His latest attempt appeared to be nothing less—or more—than an unabashed appeal to vanity.

"A commemoration," Odo repeated, "that will draw the eyes of all men, stir their hearts, and impress on them forever how great is our achievement. When you think of it, it's remarkable that no one thought to create such a memorial before now."

There were those who would argue that the great tower squatting downriver was exactly such an eternal reminder of the conquest that had swept like a deadly storm over England, Renard thought, but he did not say so. Odo had the bit between his teeth and seemed intent on running with it.

"Fascinating," Renard murmured.

Better that he had bitten off his tongue rather than utter the word, for in the next instant Odo said, "I cannot help but think that your being here today at this exact moment has a purpose. You were there at Hastings, you saw it all, and it is well known that you are a scholar in your spare time. Clearly you are the perfect choice to oversee the project."

"I think not," Renard said slowly. Odo had caught him unawares, for that he blamed himself, but now the bishop's design was clear. So the high sheriff would not report on the king's son to the king's brother? Well enough, but he certainly couldn't refuse to help the bishop devise a great gift for his liege, not if he was truly as loyal to the king as he claimed.

Will he, nill he, he would be drawn into Odo's net.

"I am not qualified," Renard said in a last-ditch effort to avoid a duty he knew would be, at best, distasteful. English needlewomen to create a commemoration of the Norman victory over their fathers, brothers, sons, and husbands? Truly there was no end to Odo's cruelty.

"Nonsense," the bishop said, "you are too modest; no man would be better suited to the task. I have absolute confidence in you. Under your supervision, the tapestry will be everything I envision and more."

The women were tight-lipped, but said nothing. As for Renard, he wished for words to sway the bishop, but he knew he would not find them. Odo's mind, once made up, was as the dead, unmovable rock from which his fortress was built.

He sighed and accepted the inevitable. "I will do my best, my lord." Perhaps he could pass much of the task along to Burgess, but no, he could imagine what the results would be. Between them, the stiff-backed women and the fiery-eyed monk would tear each other apart.

Whatever resulted, it would not be the commemoration Odo sought, unless blood, death, pain, and loss were what he meant by glory.

"Good, good," Odo said, and beamed them all a smile. It was also a dismissal. Moments later they stood outside the keep.

"Well, then," the Lady Eldgythe said, "it appears we are under your authority, my lord. Do you know anything at all about how so large and intricate a work is undertaken?"

"Nothing whatsoever," Renard replied. "I am, as I told the bishop, unqualified for the task. However, as that did not discourage him, it must not be allowed to discourage us."

His voice gentled slightly as he directed it toward the girl. What was her name? Oh, yes, Aveline. Beautiful, angry Aveline. He spared a thought for all that passion contained within the drab clothing of a religious and went on quickly to other things. "I will give you whatever help I can."

She turned to him then, looking at him directly for the first time. The light in her eyes reminded him of the great, grinding flows of ice he had seen one winter in the north. Men died trapped by them, sucked down into frigid graves, where sweet Lady Aveline clearly wished he might join them.

"I imagine," she said, "that you must be very proud."

His eyebrows rose. "Of what?"

"Why, being at Hastings, of course, and being a hero of the battle no less. Tell me, what did you do that was heroic? Did you kill a great many Englishmen? Did you loot their bodies or perhaps ransom them afterward to their grief-stricken families? Was that the start of your rise in fortune, my lord d'Agounville?"

He looked down at her, for she came barely to his shoulders, and saw that she quivered slightly, not with fear, for he felt none of that in her, but with the depth of her anguish. Distantly he marveled that it could be so fresh and strong after so many years, but perhaps Odo's pricking had revived it.

"I killed, lady," he said quietly, "as did every Norman and every Englishman on the field of Hastings that sad day."

She tilted her chin, eyes meeting his. "And you were proud?"

He shook his head. "I was fifteen years old and away from home for the first time. I took no pride in killing good men, but I accepted the will of God. You would be wise to do the same, my lady."

She did not reply, but he saw the shadow of confusion move behind her eyes, and was sorry for that. It occurred to him that he did not want to cause her pain of any kind. Such concern surprised him, for he had thought very little of women lately, unlike Burgess, who thought of them constantly even as he railed against them.

The Lady Eldgythe laid a hand on Aveline's arm. "We may have to suffer your authority, my lord, but you will understand that we do not share your opinions. You will be informed when the drawings are ready."

"As you will, my lady," he said pleasantly, for he refused to respond to her ire. He watched them go, noting as he did how Aveline's slender body swayed slightly beneath her gray robe. She was filled with life, that one, no matter how much she chose to dwell in the dead past.

He went home thinking of her and ate a good supper, which made for a pleasant change, since he'd had very little appetite for anything of late. Burgess was still out, which gave him hope that the monk had discovered something, though perhaps he was just sulking.

The long summer twilight lingered, casting soft gray shadows across the room. Dutifully Renard read through the day's correspondence, more petitions, more entreaties, more jostlings and maneuverings for a larger piece of the rich pie that was England.

The bells rang for compline, but he made no effort to pray. That need, too, had left him.

After dark, he heard Burgess come in and rattle around in the next room, but he made no effort to summon him. Solitude, he had discovered, was a precious gift he nurtured unabashedly, like a miser.

And yet, lying alone in the great bed, he saw in his mind's eye the flash of fire-torn hair and ice-born eyes, and thought again of lovely Aveline.

4

I have seen him again, the Englishman who was leaving Odo's keep when we arrived the first time. He was there again yesterday. His name is Renard d'Agounville and he is high sheriff of London. Odo has put him in charge of us. God does not hear my prayers, for all He speaks to me.

The blackbirds had a restful night. I listened to their flutterings in the eaves beyond the window of the cell I have been given. Mother Ursuline was not pleased to learn we would be staying on, but given the circumstances, she has no choice but to accommodate us.

Thorney is a Benedictine abbey, as is St. Margaret's. The sisters and their charges sleep in single cells, empty save for a rope bed, a small chest for what few belongings are permitted, and a cross. To mine has been added the luxury of a table, a stool, and a lamp.

Down the passage from my cell is the communal bath. Before prime, I made my way there. The floor is cool stone, the water drawn from a deep well that holds the chill of winter. Both brought blessed relief after the hot, close night.

Alone, I stripped off my chemise and bent, splashing

the water over me. I still had a tiny sliver of soap bought at the Canterbury fair the year before, and I used that liberally. Soon even my hair smelled of lavender.

I was done before the sisters came, sleep-eyed and grumbling. Mother Eldgythe was not among them. She was absent, too, from Mass, which is not at all like her. We were leaving the chapel when she caught up with us.

"I slept overlong," she said. The weight of her cares rested heavily on her. There were dark shadows under her eyes and her hands shook slightly as we broke bread. But her appetite was good enough, and by the time we were done, her spirits had lifted.

Taking silver coins from the purse at her waist, she said, "Go with Wulfgarth and buy what is needed. I must send word to St. Margaret's that we are delayed."

"Will you say anything else?" I asked.

Mother Eldgythe shook her head. "Not until we return. There will be too many questions, and too much anger, to do it from afar."

I nodded, struck as always by her wisdom. In the eleven years that she has been my guardian, she has taught me much. Above all, I have learned perseverance. No task is impossible if approached with proper determination.

So it was that as Wulfgarth and I made our way to the street of scriveners, all my thoughts were turned to the matter of Odo's commission and how I might reconcile it with my own ends. Suffice to say, I had come to no conclusion by the time we reached our destination.

In the old days, when England was ruled by the Witan-chosen king and his council, records were kept but sparsely. What was said mattered far more than what was written. If a man's word could not be trusted, he swiftly found himself without kin or clan, abandoned to the mercy of a merciless world. Few took the risk.

So, too, it was when William first came, but no longer. As each day passes, more clerks and scribes sprout from one end of London to the other. The scriveners' street draws them all.

Wulfgarth cleared a path for me and I kept my head down until I was in the first shop, but I was aware nonetheless of their murmurs and stares. Women are rare in such places and becoming rarer still.

I paused just inside the door and breathed in deeply. The distinctive scents of ink, parchment, and vellum are old friends to me, but I sensed something different.

The shopkeeper was a young man, most likely the owner's son or son-in-law, dressed in a neat brown tunic of good fabric. He was slightly built, as scholars always seem to be. Except for d'Agounville, about whom I must not think.

The young man flushed when I asked him what I smelled. He attention was focused over my shoulder, as well it might be, for Wulfgarth's bulk filled the small space and seemed to dwarf all else. Yet he was not being at all frightening, was smiling even, and gave the young man no cause for his unease.

Briskly I said, "Have you a new ink? Is that what I smell?"

"Y-yes, my lady, indeed." He eased a hand beneath the counter and placed a small soapstone container on the counter before us. When he removed the lid, the smell became more pronounced. I recognized the scent of the sea.

"An exceptionally fine ink," the young man boasted. "It is made from the exudate of a gigantic beast with a head as vast as a hillside and more arms than any man can count. Many have died seeking the creature and only a few have ever been caught."

Belatedly he eyed my simple clothing and said, "As a result, the ink is very rare and quite dear."

"I didn't want to buy it," I admitted. "I was merely curious. Thank you for telling me. Now, as to what I require . . ."

I described the quantity of parchment I needed, admittedly a large amount, and white this time, since Odo was paying for it, and further listed my requirements for pens, quills, and a good, reliable ink that I knew was well suited to drawing.

The young man, who had appeared chagrined by what he took to be my lack of serious intent, cheered up quickly. He went into the back to fetch the owner, his father as I had surmised, and together we chaffered over the price until all were satisfied. I left as deposit two of Mother Eldgythe's coins and went away relieved that I had struck a good bargain.

Outside the coolness of the shop, the day was hot and still. Once more the sky was clear. There has been little rain this season. It was early yet and I was reluctant to return to the cloister. Instead I convinced Wulfgarth that we should walk a little.

He was reluctant, as always, but agreed when he saw my heart was set on it. Wulfgarth has been with me for eleven years. We nursed our wounds together. Sometimes I am ashamed of how I take advantage of him.

We walked near the river. There is much building going on in London. Everywhere is the thud of hammer and mallet, the whine of saws, the shouts of men as they labor to maneuver the massive stones the Normans insist on using.

Yet much of the past still remains. We rounded a curve along the bank and there I saw it, standing stark against the sky, exactly as I remembered, the hall.

Thirty years ago and more, Godwin, then Earl of Wessex and the most powerful man in England, caused great logs to be cut in the Weald and brought along the river to London. There he raised a splendid hall, one of the finest ever built in the old style.

It stood two stories high and stretched for a great distance, surrounded by a palisade of sharp-tipped trunks. Nearby were a dozen outbuildings—stables, kitchens, quarters for honored guests, and the like. The hall was Godwin's residence when he was in London.

He lived there in such splendor as befitted a monarch, tolerating his weakling king with ill-feigned patience and dreaming of the glory his sons would attain.

The year that I was eight, my mother brought me to London. We stayed at Godwin's hall. He was dead by then, cut down in his prime while the weakling king still lived. Of his sons, one was dead, one in exile, but the rest had rallied around my father, and for them the great prize was at last within sight.

My mother came, I think, to remind my father of what he already had and what he might lose if he allowed his ambition to rule him. He did not listen, as perhaps he could not, for fate already had him in her talon grip. All else followed.

The building is used now by some of William's clerks, who, I understand, complain daily of its discomforts. It is shortly to be replaced by a more fitting, Norman structure. Wulfgarth was silent as we walked beside it. For him, the memories are even sharper.

We passed on at length and turned toward Thorney, well-named island of thorns, called also the Westminster. It has been almost twelve years since Wulfgarth stood inside the abbey. He would not do so now, but waited for me outside.

Within was cool silence, the musty scent of stone,

and dust motes dancing on shards of golden light. The soft rustling of my cotte was the only sound as I walked down the center aisle.

Westminster was Edward's abbey, built by him and consecrated as he lay dying. I have an instinctive dislike of it, but I try to contain that. It is, after all, a place of God, and more, of memory.

Twin rows of broad stone pillars support the roof. Between them is the wide aisle that leads to the main altar. There are several more small altars set off to the side but otherwise the interior is empty. Of a Sunday, crowds of reverent Normans fill it. But on this day there was not even a monk to be seen.

I knelt at the altar for a time, eyes closed, hands clasped. Anyone entering would have thought me merely a postulant at her devotions. But it was not God I sought, though I sensed His presence.

The day was stifling, yet I felt a chill. I was alone, but I felt the crowd pressing at my back. I heard their excitement, their indrawn breath, the clank of their swords, the rustle of fine garments.

Siward was there, my father's sometime friend. So were all the great lords of the Danegeld, Northumbria, Essex, and Wessex, gathered there from all the land to see the will of the council done.

It had snowed the night before, but the day was clear. Gulls called along the river. Bonfires had burned for hours and their smoke still flavored the air. Outside, a great crowd had gathered. Peddlers moved among them, musicians played, there was laughter and good cheer.

The king was dead.

I opened my eyes. The vision blurred. The clean,

brave chill of that years-gone winter vanished. I was once more alone.

Long live the king.

Renard was not at ease in the visitor's room of Thorney cloister. Twice he rose from the bench and wandered over to the window. The view was of the sluggish river. It offered little diversion.

He was hot, tired, and impatient. Odo had sent a message again that morning chiding him for the lack of progress on the thefts. There was nothing new on the merchant's death, questioning the watchman having proven fruitless and no one in the neighborhood apparently able to remember much of anything about the man who had lived among them for years.

Beyond all that, a rumor had surfaced that yet another attempted rebellion might be in the works. The mere thought of it knotted Renard's stomach. He still remembered all too clearly where the last such effort had led. The dead of York yet lived in his nightmares.

He was relieved when the door creaked and the abbess entered, all fluttering silk and nervous smiles. She extended both her hands to him in greeting.

"My lord, you honor us," Mother Ursuline said. "Please forgive the delay. I was at my prayers when I learned you were here." In fact, she had been lying down with an oatmeal pack on her face, complaining to the novice who served her about the impossible English weather.

"I apologize for the interruption," Renard said. He knew little about the abbess, but he was always cautious around such women. Unfashionable though the notion was, he sometimes thought them wilier than men, more given to subterfuge, and altogether more dangerous.

"May I offer you refreshment?" Mother Ursuline inquired.

Renard shook his head. "Thank you, no. Unfortunately I have very little time. I merely came to inquire after the Lady Aveline and her progress on the sketches. As it has been a week now and I have heard nothing, I thought—"

He broke off, seeing the abbess's confusion. "You know nothing of this?" he asked.

She shook her head and permitted herself the smallest frown. "I know of Aveline, of course, and that she is working on something that takes up a great deal of time and requires her to have a table in her cell. Also, she is using an absurd number of candles. I had no idea you were involved, my lord."

Renard smiled wryly. He had been right to come. Left to their own devices, the good women of St. Margaret's would do their utmost to circumvent Odo's orders. "The bishop asked me to supervise the project. Undoubtedly Lady Eldgythe meant to mention that to you. It must have slipped her mind."

"Along with a good deal else," Ursuline said. "I must say I am relieved to hear that they have been placed in responsible hands. Frankly, my lord, these Anglo-Saxon women are all too independent. They lack humility and have no sense of what is proper."

Renard allowed as to how that was unfortunate and came to the point. "I would like to see Lady Aveline—alone."

He held his breath, thinking the abbess might refuse, mindful of the young girl's beauty and vulnerability. But no such concern seemed to cross Ursuline's mind, or if it did, she dismissed it in light of the importance of her guest.

"Certainly, my lord. I will have her brought at once. In the meantime, can't I tempt you with this excellent cider? We make it ourselves."

Renard relented and allowed her to pour him a cup.

The chilled liquid eased his dry throat. His mood brightened slightly, only to darken again as the door opened and Aveline entered.

The look she shot him made him put the cup down. If he were to fall dead, as she clearly intended, it might as well be saved.

Mother Ursuline grimaced. She took in Aveline's wrinkled cotte, her uncombed hair, and the smudge of ink on her nose, and said, "We have certain standards here, girl, to which you are held, Eldgythe notwithstanding." Turning to Renard, she added, "My apologies, my lord. Clearly she needs a firm hand."

Renard hid a smile as he assured her he was not offended. The same could not be said for Aveline. The abbess was barely out of the room before she muttered a word under her breath that shocked Renard, and made to follow the abbess.

"Wait," he ordered, stepping forward to block her path. "You'll accomplish nothing, and besides, it isn't worth it. The woman's a fool."

Aveline eyed him suspiciously. She was in no way soothed by his apparent siding with her. "What do you want?" she demanded.

"To see you and"—he gestured toward the roll of parchment in her hand—"to see what you have been doing."

She stiffened her shoulders and looked at him unflinchingly. "Mother Eldgythe told you that you would be informed when the sketches were ready to be seen."

"Mother Eldgythe is not in charge," he said gently. On closer examination, he could see that there were shadows under her eyes and the freckles across her nose stood out starkly against the pale skin. "You have been working hard."

Her mouth tightened. She moved a little distance

away. "Does that surprise you, my lord? It shouldn't. The bishop orders and we all leap to obey. Isn't that how it is supposed to be?"

He was silent for a moment, thinking he had forgotten the precise shade of red that was her hair. It was truly remarkable. Quietly he said, "Sit down."

"I don't want to," she said mutinously.

"God's blood, woman! Do you have to argue about everything? Sit down!"

Aveline sat. It was that or fall onto the bench, and her pride would not permit such humiliation. He overwhelmed her, this tall, powerful warrior who glared at her so fiercely. Near him, she almost forget who and what she was. Almost, but not quite.

"You don't have to shout," she said.

"Don't I? I had the distinct impression that you weren't hearing me."

"On the contrary, I hear you fine. I just don't like what you say."

He laughed suddenly, surprising her. "You are honest at least," he said, standing with his hands on his narrow hips. The look in his eyes sent a tremor through her. "That is something. Now get a grip on your temper and show me the sketches."

"They are still preliminary."

"Then I will view them as such." When she still hesitated, he said gently, "It is a difficult subject, to say the least, and there are many details you cannot know. I will be glad to help you."

Her eyes were shuttered. She rose and, without a further word, spread the sheets of parchment out on the table. Renard bent to look at them.

They were, as she said, rough, but in the first moments that his eyes roamed over the drawings, he knew two things—if this early work was any indication, the reputation of St. Margaret's was in no way exaggerated, and the Lady Aveline was far more than a skilled needlewoman.

How much more he could not say, but the thought occurred to him that no young woman should—or could—have such knowledge as she possessed.

It was all there, sketched out on page after page of parchment, so many that he could barely grasp the whole. He saw, flashing before him, the panorama of a nation's end and another's beginning.

There was Harold Godwinson's ill-fated journey to Normandy, his meeting with William, Edward's death and Harold's coronation, the appearance in the sky of a miraculous portent, William's preparations for war, and finally, lightly sketched, the great clash at Hastings in which the fate of two peoples was decided for all time.

The work was vast, exhaustive in detail, filled with almost mystical power. It would be everything Odo hoped for and much more. The bishop did not deserve it, but the world did. It was a masterpiece.

It was also a mystery, especially given what he knew of its creator. Or more accurately, what he did not know.

"I am corrected," Renard said softly. "You do not need my help. But I need yours to understand how you have done this. I have never seen anything like this, yet parts of it remind me of something I have seen, not as great as this but—"

"Greater," Aveline said. His praise confused her. She had been prepared for anything but. "For the style of many of the figures, I drew heavily on a psalter kept at Canterbury that was created during the reign of the Emperor Charlemagne. *It* is a masterpiece." She gestured at her drawings. "This is merely to satisfy the bishop."

"No," Renard said, shaking his head, "it is far more.

But tell me, how are you aware of the emperor's psalter?"

"I have been allowed to study it," Aveline said. "Mother Eldgythe obtained permission for me several years ago. Since then, I have spent many hours with it."

"Astonishing," he said. "Lanfranc guards it jealously. He has allowed me only a glimpse."

She looked up, into his eyes. "You know the archbishop?"

"Slightly."

"As you know Odo?"

"Not quite. I like Lanfranc."

Despite herself, she laughed. "I am sure he would be glad to hear it."

"He wouldn't care one way or the other. When will you return to Canterbury?"

"Soon. First, I would like Odo to see the drawings."

Renard's eyebrows rose. "You are so concerned with his opinion?"

"I am concerned that he not reject the finished work."

That was a sensible enough precaution, Renard thought, particularly in light of all the time and effort to be expended on it. "I can show them to him, if you like," he offered.

She nodded. "They will be finished in another day or two. If you could return then—"

Nothing would keep him away, not missing hams, or dead cloth merchants, or rumors of war. He watched her slender hands as she rerolled the parchment and caught himself wondering how those same hands would feel against his skin.

The image that evoked unleashed a surge of power such as he had not felt in a very long time. He went away befuddled but unaccountably cheerful and eager to return.

5

"*Wake up,*" Burgess said.

Renard groaned. He'd been dreaming about Aveline and he was loath to let the dream go. It was all well and good for the monk to say; Burgess thought sleep sinful, an open door to the devil's work, and woke himself at intervals all night in order to pray. Renard thought the practice madness and avoided it at almost any cost.

"There's been another one."

Renard lifted his head and eyed him groggily. "Another what?"

"Murder. Actually there have been several, there always are. But among them there's another dead Norman with his throat cut." He took a step back and eyed his master self-righteously. "I just thought you ought to know, that's all."

The curse that broke from Renard's lips could have peeled the whitewash off the walls. He was out of bed and pulling on his clothes before Burgess had time to blink.

"Where?" Renard demanded.

"The street of the scriveners. A monk, on his way home from a deathbed, found the body. He had the sense to summon the watch without raising a hue and cry."

Renard said a silent thanks to the monk, strapped on his sandals, and headed out the door. Burgess followed, grumbling again about the lack of an escort.

Renard insisted that a lighted torch be left each night outside the entrance to his hall so that anyone in need would be able to find the place. Burgess had thought the extravagance foolish and liable to bring unwanted visitors at inconvenient hours. But he was glad enough of the torch as he seized it and followed his master.

They could have ridden, but the delay in saddling horses was too much for Renard. Besides, London was a small enough town. A man could walk from one end of it to the other in less than half an hour. They reached the scriveners' street in under five minutes.

As Burgess had said, it was quiet there, the residents sleeping snugly with no hint of what went on directly beneath their windows. A small circle of men stood near the end of the street.

The monk was there, a middle-aged man in brown serge robes looking pale and slightly ill. So, too, the watchman appeared to wish himself anywhere else. The cause of their discomfort was plain to see. Even Renard, hardened though he was to the many faces of death, paused before approaching.

The body lay near the center of the road, stretched out with the arms fully extended straight from the shoulders and the legs neatly together. The eyes were closed, the entire expression one of repose. A slashing wound across the throat was the obvious cause of death, but so, too, were the numerous stabs to the man's chest, which had caused even more bleeding.

It was impossible to be sure, given so much blood, but the scrivener seemed to be well dressed in a tunic, chausses, and soft leather boots, all suggesting he had been relatively prosperous. His neatly trimmed hair and beard supported that. He appeared to be a young man, in his early twenties, and handsome.

"What do you make of this?" Renard asked as he bent beside the body.

Burgess remained upright, staring down at it. "Diabolical," he murmured.

Renard touched the dead man's cheek, finding the skin still faintly warm. He straightened slowly. "I rather think there was a human agency involved. The limbs were arranged after death, as was the face. Someone went to considerable trouble to make him look so peaceful."

"Almost as though he accepted his death," Burgess said. "There are no signs of any struggle."

Renard pointed to the throat wound. "He was taken by surprise, as was Lagounier. The first cut was to the neck and it would have disabled him immediately. The wounds to the chest came afterward."

"The same," Burgess murmured, "but more this time."

"Exactly," Renard replied. His eyes were grim as he glanced around the street.

A few people from the nearest building had heard voices and come out to investigate. They stood in a little knot a short distance away, looking at the corpse with fearful fascination. Like the merchants' district, this was a Norman street, but among the small group Renard saw several who looked to be English. Servants, he thought.

To the watchman he said, "Don't let anyone leave. I want everyone who lives near here questioned."

To Burgess he said, "What lures two prosperous men, both presumably intelligent and worldly, out into the street at night without even a lamp? What cuts their throats without a sound and goes so far as to arrange one of the bodies so that he looks almost like—"

He did not finish, for Burgess had stiffened, his eyes returning to the dead man. He stared at the body, the arms outstretched, the head tilted slightly to one side. He made a choking sound. "No one would dare. It is a sacrilege!"

Renard laid a hand on his shoulder, calming him. "Like it or not, it is the posture of the cross. But it is also different. The wounds make it so. The throat I can understand, it was the swiftest way to render him helpless. But what about the chest? If the murderer was going to go to so much trouble, why make it different?"

"Because not even a heretic would do what you are suggesting," Burgess said, his face red and hard. "To parody our Lord in such a grotesque way is the work of an infidel or worse."

"What is worse?" Renard said, softly as though to himself. He had no answer, only further questions.

It was the same again with those who lived nearby—no one had seen or heard anything, no one admitted to knowing the man, no one had any idea why he should have been killed.

At least not until Renard came to an old, wizened woman simply dressed in the English style of a girded tunic pulled up at the sides to save trailing on the ground. A square of fabric covered her head, secured by a cotton band that indicated she was of humble class. Stray wisps of white hair showed from beneath the cloth. Her face was seamed, her body bent, but her eyes when they fastened on Renard's were bright and alert.

"Terrible," she said, clucking her tongue. "A terrible thing."

"Indeed, Mother, but then it can be argued that we live in terrible times." His use of the English honorific startled the old woman. Her smile was crafty as she looked at him with heightened interest.

"Strange for you to say, my lord. Surely one of your high position finds the world congenial?"

"Not on a night such as this. Which house is yours?"

"That one there," she said, pointing to the timber-and-wattle building directly behind them. "I am servant to the family."

Renard nodded; he had surmised as much. "It has been my observation that people rich in years sleep lightly, if at all. Were you awake this night, Mother?"

Again, the old woman smiled. She was enjoying the attention, whatever fear she had felt dissolving before his courtesy. But she was still wary. He was, after all, Norman.

"I . . . drifted," she said finally.

"And in your drifting, did you happen by chance to hear anything?"

"I can't be sure."

"You don't have to be." Gently he urged her. "A man is dead. There will be suspicions raised, accusations made. In such circumstances, those most vulnerable suffer most."

"So it has always been," she said, her voice dropping. She glanced again at the body. Renard almost felt, as well as saw, the tremor that moved through her.

"I heard a man speak. Him, perhaps. Someone replied, but it was only a murmur."

"Nothing else?"

She shook her head, her eyes still on the dead man. Again she trembled. So softly that Renard had to bend to hear her, she said, "See how it is, the old way, the sacrifice."

Her gaze turned on him, ashine with wonder and fearful awe. "Come again after all this time."

"What sacrifice? What do you mean?"

Just then, Burgess called his name. "I have found something, my lord, under the body."

"A moment," Renard said to the old woman. Burgess was holding a small piece of flint and looking very satisfied with himself. "The scrivener carried no light," he said, "again like Lagounier. But the murderer *did*."

Renard nodded slowly. A scene formed in his mind, the knock in the night, a low but frantic voice speaking perhaps of an accident, pleading for help, and the victim responding, all unsuspecting of what awaited beyond the threshold of the night.

It made sense—up to a point. People in London were cautious; even when confronted with such a scene, they might not respond as the killer wanted. What assured their cooperation?

He was mulling that over when he turned back to the old woman. The space where she had been standing was empty. Night had swallowed her as surely as it had the cries of the dying.

By morning, Renard accepted that the old woman was not to be found. She had vanished from the house where she was employed, abandoning her few belongings.

So, too, the other English servants were gone, not only those who had seen the body, but every one of them up and down the street. Not an Englishman or woman was to be found.

"They know," Burgess said as he stood beside Renard, staring down at his bent head. His master was on his knees, planting radishes. It was a queer occupation for a warrior, but Burgess was becoming inured to such sights. Besides, it was harmless enough even if the radishes wouldn't grow. The ground was too dry.

They were in the garden behind the high sheriff's residence. Renard had taken it over at the time of his appointment. He had made few changes to the stone tower with its connected rectangular hall.

The building was one of the oldest of its kind in London, having been constructed several decades before, during what some still thought of as the first Norman invasion. That one had been peaceful, brought about as it was by the fondness of King Edward, called the Confessor, for his Norman brethren.

The king had been raised in Normandy following the death of his father and his mother's treachery. He never lost his affection for the place or its people. But it was an affection not shared by the Earl Godwin, who took the first possible opportunity to banish the Normans from Edward's court.

For most of Edward's reign, only a few buildings remained to show that the Normans had ever been there. Until, that is, they returned in overwhelming force, slew Godwin's king-made son, and established themselves as sole rulers of the once-proud isle.

So much for history; the present beckoned. Renard rose and dusted his hands. Beyond the garden, a brown-sered lawn rolled away to the water's edge. Seabirds hopped about the rocks there, seeking sustenance. It was a pretty place for London, even in this dry time, and he liked it well. But other, less attractive vistas beckoned.

"They know they will be suspected," Burgess said. "As soon as there is trouble, the burden falls on us. The Normans will seize any excuse to tighten the laws yet further. Life will become intolerable in our own land."

Renard could not disagree. He had feared from the beginning what the killing of Normans could mean. Now he dreaded it even more.

"I must have answers," he said. He turned his back to the river and looked at the young monk. "Last night the old woman spoke of sacrifice and the old ways come again. Does that mean anything to you?"

Burgess frowned. He shook his head.

"Are you sure? You are a well-schooled man. In all your reading, have you come across nothing that might relate to what she said?"

"I read holy books. Anything else pollutes the mind and damns the soul."

Renard suppressed a sigh. This was availing him nothing. He tried a different tack. "Last night you spoke of something worse than heresy. Did you mean paganism?"

Burgess glanced away. "In point of fact, the Church regards the sin of heresy as worse than misguided faith in false gods. The rationale is that the heretic has been instructed in the truth and rejected it, while the pagan is merely a poor, misguided being not responsible for his own damnation."

"I see," Renard said slowly. "Then there couldn't really be any such thing as a pagan here in England because every man, woman, and child has been instructed in the true faith. There could only be heretics."

Burgess nodded, pleased that his master had grasped the point, if not its full complexity. "But, you see, there are heretics and then there are . . . heretics. Most errors of faith occur over such matters as the true nature of the Trinity, the ascension of the Virgin Mary, and so on. To reject the faith entirely, to refuse our Savior and harken back to the time of darkness—" He shivered. "That is beyond imagining."

"Yet it could happen," Renard prompted.

"I refuse to believe it. More to the point, I know nothing of it. However," he added, unbending slightly, "I could make inquiries."

Renard shook his head. The last thing he wanted was to unleash his fanatic friend on anyone who might possibly have useful information. It would be the surest way to learn nothing at all.

"Never mind," he said quickly. "I will see to it myself."

He spared a final glance for the river, thinking that the birds were having little luck, and left the garden.

"I must see Odo again this afternoon," he said as Burgess hurried after him.

"Not more hams?" the monk asked, grimacing.

"Not this time. Something of rather more significance. Also, Rufus is due back in London today or tomorrow. I will have to see him as well."

"The weavers guild wishes to meet with you. The matter with the tanners is not yet fully resolved. Although this is not a day for hearing petitions, fully three dozen people are lined up outside waiting for a word with you. I can have them driven away, but—"

Renard shook his head. "Take their petitions, I will study them later. Send the weavers my good wishes and tell them I will meet with them as soon as possible. Inform the tanners that my requirements have been clearly stated and must be met without further delay.

The alum they use to soften the hides is being let to run into several creeks that may be needed soon for drinking water. I understand the difficulty in changing this, but it must be done all the same."

Burgess nodded. He did not have to ask why his master was concerned about the fate of the creeks. They were fed by underground springs that had never been known to fail. The same could not be said for the rains, which had been sparse in the spring and even sparser since.

"I will see to it," he said. "You will be—"

"At Thorney," Renard replied as he strode through the hall, "seeking pagans."

He waited yet again in Mother Ursuline's presence chamber. Once more Aveline was summoned and once more she came, albeit reluctantly.

"I am not quite finished," she said.

"I know," Renard replied. He did not hesitate to look at her, noting as he did that she appeared somewhat better rested. Her cheeks were flushed and her hair, beneath the head covering, curled slightly at the ends. She smelled of lavender.

"I have come on a different matter," he said. They were alone in the chamber, but he could not be absolutely sure that no one was listening. Certainly he wouldn't put it past Mother Ursuline to do so.

"Will you walk with me?" he asked.

Aveline smiled, a shade wryly, he thought. "As you will."

The reminder that his will did, indeed, prevail over hers should have reassured him. Instead it merely darkened an already-darkening mood.

"I would not have come if there were anywhere else," he said as they left the cloister and emerged through a small door in the stone wall onto a path that led to the river. There they walked within sight of anyone curious enough to watch, but out of earshot.

"You have assured my interest," Aveline said. "What is so vital that only I can assist you?"

"I need information. You are a woman of learning and may be able to provide it. But . . ."

"But what?" she asked when he seemed disinclined to continue.

Renard sighed. Already he wondered if it wasn't a mistake to involve her. "But I must have your assurance that you will say nothing to anyone of what you hear from me."

She stopped walking and turned to face him. Her eyes were well hidden behind the thick fringes of her lashes. "Why should I keep your confidence, Norman?"

"Because if you don't, there could be a panic in this city that would sweep all before it."

She continued to look at him for several moments before she said finally, "All right, I will keep silent. What is it you want to know?"

"First, there is something you must know. There have been two killings in London in a little more than a week that are of special import. Both men were Norman, both had their throats cut. The first was found in the street of cloth merchants, his body hanging into an old well. Near the base of the well is an engraving of a horned god. The second body, last night, was found on the street of scriveners. This one was laid out in a particular fashion—arms outstretched, feet together, head tilted to the side—that made me think at first of the death of Our Lord. But an old woman who came out to see it spoke of sacrifice and the old ways come again after so long. She disappeared before I could find out what she meant."

Aveline heard him out in silence. She looked

thoughtful and troubled, as though she wanted to reject what he was saying but could not.

"Did it occur to you that the old woman might have been referring to the Crucifixion?" she asked at length. "After all, that was a long time ago *and* it was a sacrifice. Perhaps that is what she meant."

"Perhaps, but it just didn't sound that way. For one thing, we are taught to regard the Crucifixion as *the* sacrifice, the ultimate act of redemption for mankind. She said *a* sacrifice, as with something that is repeated more than once. And she spoke of the old ways. Nobody refers to our faith like that. No, she meant something else."

"You are making much of a handful of words spoken by an old woman who may well have been confused, if not addled."

"I am grasping at straws," Renard admitted, "and I probably shouldn't be. If it hadn't been for the second death, I would have thought nothing of what I saw at the well. And if it hadn't been for that horned god, I would have thought much less of what the old woman said. But taken together, they worry me. These are difficult times. It would require little to turn worry into terror and resentment into violence."

"Why do you care, Norman?" Aveline asked. She stood with her hands folded, her face expressionless. He could read nothing in the shadowed depths of her eyes. "If there is violence, it will be against us English. Why should that trouble you?"

"I am high sheriff," he replied, because that was easy as well as true and safer than any other explanation he might have given. "When the king gave me my post, he didn't say, 'Keep the peace for us Normans.' He just said, 'Keep the peace.' I take him at his word."

Slowly Aveline shook her head. She looked as though she was tempted to laugh. "Does he know that?"

"I certainly hope so," he said, a little stiffly, for she put him on his dignity.

She smiled, ruefully this time. "All right, then, I will help if I can. You said the first victim was a cloth merchant. I know some of them. Which one was it?"

"Bertrand Lagounier."

Her smile faded. "I do know him . . . did know. He sold silk to the abbey last year. What a shame. He was a good man."

"For a Norman?"

"I didn't say that, did I? What about the other one, the scrivener?"

"I have no name for him as yet."

She nodded and her expression softened as she looked at him. He could feel her sympathy. "I am truly sorry about Lagounier," she said. "Whatever help I can give you, you will have. But first I want to see this horned god of yours. Will you take me to him?"

He wanted to shout his relief, but instead said only, "Shouldn't we go back for your shadow?"

"Wulfgarth?" An image flashed between them, the one-eyed giant trailing protectively after his mistress, watching Renard's every move and plotting his swift demise on principle alone. "I think not," Aveline said.

Nearby, rushes grew in thick abundance. Just beyond, a small wooden bridge spanned a narrow eddy of the river. She walked toward it. Renard delayed a moment to admire the proud carriage of her body and the straight, supple line of her back.

He followed quickly.

6

The stone beneath my fingers was cool despite the heat of the day. The lines cut into it were blurred, worn down by the ages, but still discernible.

Above me, I was aware of d'Agounville watching. His presence was oddly reassuring, but then he is such a surprising man that I shouldn't be startled by anything to do with him.

He was right, the face was topped by horns, but he was wrong about what that signified. I stood slowly and avoided looking at him. Not that it helped. My thoughts whirled in confusion. I had never felt that way before, so excited and unsure. I did not like it.

"Old indeed," I said, still staring at the stone.

He waited, silent. Few men I have known can do that. They always seem compelled to jump in with an explanation or, more likely, a directive. D'Agounville is different. I do not like that either. Different is dangerous, especially when it makes me feel as I do.

"Let us walk," I said. "We will draw too much attention if we stay here."

We strolled a short distance along the cloth merchants' street, but quickly veered north toward one of the city gates. It stood open at that hour. Wagons, horses, and people passed through it at a steady pace.

We walked west away from the city, following the course of a pleasant stream. It was much quieter there and a little cooler.

D'Agounville was very patient, but there was a limit to how long even he would wait. Finally he said, "Well?"

"It is not a god," I replied. That much I had resolved to tell him. He waited again. I watched a hawk turn lazily on currents of heated air before I continued. "A short while ago, you asked to speak in confidence. Now I must ask the same. What I tell you must not be repeated."

He looked at me as he does from those gray eyes that appear to see everything. "All right."

Almost I had wished he would refuse. That would have been an end to it, for truly I would have kept silent. What I had to say could, in the wrong ears, wreak havoc, not merely with my own life but with the peace and safety of St. Margaret's.

"I am no heretic," I said plainly, lest there be any doubt of that. "But I have learned many things, some of which are disapproved of by the Church."

"I am not here to sit in judgment of you, Aveline. I came only because I fear what these deaths could cause. Any help you can give me will remain between the two of us."

I believed him not because of who he is or even—I hope—how he makes me feel, but because of a very simple thing: he sounded so tired, like a man wrung dry with weariness and fearing that he will not be able to muster the strength to face the challenge that is coming.

My heart tugged at me. Softly I said, "Long ago

before the word of the Christ was brought to this land, there was another faith here. It was the same in Normandy and most everywhere else. The earth was worshiped for her bounty and rituals were performed to win her favor. The carving on the well has to do with this."

He looked puzzled. "You said it wasn't a god."

"It isn't. It is a man. The Green Man, he was called. It is a very old name, but before that there was another." I glanced at him from the corner of my eye, trying to guess how he reacted so far. His face with all those hard lines and chiseled planes was unreadable.

"He was called the Stag King. In days long gone by, he was chosen from among the strong young men of the clan to be the queen's consort. Between them they were believed to possess great magic and they lived honored by all. But there was a price to pay. In times of crisis, the life of the Stag King would be given to the Mother in sacrifice."

"I see," he said slowly, although I suspected he did not. How could he when the Church bans all such knowledge? In their telling, before the coming of the Savior, there was only darkness. This is not true, though it can be death to say so.

"Your horned god is the Stag King."

"And the dead scrivener?" he asked.

"There is a link," I admitted. "When the Stag King had to die, he was hung from a tree with arms outstretched and his body was pierced by arrows."

At his look of mingled shock and distaste, I added, "It was regarded as a holy death for the good of the clan, and while no man deliberately sought it, the honor was great."

I saw then what passed through his mind in the flicker of an instant, the thought that this should not be, for it was too similar to the death of our Lord, and if it had happened long before that time, then what did it say for the events on Golgotha?

I wondered how far he would let himself pursue such a thought, but he gave no indication, saying only, "A false honor, for surely no such pagan death ever redeemed a suffering people."

I shrugged, hoping he would sense nothing in my answer. "Who is to say? The point is that your concerns are not completely unfounded. I want to believe it is all coincidence, but the possibility exists that someone is going about London trying to create the impression of pagan sacrifices."

"Do I have to tell you what the response to that will be?"

I shook my head, my stomach clenching at the thought. "It is madness."

"Or meant to look as such."

We walked a little farther. Among all the surprises regarding him was how comfortable he was to be with. Comfortable, yet not, for I felt safe and endangered at the same time. More madness.

"Let us say," he went on, "that we are right and someone is deliberately arranging deaths to look like pagan ritual. How are the victims selected? Who is likely to be next?"

"Another Norman," I ventured, "and not a poor one but someone who has benefited—" I realized too late the import of my words.

The gray eyes glittered. "Exactly. Someone who has grown prosperous as a result of the conquest. Someone an Englishman would have good cause to hate."

"But why a merchant then or a scrivener? Surely a government official would be more appropriate? Or was the scrivener a clerk?"

"I don't know yet," d'Agounville said. "We haven't learned his name, but we should have it soon. Aveline, are you sure of all this you have told me?"

I nodded, not resenting the question, for this was a case where truth mattered even more than usual. "I am sure, my lord."

He used my name often, as though he liked the sound of it. He said it again as we walked back toward the city.

"I will call on you tomorrow, Aveline, if you think the drawings will be ready then."

"They will be." Curiosity, ever my curse, prompted me further. "What will you do in the meantime?"

His smile was self-deprecating. "What I do best, juggle."

My eyebrows rose. "You sound like a player such as are brought to amuse noble guests."

"You are too kind. Another would have remembered it is the fool who juggles and said as much."

I had remembered, but I could not credit him with such a notion. He was a hero of Hastings at fifteen, the scourge of York scant years later, trusted servant of the King, well rewarded for his faithful service. And he likened himself to the fool?

Surprising man.

He left me at the side door to the cloister. For the briefest instant our hands touched. He was gone before I could resist, which I most surely would have done had I thought of it.

I was still smiling when I reached my cell, but the smile faded quickly when I saw who sat on my narrow bed, her hands tightly clasped and her face drawn.

"Where have you been?" Mother Eldgythe asked. Her voice was thick with worry.

I was instantly contrite. She has been so good to me

for so long, it is the worst sort of ingratitude to cause her a moment's concern.

"The Englishman came again," I admitted, for I cannot even think of lying to her. "I went for a walk with him."

She stood up abruptly. "I knew it! That stupid bitch Ursuline! She would like nothing better than to see you hurt by him."

My mouth fell open. I had never heard her speak in such a way. Her disdain for Thorney's abbess was well known but to use such words—

"He did nothing wrong," I said quickly, "and neither did I. For a Norman, he is very unusual."

Her hands twisted. Color stained her cheeks. "No, he is not! He is only craftier than the rest, lulling you into a false sense of safety so that he can—" She broke off, staring blankly at the far wall.

Silence. I could hear her breathing, but she stood unblinking and seemed suddenly removed from all around her.

I stretched out my hand. "Mother?"

Her eyes closed, opened. She was back. "I'm sorry," she said quietly. "I am tired and anxious. You have a good mind, but there are things you know nothing about. I do not want you to see the Norman again. You understand?"

I did and I didn't. Her concern seemed excessive. I am not so innocent as she imagines. No one could be allowed to read as I have done and not understand what humans are capable of, both the good and the bad.

Gently I said, "I cannot avoid seeing him again. He has been put in charge of the tapestry."

"Then do not see him alone! If he comes, fetch me

or, better yet, Wulfgarth. Yes, let Wulfgarth deal with him."

My back stiffened. She was going too far. "If Wulfgarth *deals* with him, Wulfgarth will die, either at Renard's hand or in punishment for whatever happens to him. Is that what you want?"

She looked at me then with such anger as I have never seen or hope to see again. "Is it *Renard* now? Foolish girl! Do you want to end up like your mother? Is that it? You want to die as she did, because of them? The Norman is the enemy, he will *always* be the enemy. You cannot forget that!"

Tears threatened to choke me, so abandoned did I feel in the face of her rage. But I would not yield to them.

"I have forgotten nothing. My mother died because she lost the man she loved above all else in the world. I lost, too, everything I had ever known or cared about. But life goes on! Not easily or simply or even rationally, but we survive. Yes, we have much to blame the Normans for, but that doesn't mean every single one of them is evil."

"You are just like your mother, blinded by your feelings for a man. You can't see what he is leading you into."

Her voice broke. She reached for me with open arms. "For the love of God, Aveline, have I kept you safe all these years only to lose you now?"

I had no answer for her. Close within her arms, I was again the terrified child whose world had vanished in a single cataclysmic stroke and who saw nothing ahead but darkness. She had saved me from that, loved me, educated me. I owed her everything.

"I am sorry," I murmured against the rough spun

wool of her robe. "I will be more careful in the future."

She held me a moment longer as though she would hold me forever, but then, with a sniff, she let me go. "See that you are."

She blinked back tears and managed a smile. "You have work to do. I will leave you to it." At the door she turned and looked at me again. "Will you always remember that I love you?"

I nodded, not trusting myself to speak, so caught was I between guilt and confusion. She was satisfied. I heard the sound of her pattens echoing faintly in the passage until they faded away.

Which should have been the end of the matter, but was not. I tried for a time to work, but concentration escaped me and finally I gave up. It was after nones, the heat of the day was easing. I decided to go for a walk.

Behind the cloisters is a dairy, where cows are kept for the fresh milk Mother Ursuline requires, and which, to be fair, her sisters also enjoy. I was approaching there when I caught a glimpse of Wulfgarth standing to one side of the path that leads to the river. He did not see me.

A line of thick-leafed oaks separated us. I passed scarcely twenty feet from him without his knowing. Wulfgarth was not alone. Mother Eldgythe was with him.

"Are you sure?" she asked.

Wulfgarth nodded. "Oath Bearer rises, as he said he would. The time comes."

"It has been tried before," Mother Eldgythe replied, "and with what results? Why should this be different?"

Wulfgarth shrugged. They moved on, out of my hearing. A chill breeze blew through the old oaks. I wrapped my arms around myself and sought the sun.

* * *

"Oath Bearer," Odo said, snarling. "Whoever heard a more ridiculous name? That's the trouble with these English, always melodramatic, posturing and declaiming instead of doing."

"If your information is correct," Renard said quietly, "they are prepared to do a great deal. At least four hundred men have disappeared from their farms and towns in the west country and are believed to be training in some hidden location? That is ominous indeed."

"It is absurd!" Odo insisted. They were in the bishop's private chamber on the second floor of his residence. Odo had dismissed his servants. Guards were posted at the outer doors. Every precaution had been taken to assure that they would not be overheard, a necessary course given the explosive nature of what was being said.

"Do they seriously expect to put an army into the field against us?" Odo demanded. He was seated in what looked to be a copy of the thronelike chair in his receiving room. His scarlet robes were disheveled. Agitation had knit a crease between his brows and turned his eyes to slits of glittering contempt. "Us, the greatest military force ever assembled? Fools!"

"They did it before," Renard pointed out. He stood by the window, catching what slight breeze there was. His head hurt, but his impatience at the bishop's summons had faded. Truly this news did merit attention.

"We almost lost at Hastings," he went on bluntly. "And there we met an army that was facing its *second* invasion in less than three weeks. They won a major victory against Hardrada of Norway, made a forced march down the length of England, and went directly into battle against us. We had every advantage and yet they came very close to winning. Do not discount them now, my lord."

"I'm not," Odo said, still scowling, "that's why you're here. I need more information."

It was Renard's turn to frown. "You want me to go to the west country?"

"No, I have agents there already, good men for the most part. That's how I learned as much as I have. No, I want you here in London."

He wheezed, pushing on the arms of his chair, and rose laboriously. "If this Oath Bearer actually exists and if he is planning what he seems to be, someone in London will know about it. You've always gotten along better with them than the rest of us. Find out what they're saying, what bloody dreams they're hatching."

"*They* are well aware that I am Norman," Renard said, "and they don't trust me an inch. What makes you think I'll be able to find out anything?"

"I have total confidence in you," Odo said automatically.

Renard sighed. He passed a hand before his face. "Forgive me if I do not thank you."

The bishop laughed, or tried to. He fell to coughing. When he regained his breath, Renard asked, "Does Prince Rufus know of this?"

Odo looked at him slant-eyed. "Why do you ask?"

"We are speaking of rebellion. In the absence of the king, surely the heir apparent should be informed."

"Do you actually imagine Rufus would lift a finger to protect his father's sovereignty? He doesn't see beyond the tip of his own nose and he doesn't feel except to hate. If he learns of this, all he'll do is find some way to use it to his own advantage."

Indeed, Renard thought. He had no doubt that Rufus would crush the rebellion with vicious thoroughness, if only to protect his own claim to the throne.

But he could also use it to try to discredit Odo, not without cause, for the bishop was thought to believe that the youngest of William's get, Henry by name, was the only one worthy of inheriting his father's great prize. That wasn't known for sure, Odo being far too discreet, but the suspicion alone would be enough for Rufus.

"I have heard the prince will be back in London tonight or tomorrow," Renard said.

"He is back now. He arrived an hour ago and is at his residence."

Despite himself, Renard looked amused. "Is there anything you don't know?"

Odo smiled. "Nothing of merit. Be watchful of him, my young friend. He is not to be trusted, not ever."

Are any of us? Renard wondered silently. He caught himself thinking of Aveline and the trust she had shown when she went with him. The thought that such faith might be misplaced pained him even as he admitted the possibility.

Odo left him by the window and went over to a small, ornately inlaid table set with a flagon and two cups of chased silver. He poured cool Rhenish wine for them both and handed one of the cups to Renard.

"By the way," the bishop said, "are you making any progress on those murders?"

Renard lowered the cup without drinking and met the narrow, rheumy gaze. "Some," he said cautiously.

"Good. We can't have some idiot running around killing Normans, especially not now."

Renard waited, thinking he would say something more about the scrivener, perhaps, and the strange posture of his body. But if Odo knew of that, he did not choose to comment.

Instead he asked, "And the ladies of St. Margaret's, how are you faring with them?"

"Well enough. The preliminary drawings are almost done. Would you like to see them?"

Odo waved a hand dismissively. "I think not. You approve them or not as you find fit. I have too much to concern myself with at the moment."

Renard nodded, puzzled as to why he was gladdened that Odo would not see Aveline's work, at least not yet.

They drank in silence. Outside, Odo's guard was drilling, rather ostentatiously, Renard thought, in the bailey before the tower.

No one had ever accused the bishop of being subtle. He was giving fair warning to any Englishman who might entertain unsavory notions toward the prelate's august person.

Odo smiled over the rim of his cup. "The little red-head, what's her name?"

"Aveline," Renard replied reluctantly.

"Ah, yes, I remember now. How is she?"

"Well enough, I suppose. She is working hard."

The bishop's eyebrows rose. "Working? Is that all? I would have thought you'd have bedded her by now. But wait, I forget, you live more purely than many a monk. At least so far as women are concerned."

He took a drink and eyed his guest again. "Either that or you are the soul of discretion. Which is it?"

Renard smiled. "It would be indiscreet to say, my lord."

Odo looked surprised, which was reward enough for Renard. "If there is nothing else—" he said.

"You may go, but remember what I said about Rufus. Don't trust him. And find out what you can about this Oath Bearer fellow. He could be genuine trouble."

"You may be wrong about London," Renard said as he prepared to leave. "The people here are very practical. They go where the power is and the power is Norman.

They may know nothing of him here."

"Then where?" Odo demanded. "He has to be known somewhere."

"You have men in Wessex already, the old Godwinson stronghold. What about Canterbury?"

Odo hesitated. He appeared to smell something bad. "Canterbury is Lanfranc's."

Renard hid a smile. It was no secret that the ambitious Odo had no truck with the equally ambitious, but some said wilier Archbishop of Canterbury.

"Lanfranc sits atop the heap, but the heap itself is English. There have always been stirrings in the abbeys and elsewhere in that town."

"Are you suggesting you go there?" Odo asked, clearly not dismissing the idea out of hand.

Renard shook his head. "Not yet. I have two dead Normans and no clue as to who killed them. As you said, that can't be allowed."

"No, no, of course not, but it's damnably inconvenient. The deaths don't necessarily have anything to do with each other, do they?"

"I think they do," Renard said.

Odo grimaced. "Oh, very well, stay here for the moment, but do whatever is needed to find the killer. We may have very little time."

Renard agreed. The Rhenish wine, pleasant though it was, settled uneasily in his stomach. A sense of urgency gripped him all the way downriver to his own hall.

It grew stronger when he saw that Burgess was out by the water steps waiting to greet him. The look on the monk's face told much, if not all.

7

"*Crispin LeMeux,*" Burgess said with satisfaction, "that's his name, a scrivener for at least three years past according to his landlord, who says he was prompt with his rent and never caused any trouble."

"Bound for paradise then," Renard said, "at least in the landlord's eyes." They were walking up the broad sweep of lawn toward the house. The sun beat down unmercifully. When had it last rained?

"Why can't you find out the same sort of thing about Lagounier?" he asked, knowing he sounded vexed but not caring. His head throbbed.

"Because he owned the building in which he had his shop and there were no tenants," Burgess replied, not unreasonably. He cast a worried glance at his master. "Are you having the headache again?"

"No," Renard lied. "I am merely tired. I have been with the bishop."

"Surely enough to weary any man. Come in and lie down for a while."

"I can't. Rufus has returned. If I don't call on him, he'll

take offense and make trouble. You know how he is."

"I know how you are when you get the headache," Burgess said. "You need a dark room and quiet. Don't be stupid about it."

Renard wanted to argue, but colored lights were dancing in front of his eyes. He could feel himself stiffening in anticipation of the pain to come. Resigned, he let himself be led inside.

The pain came and it went, but by the time it was gone, a full day had passed. Renard rose gingerly from his bed. As always, the piercing agony in his head had left him dazed and lethargic.

He fought the desire to lie down again and forced himself to walk across the room to where a basin was laid out with warm water, a fresh towel, and soap. Above it was a square of polished metal. Gazing into it, he saw himself bedraggled, bewhiskered, and looking, he thought, twice his age.

He cursed and yelled for Burgess. The sound of his own voice exploded in his head, making him almost double over. The monk came on the run, but not before Renard managed to regain control of himself. He eyed the young Saxon impatiently.

"Get this beard off me and order water for a bath. Have I died that nothing is done around here? I need clothes, food, and while you're at it, news. Has anything been happening?"

"Nothing out of the ordinary," Burgess said, laying out the implements for shaving. He honed the razor methodically on the strap of leather that hung beside the basin, then turned his attention to the lather.

When his master was ready, the monk began slowly and carefully to scrape away the soap, taking with it the night's growth of whiskers. When he was done, Renard stretched and smiled slightly. He was feeling better, as he inevitably did, and he didn't mind chiding Burgess a little.

"You should be honored, friend. Not many Normans would bare their throats to a Saxon, especially not now."

Burgess rinsed the blade clean and dried it carefully. He did not appear to be amused. There was worry in his eyes and something else—

Renard sat upright in the chair, one hand still holding the towel he was using to dry his face. "What is it?" he demanded. "What's happened?"

"Another killing," Burgess said. Hastily he added, "I was going to tell you, I just didn't want to do it while I was shaving you. You could have jumped and been hurt."

"You said nothing out of the ordinary occurred," Renard said, glowering.

"It's the third such death in ten days," Burgess pointed out, not unreasonably. "Like it or not, it is becoming ordinary."

Renard exhaled sharply. The monk was right. Not only were the killings mounting in number, they were also occurring more frequently. There had been a week between the first and second, but only two days between the second and third.

The murderer, whoever he was, was growing hungrier or perhaps simply more daring.

"Who knows of this?" he demanded as he stood, tossing the towel aside. The bath would have to wait. Already, he had lost too much time.

"Prince Rufus, for one. He wants to see you."

"Send word I will come, but first I want to see the dead man. Who was he?"

"Hillard Valerian, a clerk in the royal counting office. He was found near his residence not far from the tower."

William's very seat of power, Renard thought, the heart and soul of Norman rule in England. Truly the murderer was growing more audacious.

"How did he die?"

"The same as the others; his throat was cut. There were no chest wounds this time, nor did the killer appear to have arranged the body, but there was something interesting all the same. An oak branch was draped over the chest. There are no oak trees anywhere in the immediate vicinity of where the crime occurred, so the killer had to have brought it with him."

Renard's breath was tight in his throat. He did not need Aveline to tell him that the oak was a pagan tree. "Where is the body?" he demanded.

"Prince Rufus has taken custody of it. If you want to see it, you will have to see him."

Renard nodded. There was no escaping what had to be done. Rufus was capable of using the murders as an excuse to crack down even harder on the English. If Oath Bearer was truly raising an army, the last thing Renard wanted was to encourage more recruits.

In his royal father's absence, Rufus had taken over William's tower, a large but roughly made and generally uncomfortable fortification built the year after the conquest. It was in a strategic location on a bend of the river, well sited for advance warning of any enemy coming by water.

Not far away, men were laboring over an immense pile of pale stone blocks brought from the quarries of Kent and Caen. Renard had seen the plans for the great tower to be built from them. When finished, it would be one of the largest and most indomitable fortifications in all of Europe. But its completion was decades off and no certain thing, especially not with the rumblings from the west.

Rufus was holding court in the great hall, surrounded

by hangers-on and retainers, when Renard entered. A herald stepped forward to announce him, but Renard did not wait. He proceeded through the vast chamber with its smoke-stained rafters and up the short flight of steps to the solar where Rufus sat.

The prince was a short man, almost a foot less than Renard in height, stocky and red of face. He was elaborately dressed in a purple overtunic embroidered in gold, yellow chausses, also lushly stitched, and a yellow mantle hemmed in gold and attached to his right shoulder by a jeweled brooch.

His ruddy hair was cut very close to the scalp, so that from a distance he appeared almost bald. He had a large, blunt-featured face with a thin mouth and slightly protruding blue eyes.

The young men clustered around him were laughing energetically at some remark the prince had made. They broke off when they saw Renard.

In the silence that followed, Rufus waved a languid hand. "D'Agounville, you have remembered us at last. I am touched."

"Your pardon, my lord," Renard said. He inclined his head the bare minimum required by Rufus's rank. "I have been indisposed."

Rufus looked at him skeptically. "While you've been in your sickbed, some madman's been running around killing Normans. What are you doing about it?"

"Actually, sir, only one death occurred since I was taken ill, but I don't suppose that matters. Obviously we must do everything possible to stop it."

"Good, I'm glad you agree. Round up two or three hundred of the scum, make it clear punishment will be severe unless the culprit is surrendered, and we'll have him before nightfall."

"I don't think that's advisable," Renard said. "Instead of the murderer, we would be more likely to have civil upheaval on our hands."

Rufus sneered. "Squeamish, d'Agounville? I wouldn't have thought it of you. Besides, what about these rumors?"

"What rumors?" Renard asked cautiously.

"That there's something unclean, something impure about the killings. That we could be dealing with a spawn of Satan."

Renard repressed a groan. So it was happening already. The old woman had realized what she saw when she looked at LeMeux. Though she was gone, her suspicions were still very much present and, by the sound of it, spreading rapidly.

"The killer is human," he said, raising his voice enough to make sure everyone in the solar would hear him. "Let no one have any doubt of that. As for the rumors, they are as chaff on the wind. The wise man lets them go without notice."

Rufus frowned, unsure as to whether or not his own intelligence had just been questioned. Before he could ponder that unduly, Renard said, "I would like to see Valerian's body, if I may."

The prince waved a languid hand. "Go, go, stare at it all you want, but I doubt you'll get anything from him. He's dead, you know." Rufus laughed loudly. The others joined in.

The sound had not yet fully died away before Renard had forgotten it. What Rufus thought of him made no difference. It was the father he served, and no one, especially not an ambitious son, would be allowed to forget that.

Beneath the tower was a labyrinth of chambers and

passageways where supplies were kept stored against the possibility of siege. In the eleven years since the conquest, they had never been needed, but they were kept all the same at William's direct order. He was not a man to take chances he could avoid.

Hillard Valerian—or what was left of him—lay on a stone slab in the chill room. Great blocks of ice covered with straw lined the walls. There was a steady trickle of frigid water across the floor. Burgess stepped gingerly after his master.

Together they looked at the body. The clerk had been in his early twenties, a well-set-up man, dressed as befitted his privileged position, with neatly trimmed blond hair and clean shaven. His eyes were closed, his mouth slightly agape, the expression not as peaceful as with LeMeux but showing no clear sign of fear.

Like the others, he'd had little warning. Aside from the jagged cut across his throat, he showed no sign of injury.

"Where is the oak branch?" Renard asked.

"Not here," Burgess said, glancing around. "They must not have thought it worth bringing."

"Then it will still be where he was killed. I want to see it."

One oak branch looked much the same as another, Renard thought as he stood, not far from the tower, holding the branch that had lain across Valerian's chest. It was large and sturdy, cleanly cut at the base, and still with a tuft of leaves at the top. The leaves themselves were just beginning to curl at the edges, indicating that the branch had not been long removed from the tree.

"Look at this," Renard said, turning the branch upside down so that the bottom was exposed.

Burgess peered at it and shrugged. "At what?"

"There is dirt here where the cut was made as though it had been pressed into the ground."

Still, the monk was puzzled. "I don't see the significance of that."

"It's been used as a walking staff, that's why the rest is trimmed clean up to the tuft of leaves at the top." He turned the branch again, pressing the bottom into the ground. "See here, it is just right for the purpose."

"Not quite," Burgess said. "It's not tall enough for you."

"True, so we may be looking for someone shorter or perhaps not. Who would carry such a staff?"

"Someone who needs help walking," Burgess ventured.

"Possibly, but then why leave it behind?"

"I see . . . but if it wasn't needed, why bring it?"

"To leave," Renard said. He hoisted the staff again in his hands, feeling its weight. "Come," he said abruptly.

"Where are we going?" Burgess asked. He had to run to keep up with Renard.

"You're going back to the scriveners' street to learn anything you can about Valerian. I'm going to Thorney. I want to talk with someone there."

Aveline received the summons while she sat at the table in her cell, putting the last touches on the drawings. She listened to the novitiate who had been sent to fetch her, but made no move to go. Instead she asked, "Where is Mother Eldgythe?"

"I don't know," the whey-faced girl said. She looked at Aveline resentfully. "The abbess said nothing of her, only that you were to come at once. You can't keep the high sheriff waiting."

Still, Aveline remained where she was, holding the pen she had been using. Her fingers were ink-stained, her shoulders weary. She was thinking about what Mother Eldgythe had said about not seeing d'Agounville alone again. While Aveline had not actually agreed to that, she did not want to be guilty of disobedience.

"I must find Mother Eldgythe first."

"Do what you want," the girl said, "but I won't be blamed for it." She turned on her heel and departed.

Mother Eldgythe's cell was empty. So was the cloister garden immediately beyond. Nor was there any sign of her in the chapel.

Aveline knew she could summon Wulfgarth, but she shrank from doing so. A confrontation between him and d'Agounville would be almost certain.

Trying to ignore the spurt of gladness she felt at the thought of seeing Renard again, she entered the visitors' chamber.

"Lady Aveline," he said, "I apologize for disturbing you, but a new matter has arisen."

He gestured with the staff. "I wanted to ask you about this."

"What is it?" she asked.

"You tell me. It was found on the body of the third victim."

Aveline blanched. She had been so busy with her work that she had not heard of an additional killing.

"Another one?"

Renard nodded. "Last night near the tower. He was a clerk named Hillard Valerian." As he spoke he remembered what she had said about it making more sense for an angry Englishman to kill Normans more directly involved in the government. Now it had happened.

Gingerly Aveline took the branch and studied it. Her hands trembled. "I was afraid of this."

"Explain."

"The question that occurred to me was whether the murderer intended from the beginning to give the impression of pagan ritual or if it happened in some other way. The first killing by the Stag King's well may have simply been a coincidence. The carving is low down and hard to see. The killer may not even have known it was there."

"What about the second, LeMeux's wounds, the way his body was arranged?"

She frowned. "LeMeux? I know that name. Not Crispin LeMeux?"

He nodded slowly, his eyes watching her closely. "How do you know him?"

"He bought some of my drawings a few months ago for use in an illuminated manuscript he was working on."

"Did he pay you?"

"He paid St. Margaret's, as is proper, and he paid well. Like Lagounier, he was a good man. And don't ask 'for a Norman?' again. I dislike that heartily."

"Your pardon," he said gravely. "I assure you, I wasn't even thinking it. Does it strike you as odd that you knew both men?"

"Not really. In my work for St. Margaret's, I've come into contact with many of the cloth merchants in the city. Lagounier was among the best, so it was only natural that we would deal with him. As for LeMeux, that is more unusual, but we do get approached from time to time by scriveners wanting to use our drawings. He was one of perhaps half a dozen in the last several years that I can recall."

"Besides their casual acquaintance with you, do you know of anything else the men had in common, any enemy they might have shared?"

"No, absolutely not. As I said, they were both good men. I can't imagine why anyone would have wanted to kill them."

"All right," Renard said, "we were speaking of LeMeux's wounds and the way the body was arranged. Surely you don't think that was an accident?"

"Of course not, but we may be misunderstanding it. The chest wounds suggest that the murderer may have been angrier than before, more eager to inflict damage. The arrangement of the body must have been deliberate, but it could have been some sort of twisted kindness for the victim once he was safely dead."

"How do you explain away the oak staff?"

Aveline shook her head. Her eyes were grim. "I don't. There is no mistaking this. The old ones used such a staff as a symbol of their authority. It connected the priest or priestess to the holy earth. This message is clear."

"I understand what you're saying, I think. The pagan link could have been an accident in the beginning, but then the rumors about it began to spread and the murderer decided to take advantage of them."

"Rumors?"

Renard nodded. "They are all over London." He smiled slightly. "If you spent less time at your work, you would know of them."

"This is very bad," Aveline said.

His smile faded. She was right, of course. "There's nothing to be done about it now except to hope that we can catch the killer quickly."

"Is that likely?"

"I don't know," he admitted. "The trouble is that he hasn't made any mistakes. No one has seen him or at least is willing to admit it. He hasn't bragged of his exploits to anyone who would repeat them. He hasn't left any indication of who he might be except as regards the pagan aspect of the killings, and as you said, that may not even have been his idea to begin with."

Aveline returned the staff to him. She wiped the hand that had held it down the side of her robe as though to erase the stain left by death.

"What will happen if the killings continue?" she asked.

Renard sighed. "Rufus will try to do something stupid. It will be up to me to stop him."

She looked up, meeting his eyes. "Can you?"

"I don't know," he said candidly, "but I have a feeling we are going to find out." Deliberately he changed the subject. "How is your work progressing?"

The sudden shift did not discompose her, but then he wondered if anything would. "The drawings are finished," she said evenly. "You may see them now, if you like."

"That would be fine."

She turned toward the door but hesitated. "Then you will take them to Odo?"

"No, he has decided that I can approve them for him."

A flicker moved behind her eyes, but her expression did not change. "As you will."

Her hand was on the door, but she stopped when he said, "Aveline, after I have seen the drawings, I would like you to return to Canterbury as soon as possible." Lest she take offense at his giving her orders, he added, "It will be safer there."

He saw her wince and regretted having to confront her with so harsh a reality. But that was better than what might happen to her if she remained. That, above all, he could not bear to contemplate.

8

A fortnight after we left Canterbury, we are back. The River Stour, which separates just south of the walls and flows in two arms, one directly through the town and the other next to Westgate, has fallen alarmingly in depth. Whole swaths of the banks never before seen in living memory lie exposed now to the unrelenting sun.

It is very hot. The gardens beyond my window are silent; not even the bees are about. But the silence is deceptive. The sisters think loudly.

I can hardly blame them. Yesterday evening, a few hours after we returned, Mother Eldgythe broke the news of what Odo expects from us.

The response was as anticipated, much anger, defiant words, insistence that we have no part in his loathesome scheming. Supper was delayed long past vespers, but in the end agreement came swiftly.

Later, in my chamber, I knelt in a ribbon of moonlight and prayed to God that I had done right.

It is morning now or almost so. The sky in the east is

gray. Soon the bell will ring for prime. We will breakfast, and then, in the great sewing room of the abbey, we will gather to begin the work.

Last night I dreamed of d'Agounville. He sat under an oak tree, his hair damp as though he had been swimming. He looked more relaxed and happy than I have ever seen him. He said something that I could not hear.

St. Margaret's is a larger abbey than the one at Thorney. We lie just on the other side of the river to the west of Canterbury proper. At the center is the church itself, a graceful stone structure built in the reign of the great Canute and now almost half a century old. It puts the lie to the Norman claim that the English could only build with wood.

Around the church are an assortment of other buildings—the cloisters where my sisters and I live, the abbess's house, the infirmary, the kitchens and bakehouse, the brewery, the laundry, and so on.

Beyond lie vast fields and orchards that produce virtually all our food as well as flax for linen. Sheep graze in the meadows. Their wool is used for our garments and in our work.

We are self-sufficient, as all such communities are supposed to be. Almost nothing is brought in from outside except a few of the dyes needed to color our wool and some medicines for the infirmary. All else is kept at bay.

Very little has changed here since the coming of the Normans. There are few other places left in England that can make that claim.

Next Candlemas, we will celebrate Mother Eldgythe's twentieth year as abbess. It is to her that the credit goes for preserving our ways in the face of such terrible adversity. I was glad to see that since our return she seems more at ease.

*   *   *

Later—

I see now that I was wrong about Mother Eldgythe. She is, if anything, more worried and preoccupied than she was in London. Or at least she is now that Lanfranc has come calling.

We were in the sewing room. It runs the entire length of the cloister and faces south, so that the light is good. Large windows are cut into the stone along the outer wall. In bad weather, heavy wooden shutters can be pulled shut across them, but on this day they stood open.

The room is always swept clean, every nook and cranny dusted so that no mark might fall on the materials we use. The floor is bare of rushes. In the winter, heat is provided by charcoal braziers, but they are stored away for now.

The furnishings consist of a large table set against one wall, several chests of materials, a dozen stools and racks for holding wool, and an equal number of the high wooden frames we use for stretching fabric while we sew.

Near one window is a high-backed chair where Mother Eldgythe sits. It is a pleasant place smelling of linen and wool, herbs from the garden below, and the lingering scents of beeswax candles and incense from the church immediately next door.

I sat on the floor separating strands of wool. Beside me, Sister Gleda hung each group on a wooden rack as I handed them up to her. The wool is cut into short lengths to prevent fraying as it is stitched. By the time we were done, all the racks would be covered, row upon row of bright-hued thread waiting for the needle.

But we had barely begun when Sister Ann burst into the room.

"Mother," she said breathlessly as she bowed to Eldgythe, "the archbishop is coming. He will be here any moment."

There was an indrawn gasp throughout the room. As one, my sisters looked to the drawings stretched out on the worktable for all to see. I jumped to my feet, shoved a handful of wool at Sister Gleda, and hurried to conceal them.

I was too late. Barely had I begun to wind the long, narrow sheaves of parchment than the door burst open and the archbishop swept in.

He is a tall, thin man with a gentle face, farseeing eyes, and thinning gray hair. Despite his high office, he dresses simply. As usual, he wore a plain black robe that hung to his ankles and was unadorned save for the wooden cross worn around his neck.

In his youth, Lanfranc was a monk. There are those who say that left to himself he still would be. Yet it seems a strange occupation for one who so plainly loves the world.

"My dears," he said, smiling broadly, "how good to be among you once again. I have been far too neglectful of late. You are well, I hope?"

His gaze, encompassing us all, was shrewd. It missed nothing, including the half-rolled parchment I held. For a moment our eyes met. His smile deepened.

"Abbess," he said, going over to Mother Eldgythe. He took her hand in his and held it gently before returning it to her. She remained seated, her mouth firmly set, but with no outward sign of alarm.

I never really know what to make of Lanfranc. On the one hand, he possesses great power and has a concrete vision of how to use it, a truly formidable combination. On the other, his good humor and kindness seem genuine.

He is a lawyer and teacher as well as a priest, a highly moral man who has great patience for the frailty of lay people but no tolerance whatsoever for the corruption that plagues the clergy. This puts him firmly at odds with Odo, whom he has been said to liken to a fishmonger loudly proclaiming the value of his wares even as their stink rises to offend heaven.

The two do not get along.

"You found London pleasant, I hope," he said, waving aside Mother Eldgythe's halfhearted attempt to vacate her seat and instead taking the one next to her. The rest of us clustered around, unsure what to do.

"It is a cesspool," she said, resigned to frankness. There is no point in anything else where the archbishop is concerned. "I breathed the sweet air of Canterbury with even more relief than usual."

Lanfranc nodded. He, too, had a poor opinion of London. "Not as sweet as it should be. The drought hits here, too."

Neither spoke for a moment. This is one matter against which all prayers and entreaties seem useless. Rains fail or they come in too-great abundance. Crops perish, people die.

We must believe it is all part of the divine plan, and yet I wonder. A God who claims not to know whether I am right may not be paying as close attention to other matters as we wish Him to.

Truly I grow bold in these pages, for that is blasphemy.

"Ah, well," Lanfranc said, moving on, "it is enough that you have returned, for truly this place grows dull without you." He looked at her affectionately. "I haven't had a good argument since you left."

Mother Eldgythe snorted. There was a suspicion of pleasure in her eyes, but she subdued it. "Flatterer, you keep yourself well occupied berating the poor monks in your care. Have you given them a moment's peace?"

"I give them what they deserve. How is Mother Ursuline, by the way? Still proclaiming her holiness to all who will listen?"

"Don't mention that woman. I have come to the end of my patience so far as she is concerned. Do you know she practically tried to throw Aveline at a damn Norman who—"

She broke off, belatedly aware that Lanfranc had, as usual, provoked her into saying more than she intended.

His eyebrows rose in mock reproof. "Indeed, a *damn* Norman? Is there any other kind? But tell me, Aveline, who was he?"

"It doesn't matter," I said very low, and turned back to the wool. My cheeks were hot.

"But it does," Lanfranc insisted. "If Ursuline must play matchmaker, at least tell me her taste is good. She wasn't trying to palm you off on some villein was she?"

"She wasn't trying to do anything," I said with a cautious glance at Mother Eldgythe. I do not often contradict her. "She only consented when the high sheriff of London asked to meet with me for perfectly proper reasons."

"You mean d'Agounville?" the archbishop asked.

"You know him?"

"I do. A fine young man, very sensible. But what has he to do with you?"

I hesitated. It was not for me to tell him.

Reluctantly Mother Eldgythe said, "As you know, when the summons came from Bishop Odo, I believed it concerned the property he holds near ours. I told you that at the time."

Lanfranc nodded. Odo holds land throughout England. He seized some of it in the days immediately following the invasion and has acquired more since. Some say he is the largest property owner in these parts, surpassing even the king himself.

"But it did not?" Lanfranc asked.

"No," Mother Eldgythe said. She looked around the room at my sisters, who sat, pale and watchful, white cowls gleaming in the too-bright light. Alone in the room, my head was uncovered. No vows shield me save those I have made to myself.

"He had a different purpose." She took a breath and let it out slowly. "Odo wants us to do a work for him to commemorate the conquest. He has put the high sheriff in charge of it."

The archbishop stared at her for a moment, as though trying to determine whether or not she was serious. Finally he said, "I have never been able to decide whether the bishop is merely callous or genuinely stupid."

"He would not be where he is today if he were stupid," Mother Eldgythe said wearily. The days in London had taken more out of her than usual. "He knows we cannot refuse. To do so would be a direct insult against the king. Not even you would be able to protect us in such a situation."

"That is true," Lanfranc said reluctantly. "But still, to expect Englishwomen to glorify the Norman victory is asking a bit much, don't you think?"

He looked around at us all as though gauging our

reaction. I kept my eyes averted, as did my sisters.

Into the silence Lanfranc said, "Can you really manage it, Aveline?"

I was not surprised that he directed the question to me. Lanfranc knows that I draw much of the work my sisters stitch. To that end he has allowed me access to the great scriptorium at Christ Church in Canterbury. Now that I am in Odo's employ, I fear he may revoke his permission.

"I must," I said. "As Mother says, we have no choice."

He stared at me a moment longer before he seemed satisfied that I spoke the truth. I thought he might ask then to see the drawings I still held, but he did not. Instead he turned the talk to other matters all related to the lack of rain.

The crops languish in the fields. Unless rain comes soon, there will be real hunger this winter. As we must expect in such times—or indeed at any time—there is illness in the town. But so far it has been contained.

A serving woman brought cool cider. Lanfranc stayed on another hour, but he declined an invitation to join our midday meal.

"Alas," he said, "I must return to my own work, but another day I will be pleased to join you."

He took his leave after saying a short prayer over us. Lanfranc's prayers are always short and to the point. He and God seem to understand each other.

Scant minutes after returning to his residence, the archbishop summoned his cleric. His orders were as succinct as his prayer has been. Before nones, a messenger was galloping north to London.

It took him three days to reach the capital. When he

did so, he went directly to the residence of the high sheriff. Renard was out, but the message from Lanfranc was waiting for him when he returned a few hours later.

He sat down, kicked off his sandals, took a long swallow of water to ease his parched throat, and picked up the single sheet of parchment emblazoned at the bottom with Lanfranc's seal.

The curse that broke from him caused a passing servant to drop a tray of crockery. Renard did not notice. He was too busy contemplating what Lanfranc's summons would mean.

It could not have come at a worse time. He was no closer to finding the killer Londoners were calling—with delicious horror—the "pagan slayer." Although no further murders of the kind had occurred, Renard would not rest until the killer was in custody.

Added to that were the rumors of rebellion that seemed to grow with each passing day. Yet information on Oath Bearer remained elusive. As he suspected, no one in London would admit to knowing of him.

He had told Odo that Canterbury might be a better place to seek such information, but he hadn't expected to do it so soon. Now he had no choice.

Only one bright spot served to improve his dark mood. Aveline was in Canterbury. He could seek her out on the excuse of Odo's scroll. He could speak with her, hear her voice again, see again the fire that dwelt behind the ice shards of her eyes.

See and be warmed by it, for truly she did rouse his blood, this slender, flame-haired Englishwoman whose spirit he seemed in some strange way to recognize.

To Canterbury then and the pagan slayer be damned. If he stirred while Renard was away, Rufus could have him.

He rose, picked up his sandals—for he was an

instinctively tidy man—and went in search of Burgess, finding him as usual laboring over the accounts Renard himself found so tedious.

A stab of guilt moved through him as he thought how tirelessly the monk worked. He deserved a holiday.

"We are going to Canterbury," he said. "See to it, but quietly. I would rather it was not known that I have left the city."

Burgess sighed. He knew what that meant. "No escort, I suppose? No proper livery? Just the two of us plodding along, finding shelter wherever we can, subject to every mishap the road throws our way?"

Renard grinned at him. "That's about right, except for one thing."

"What's that?" Burgess asked, peering suspiciously. He would put nothing past his master.

"We won't be plodding. I intend to be there the day after tomorrow."

The monk groaned. "Leave me here, I beg of you. I am not equipped for such suffering. A donkey was good enough for Our Lord and it should be good enough for any man."

"Nonsense," Renard said, and slapped him on the back, just a shade more heartily than he might have. "You sit a fine horse. Get us packed up while I tend to a few matters. We'll leave in an hour."

"Where will we be staying?" Burgess called as Renard left the room. "What clothes will you need? How long will we be there? Wait, how I am supposed to—"

He gave up, contenting himself with a further groan. That done, he put his pen aside and hurried to do Renard's bidding.

*   *   *

Lanfranc's summons reached Renard on a Tuesday. It was late Thursday when the archbishop walked into his private receiving chamber to find his young friend waiting for him.

"There you are, then," he said, holding out a hand. "Pleasant journey?"

"Tolerable," Renard said. He had shaken the worst of the dust from him while still outside, but he still felt tired, hot, and grimy. Lanfranc's knowing smile did nothing to ease that.

"It would have been better without Burgess. When you convinced me to take him on, you didn't mention that he can complain about anything and everything, and unfailingly does."

The archbishop laughed. They clasped hands before taking seats near the window. It was slightly cooler there, but not much. Canterbury, like London, sweltered.

"But he is loyal, is he not? And meticulous in his work. You won't find better."

"I suppose," Renard said without much conviction. He was feeling better disposed toward Burgess now that he did not have to listen to him constantly. Upon closer examination, he thought that Lanfranc also looked weary.

The prelate was in his sixty-fifth year, a great age, but he normally appeared more youthful. Something seemed to be wearing him down.

"Are you well?" Renard asked quietly.

"Well enough. I live a simple life and I take care of myself, which is more than I can say for Odo. Is he still bolting down hams?"

Renard laughed. He was feeling better for having come. "And still having them stolen. I am supposed to be seeing to that, but I haven't had much of a chance lately."

Lanfranc nodded. "I heard about the killings."

Renard was not surprised. The archbishop heard everything and usually sooner than later. "I am no closer to solving them than I am to finding Odo's thief. But at least there have been no more for the moment."

"That is fortunate, for you have yet more matters to see to, don't you?"

It took Renard a moment to realize what he meant. When he did, he sighed. "You mean Odo's great work? The one he is having made for the king? I am supposed to be supervising it, although exactly how remains unclear."

A servant entered with chilled wine. Each man accepted a goblet before they continued.

"What do you make of the good women of St. Margaret's?" Lanfranc asked.

"I have met Abbess Eldgythe and the Lady Aveline, but I know little about them."

The archbishop smiled and complied with what he rightly took to be a desire for greater knowledge.

"Mother Eldgythe is a remarkable woman. Her origins are humble and I am not clear on them myself, but early on she came to the notice of those who matter. She has been abbess of St. Margaret's for almost twenty years now and she has done an exemplary job. She possesses great intelligence, an indomitable will, and a gift for strategy that many a battle commander would envy. In short, she makes a formidable adversary."

Renard frowned. "Surely she is not yours?"

"Certainly not. We get along splendidly." Lanfranc leaned forward slightly, amusement tugging at his mouth. "I am talking about you, dear boy. The girl, Aveline, is very precious to Mother Eldgythe. She has been her ward for eleven years and the abbess guards her jealously."

"I see," Renard said slowly. "What makes you think Mother Eldgythe would have any reason to believe I am a threat where Aveline is concerned?"

"Instinct, that's all. She is a lovely creature, don't you think?"

Renard looked into the wily gray eyes and suppressed a laugh. Lanfranc liked nothing better than to stir the pot. "If you have a taste for red hair," he replied with deliberate casualness.

"And you don't?"

"I didn't say that."

Lanfranc sat back, satisfied. "Very well then. Odo wants this scroll made to commemmorate the victory. What I want to know is why?"

Renard frowned. It was obvious, wasn't it? "To honor his brother."

"To flatter him, you mean?"

"It's usually the same thing, isn't it? He intends to give the scroll as a gift to William."

"Again, why? Odo does nothing—gives nothing— unless he expects something in return. So the question becomes what does Odo want?"

"What he has always wanted," Renard said promptly. "To be pope. To sit on the throne of Peter."

Lanfranc grimaced. "It is a loathsome thought, but you are right; that is his objective. So he imagines giving William this great gift will better dispose the king to helping him achieve the papacy. Is that it?"

"I suppose, but what does it matter? William won't agree, he can't. He's stretched too thin now protecting what is already his."

"Precisely," Lanfranc said. His voice took on new urgency. "But Odo refuses to acknowledge that. Indeed, his decision to have this scroll made shows beyond doubt he still believes William can be persuaded to help him despite all the evidence to the contrary."

"It can be seen that way," Renard acknowledged.

"Can and will. William and anyone else who is interested will think that this is how Odo means to gain the papal throne, by first flattering his brother into supporting him and then using William's might to take what he believes should be his."

"But when the king denies him such support, that will be the end of that," Renard said.

"No," Lanfranc replied, "it won't, because it was never that to begin with. Odo is many things, most of which I despise, but he is no fool. He can't believe that William will be swayed by any gift, even one so great. He knows William will stand firm in his refusal to help him."

"Then why bother?"

"Because it gets everybody looking in the wrong direction. It will take months to complete such a work and months more for it to become clear that William hasn't changed his mind. In the meantime, no one expects Odo to be doing anything. But I think he will be. I think he has an entirely different plan for advancing himself that has nothing whatsoever to do with the scroll."

"Then what does it have to do with?" Renard asked. His mind turned over what Lanfranc had just said. Like it or not, it made sense.

"I don't know," the archbishop admitted, "but it is linked to this talk we're hearing of rebellion; it has to be. Whether the talk is true or not, it can be used as an excuse to raise more troops here in England and keep them at the ready. Those aren't just the conditions for putting down rebellion, they are also the conditions for seizing a throne from its lawful ruler. Odo has spent very little time in England of late, but he is here now. So is Rufus. Meanwhile our king remains in Normandy, fighting a treacherous son, with little time or inclination to think of what we are facing here."

"You realize," Renard said slowly, "that you are suggesting Rufus and Odo are in league against the man who is father to the one, brother to the other, and king to both."

"None of which would matter to either of them if they saw a chance for personal gain. Mark my words, the scroll is a diversion, something to draw the eye from where it should really be. But it may have unintended consequences."

"How so?" Renard asked.

"I am not prepared to say as yet." Hastily he added, "That is no reflection on you. I simply haven't put it all together in my mind. But I will tell you this, Aveline bears watching—and protecting. She is too close to the center of this, whatever *this* is."

Renard sat back in his chair. He had drunk little of the wine, but his mind felt fogged. What was the archbishop telling him?

"Surely it is up to the Church to protect her."

"Why so?"

"She lives at the abbey, the abbess is her guardian, isn't she under some sort of vow?" She wasn't a nun, he knew that, or even a novice, but she must surely be a postulant.

"You'd think so, wouldn't you?" Lanfranc said genially. "But you'd be wrong. Aveline came to the abbey eleven years ago. Her family had been killed in the conquest. It is a common story, though a sad one. At any rate she was lucky. Mother Eldgythe took her in. She has been there ever since, but she has never taken holy vows. Her status at the abbey remains strictly unofficial."

Renard did his best to conceal the surge of relief that went through him at this news. He did not entirely succeed.

Lanfranc drank sparingly from his cup and set it aside. He looked as though he was enjoying himself. "Perhaps you would care to see her? She is here now in the scriptorium. I believe you know the way."

Renard remembered it without difficulty. He reached the stone-vaulted chamber just as the bells of Christ Church were ringing the call to vespers. The few monks who had still been at work laid down their implements and filtered out.

In all the chamber only one desk remained occupied. There a bright head bent, red gold in the waning light.

"You will strain your eyes," Renard said.

Aveline started. She looked up at the big, hard man looming above her. His dark hair was disheveled and he needed to shave. The tunic stretched across his powerful chest was travel-stained and wrinkled. There was a sword strapped around his taut waist. He looked exactly what he was—a warrior, proud, indomitable, dangerous. The enemy.

Without thought, she reached out her hand to him.

Wulfgarth stepped from the shadows. At once Aveline dropped her hand. She looked away from Renard, her face pale.

"What are you doing here?" Wulfgarth demanded. He was as tall as Renard and as powerfully built. The long scar across his face and the cavern where his right eye had been only added to his fierce demeanor. His voice was a low growl. He made no pretense at courtesy.

"Speaking with your mistress, English," Renard said.

"What I have to say to her does not concern you. Get out."

Instead, Wulfgarth took a step forward, his fighting arm raised. "Why you—"

"No!" Aveline cried. She stood up, putting herself between the men. "This is nonsense. You are acting like children trying to bully each other. Go outside, Wulfgarth. If I need you, I will call."

He went, but he made it clear he did not want to. Barely had the outer door slammed behind him than Renard shook his head in wonder. "How are you with lions if you can control a bear so well?"

Aveline whirled on him. "Is that what he looks like to you? A bear to be baited and tormented? He is a man and a good one. I would not be alive were it not for him. I will not hear him insulted or threatened in any way."

"I meant no harm to him," Renard said softly. He admired her defense of her friend, but he could not help but wish that some of that loyalty might be for him.

"What are you working on?" he asked, intending to distract her.

Aveline hesitated. She was still smarting over his attitude toward Wulfgarth, but she calmed quickly enough. Quietly she said, "I am putting the final touches on the drawings for the first panel."

"Then work hasn't actually begun yet?"

"On the contrary, the ornamental borders are being done right now. They will frame the work and draw the different parts of it together."

Renard nodded, seeing the sense in that. He looked down at the parchment spread out over the worktable. "Why do you come here to work?"

"I needed to check a few details. There are numerous illustrated manuscripts here. The archbishop is kind enough to let me use them."

"To further the work on Odo's tapestry?"

"I am surprised by that, too," Aveline admitted, "but the archbishop is a very kind man."

Renard did not disagree with her, but privately he thought a different interpretation could be put on Lanfranc's generosity. By still allowing Aveline access to the scriptorium, he had a ready means of keeping tabs on her.

He glanced again at the drawings. Here and there he could see where she had added detail or changed a line. The whole flowed together beautifully, from the very first scene, where a man he supposed was Harold could be seen talking with the aged King Edward.

"What is happening here?" he asked.

"It is the spring of 1064," Aveline said softly. Her fingers traced the lines on the parchment. "The Earl Harold is going to Normandy. He visits King Edward first, then rides to his manor at Bosham. A short while later he departs with his thegns. An ill wind blows them off course and they land at Ponthieu, where they are taken captive by the Comte Guy."

"I remember that," Renard said suddenly. "When word came that Guy was holding Harold, it caused an uproar."

"You were with William then?" Aveline asked.

He nodded. "I was thirteen years old that spring and a page in William's court. I'll never forget the look on the duke's face when he heard Harold had come, and worse yet, that Guy had arrested him. It was an act of dishonor."

Aveline said nothing, but he sensed she wanted to. He turned his attention back to the drawings. "Here, this is where William ordered Guy to release Harold and they all rode to Rouen?"

"That's right, and here they all fought together in Brittany and Harold saved two of William's soldiers from the quicksand."

"A noble act," Renard said. "It set the stage for what followed."

"Oh, yes," Aveline murmured under her breath, "the swearing of the oath. Were you there for that, too?"

Renard nodded. "As it happens, I was."

She looked surprised. "I thought it was done in private."

"It was, but I was there. I heard and saw it all."

"You heard the Earl Harold take an oath of vassalage to William?"

Renard hesitated. He knew what men said about the oath now—what they were encouraged to say—and he knew what had actually happened. The two were not really the same.

Slowly he said, "The exact wording of the oath doesn't matter, not anymore. The point is that Harold violated it, and for that he died."

Again, he had the impression she was about to speak, but she remained silent. Without a word she rolled up the parchment and tied it with a length of string. Vespers had long since stopped tolling. Off in the distance they could hear the monks chanting their prayers.

"It is getting late," Aveline said. "I must return to St. Margaret's."

"I will be in Canterbury for a while. Have I your leave to call on you?"

For most of the time they had been talking, Aveline had kept her gaze studiously away from him. But now she faced him directly. "You do not need that, Norman, and we both know it."

The bitterness in her tone was unmistakable. He could only wonder at its cause. She had lost her family in the events that began with that ill-advised journey to Normandy. He could not blame her for being upset by the memory of it.

He stepped aside. Aveline did not so much as glance at him again as she left the scriptorium. But he saw how her hands trembled and had to resist the impulse to sweep her into his arms, to comfort and cajole her, to put the past behind them and think only of what could be.

He did not because this was a sacred place and because she would undoubtedly scream for Wulfgarth. Not that he feared the Englishman, far from it. He relished the thought of taking him apart. Except that would upset Aveline.

He frowned. This business of caring for a woman's feelings was more complicated than he had expected. At least when the female in question was a high-tempered Englishwoman who should have been safely under the protection of holy vows but wasn't.

He could have her. That thought burned in his loins as, outwardly calm, he walked out of the scriptorium. There was no sign of Aveline and Wulfgarth; they would waste no time returning to St. Margaret's.

The monks were at their evening meal. Renard could join them, but he had no desire for their company. Instead he turned in the other direction. He would walk into the town, find a congenial inn, buy a few drinks, and talk. More important, he would listen. With luck, he might hear something that could be useful.

With even more luck, he might drink enough to sleep that night, but he doubted it. Grumbling at the vagaries of women, he went on his way without seeing the flicker of movement at the archbishop's window.

Lanfranc smiled as he observed his young friend's mood and rightly judged its cause. Truly he had set a hound among the hares.

Or was he wrong to think of the ladies of St. Margaret's in such terms? The old stone abbey harbored many secrets, of that he was sure. Aveline was merely one, but she was far and away the most tantalizing.

He would know the truth for better or for worse. The fate of this poor, blood-drenched land might well depend on it. He sighed deeply and left the window.

His monks were waiting for him at supper; they would not begin without him. Slowly he made his way down the steep stone steps to the refectory. Memory, he thought, was a funny thing. It played games with a man.

Yet he was not so old or so worn that he could not clearly remember the time when so much hung in the balance and any act—any act—had seemed justified, given what was to be won.

The problem was that others remembered it, too. And there was no guarantee they would keep silent forever.

He entered the refectory and took his seat at the high table. To each side of him, the monks of Christ Church bowed their heads in prayer, then raised them to break bread. Lanfranc went through the motions. His appetite was gone. Only fear remained.

While the last man lived who knew the truth, there was no safety. And when he was gone, then what? When they were all dust, what voice would still be heard?

Odo's tapestry, perhaps. Would it be what told the tale? A tapestry created by a woman of skill and daring who was herself no stranger to inconvenient truths.

Despite the warmth, he shivered. The air felt chill on his old skin. He closed his eyes and heard again the cry of falcons diving for their prey against a bloodred sky.

⅊ The Journey ⅋

The Lady Edythe was smiling. She stood at the top of the steps leading to the great hall, a slender, flame-haired figure in a shimmering white tunic girded in braided silver, her green eyes aglow as she watched the man striding toward her.

He was tall, with the sinewy, muscled body of a warrior, broad of chest, narrow of waist, lean at the hips, and long of leg. On this fair morning he was luxuriously garbed in a scarlet tunic embroidered in gold and a short scarlet cape held at his right shoulder by a brooch of beaten gold set with precious gems.

Behind him, his sleek black palfrey pawed the ground, nostrils flaring as he snorted from the hard ride. The dark-haired young thegn holding the palfrey's reins watched as his master climbed the steps two at a time.

Harold Godwinson, Earl of Wessex, was eager to be reunited with his beautiful handfast wife. Wulfgarth could not blame him.

When the earl had vanished into the great hall, the Lady Edythe with him, Wulfgarth led the palfrey around to the stables. He took his own horse as well, a good mount not quite so noble as the earl's, but strong and dependable, not unlike Wulfgarth himself.

A groom ran up to assist. "Walk them well," Wulfgarth instructed as he handed over both sets of reins. He waited a moment to make sure the boy obeyed. Such caution really wasn't necessary, all the servants at the earl's manor of Bosham and elsewhere were superbly trained, but it was in Wulfgarth's nature always to be sure.

Only when his responsibility for the horses had been properly discharged did he see to his own needs. He and the earl had ridden from London, covering the distance in four arduous days.

With them had come the usual escort of thegns, men-at-arms and the like, all mounted and fully armed. Even in these days of relative peace, Harold Godwinson did not let down his guard. In his midtwenties, Wulfgarth had seen enough of life to be sure that if anything could go wrong, it most likely would. He approved of the earl's caution.

But enough of that for now. The day was brilliantly clear, warm without being oppressive, and he welcomed a rare chance to relax. As one of Harold's ranking thegns, Wulfgarth had the privilege of private quarters set a small distance from the main hall.

The single room was of rough-hewn wood rising to a domed ceiling. The walls were brightly painted and hung with Wulfgarth's own shields as well as those of his father and grandfather. The large rope bed was covered with wolf pelts. Several carved chests held clothing and other belongings.

Already his servant had gone ahead to air the room and begin unpacking. The weapons would be taken away for polishing, the clothing washed; by the end of the day everything would be back exactly where it should be.

A wave of contentment washed over Wulfgarth as he stooped his head to pass through the door. He liked order, discipline, and purpose, all of which he found in his service to the earl.

With clean clothes in his hand, he made his way to the sweat house. The low stone structure was a legacy of a far earlier time, when the earl's grandfather, a wily Danish pirate, had come plundering in the area only to decide he liked the place enough to stay. It was he who built the first hall, of which nothing now remained. The sweat house had proved more durable.

Wulfgarth left his clothes outside and entered through the low doorway. The room was circular in shape, small and dark with only a few chinks of light let in from the outside. In the center, surrounded by low benches, a bed of coals glowed red hot. Beside it was a bucket of water and a ladle.

Throwing water on the coals, Wulfgarth sat back to enjoy the steam. He breathed in deeply, feeling his pores open and the sweat begin to rise. It purified his body, but it did nothing to ease his mind.

The journey to London worried him. Not that there was anything unusual about it; the earl went often to confer with the king, although perhaps confer wasn't the right word.

It was open knowledge that England's greatest earl held more real power than his king could hope to muster. Despite the courtesy he still showed Edward, Harold was more likely to inform his sovereign of what he intended rather than ask his permission.

Wulfgarth had been present when the earl informed Edward that he would shortly visit Normandy. The king's response had been immediate and more vigorous than usual.

"Why?" Edward demanded, his pale face agitated. He was a small, slightly built man with a long gray beard and an expression some took to be holy. Wulfgarth thought otherwise. He believed the king to be weak and vindictive, and he awaited the day God would see fit to take him.

"Why would you go there?" Edward went on, his voice more petulant than anxious. He had a slight accent, the legacy of his years in Normandy. Except for the beard, he looked like a Norman as well. Thought like one, too, always scheming and plotting.

No, Wulfgarth did not like his king or trust him. He was glad the earl was there to keep him firmly in check.

Harold shrugged and twirled the goblet of chased gold between his fingers. He was comfortably seated on a cushioned chair not quite as ornate as the king's but in keeping with his high rank.

They were in Edward's retiring room next to the chapel, where the king seemed to spend most of his time. Certainly he had never spent it in bed with his wife, Harold's sister.

If he had, he might have gotten himself the heir England so desperately needed and no trip to Normandy would have been in the air.

"I want to meet William," Harold said. He glanced away negligently, gazing out beyond the palace to where the laborers were at work on Edward's great abbey. The Abbey of the Westminister, as it was called, was being raised to the greater glory of God and the salvation of Edward's soul.

In the earl's view, God had no need of the former and Edward had no hope of the latter. But there was no point in dwelling on that.

"Why?" the king demanded again. His face was pale, the lips bloodless. Only the brilliant black eyes revealed the frustrated will buried deep within. He had never been able to win against the bold, brash, thundering Godwinsons, the Viking spawn that had long ago shattered his hopes and destroyed his peace. Once, years before, he'd thought he had them, but they came rampaging back, seizing even greater power and leaving him to fend for himself as best he could.

He had kept his throne but little else. Even his pride was gone. He feared the hard, virile man who faced him, feared where his strength of will and his vision of greatness would lead them all.

"What have you and William to talk about?" Edward asked.

Wulfgarth wondered about that himself. He was standing by the door on guard. The fact that they were in the king's residence, but it was the earl's man who stood watch, put the situation neatly. He leaned forward to hear what Harold would say.

The earl smiled. More correctly he bared his teeth. There was no humor in his brilliant blue eyes.

"You forget," he said softly, "William holds my brother Wulfnooth as well as his family. They have been hostage in Normandy for thirteen years despite all our attempts to negotiate their return. It is my opinion that a personal visit is needed to settle the matter."

Had there been any color in Edward's face to begin with, it would have vanished. He gripped the arms of his chair so tightly that Wulfgarth thought his blue-veined knuckles would crack.

"You are wrong to think I have forgotten Wulfnooth," Edward said. "He is daily in my prayers."

"As well he should be," Harold replied. The words

hung between the two men. Both knew that Edward was responsible for the fate of the youngest Godwinson. In that brief time thirteen years before when the king had managed to evict the Earl Godwin and his sons from England, Edward had held on to the youngest of them. Wulfnooth had been twenty-one, newly married and with an infant son. That proved his undoing, for he refused to leave his wife and child, instead allowing himself to be taken prisoner.

Within weeks of the Godwinsons' defeat, Duke William was in England to visit Edward. All these years later no one knew what had been said between them, but when William left, he was not alone. Wulfnooth and his family went with him.

Since then, every effort to secure their return had failed, as Harold said. Apparently the earl had grown tired of waiting.

"No good will come of this," Edward said. "William will simply refuse."

"Perhaps," Harold replied, "but that would be regrettable. After all, I go to Normandy in friendship, anxious to hold out the hand of peace and secure better relations between our peoples. This matter of hostages has hitherto been political, but if William refuses me face-to-face, he makes it personal. I would have no choice but to respond appropriately."

Wulfgarth turned his head slightly to hide his smile. Did any man serve a wiser or more clever master? Should the earl return from Normandy without his brother and the others, he would be perfectly justified in asserting that William had hostile intentions toward him and therefore toward England. Under those circumstances, no man would resist the call to arms.

If he succeeded in his mission, he restored members

of his family to their rightful place. But if he failed, an argument could be made that he accomplished even more.

Clearly Edward thought so, for he rose suddenly and jerked down the few steps separating the seating area from the rest of the small room. His body shook and he appeared to be in the grip of emotions he could not control.

"You think me a fool," he said. "You think I don't understand what you're doing, but it is all too clear. Nothing matters to you except your own power. For it, you will bring this country to ruin."

Harold did not respond at once. He set his goblet down and stood unhurriedly. Gathering his cloak about him, he walked down the steps and came toward the door.

Preparing to leave, he said almost as an afterthought, "No, sire, that is not what I am doing. I am preparing this country to fight for its life. God willing, there will be no need, but the world is full of ambitious, greedy men, and too many of them have been encouraged by what they perceive as England's weakness. Given the opportunity, they will fall upon us without mercy."

Edward clasped his hands in front of him to hide their trembling. "Then we must pray to almighty God for deliverance."

"You pray," the earl said. "I fight." He gestured to Wulfgarth, who flung open the door and quickly followed his master through it, as he would follow him into the very gates of hell, if need be.

The steam was growing too hot. He rose, wiped the sweat from his eyes, and left the low stone house. Beyond it was a small pool fed by a crystalline stream.

Wulfgarth took a breath and launched himself into space, landing with a resounding clap in the middle of the pool.

Even on a warm day, the water was cool. He swallowed a shout of shock and dove deep, holding his breath until his lungs burned. Only then did he surface, shaking the water from his hair like a great, unruly dog.

Refreshed and cleanly garbed, he made his way to the hall in search of food. The Lady Edythe was nowhere to be seen. He would hardly expect her to be, with her lord newly returned. But her absence in no way detracted from the smooth running of her household.

Barely had Wulfgarth taken his seat at one of the long trestle tables than a servant appeared to pour ale. Another set a trencher of stewed meat and vegetables in front of him.

He was well into the food when he became aware that he was no longer alone. A child had appeared at his side. She was delicately made, with an elfin face in which blue eyes shone brightly. Her hair was a riotous shade of red. Despite the luxuriousness of her tunic, she looked rumpled and disheveled, as though she had been hard at play.

Wulfgarth smiled. He liked the seven-year-old Lady Kendra. Of all the earl's children, he thought her the most spirited and, perhaps, the most like her father in the cleverness of her mind and the strength of her will.

"What brings you here?" he asked, making room for her on the bench. "Are you hungry?"

He would gladly have shared his food with her or sent the servants for more, but Kendra shook her head. She leaned against him companionably. He was a familiar figure in her life, the great lumbering bear of a man who followed her father so devotedly. She took it for granted that his loyalty extended to her and she was not wrong.

"Mother and Father are arguing," she said.

Wulfgarth was surprised. It was well known that even after more than fifteen years together, the earl and his lady were powerfully drawn to one another. He had presumed them otherwise occupied.

"What makes you think that?" he asked cautiously.

"I heard them as I went past their quarters." She made a face. "Mother was yelling. She said he is a fool to go to Normandy, it is too dangerous."

Wulfgarth sighed. In hall or anywhere else in public, the Lady Edythe deferred to her lord, as was proper. But in private she did not hesitate to give him her opinions.

"You shouldn't eavesdrop," he said.

Kendra drew back, offended. "I wasn't. She was shouting so loudly anybody could have heard her." She paused before adding, "I guess she's really worried." Huge eyes fastened on Wulfgarth, seeking reassurance.

He gave it without hesitation. "The earl is a great and wise man. He knows what he is doing."

"But why go? What does he hope to gain?"

Wulfgarth chuckled. Truly she was the earl's child. "If I tell you, will you promise not to repeat it?"

"Of course."

Most children he would not have so trusted, but this one he did. Even at seven, there was a stillness at the center of her being that boded well for the women she would become.

"The earl goes to Normandy to free your uncle and his family."

"Wulfnooth? But he's been there forever. Why would father go to get him now?"

"Don't you think it's time?"

She tilted her head to one side thoughtfully. "Probably. Will he take a great army with him?"

"No."

"Then how does he expect to win?"

"He will ask William to return them."

Her brow furrowed. "Can that work?"

Wulfgarth thought about it for a moment. Slowly he nodded. "If William is half as smart as he needs to be, I think it will."

She sat awhile longer, as though in thought, before darting off as swiftly as she had come. Her smile lingered, warming Wulfgarth, but the niggling suspicion that he had said something he oughtn't have troubled him.

By evening, the earl and his lady appeared to have made their peace. When they appeared in the hall, there was no sign of rebellion in Edythe's clear green eyes. She sat beside Harold at the high table, a vision of beauty and grace, and was attentive to his every word, though she said little herself.

Wulfgarth was relieved. Though Edythe was barely ten years older than he and the earl only seven more than that, they were the closest to parents that he had ever known, his own having died when he was still in swaddling clothes. The thought of trouble between them made him feel like a hurting child.

He drank a little too much ale that night and woke the next morning with a head that felt bigger than it was. But the clear sky and freshening breeze cured him quickly enough. Excitement stirred within him. He had never seen Normandy and he was looking forward to it. More, he was looking forward to seeing the earl best Duke William.

That had to wait a few days more as the earl had

business to attend to in Bosham. But less than a week after their return from London, they were ready to depart again. Wulfgarth rose early on the appointed day.

He dressed quickly, ate a spare breakfast, and made his way to the shingled beach. He was there, watching the boats being dragged into the water, when Harold and the rest of his party rode up.

Bosham overlooked the sea and, immediately beyond, the Isle of Wight. Even in the worst of seasons, it was well protected and had therefore grown into a prosperous port. A few gulls wheeled overhead while pipers scurried at the water's edge. All signs were for a fair sail.

The Lady Edythe did not come to see them off. Presumably she had said her farewells privately. The earl dismounted, but stayed to pat his horse and speak a word of encouragement as the beast was led up the ramp and into the first boat.

Nearby, men strained at the ropes as the foreman called forth the chant. Working together to the rhythm, they pulled and tugged until the second high-prowed vessel slid into the water.

Wulfgarth stood near Harold but a little apart, watching all the preparations. He had a keen eye for detail and was not afraid to use it. All appeared to be in order. The horses were stowed, oars were lashed to the sides, even the falcons and hounds had been brought on board. It looked as though they were going on holiday.

The thought amused him. Harold turned in time to see him smile. "A rare occurrence," the earl said. "I thought you'd be dourer this morning."

So Wulfgarth's imbibing had not gone unnoticed. He was not the only one with an eye for detail. Flushing slightly, he said, "I enjoy traveling, my lord."

"Good thing," Harold said. "Sometimes I think I've walked every inch of this kingdom, and with you beside me most of the way." He reached out a strong hand and clasped Wulfgarth's arm. His eyes were suddenly serious. "It hasn't been unappreciated, my friend. There is no one else I would rather have with me."

Wulfgarth's flush deepened. Praise from the earl was rare and all the more treasured for that. Humbly he inclined his head. "Thank you, my liege."

A moment more the two men stood on the shingled beach, locked in understanding. Then Harold turned away, heading for the lead boat, and Wulfgarth trotted after him.

The tide turned with the hour. The oars dipped, the helmsman called the pace, and soon Bosham was but a memory behind them.

Wulfgarth settled down comfortably toward the bow. He could see the earl clearly and could respond to any command that might be given, but Harold seemed disposed simply to enjoy the voyage. He was chatting casually with several of the thegns.

As always, the salt air raised an appetite. Servants brought out a keg of ale along with rounds of cheese and slices of the good sweet ham for which Bosham was rightly famous.

Wulfgarth did credit to his share. His head no longer throbbed and his stomach was, as always, steady. Not until he glanced to the east did he realize that the fair weather of the morning was changing rapidly.

The earl realized it at the same time. He went forward and had a word with the helmsman, but gave no indication of concern. His vessel, *Stormflyer,* had been through far worse, as had her sister ship, *Wavecatcher.* There was no cause for alarm, not even as the clouds thickened and the pleasant breeze turned to chill wind.

Rain began to pelt the ships. Wulfgarth pulled his cloak more securely around him, but otherwise did not move. He was long accustomed to discomfort.

Not so the small boy he noticed only then, who had appeared among the servants. He was a slight thing, dressed in rough garb too big for him, with a cap pulled down almost over his eyes.

As the ship lurched into the trough of a wave, the boy stumbled and fell forward. He would have been hurt had not Wulfgarth caught him.

"Easy," he said to the child, not wanting him to be alarmed, "it looks as though you don't have your sea legs yet."

The boy gasped and tried to pull away. Surprised, Wulfgarth instinctively tightened his grip. A cry broke from the small, pale lips.

"Let me go!"

Wulfgarth obeyed, instantly and without thought. He could hardly do otherwise. Surprise overwhelmed him, followed hard by shock.

"Lady Kendra!"

She was bent on getting away, but Wulfgarth recovered enough to stop her. Hauling her up against him, he peered down into the ashen face.

"Sweet Lord," he said, "it *is* you. What in the name of heaven are you doing here?"

"I wanted to see Normandy," she said, eyes defiant, "and I wanted . . . I wanted . . ." The defiance ebbed, replaced by doubt and tremulous yearning. "I wanted to spend some time with Father," she said finally. "All he ever notices are the boys. He never takes me with him."

Wulfgarth sighed. He knew his master to be an unusually loving and devoted father, but Kendra did have a point. Naturally enough, Harold was more involved with his sons than with his daughter. For one thing, she was the youngest, but more than that, she was expected to learn what she would need in life from her mother. The battle-hardened earl undoubtedly thought he had little to offer so tender and delicate a flower.

Kendra thought otherwise. She tossed her head so that the cap slid precariously. A riot of red peeped from beneath it. "It's too late to take me back," she said.

The storm made her right. In another moment it was hard upon the ships. Wulfgarth scarcely had time to pull Kendra within the shelter of his cloak before the fury hit.

"Hang on," he yelled as yet another wave, larger than the last, hit *Stormflyer.* Kendra screamed and burrowed against him. He held on to her as the ship bucked, planks shrieking.

The oarsmen cursed as they fought to turn into the wind. For long moments they hovered between success and failure, backs straining, muscles bunched beneath their leather tunics, faces contorted with their effort.

Slowly, inch by inch, *Stormflyer* twisted, sails filling until it looked almost as though they would triumph. But then, without warning, the wind redoubled its efforts and they were flung, helpless as a bit of flotsam, pell-mell into a wall of water that loomed above them full fifty feet, gray and surging, thunderous in its power, white foam flecked with the face of death.

Wulfgarth murmured a silent prayer, dragged Kendra under him, and said what he knew might be his last words. "Breathe in, my lady, as deep as you can, and for the love of God, hold it!"

The child shuddered against him but obeyed. *Stormflyer*

hit the wall. The full weight of the water fell upon them. Light, air, life itself all vanished beneath its implacable rage. Wulfgarth forced his eyes open despite the stinging salt. High above him he saw the last faint flicker of the sky before it vanished into darkness.

Desperately, with all his strength, he held on to Kendra. If he let her go know, she would be lost in the pounding fury. His lungs burned and his muscles felt stretched to tearing, but he would not let go. He would die a hundred deaths himself before he let this bright-eyed, sprite-spirited child perish.

Just when he thought he could bear it no longer, another might surge sent *Stormflyer* hurtling upward. Wulfgarth dragged in breath, aware of Kendra doing the same. She shifted, trying to get free. Realizing that his grip must be hurting her, he relented slightly but did not let her go.

"Are you all right?" he asked.

She nodded. Her eyes were wide and dazed. He could see the sky reflected in them. And the fear that he knew to be his own as well as hers, for what sane man would not fear the terrible strength of the sea in primal fury?

Anxiously he glanced around as Kendra did the same. The storm had flung them across the deck of the boat and brought them hard up against the mast. All around them, they could see men trying to right themselves.

The first to stand was the earl, sopping wet as they all were, but still very much in command. He looked around quickly, assessing the damage, and barked a sharp order.

"To oars! Heave to! Look sharp or we'll be on the rocks! There's good lads, put your backs to it. Heave . . . heave . . . !"

The helmsman spat water, filled his lungs, and took up the cadence. Harold took another look across the surging sea. A hundred yards off their port, *Wavecatcher* rose battered but unbowed.

Relief filled his eyes, but it faded quickly when he glanced toward *Stormflyer*'s mast and saw Wulfgarth there, a flame-haired child snug in his lap.

"God's blood!" Harold muttered, loud enough to make the men nearest jump. Their gazes all turned in the same direction.

"Kendra! What are you doing here?"

She had answered Wulfgarth readily enough when he asked the same question, but faced by her father's anger, she was mute. Nor did she try to get away when Harold seized her, holding her with one hand, her feet dangling well above the deck.

"By all that's holy! Have you lost your senses?"

"Sir," Wulfgarth said, leaping up, "she may be hurt!"

Harold glared at him, but it took only a moment for the truth of that to sink in. With a groan, he clasped his tiny daughter to him, holding her with infinite tenderness.

"Kendra, sweetling, Wulfgarth is right. Are you hurt? Does anything pain you? For the love of God, speak!"

She did so, clearly and persuasively, with a smile so radiant that no man who saw it could fail to be moved. "I am fine, Father. Wulfgarth held me through the storm. It was most exciting."

For a scant instant there appeared to be tears in the earl's eyes, but they must have been a trick of the light. Still holding his daughter, he extended a hand to his faithful thegn.

"I thank you," he said gruffly. "When we return to England, you will name your reward."

The other men nodded approvingly. With those

words, the earl both acknowledged the service done him and signified the value he placed on his young daughter. Wulfgarth was to be envied. He could claim land, manors, men-at-arms, and clearly the earl would grant them gladly.

But first there were other matters to be dealt with.

They were, as Harold had guessed, very near the coast. Even as they watched, an indistinct line on the horizon became a rocky beach. They drew closer and, with caution, anchored. *Wavecatcher* did the same.

The earl was the first ashore, splashing knee-deep through the surf with Kendra in his arms. Wulfgarth followed, as did the other thegns. Groomsmen unloaded the horses that shied and kicked their hooves but made no attempt to bolt.

"Where are we?" Wulfgarth asked, coming up beside his master. He set Kendra down carefully with an admonition not to wander far. For once, she seemed disposed to listen.

"I'm not sure," the earl said. "We were making due south for the Norman coast, but the storm blew us eastward."

"Flanders?" Wulfgarth suggested. That would be all right. The earl had friends and allies in Flanders.

Reluctantly Harold shook his head. "Not likely; there wasn't time. We are either at the eastern-most reaches of Normandy or just across the border into Ponthieu."

Wulfgarth frowned. Ponthieu lay between Normandy and Flanders, a small province ruled by a rapacious count. Their presence there could mean trouble.

"Organize the men," Harold directed. "The ships must be inspected. If they are undamaged, we will wait for the storm to blow itself out and then set sail at once. I do not want to linger here."

Two hours later, the storm was gone, but they were

no closer to leaving. *Wavecatcher's* mast was badly cracked near the base; it was a miracle it had not given way.

As for *Stormflyer,* the gash in her hull made it clear that all aboard her had escaped death by only the slimmest margin. In their present condition, the ships were unusable and there were no means to repair them.

But help—if that was what it was—appeared to be at hand. Even as the men stood around the ships, shaking their heads at their close escape, a line of riders appeared from the nearby hills and made their way toward the English at a rapid pace.

Watching them, Harold said, "Put your cap back on, Kendra, and keep it on." As she hastened to obey he turned to Wulfgarth. "Keep her close."

The order proved wise, for within minutes after their arrival on the beach, the riders made their intention clear. They came at the gallop, pennants flying, and did not draw rein until they were almost upon the English. A shower of sand struck the earl in the face as the lead rider halted directly in front of him.

Harold stood unmoving, looking at the man. He was tall and well built, dressed as befitted a member of the high nobility. His face was handsome, his hair trimmed in the short Norman style, cut high on the back of the neck. His expression was cold, with a glint of malicious pleasure.

He inclined his head tauntingly. "I am Guy, Comte of Ponthieu, and you, English, stand uninvited on my land."

Wulfgarth made a quick motion toward his sword, but the earl stopped him with a gesture. Apparently unperturbed by Guy's rudeness, he said, "I am Harold Godwinson, Earl of Wessex. We had no intention of trespassing, my lord count. The storm blew us off course. Our destination is Rouen and the court of Duke William. With your assistance we will be on our way as quickly as possible."

Guy raised an eyebrow. "Assistance? Oh, but, of course, my lord earl, I will not hesitate to offer you assistance."

He laughed, a most unpleasant sound that drew Kendra even tighter against Wulfgarth's side. "You will be my guests until your kinsmen in England decide what they will pay for your return. Perhaps your king will give a good price for you. Or perhaps not. It will be interesting to see."

He raised his sword arm and his voice as one. "Seize them!"

In the mad scramble that followed, Wulfgarth kept a tight hold on Kendra. All around him, Harold's men were going for their swords, but they had no opportunity to use them.

Above the confusion, firm and steady as a rock, the earl shouted, "Stand down! No bloodshed. This fool of a pirate isn't worth it!"

"Indeed?" Guy demanded unpleasantly when the English were disarmed. "Mayhap I should forget the notion of ransom and simply let you rot in one of my prisons."

Harold sighed. He showed no anger and certainly no fear. His biggest difficulty seemed to be holding on to his patience. "No," he said calmly, "you won't do that. Your greed won't allow it."

Guy stared at him for a long moment. Abruptly he laughed again. "Luck doesn't favor you, English, but you aren't without sense."

He gestured to the black palfrey that had been brought up next to Harold. "Mount, but first remove your stirrups and do not think to seize the reins. Any attempt to escape and I will kill every one of your men."

This the earl did not deign to answer. Wulfgarth knelt, without having to be told, and carefully unfastened the stirrups. Harold threw him a quick look that slid to Kendra. Wulfgarth nodded. He held the reins as the earl mounted.

The journey to Guy's stronghold was made in silence. Although the storm was over, an ominous quite lay over the land. Tendrils of fog seeped from the marshes just beyond the beach. The road they followed was an old one, much worn, that wound along in sight of the water for several miles until it came to the town of Beaurain.

Guy rode at the head with several of his men ranging on either side around the mounted English. Farther back, more of the crews from the two vessels were coming on foot, also surrounded by guards. Kendra rode with Wulfgarth, who kept a stern eye on her cap. He did not need to be told that everything must be done to conceal her identity.

They passed through the gate in the town walls to the startled stares and murmurs of the residents. Wulfgarth noted that the people seemed afraid of Guy; no one cheered him and all kept their eyes averted.

The count's keep stood near the center of the town. They drew rein in front of it. The English were led inside. It was there, immediately inside the keep's main hall, that one of Guy's men noticed Kendra.

"You there, boy," he said, "what are you doing here? You should be back with the rest of the crew."

He took a step forward only to be stopped when Wulfgarth said, "The lad is with me. He stays."

The knight looked disposed to argue, but something in the stamp of Wulfgarth's face, the unrelenting light in his eyes and the slight smile playing around his mouth—as though he would welcome combat, was in fact itching for it—stopped the man. Muttering under his breath, he went away.

"Close," Wulfgarth murmured. "Stay right with me and say nothing to anyone."

Kendra nodded. Her eyes were wide with excitement and a flush of color stained her cheeks. She appeared fully recovered from the storm and seemed to be enjoying herself. Wulfgarth suppressed a sigh. He had become nursemaid to a girl child with the spirit of a warrior, Mary and all the saints help him.

They slept that night in the great hall of Guy's keep, bedded down on straw pallets. Harold was in private quarters as befitted his rank. Kendra slept beside Wulfgarth, her stomach filled with the count's bread and meat, her mind untroubled. Not so Wulfgarth himself, who dozed lightly, if at all.

The next day passed with aching slowness. All the English, Harold included, were kept confined within the keep. They were provided with food and drink, but the inactivity chaffed at their nerves.

Kendra proved unexpectedly resourceful. She searched about in the remnants of the fire until she found several pieces of charcoal. With these, she began to draw on the flagstone floor, first simple scenes of birds and other animals, then the ships they had sailed in, and finally sketches of the men themselves that had them all looking on admiringly.

"For true, Lady Kendra," one of the thegns said, "you've a gift for that sort of thing."

She smiled at the words, but he did not see it, for the glare Wulfgarth shot him froze his blood in his veins. Realizing what he had done, the man stammered, "S-sorry, I wasn't thinking . . . her name . . ."

"It's all right," Wulfgarth muttered, relenting. "There

are none of Guy's men about. But keep sharp. We can't afford mistakes like that."

The man nodded, glad to have been let off so lightly, and Kendra returned to her drawing. Wulfgarth was glad she had found something to keep her distracted as well as amuse the men. He watched with some amazement as she began sketching familiar scenes of Bosham, the hall there, and even her favorite pony.

It was then that he thought of the Lady Edythe and felt his stomach clench. By now Kendra's absence would be known. Her mother would be frantic with worry. Guy's mischief was as nothing compared to what they would face when they got home.

Under his breath he murmured, "They'll be missing you."

Kendra shook her head. As softly she said, "They know where I am."

Wulfgarth thought swiftly. Could she have confided in a servant? If so, the man or woman who had not immediately reported her intention had to be a fool and would rightly pay a terrible price.

"I left a message," Kendra said, still busy with her drawing. "Like this." Quickly she sketched a child whose hair somehow held a hint of flame, a boat he recognized as *Stormflyer,* a man who resembled Harold, and another who was clearly Norman.

Despite himself, Wulfgarth chuckled. He was relieved that the Lady Edythe would at least know where her daughter had gone.

That relief ebbed over the three days that followed. It was replaced by gnawing impatience he was hard-pressed to control. Harold was holding negotiations with Guy, apparently to bring about their release, but they were taking longer than they should have.

While they dragged on, the English were finally allowed into the town under guard. They wandered about, taking in the sights and sounds. Wulfgarth privately thought Beaurain a poor place, lacking the vitality he expected of English towns. That didn't surprise him. Guy's heavy hand lay everywhere.

He had returned to the keep with Kendra close beside him when a clatter in the yard beyond drew him to the window. A dozen horsemen were drawing rein. He needed no more than a glance to see that they were Norman and that the two in front were clearly lords of high degree. They were big, hard men, richly dressed, with horses of exceptional beauty and spirit.

Wulfgarth's guess about them was confirmed when Guy himself emerged to greet them. They spoke for a brief time. Guy laughed and gestured toward the keep. He appeared pleased with himself. A moment later they entered the hall.

Wulfgarth had no way of knowing what happened next, since it took place in a private meeting of Guy, the Normans, and the earl. But when they emerged, they all looked satisfied.

"We will ride to Rouen," Harold said quietly. Wulfgarth nodded. The duke had interceded on their behalf. That was both good and bad. On the one hand, they were free to continue on their course. On the other, they were indebted to the very man Harold had come to best.

If that had occurred to the earl, it did not seem to trouble him. He talked easily with the Normans and, when the time came, bade Guy a courteous farewell. Wulfgarth was not so easy in his own mind. Glad though he was to see the last of Beaurain, he could not shake off the feeling that it had all happened too smoothly.

The messengers from William had arrived so quickly. Try though he did, he couldn't imagine how the duke could have received word of Harold's whereabouts and dispatched his messengers in so short a time. It didn't seem possible, not even with the best horses and riders in Christendom.

At the very least, William would have had to make up his mind what to do the moment he learned of Harold's presence in Ponthieu. Certainly he would have had no time to waste wondering about the earl's arrival, the purpose of his visit, or whether or not it was wise to receive him.

Did such questions truly not arise or had they somehow been answered before word came from Guy?

When he had the chance, Wulfgarth drew up beside the earl and spoke quietly. "What do you think we can expect in Rouen, my lord?"

Harold cast him a quick glance. His eyes were sharp and clear. "Whatever is unexpected," he said. A smile tugged the corners of his mouth when he looked at Kendra in her perch before Wulfgarth. Her cap was still in place. The Normans knew nothing more of her identity than Guy had and that was the way it was going to stay.

"Behave yourself," the earl admonished her gently. "Do as Wulfgarth tells you."

"Yes, Father," she murmured. She turned her head slightly to make sure they could not be overheard. Softly she asked, "Is William a good man or a bad one?"

"That is what we are going to find out," the earl said, and spurring his horse lightly, rode to the front to chat a little more with William's messengers.

The duke himself rode out to meet them as soon as they crossed the border into Normandy. He was a tall, strongly built man with a barrel chest, broad shoulders, and a ruddy complexion. His hair was brown with a hint of red. He had an air of command about him that was unmistakable, but he greeted Harold with grave cordiality.

Wulfgarth watched them, the golden-haired earl and the darker duke, as they rode side by side, talking comfortably. No one watching them could have guessed at the tensions swirling around the two men. They both appeared perfectly at ease.

William had brought his hawks and his hounds. He and the earl hunted well as they progressed through the fresh Norman countryside. By the time they reached the duke's residence at Rouen, Englishman and Norman alike were behaving as the best of friends.

Or at least most of them were. Wulfgarth instinctively kept his distance. He had Kendra to watch over and he didn't like the way things were going. It was all too friendly, too relaxed. Life was never this easy. Something was bound to go wrong.

Within hours of their arrival at Rouen, it did.

9

Renard is here in Canterbury. I saw him yesterday at the scriptorium. His presence affects me strangely. I should despise or—at the very least—distrust him, but I cannot manage either.

On the contrary, I came very close to telling him far more than I should. He looked at the drawings again and asked me a few questions, but he did not press for answers. There seem to be other matters on his mind.

As there are on mine. Even at this moment I should be working on the drawings. There is much yet to be done before they are complete. Yet I sit here, dithering over this secret book of mine and thinking of the one man I should never think of at all.

Since seeing him, I have been trying to remember. There was a boy at Rouen, dark-haired, gray-eyed, big for his age. Was that Renard? Wulfgarth might know, but I do not want to ask him. If I do, he will watch me all the more closely just when I most want not to be watched at all.

Indeed, last night I was the watcher. Something strange happened here. I am no nearer to understanding it even in the fresh light of day. Several hours after lauds, when all the cloister lay wreathed in silence, I woke suddenly.

It was very dark. The moon was new and clouds obscured the stars. A sound drew me from my bed. I went to the window and from there I saw a man and woman crossing the garden below.

The man was Wulfgarth, I am sure of that. Few men are ever admitted here and none other is so large as him. The woman was Mother Eldygthe. I know her walk too well to have any doubt. They went out through the garden gate in the direction of the stables.

That would be odd enough at any hour, for the truth is they do not get along very well. I think Mother Eldgythe only tolerates Wulfgarth here because of me. At any rate, for them to be abroad together at night is even stranger. It gives rise in my mind to what I over-heard at Thorney.

Who is Oath Bearer?

This morning, I traced their steps. The stables are, as always, hay-scented, sun-dappled. But in the loft above, I found a pile of hay crushed as though a man had lain upon it.

Crouching there in the stillness, I felt the hair rise at the back of my neck, and for the barest instant a flood of memory washed through me so powerful that I came close to crying out.

God save me from it.

Later—

I went back to the sewing room, to sorting wool and looking over shoulders at the borders being swiftly laid. My sisters worked more cheerfully than I had expected. They are at peace with what we do. That is the true power of prayer. I wish I could find it for myself.

I stayed an hour or so, answering any questions that I could, and then excused myself. My intention was to return to the scriptorium to continue work on the drawings.

But as I was crossing the yard in front of the cloister, I saw Wulfgarth emerging from one of the workshops scattered about the abbey. This particular one had gone long unused and I could not imagine why anyone would be bothering with it now.

The set of Wulfgarth's shoulders, the tension in his face, some element of change within him that was clear to me even across the distance separating us, kept me from taking another step toward him. Instead I drew back against the nearest wall and waited there until he was gone.

And then I went to the workshop, around to the far side where no one else passing by would see me. The windows were shuttered, but through a chink in the wood I could see the small, dim interior. A man lay on a bed of straw, his face turned toward me.

His face. Hard, unyielding, a man's face yet scarce older than my own. Heart-shaped, surrounded by unruly red hair, and the eyes—green as the sylvan glade, eyes so well remembered.

A ghost face.

I turned and ran as though demons were lapping at my heels, not stopping until I had reached the inner sanctuary of the abbey. There, breathless and heart pounding, I fell to my knees before the altar. Long moments passed before I dared to open my eyes.

Some part of me half feared that I would see him again suddenly before me. But there was only the long table set with candles and the holy cloth, and beyond it the simple cross that adorns the wall. All safe, familiar things.

Not like what was in the workshop.

I was wrong, I had to be. Never mind what I thought I

saw, it was a trick of memory, of yearning, of never quite being able to accept what had been.

Or was it?

There was only one way to find out. I had to return to the workshop.

If he was a ghost, he would be gone, for they do not linger. But the man was still there, stretched out on the bed of straw, one arm thrown over his forehead.

The door to the workshop was locked. I found a length of sturdy wood and forced the window. It was just big enough for me to wiggle my way in.

In the process I hardly noticed the grime that covered my robe and smeared my face. But the man must have, for when he saw me, he started violently, even as I had done when I first saw him.

"W-who . . . ?" he gasped, and struggled to rise from the pallet, only to fall back when his strength failed him.

Fear left me the instant I heard his voice. For the moment there was only a great rushing sense of gladness that banished all else. Joyfully I ran to him.

"Magnus, it is I, Kendra! Dear brother, I thought you dead!" My voice failed. I knelt beside him and hugged him fiercely.

When I drew back at last, he was staring at me blankly. The fever that gripped him undoubtedly had something to do with that, but there was more. He appeared unable to understand what was happening.

"K-Kendra?" he said wonderingly. "It can't be . . . surely . . . you . . ."

"It is, I promise." I sat back on my heels and smiled at him adoringly. He really was Magnus, the youngest of my brothers and always my favorite. Not dead these long years as I had thought, but here at St. Margaret's, safe and sound except for a fever Mother Eldgythe would undoubtedly swiftly cure.

My brother. Alive. When all this time I had thought myself without family to call my own.

"Oh, Magnus," I said, tears sliding down my cheeks, "how can this be? We had word so long ago that you were dead along with Edmund and Godwin . . . and M-Mother. . . ." A sob broke from me, the first of what I admit were many.

Magnus, my brother, put his arms around me and held me close. He patted my back a little awkwardly as he murmured, "There now, Kendra, sweetling, obviously I'm not dead. Just a bit battered. The others . . . surely we've done our weeping for them and they're in a better place by now. They want us to be brave, don't you think?"

His arms tightened around me. More fiercely he said, "Sweet Lord, I truly never thought to see you again. You were just a child when we parted and now look at you, a woman grown."

I sniffed and sat back slightly, the better to see him. "I was a child? What about you? You were hardly ten and already trying to be a man in that terrible time. Oh, Magnus, how I remember. That last night, the parting—"

We had scattered to the winds like the geese who feel the frost coming. Father was dead, buried in a hidden grave. His brothers, too, had perished, save for Wulfnooth, who had been little alive anyway. In that moment of wrenching anguish so great as not to be borne, thought had to be given to the survivors, to us.

The boys were to go with her to Ireland, Mother said. They would find sanctuary there. But I . . . I was to go with Wulfgarth to Canterbury, where Mother Eldgythe would hide me.

I protested, crying that I did not want to be separated from them, but Mother stood firm. I could not understand her decision then, but now I do. She was a woman of incomparable strength. Even as she mourned the death of the man who had been her life, she plotted to keep his seed from perishing.

Treachery was everywhere, the sanctuary they found in Ireland might prove slight. If they did not survive it, I would still be alive and safely hidden. So long as I was, the blood of England's last Anglo-Saxon king would endure.

But now—oh, thank you, God—I am no longer alone.

"Kendra," Magnus said gently, "I knew you were here, of course, that's why I came. We must talk."

"Not now," I said, for I saw the weariness that etched a white line around his mouth and cast deep shadows beneath his eyes. "First you must rest and recover. Then we will talk about so many things. We'll find a way for you to stay here, I know we will. Truly I want never to be parted from you again."

He looked at me in such a way that I knew something was wrong, but I refused to think what it could be. He was alive; beside that all else was insignificant.

Or so I thought.

However, not even I in my haze of happiness could ignore the meaning of what I saw when I stepped out of the workshop just as Renard was arriving at the abbey. He dismounted agilely and strode, long legs eating up the distance, in the direction of Mother Eldgythe's house. Whatever he had come for, he would expect to see me before too long.

I remembered then the condition of my robe, not to mention the grime that covered my face and arms, and ran for my quarters. There I seized clean clothes and raced again to the bath house. It was thankfully empty.

My hands flew as I tore off my dirtied robe, splashed

water on myself, and scrubbed vigorously. When I was done, I dressed quickly, ran a hawthorn comb through my hair, and as calmly as I could, went back outside.

Mother Eldgythe was crossing the yard with Renard beside her. Her mouth was thinly drawn, her eyes shuttered.

"There you are," she said when she saw me. "We were at the sewing room. Sister Gleda said you'd gone into town."

"I was going to spend a few hours at the scriptorium," I acknowledged, "but I was . . . distracted." Quickly I inclined my head to Renard, who, I thought, was looking at me rather oddly. "My lord d'Agounville, if you wish to see the drawings again, I will be glad to show them to you."

Mother Eldgythe frowned as though she thought I sounded too eager, and perhaps I did, for a light flared in Renard's gray eyes that sent a tremor through me. He smiled gravely. "Thank you, Lady Aveline, but I haven't come about the drawings."

"You haven't?" Mother Eldgythe asked. Clearly she felt misled.

"Aveline was kind enough to help me with another matter when you were both in London. I'm hoping she will be able to help again."

"What matter?" Mother Eldgythe asked before I could say anything.

"Three men have been killed," Renard said, "all Norman, all with their throats cut. There were certain details about the murders that needed explaining. Aveline has tried to help me understand them."

"Why didn't you tell me about this?" Mother Eldgythe demanded, turning to me. "And how could you possibly know anything about murders? This is absurd." She shifted her attention to Renard angrily. "You had no right to do this, to involve her in such a thing, especially without my knowledge. It is always this way with you Normans. You think you can do anything, ignore any propriety, do exactly as you please. But you can't, not this time, not while I have something to say about it!"

"Please," I said quickly, laying my hand on her arm, "there's no reason to be so upset. If these murders go unsolved, there will be trouble for everyone, Norman and English alike. And there are certain elements to the deaths that needed looking at. Renard was right to ask for my help and I was glad to give it."

Mother Eldgythe was not convinced, but at least she calmed down a little. Perhaps she had thought, as I had, that whatever trouble might come could start right here at St. Margaret's. If Renard became angry in turn, if he chose to use any of his considerable power, how long could Magnus remain hidden?

She took a deep breath and nodded slowly. "All right, you helped him. But what is so strange about the murders that you could possibly explain?"

I was about to answer when Renard caught my eye. Almost imperceptibly he shook his head. Mother Eldgythe did not see it, but I did, and I knew then that I faced a terrible choice.

Did I continue to obey the woman who has been my guardian and teacher these eleven years or did I instead obey this man, this Norman, who makes me feel in such new and disturbing ways? For seconds I teetered, not knowing which to do. In the end I obeyed neither but instead followed my own instincts.

"It was a coincidence," I said. "The first man killed was a cloth merchant, Bertrand Lagounier. Perhaps you remember him? I bought silk from his shop last year. The second death was that of a scribe, Crispin LeMeux.

Several months ago he asked to use some of my drawings in an illuminated manuscript he was preparing."

"I remember that," Mother Eldgythe said slowly. "He paid well for them."

"That's right, and Lagounier always asked a fair price for his goods. They were both decent men, for all that they were Norman. Lord d'Agounville simply wanted to know if I was aware of anything that linked them, any common enemy they might have shared."

Mother Eldygthe considered that. Slowly she shook her head. "As Aveline says, they were fair in their dealings. It is difficult to imagine why anyone would single them out."

"There has been a third death since then," Renard reminded them all. "A clerk who, so far as I can tell, has no connection to Lagounier or LeMeux, but I may be wrong. That's what I wanted to talk with Aveline about."

He inclined his head respectfully to Mother Eldgythe. "I would have asked you directly, but my impression is that Aveline had more dealings with Lagounier and LeMeux than you did."

"That's true," Mother Edlgythe said grudgingly. "I only met them in passing. Very well then, you may speak with her about it, but in future I expect to be kept informed about these things. Is that understood?"

I nodded quickly and hoped I did not appear too relieved. I had no doubt that her decision had been made at least in part because she could not afford to anger Renard, not now at least. If I needed any proof of this, it followed quickly.

"The day is too pleasant to be cooped up inside," she said. "Why don't you go for a walk? If you must discuss such unpleasant matters, it may as well be in pleasant surroundings."

Renard was surprised, but he wasted no time accepting.

I flung my mind wide, thought of the place farthest from the shuttered workshop, and said, "The orchards are very nice this time of year."

He agreed. We walked beyond the cloister walls, following the deeply rutted path the ox carts take to and from the fields. There is a narrow grass verge next to it, and it was there that we actually walked. It is just wide enough for two people.

For a time neither of us spoke. I was curiously content in his company, despite all that had happened, and was glad of the chance to gather my thoughts. As for Renard, I cannot say what was passing through his mind, but it must have amused him, for when he did speak, he sounded amused.

"I'm not sure who to be more surprised by," he said, "you or Mother Eldgythe. You think quickly on your feet, while she seems able to change her mood with astonishing speed."

"You gave me no choice," I protested. "I saw that you did not want me to tell her about the pagan signs and I was willing to believe you had a good reason for that. But now I'd like to hear it."

He shrugged and bent slightly. His strong brown fingers snapped the stem of a daisy beside the road, one of the few that grew in this dry time. Solemnly he handed it to me. "Put it in water when you get back and it will live longer than it will out here, unless it rains soon."

As one, we looked at the sky. You see people doing that these days, taking quick glances upward when they hardly seem aware of it. We all hope for the same sight, great fat clouds of rain rolling toward us, but so far at least they have failed to appear.

I took the flower, holding it gently between my fingers, and tried not to think the last time anyone had given me such a thing. It was so long ago, in another world, when I might as well have been a different person.

Except that is not completely true now. A part of that world has returned. I must protect Magnus at all costs.

"Thank you," I said. "Now please tell me why you didn't want Mother Edlgythe to know."

"I don't want anyone else to know," Renard said, "the precise details. Right now they are known only to myself, Burgess, you, and the murderer. The arrangement of LeMeux's body can't be kept hidden. The old woman saw the significance and has spread it about. But the rest—the Stag King at the well and the oak staff on Valerian—that we can keep silent about. If no further fuel is added to it, the talk of pagan killings may burn off before too much longer."

"You are optimistic," I said, "but you are probably also right. At least it's worth taking the chance."

He nodded. "Besides, I really did want to speak with you about this. When we talked before, I mentioned the third man's name—Hillard Valerian. Did it mean anything to you?"

I shook my head. "Nothing, or I would have said so."

"That's what I thought, but I wanted to be sure. Will you think about it, see if anything occurs to you?"

I agreed, although it was unlikely I would remember anything more. We had reached the orchards. Strictly speaking, I should have suggested returning to the abbey. But I was unsure there had been enough time to smuggle Magnus to a safer hiding place. It was better to stay where we were.

"It's lovely here, don't you think?" I asked, looking around at the stands of low-branched apple trees. Their fruit was less than usual this year because of the drought, and what there was looked small and hard. But the trees themselves were graceful and the slow-moving river that crept through the orchard offered a refuge of coolness and shade.

Without looking to see if Renard would follow, I went over to the bank and sat down. Reaching beneath my robe, I undid my sandals. When my bare feet sank into the water, I couldn't help but laugh with delight.

"You should join me," I said.

He did, but cautiously, I thought, as though our new-found friendliness unnerved him.

No, that isn't right. In truth, I cannot imagine Renard being unnerved by anything. He was merely thinking, as he seems to always do. Warriors are for the most part impulsive men, given to swift action. Only a very few are different—my father for one, William for another, and Renard, too, I think, whose mind may be his greatest weapon.

Not that his body isn't at least as formidable. I would be the worst sort of hypocrite if I claimed I wasn't vividly aware of the long, hard length of him stretched out beside me on the grass.

His black hair was slightly tumbled by the breeze, there was a small cut on his chin just below the fullness of his lower lip. His mouth can look so hard sometimes or soften to gentleness. And when he smiles . . . Ah, then I feel warmed clear through, as though he has captured a tiny ray of the sun itself and given it to me.

Poesy, Mother Eldgythe would call that, and mock me for it. But I had never known anything quite so real.

I did not feel him move, but he was closer suddenly, looking at me so intently that I could not look away. His hand, stroking my arm, was slow and cautious. He rushed nothing, presumed nothing.

In the end, it was my body that swayed to his, my hand that reached out, my lips that trembling slightly, touched his own.

10

Her mouth was warm, sweet, and infinitely desirable. Renard tried to hold himself in check, but he could not long resist what he had so long desired. His arms closed around her, steel embracing silk. She bent, supple as a willow.

He pressed her gently onto her back, holding his weight above her, and probed with his tongue into the moist recesses of her mouth. She moaned softly but made no attempt to pull away. Instead her hands tightened on his broad back.

The plain linen robe she wore was no hindrance to his touch. His big hands, the palms callused, cupped her breasts tenderly. He could feel her nipples hardening and longed to taste them, but she was so new to this and it had come so unexpectedly, he did not want to frighten her in any way.

She trembled beneath him as he lifted his head, gazing into blue eyes smoke-tinged with passion. "Aveline," he murmured, "sweetling, so beautiful . . ."

His voice was low and rough, the words only semicoherent. Passion raged through him. It had been so long, so very long, since he had known a woman, and even then, he had never felt what he was feeling now. He was alive in a way he had not hoped to be again. After so many years, so much blood and death, so much struggle and despair, magical Aveline on a summer day woke him to wholeness again.

He laughed, suddenly elated, and watched her mouth curve in a smile. A prayer rose in him—unholy perhaps but no less sincere—thanks for the simple fact that she had never taken vows.

Touching her, tasting her, yearning to possess her, he did not rob God. On the contrary, deep within him a sense of rightness flowered. This woman, this fire-haired beauty of strength and courage, fitted so perfectly into the empty space within his soul that truly they must have been made one for the other.

His dark head bent, blotting out the sun. Ravenously he kissed the delicate skin behind her ear, the long slim line of her throat, the sweetly scented hollow at its base. He could not get enough of her. She smelled of lavender, sun, fresh country air, hope, of all good things. He was engulfed by her, senses reeling, reason fading.

They were alone, there beneath the sheltering apple tree. He ached with need, the life force driving within him, demanding release. The maid was fair, warm, willing. Surely there was nothing to stop them from—

Maid. The thought stabbed through him. Beautiful, passionate Aveline was most certainly a virgin. Her years in the cloister had not dampened her fiery nature, but they had preserved her innocence.

If he took it now, what else did he take? Her right to stay untouched behind the wall of her own inviolability. A single act, born of raging need, would forever change that. Like it or not, he had to admit she would be hurt.

Yet he hurt now. The blood pounded through his veins, his breath came in gasps, and he was a hair-breadth away from losing all control. He had seen that happen when men in the brutal aftermath of battle turned on those most helpless. He remembered York—and other places across this war-ravaged land. In his sleep he still heard the screams.

I killed, he had told her when they spoke of Hastings, but in a fair fight, man-to-man. He had never in his life hurt a woman. Not for any reason.

To begin now, to begin with her, would in an instant rob him of the wholeness he had only just found again. His burdened conscience would surely shatter under the weight of that.

He stood and silently cursed the God who gave and took away with the same hand.

Aveline lay on the ground at his feet, her red-gold hair spread around her in glorious disarray. Her mouth was slightly swollen, her eyes deep and impenetrable. She looked neither shocked nor dismayed.

"What's wrong?" she asked softly.

His smile was bitter. "You mean of all things wrong here, which exactly troubles me?"

Slowly she got to her knees. A few stray bits of grass had gotten into her hair. She plucked them away absently as she studied him. He thought he saw a flicker of embarrassment behind her eyes, but he couldn't be sure, it was gone so quickly, absorbed into the stillness that was always with her, in passion, in rage, always. He envied her that.

"Yes," she said, "which?"

"I am Norman. You have told me several times what you think of that. You are English, with all the proud defiance of your people. Yet now you suddenly expect me to believe that you want me to be your lover."

She did blush then. Softly she said, "I didn't think it out quite so plainly."

"You should have."

"Perhaps, but I do understand something now that I never used to."

He didn't want to hear it, didn't want to know anything more about her motives for wanting him. Yet he could not stop himself from asking. "What?"

She hesitated and he could tell she was choosing her words carefully. No more impulsiveness, not for the moment.

"My mother and father," she said finally. "I never really understood about them before."

He frowned slightly. She came of good family, he was sure of that. Such unions were arranged for profit, not passion. What was she talking about?

"They married for love?" he asked in an effort to understand.

Aveline shook her head. "They weren't married, at least not in any way a Norman would recognize. My mother was my father's handfast wife under the old Viking law. He shared everything with her, honored her, protected her, fought for her. She was his lady in every sense, but because they lacked a Christian union, a Norman would consider her to have been a concubine."

Renard understood the distinction well enough, but it mattered little to him. What counted was how Aveline felt. "You loved them," he said.

"Oh, yes. There was something about them that was so special. You could feel it whenever they were together. It was like . . . like the sun shining right through you."

She stood gracefully and brushed off her robe without looking at him. He followed her every movement with his eyes, ravenously. Need twisted in him. "The Normans killed them," he said.

She raised her head. Her eyes were suddenly full of pain. "Yes."

He stood, his legs slightly apart, fists clenched with the effort to keep from touching her. Harshly he said, "I am Norman. I will always be Norman. Go back to the abbey, Aveline."

Her chin tilted, her eyes flashed. A door opened in his mind, a memory. Those eyes . . .

It was gone as quickly as it came. He took a step toward her. "I am a warrior, that is all I have ever really known. If I take you, you will be hurt. Go, now."

She stood her ground just long enough to make it clear she was not retreating from him in fear. Indeed her voice was gently regretful as she said, "I will go, Renard, because you are a good man and I would not wish to see *you* hurt. It works both ways, you know. Only think on this. . ."

"What?"

"That there are worse fates than hurting. The worst of them is not to feel anything at all. I know what that is like, in fact I cultivated it for a long time. I think you know the same."

Her eyes held his for a heartbeat. She turned, fire-born hair fluttering in the breeze, and walked away from him across the drought-sered fields to where the gray stone abbey stood, stark beneath the unrelenting blue sky. He watched her until the waves of heat-simmered air swallowed her up and she vanished from his sight.

* * *

Renard was getting drunk. He went about it purposefully, determined to tolerate no interference. To that end, he had left the guest house where he and Burgess were staying and gone into town. The first tavern he saw suited him fine. Any would have.

He found himself a seat at one of the rough trestle tables toward the back. Though he had left off the usual raiment of his class and dressed simply in the tunic of a scholar, he was served promptly enough. Once the serving girl saw the color of his coin, she kept the mugs of ale coming regularly.

It had been a very long time since he had drunk to excess. Two lost needs resurrected in a single day; he supposed he should be grateful. He smiled at the thought, but there was no humor in his manner.

Indeed the big, hard man looked so intimidating that he had the table to himself. Even as the tavern began to fill up no one attempted to join him.

That suited Renard. He was in no mood for company. He sat, glowering into his ale, and berating himself for being a fool. Who did he imagine he was, one of those noble knights the troubadours prattled on about, sacrificing all for a chaste smile from his lady love?

He could have taken her right there in the orchard, slaked his thirst for her and not looked back. She was only a woman, after all, and an overly proud one at that. What right did she have to look at him as she did, with the light of ancient knowledge in her eyes?

There was nothing timid about her despite her virginity, and there was certainly no deference as there ought to be between a maid and a man, particularly when the man was—as he had seen fit to stress—a Norman here in this conquered land.

He almost laughed out loud as he tried to imagine

Aveline being deferential to him or anyone else. He couldn't do it. Whoever her mother had been, the unnamed father's concubine, she had borne a daughter for whom none of the ordinary rules seemed to apply.

The serving girl brought him yet another mug and smiled encouragingly. Renard ignored her. His head was pleasantly fuzzy. He emptied the mug and set it down with a thump.

The tavern was almost full now. Men clustered in groups, talking and laughing. Good fellows all, he thought, know what counts in life. None of this woman stuff for them.

He stood, somewhat unsteadily, and gestured to the serving girl to bring another mug. But first, nature called. A man jostled him on the way out the back. They were bound for the same purpose.

"That's the thing about beer," the fellow said, grunting, "you can't really buy it. All you can do is rent it."

It was an old joke, but Renard chuckled all the same. Outside in the fresh air, he realized he wasn't as drunk as he'd thought. Indeed he was rapidly sobering. That was the problem with being as big as he was. Long before he could imbibe enough to get drunk, he lost interest.

The other man had gone back inside. Renard was alone in the alley behind the tavern. He was about to return to pay his bill when a voice suddenly stopped him.

The voice came from a small window to the far side of the rear of the tavern, a private room, Renard guessed. It was a man speaking, young by the sound and not uneducated. Not his voice itself but the words he uttered drew Renard up short.

"Oath Bearer," the man said. Something else followed that Renard could not make out. He moved down the wall of the tavern, closer to the window, and crouched below it.

A second man spoke. "Bad luck, the fever, but not as bad as it could have been. He's well cared for."

"He damn well better be," the first man said. "If he's not in London on time, this whole thing could fall apart on us."

"You worry too much," the second man said. "He'll be there, and when he is, it'll put an end to the doubts. He only has to talk to a few of our people, let them see him and hear what he has to say. The word will spread like fire on the wind. They'll be rallying to him as they never have to anyone else. We'll have the keys to the city, my friend, and the Normans will die in their beds, God speed them to the hell they all deserve."

"Aye," the first man replied, "Godspeed." There was a clink of mugs being touched together. "To England, old friend, and to the sacred memory of King Harold, God's glory to him."

"And to his line," the second man said solemnly. "Long may it endure, kings over all."

They drank, and shortly thereafter Renard heard them depart. He went back into the tavern quickly but wasn't in time to see who came out of the private room. Whoever they were, they blended quickly with the rest of the patrons in the tavern and were quickly gone.

He settled his bill as swiftly and set off back to the guest house. It was getting on for matins, the midpoint of the night, when one day turned to the next. Burgess was soundly asleep on his pallet. Renard had no compunction about waking him.

"Where are we going?" the monk muttered as he was dragged unceremoniously from sleep.

"To London," Renard replied.

"What, now?"

"No, in an hour. Get up and get us packed."

Burgess groaned. Now or in an hour, it made no difference. No decent man—much less a God-fearing monk—should be dragged from his bed in the dead of night.

"What's the hurry?" he demanded grumpily. "Has there been another murder?"

"Not yet," Renard said. "But if we don't get there in time, there will be a great many murders. I'm going to have a word with the archbishop. Get busy on that packing. There's no time to waste."

Burgess stared at him goggle-eyed, trying to absorb the fact that his master was going to wake Lanfranc as abruptly as he had himself. That made him feel better and he fell to his task with a will.

Renard was grim as he addressed the men he had summoned to him. There were a dozen in all, each of them well known to him, men he had campaigned with, marched with, dreamed with.

Of all the several hundred Norman soldiers in London at that moment, these twelve were the ones he believed he could trust. He was risking much by choosing them, but he had no regrets. They were the best.

"I have informed Prince Rufus and Bishop Odo," he said, "that in light of the worsening drought, I am assembling a group of deputies to assist me in any matters that may arise concerning the public safety of London. They have both given their approval for this."

The men nodded. Most were older than Renard, a few were close to his age. Among them, they had decades of experience with violence and treachery. They knew Rufus and Odo well, and they understood what lay beneath Renard's carefully chosen words.

"We report to you?" one of the men asked.

Renard nodded. "Only to me. If there are any among you who aren't comfortable with that, now's the time to leave."

No one stirred. They merely waited for him to get on with it.

"A man is coming to London," Renard said. "In all likelihood, he will be here soon. When he gets here, he will meet with various people in an attempt to convince them to support a rebellion against the throne."

The men exchanged glances in which irritation and amusement mingled equally. "How many rebellions will this make?" one asked.

"I think this one could be different. It seems better organized, for one thing, and the man who is coming— well, let's just say there may be a special reason for them to listen to him."

"What's his name?"

"He's called Oath Bearer."

Several of the men shifted slightly. Renard looked at them. "You've heard of him?"

"Rumors only," a grizzled veteran said. "You know how it is."

"All right, then, this is what I want you to do. Go out into the town, mingle with the people, visit the taverns, the markets, and so on. Wear ordinary clothes and don't carry your swords. You should appear as unthreatening as possible. If any of you can pass for English, do it. Keep your eyes and ears open. When Oath Bearer comes, I want to know about it. But *only* me. If Rufus or Odo gets word of this, there will be more trouble than we've seen in a very long time."

They nodded, accepting what he said, for they knew

him as well as he knew them. When they were gone, Renard sat staring off into space. He hoped he was doing the right thing, but he wasn't anywhere near sure.

He had very little on which to base all his hopes of averting yet more bloodshed. If he'd heard wrong that night behind the tavern, or if his men simply couldn't find the mysterious Oath Bearer, then what?

It didn't bear thinking about, but he did anyway because that kept him from thoughts of Aveline. Since those few moments in the orchard, she was constantly in the back of his mind, tormenting him with images of what might have been.

It was just as well she was safe in Canterbury behind the high walls of St. Margaret's. That was where she belonged and where she should stay. His self-control was exhausted. If she came near him again, he very much doubted he would be able to keep from doing everything to her that he dreamed about, and quite possibly more.

He spent the remainder of the day going about his duties as best he could. The three hours between sext and nones were allotted for petitions. That done, he went out into the streets and strolled around, letting himself be seen.

His presence had a good effect. Several arguments were broken off when he appeared, the participants preferring to slink away rather than contend with London's formidable high sheriff. After vespers, he ate a simple supper and indulged himself in a new book freshly sent from the continent.

He went to bed early and slept well.

Until shortly before sunrise when Burgess woke him with the news that there had been a fourth murder.

11

"*I am tired of this,*" Renard said. He was standing with Burgess near the bank of the Thames. The body of a middle-aged man lay on the soft mud.

All around the body a circle had been drawn and in the circle were various symbols—the horned moon, the five-pointed star, the stag head—whose meaning Renard now knew all too well.

"It is a bit much," Burgess agreed. "I'd hoped it was over. What do you suppose prompted him to start up again?"

"I have no idea." Renard glanced over toward the bridge, where a cluster of townspeople had gathered. They were pointing and talking among themselves.

"Get those people out of here," he ordered the guardsmen, "and move the body as quickly as possible. Smooth over the ground. Leave no sign of what happened here."

The guards obeyed, although he noticed that they eyed the circle nervously. There was some discussion among them as to who would erase it. That ended when they caught his stern look.

"The leaders from the water brigades are waiting for you," Burgess reminded him quietly.

"I'm going." He glanced again at the body, now lying in the back of a wagon. "Meanwhile you find out who he was. Learn everything you can. Dig hard. Look particularly for any possible link to Lagounier, LeMeux, and Valerian. I want information and I want it quickly."

The young monk's face was somber. He hesitated a fraction before he said, "It's coming to a head, isn't it?"

Renard nodded. "Aye. Rufus, Odo, the killings, all of it. But what worries me the most is this damn drought. I should be spending every moment of the day dealing with it, not being pulled in every other direction."

"You could save time," Burgess ventured, "if you would just order a few proclamations instead of meeting with everyone in person."

"I'm about to tell these people that they will have to accept truly severe hardship. I can at least look them in the eye when I do it."

The words were simple enough and sincerely meant, but a short time later, when he had returned to his residence, he realized how hard they were to put into action.

The leaders of the water brigades were gathered in the main hall. The hour was still early; most had come directly from their breakfasts; some were rubbing sleep from their eyes. They were all working men, settled and responsible, chosen because they had homes and businesses within the city that they presumably would not want to see destroyed.

They were also overwhelmingly Anglo-Saxon. Only a handful were Norman. That suited Renard fine. Most of the population of London remained Anglo-Saxon. It made no sense to exclude them from its protection.

"Gentlemen," he said as he took his place at the head of the long table, "I don't have to tell you the situation we confront. You're all as aware of the drought as I am. From this day there will be new regulations governing the use of all fires in the city. I count on you to enforce them. Every fire, whether in a home or shop, must be constantly watched. Buckets of water must be positioned within easy reach and kept full at all times. Night patrols are to be doubled with particular attention given to any hint of smoke or flame where it should not be. Is that clear?"

Slowly the men nodded. They were not accustomed to being dealt with in this way. As Burgess had said, orders were usually given by proclamation. But the high sheriff spoke to them directly, man-to-man, and his words had all the more impact for that.

"I cannot emphasize too much," Renard went on, "the need for the greatest care. However, I must also tell you that if this drought does not break soon, even more stringent measures will have to be taken."

"Like what?" one of the men asked.

Renard's face was set, the eyes unyielding. "All the fires in London will be extinguished," he said.

Confusion erupted around the table. "God's blood," another said, "you can't do that! How would people cook or heat water?"

"What about the shops?" demanded another. "Every bakery would have to shut down, every blacksmith, every brewer and malt maker. No cooper could work or wheelwright, there'd be no kilns, no glassmakers, no coalers, no smokehouse. How would we live?"

"Better than you will if you burn," Renard said flatly. "With luck it won't come to that, but you should begin preparing for it now. There's been no rain in two months, and before that barely a trickle. Eight wells have failed in the city in the last fortnight. If very many more of them go, I will do as I have said. Better that than see London burn."

"Does the Prince Rufus know about this?" one of the Normans asked.

"Rufus is not responsible for the safety of London," Renard said. "I am, by the king's order. Let none forget that, for I surely will not."

They fell silent, thinking about what he had said and even more about what they should make of it. Rufus wouldn't care if London burned; he'd probably enjoy the spectacle. The same for Odo, so long as his own keep was spared.

But London's high sheriff did care. He was willing to impose the toughest measures—and take the anger that came with them—in order to protect the city.

Grudgingly they weighed that against the hardship his orders could bring. In the end they judged him right.

By the time the men left, Renard felt reassured that they would do what was needed. That much at least he had accomplished, but there was so much more to do.

Odo had sent a message saying he wanted to talk with him. It wasn't likely to be about hams this time. The bishop no doubt had discovered his trip to Canterbury and wanted to hear his explanation for it. He would have to wait.

There was still the fourth murder to deal with. Burgess should be back soon. With any luck, he would have some information. And then—

But it was not Burgess who interrupted Renard's thoughts. Instead it was one of the men he had sent out to look for Oath Bearer.

"Lord," he said, "I have news."

Renard sighed. He should be glad of this, but instead all he felt was that tightening in his soul that heralded the coming of battle. Every sense he possessed told him the waiting was near its end.

"Tell me," he ordered.

"This morning I was in the old quarter down by the river, dressed as you see me. I can speak English without an accent and I took care to do so. I told several people that I was newly arrived in the city from Wessex and was looking for a place to stay. On that excuse, I visited the nearby taverns as well as half a dozen rooms in private houses that are available to rent. Everywhere I went, I kept a careful eye out for anything unusual."

"And did you see it?" Renard asked, trying not to sound impatient.

The man nodded. "Scarce an hour ago, I was coming out of one of the houses after thanking the owner for showing me the room. The house does not face the street directly but is on a small alley. There are several other buildings nearby. I saw a group of men going into one of them. They were moving quickly and being very cautious. When they were inside, I followed. The windows on the first floor were shuttered despite the warmth of the day. I went around to the back. Someone has made a garden there. Much of it has died because of the drought, but there is still a piece of latticework set up against the house. From it, I was able to see into a window on the second floor. There was a man, young, reddish hair, with a look to him as though he may have been ill recently. The men I saw go into the house were with him. They were all embracing and talking eagerly. From their manner, I saw that he was the leader. They were very respectful to him."

"I see," Renard said slowly. "Did anything else happen?"

"Another man came, older than the others and badly scarred around the face. A big man, very hard. His manner was different. He looked worried, even angry. He and the leader spoke between themselves. I could not hear what was said. After a few minutes the scarred man went away and I came here."

"Would you recognize this man again?" Renard asked. "The one who seemed to disagree with the leader."

"Definitely. He is tall, strongly built, shaggy black hair, and a scar like this—" He ran a hand down the left side of his face. "He's missing an eye."

Renard exhaled sharply. Somewhere in the back of his mind he had known or at least suspected that this would happen. With all the different tendrils of worry and danger swirling around London, at least some of them had to be connected somewhere.

He rose, his features set. "You have done well. Now go to Thorney cloister. The abbess there is Mother Ursuline. Find out from her what visitors she has and when they came, but be discreet."

"Aye, lord, and the house?"

"I'll go there myself and keep watch. As soon as you can, round up the others and come to me. We must not let the Englishman escape."

"Your pardon, lord, but you are well known in the streets. As soon as you are seen, the English will be warned."

Renard grimaced. The man was right. "All right, *you* go to the house, but be careful. They must not be alerted before we are ready to move. I'll go to Thorney and then find the others."

"If something happens before we are ready, what then? Do I kill this Oath Bearer or do I let him go?"

The question hung between them. In theory, there

was only one possible answer. Any rebel against the throne deserved to die.

Yet Renard hesitated. He was so very tired of death, and this man, whoever he really was, at least was fighting for something he believed in. He wasn't like Rufus, who would slay his father for his own gain, or like Odo, who would betray God himself to get what he wanted.

And then there was that strange comment he had overheard at the tavern about the line of Harold Godwinson. Surely the line was dead, wasn't it? Whatever else could be said about the old Earl Godwin, he hadn't been lucky in his progeny.

The eldest son, Sweyn, had died in disgrace years ago. Tostig was dead in the same year as the conquest, caught in rebellion against his brother. Gyrth and Leofwine had died with Harold at Hastings. The youngest son, Wulfnooth, long William's prisoner, was a mere shadow of a man. Surely no one could expect him to lead the realm.

As for the only daughter, Edith, she had lived a sterile life as Edward's queen, gone into a nunnery after his death, and finally died herself two years before. She had no children.

But Harold had—three sons, as Renard recalled. They, too, were dead, killed in Ireland by treachery, disease, and perhaps, in the end, simple despair. Who then was Oath Bearer? He had to know. Slaying him would bring no answers.

"Let him go," he said. When the man looked surprised, he added, "If you try to take him yourself, you could prompt a riot. This city's on the edge now. We can't afford any trouble. We'll take him if we can, quietly and quickly, but we need force for that."

The man was satisfied. He hurried off, intent on his

duty. Renard did the same, if less eagerly. He was still hoping that he was wrong, that there were two big, shaggy, one-eyed Englishmen, but in his heart he knew better.

Mother Ursuline confirmed it a short time later. "Why of course, my lord," she said after she had greeted him, "I'm delighted to be of assistance, but to be frank, I'm surprised you don't already know. Surely Mother Eldgythe would have the courtesy to inform you that she and Aveline had returned."

She smiled mirthlessly. "But then, perhaps I should have expected such a lapse. They came yesterday without informing me ahead of time. Apparently Mother Eldgythe sees nothing amiss in coming and going as she pleases."

"Apparently," Renard repeated. Mother Ursuline went on talking, but he no longer heard her. Aveline here in London, Mother Eldgythe and Wulfgarth with her.

Why? The journey was long enough that no one made it without good reason. Odo could have summoned them, but Renard doubted it. The bishop was too involved in other matters. Why then had they come?

"Are they here now?" he asked, interrupting Mother Ursuline.

"Mother Eldgythe may be. Would you like me to summon her?"

Renard shook his head. "What about the Lady Aveline?"

"She went out a short time ago. I saw her leave."

"Was Wulfgarth with her?"

"Not that I recall." Her small eyes narrowed. "Indeed that is so unusual that I can only think it was deliberate. Perhaps she wants some time to herself."

Renard cursed under his breath. He ignored Mother

Ursuline's startled look, thanked her for her help, and left on the run. He had to be wrong, he had to be.

She was out somewhere buying thread or cloth, or sitting under a tree sketching, or simply strolling through the markets, or a hundred things none of which had anything to do with Oath Bearer.

He moved quickly through the street and before long found three of the men he was looking for. Sending them for the rest, he returned to his hall. By the time the rest of his men reported in, Renard was ready.

He stood in the center of the hall wearing chain mail, his battle sword strapped to his side. Under the crook of his arm was his helmet. It glowed dully in the light.

"Arm yourselves," he instructed. As they did so, he explained what was to be done. "I want this clean and quick. The English must have no warning. If we move swiftly enough, no one will realize what's happening before it's too late. The man we're looking for is young, red-haired, the leader. Bring him to me alive. As for the others, defend yourselves as you must, but I want as many of them left alive as possible. We'll get no information from dead men."

This time Renard did not hesitate to ride through the streets of London. He and his men took their swiftest mounts and spurred them to the gallop. People scattered before them, screaming in surprise and fear.

They reached the alley and in seconds had the house surrounded. With no time to waste, Renard pulled his sword from its sheath, shouted his command, and kicked open the front door.

Pandemonium broke out inside. He took the steps to the second floor while his men pursued the English below. He had reached the top and was about to enter the room there when the door before him suddenly opened. Before him, wide-eyed and ashen, stood Aveline.

She took one look at him—and at his raised sword—and did the last thing he could have expected. Without hesitation, without a thought to her own safety, she flung herself straight at him. Even as she did so she screamed a single word: "Run!"

Her slim weight was not enough to knock Renard off balance, but it did slow him for a few crucial instants. Had he been willing to thrust her savagely aside, or even to kill her, it might not have mattered. But he could do neither.

It took several moments for him to shake her off. She fell panting to the floor as he raced into the room. It was empty. From below in the alley, he heard the pounding of hooves. Oath Bearer was gone.

But Aveline remained. Back on the landing, Renard pulled her to her feet. His hand was an iron clamp around her wrist as he dragged her down the stairs. His men were below, looking anxious.

"Damages?" Renard demanded.

The man who replied was pale and looked deeply troubled, as did all the others. "Four dead, sir, all English. We killed two, but the other two took their own lives before we could disarm them. The rest escaped."

Renard looked around at the bodies on the floor. A chill went through him. Suicide was a mortal sin. What kind of man inspired such loyalty that men would condemn their souls to damnation in order to protect him?

He turned his gaze to Aveline. She was still struggling against his strength, but the effort was useless. She would never escape him. Never.

"Clean up here," he ordered through gritted teeth. "Quiet the street. One of you take a message to Prince

Rufus. Tell him I apologize for the disturbance, but there were illegal fires that needed putting out."

"Aye, lord," the man murmured. He cast a nervous glance at Aveline. "What about her?"

Renard bared his teeth. "She comes with me."

"No!" Aveline said, and renewed her struggles. Renard didn't hesitate. He seized her around the waist and, ignoring her attempts to land her fist in his face, hoisted her unceremoniously over his shoulder.

She was still fighting when he thrust her onto the saddle in front of him. He evaded a blow that would have blackened his eye and grabbed both her hands in one of his.

"Stop it," he ordered tersely. "My patience is at an end. If you have any sense, you will sit still and say nothing, or I promise, by the time we reach my hall, you won't be able to sit at all!"

She sat, unmoving and unspeaking. He kept a firm hold on her nonetheless. In the back of his mind, the horrible image lingered of the dead men. He would move heaven and earth to keep her from their fate.

But for the moment it suited him not to let her know that. By the time they reached his hall, he could see the fear stamped stark in her eyes. She did her best to hide it, but she was plainly terrified. As she ought to be, he thought grimly.

Several of his servants were in the main hall. They gaped in astonishment as he carried Aveline, all but crushed in his arms, up the steps to his own quarters. There he deposited her without ceremony on the bed. She scrambled upright and glared at him as he stood above her, iron hard and implacable.

"Bastard," she said.

He raised a hand and brought it toward her face. She

did not flinch. He laughed humorlessly and let his fingers close around her chin.

"So brave, sweetling? We'll see how long that lasts." Deliberately he set out to increase her terror yet further. It was the surest path to getting what he needed in the quickest and safest way possible.

"Your friends escaped into the street or into death. You won't be able to do either. You are going to tell me everything I want to know starting with Oath Bearer. Who is he?"

She wrenched herself away and refused to look at him. Silence reigned.

Renard sighed. She was such a stubborn wench. Even now, when she should have been pleading with him not to hurt her, she refused to give an inch. He admired her spirit even as he determined to break it.

"Aveline," he said quietly as he sat down on the bed beside her, "you will tell me. You realize that, don't you?"

Silence.

"Indeed," he said, still matter-of-factly, "you will want to tell me."

That earned him a darting glance before she looked away again. Her lower lip trembled.

"Stand up." Renard's voice was low and hard, masking his own turmoil. He had to act quickly before his resolve weakened.

She ignored him. He might as well not have existed for all the notice she took.

He pulled her upright. Holding her with one hand, he moved the other down her back to the curve of her buttocks and beyond.

"Stop it! What are you doing!" She struggled, her face flaming, but her efforts were useless. He continued unrelentingly, touching her over every inch of her body until he was convinced that she concealed no weapon with which she might harm herself.

"You won't do what those men did," he said grimly. In his eyes was the memory of how she had thrown herself at him with no thought to her safety. Terror filled him at the thought that she, too, would die rather than tell him what he had to know.

"You are going to live, Aveline," he said implacably, "whether you want to or not. And you are going to tell me who is plotting to bring yet more death and destruction to this poor land."

The color had fled from her face, leaving her ashen. Only her eyes shone, unflinching in their courage, deep blue eyes like the sky on those days of utter clarity when nothing stands between a man and the merciless gaze of Heaven. Her eyes . . .

She was all sky and flame, the bright red hair curling around his hand as he wound it taut and pulled her head back. He hesitated, struck by the sudden sense that he was about to confront something he was not ready to deal with.

But there were no choices left, truth was his only armor and the only weapon he had to stop the cataclysm he saw sweeping down on them all.

He took a deep breath and met her gaze, knowing in that instant what had been slowly growing in him since that first meeting on the quai by Odo's keep. He had seen her before, long ago in a different place and a different self. Different for both him and her.

He had not been Lord Renard d'Agounville, a man full grown, a warrior of proven strength, possessor of wealth, power, and the sacred trust of his king. He had been a boy of no particular account, uncertain, sometimes afraid, and she . . .

"Renard."

Far in the back of his mind, he heard the call borne on the wind. The sun shone on grass damp with the morning rain, seabirds whirled in the sky above, and he was thirteen again, astride the horse he had loved almost more than anything in the world.

He turned toward the voice. Excitement surged through him. Sir Turold himself, close companion of the duke, was beckoning to him.

He put his spurs to the horse and moved out of the line of march toward the knight.

⚜ The Oath ⚜

    "A fair day," Sir Turold said. He smiled as he spoke. His sharp brown eyes beneath his peaked helmet were filled with good humor. He was a handsome man, well built and steady in his manner.

William was said to trust him as much as he trusted anyone. "A good day for battle, don't you think?" Turold asked.

Renard nodded, hoping he looked as though he meant it. He had never been in battle before and wasn't sure he was ready for it now. Not that there was any choice.

Duke William was angry at one of his vassals, Conan of Brittany, and had decided to punish him. Renard wasn't sure what Conan had done to make the duke angry, nor did he know why he had to be punished just now when the English visitors were on hand, but then thirteen-year-old pages weren't kept informed about such things.

The mere fact that Sir Turold was speaking to him at all was sufficiently out of the ordinary to make Renard cautious. He might be one of the younger males at William's court and a not particularly well-connected one at that, but at least he had the sense to know there was a great deal going on that he didn't understand.

Best to keep his mouth shut, go along, and hope not to make too many mistakes.

"You keep your own counsel, boy," Sir Turold said. "I've noticed that about you."

Renard flushed slightly, embarrassed to think that the great knight had noticed anything at all about him, yet also flattered. "Thank you, sir," he murmured.

Turold shot him a quick, assessing look. He must have liked what he saw, for his smile deepened. He leaned nearer and asked confidingly, "What do you make of these English?"

Renard hesitated. Like everyone else at William's court, he was consumed with curiosity about their unexpected guests. The Godwinsons were notorious. Everyone knew about their lust for power, their disrespect for old King Edward, and their determination to banish Norman influence from England.

Harold was said to be the smartest and strongest of this clan of eagles, so naturally people were eager to see him.

Yet barely had the earl and his party arrived in Rouen than William announced it was time to deal with Conan. Cordially he invited his English guests to come along, suggesting they would find the campaign amusing.

The earl accepted readily, leaving the impression that he was as eager to judge firsthand William's war-making skills as William was to judge his. So here they all were, a merry band of two hundred Normans and a handful of English, trudging their way to Brittany.

They were approaching the river Couesnon. Here the

marshes grew wider and deeper. The air seemed to become more still and the light conversation that had gone on up and down the ranks began to die away. Men looked over their shoulders more, knowing themselves to be in the abode of spirits and other unclean things.

How did he find the English? He thought about that for several moments before he said, "They seem very easy in themselves. Not what I'd expect of men who have been shipwrecked, captured, and turned over to someone who, if not precisely an enemy, can't be counted a friend either."

"What do you suppose accounts for that?" Turold asked.

"I don't know," Renard said honestly. "But at least some of it must be pretense. They would want to appear more confident than they necessarily feel."

Turold nodded as though pleased by his response. "Indeed, it's always wise to make your opponent believe that you are without fear. Why do you think the earl has come?"

"No one has said, sir."

"You must have heard some speculation."

Renard shrugged. His shoulders were already too broad for his tunic. He would have to see about getting a new one when they got back.

At thirteen, he was as large as many of the grown men. Since the age of six, he had spent most of his waking hours on the training field. His muscles were powerfully developed, his reflexes lightning quick; even old Ragnar, the sword master, had expressed himself pleased with him.

Perhaps that was how he had come to Sir Turold's notice. Something had certainly caused the knight's eye to fall on him. Renard had the feeling it was not by chance.

"There are always rumors," he said.

"You put little store in them?"

"I have little time to listen to them, sir." That was truth. Of late, Ragnar had kept him even longer at his training, demanding ever more of him. There were days when he thought he could not possibly continue, yet something drove him on.

He did not question this, but lived with it as he lived with all else, the constant pain of aching muscles and bruised limbs, the endless rounds on the practice field that left hardly a moment to call his own, the lumpy mattress where he fell each night exhausted, the meals caught on the run, and of late, the torment that shot through him when he glimpsed some of the girls around the castle, flitting past him with a toss of their hair and a look in their eyes that spoke of secret woman things.

"Harold has come to ask the duke for the release of his brother, Wulfnooth and his family," Turold said.

Renard's eyes widened. He was surprised enough to say the first thing that came into his mind. "Why now?"

Turold laughed, a great pealing sound that drew attention to them. "Ragnar was right, you are intelligent."

"Sir?"

"He said you were more than a strong arm and a strong back, a warrior in the budding. He said you had a brain. You've put your finger on the question that confronts us all—why has Harold come now?"

"King Edward is old," Renard said slowly. Later he would think about all this, about what Ragnar had said and Turold, too. For the moment he knew now that he was being tested. Turold spoke for the duke; satisfy him and all things might be possible.

"And sonless," Turold said. "When he dies, the Witan is likely to chose Harold as king."

Renard acknowledged the truth of that even as he regretted it. There had been a time when the closeness of Edward to his Norman kin had raised hopes for a different line of succession to the English throne. But the power of the Godwinsons had ended that.

Or had it?

His mind reeled at the implications. Had William truly given up all thought of one day being not merely duke but king over the water?

"If the duke surrenders Wulfnooth," Renard said slowly, "he and the earl will become friends. That would bode well for the peace between our lands once Harold does become king."

"And if he keeps him?"

"Then they are enemies." Renard thought again and said, almost to himself, "Friendship is fleeting, particularly among men of ambition. But enmity lasts. If William refuses to release Wulfnooth, he puts Harold on his guard. No," he corrected quickly, "he is already on his guard and will remain so. If he leaves without Wulfnooth, he will have the means to put all England on its guard."

"Precisely," Turold said. "But if he releases Wulfnooth, he shows that he is a friend of Harold's, even that he approves of him. How could he then turn around at some later date and say that Harold should not be king?"

"He could still do that," Renard said, "but it would smack of dishonesty."

Turold sighed and shifted slightly in the saddle. "There was a time when things were simpler. Power ruled through the sword. Now it is all opinion, politics, and the vagaries of fortune. I like it not."

Renard had no answer for that. The world was as it was. Men did the best they could.

JOIN THE
TIMELESS ROMANCE READER SERVICE AND GET FOUR OF TODAY'S MOST EXCITING HISTORICAL ROMANCES FREE, WITHOUT OBLIGATION!

Imagine getting today's very best historical romances sent directly to your home — at a total savings of at least $2.00 a month. Now you can be among the first to be swept away by the latest from Candace Camp, Constance O'Banyon, Patricia Hagan, Parris Afton Bonds or Susan Wiggs. You get all that — and that's just the beginning.

PREVIEW AT HOME WITHOUT OBLIGATION AND SAVE.

Each month, you'll receive four new romances to preview without obligation for 10 days. You'll pay the low subscriber price of just $4.00 per title — a total savings of at least $2.00 a month!

*Postage and handling is absolutely **free** and there is no minimum number of books you must buy. You may cancel your subscription at any time with no obligation.*

GET YOUR FOUR FREE BOOKS TODAY
($20.49 VALUE)

FILL IN THE ORDER FORM BELOW NOW!

YES! *I want to join the Timeless Romance Reader Service. Please send me my 4 FREE HarperMonogram historical romances. Then each month send me 4 new historical romances to preview without obligation for 10 days. I'll pay the low subscription price of $4.00 for every book I choose to keep — a total savings of at least $2.00 each month — and home delivery is free! I understand that I may return any title within 10 days without obligation and I may cancel this subscription at any time without obligation. There is no minimum number of books to purchase.*

NAME_____

ADDRESS _____

CITY_____STATE____ZIP_____

TELEPHONE_____

SIGNATURE_____

(If under 18 parent or guardian must sign. Program, price, terms, and conditions subject to cancellation and change. Orders subject to acceptance by HarperMonogram.)

GET 4 FREE BOOKS
(A $20.49 VALUE)

TIMELESS ROMANCE
READER SERVICE

120 Brighton Road
P.O. Box 5069
Clifton, NJ 07015-5069

"Harold, too, is intelligent," Turold said after a bit. "He has us neatly caught. We need to find a way out, a lever, if you will. It doesn't have to be much, just enough to help us with a tricky situation."

"I don't see how—"

"The boy," Turold said, cutting off his protestations. "The one the English brought along, you've seen him?"

Renard nodded. He had noticed the child once or twice. It was impossible not to when he was kept so close in the earl's train.

"They were invited to leave him in Rouen, where he would have been both more comfortable and safer, but they insisted on bringing him along. Why do you suppose that is?"

"They don't trust us."

"With the child of a servant or some such? He's roughly dressed and no honors are accorded him, yet he also doesn't seem to perform any duties. And that big Englishman, the one with the black hair, always has an eye on him."

Renard moved uneasily in his saddle. He disliked the idea that he, a budding warrior with a brain, might be delegated to spy on a child.

"What are you saying?"

"There's something odd about that boy being here. I want to know what it is. Truthfully it will probably amount to nothing, but in the situation we're in, we can't let any possibility go by. You're the closest to him in age. You've got the best chance of getting near him. Do it."

Renard knew an order when he heard it. No further discussion was possible. For all that Turold flattered him, he wanted him to play nursemaid to a babe. It was all he could do to hide his disgust as he fell back into the line of march.

All the rest of that day, he tried to do as Turold wanted, but despite his efforts, he could not get anywhere near the mysterious boy. The black-haired Englishman kept him too close. Finally, toward evening when they were about to make camp, Renard saw his chance.

There was sudden confusion in the ranks, shouts and men running. In the midst of that distraction, he rode closer to the English and for the first time got a clear look at the boy.

He was . . . pretty, that was the only word for it. A heart-shaped face was dominated by eyes of startling blue. A cap pulled down low over the brow hid his hair, but by the look of his skin, he was fair. He was dressed as befitted a servant, but his hands were soft and well cared for. Turold had been right to think him odd.

There were more shouts and Renard turned his head. What he saw sent a shock through him. Two bowmen had stepped a little distance off the road. That was foolish, given the marshes that surrounded them, but in this case it might well prove deadly.

Even as he watched, the ground pulled at them. Brittany was well known for its shifting quicksands. All unknowing, they had stumbled into them.

The line of march had halted. Renard could hear the duke shouting orders. But there was no time. The men were sinking fast. Already they were up to their waists. In seconds, the quicksand would squeeze the air from their lungs and they would die.

If there was only more time, if only he could get closer, if only—

A horse surged past him hard at the gallop. Renard barely had a chance to pull his own mount to the side to avoid being bumped. He caught a glimpse of a handsome man, fair-haired, big, richly dressed, with a look of ruthless determination in his compelling blue eyes.

"The earl," he murmured under his breath, and shook his head with wonder. Harold did not hesitate. He drove his horse off the road directly into the marshes. The stallion pranced nervously as though he sensed the danger, but the earl urged him on, step-by-step.

Renard held his breath. The peril was acute. One false step and horse and man would meet the same fate as the others.

He was not alone in thinking so. All eyes were turned to the life-and-death drama being played out before them, but one set of eyes was especially riveted. From behind him and slightly to the side, Renard heard a choked cry.

"Father!"

He turned toward the sound just as the big Englishman scooped the boy into his arms and walked quickly away. The child struggled as though he wanted to be put down, but the Englishman would not relent. He carried him out of sight of what was happening in the marsh.

Renard was torn between his duty to Turold and the excitement of the moment. Excitement won, on the excuse that he couldn't get close to the boy after all. He watched, hardly breathing, as the earl edged closer and closer to the men.

Just as it seemed he must surely join them in their terrible fate, he stopped, holding his horse rock steady, and unwound the length of rope he held. One end each he threw to the men, then wound the middle around his saddle pommel.

A great cheer went up as he began urging the horse backward along the same perilous path, pulling the men inch by inch with him.

Renard joined in the cheering. He had never witnessed a greater act of valor, yet in the back of his mind there lingered the thought that the earl was either a man liable to take great chances or one so certain of his ultimate success as to be free of the fears that plagued lesser mortals. Whichever was the case, it made him a formidable foe.

William arrived on the scene just as the bowman were being helped to stand upright on the road. They were covered in slimy gray mud and terror still stamped their features, but they were indisputably alive.

Above them, seated easily on his great stallion, the earl casually rewound his rope and looked as though nothing in particular had happened.

"Well done," the duke called across the small distance separating them.

The earl shrugged. Again, Renard was struck by the intensity of his eyes. "A small thing," he said. "You would have done the same."

The Normans smiled at that and cheered again, for they took it as honorable praise of their lord. But William's manner remained somber. He smiled humorlessly, and as soon as he decently could, he started the line of march moving again.

Renard could not help but notice that while Harold looked well satisfied, William looked anything but. The duke's face was dark with thought as they continued on a short distance until they passed the quicksands and it was safe to make camp for the night.

The tents were up and the fires had been lit, good smells suffusing the air, before Renard sought out Turold. He found the knight by his own tent, scarlet and gold in the pale light. Turold was sitting on a small stool. He had taken off his armor and was dressed in a tunic of fine wool emblazoned with the lion that was his emblem. He should have appeared relaxed, but he did not. There was tension in the set of his shoulders and the hard line of his mouth.

"Sir," Renard said, "about the boy—"

"What about him?" Turold demanded. He sounded tired and impatient.

"I think he may be the Earl Harold's son."

Turold's eyebrow rose. He looked at Renard skeptically. "The earl has three sons, his get by his concubine, all older than this boy must be."

"Yet the boy called out to him as the earl entered the marsh. He called him father."

The skepticism gave way to interest. "Indeed? You're sure of this?"

Renard nodded. "I heard him clearly. There is no doubt what he said or who he was looking at when he said it."

"Extraordinary. Why would the earl conceal his son among his train, make him appear as a servant?"

"Because he doesn't want us to know the boy's identity."

"That's obvious, but why not?"

"He wouldn't need a clear reason, would he? Instinct would be enough. A child has no business being involved in what's going on here."

"Then why bring him?"

"Perhaps he didn't intend to," Renard suggested. "The boy looks to have spirit, for all that he's delicately made. He might have decided on his own to come along."

"Possibly," Turold said. He looked deep in thought. "All right then, you've done well. See what else you can find out."

Renard suppressed a sigh. It had been too much to hope that Turold would be content with what he had already learned. Around him, the camp was settling down for the night. There would be no chance to see the boy again before morning.

In the meantime he would be smart to get some rest. They were deep within Brittany now and close to Conan's fortress of Dol. For William, Turold, and the others, that might mean little. But Renard lay wrapped in his blanket by the dying fire and prayed that God would send him courage in battle.

Above all, he did not want to disgrace himself.

As it turned out, he got no chance to do so. Conan was cornered two days later at the fortress town of Dinan. There was fighting, but it was very brief. Renard had barely any chance to realize he was in combat before it was over.

Conan surrendered, and in the aftermath of the battle, William took the opportunity to award arms to Harold in recognition, as he said, of a brother warrior's courage.

All in all, a pleasant outing, although not quite what Renard had expected. In truth, it had been something of a letdown. His mood was dim as Dinan faded behind them. William had decided next to visit his half brother, Odo, at his bishopric of Bayeux. He wanted him to meet their distinguished guests.

Renard found quarters for himself in the stables and considered skipping supper. He was tired, a sharp pain was building behind his eyes, and he felt out of patience with the scheming of the great. He wanted a wash, a soft pillow (no chance of that), and some peace and quiet.

If he fell asleep before the other pages came back, he might be able to avoid the worst of the headache. Or so he hoped. As it happened, it was not to be. They were back before he expected, grumbling that the duke had dismissed everyone early because he wanted to be private with the earl.

Lying on his pallet, trying not to listen to the noise and confusion that made his headache worse, Renard thought of what the two men would be discussing. This would be the time when the matter of Wulfnooth would finally have to be settled. Yea or nay, which would the duke decide? He seemed to lose with either.

The headache worsened. When he'd had it in the past, sometimes a draft of dandelion tea had helped. He had the dried leaves in a small bag he kept, but he needed hot water. Rising gingerly, he kept a hand to his head to prevent it from exploding and went to find some.

His search took him to the kitchens that were out behind the back of the main hall. He had delayed going longer than he should and the hour had become late. The kitchens were deserted, but embers still glowed in the fire. He filled a small pot with water from the well and hung it over the coals to heat.

While he waited he wandered around, looking for something to distract him from the pain. A door of the kitchen led directly to a backdoor of the hall, the better to bring food quickly. Both doors stood open. Renard heard raised voices.

One belonged to William, the other was less well known to him but equally implacable. He guessed it to be Harold's. Both were clearly angry.

"It is a small thing," William said, "especially in return for so much. You receive back your brother and his family, and all I ask in return is that you acknowledge me as ruler of Normandy and that you vow never to attempt to usurp what is mine by right of inheritance. Is that so much?"

"You want me to swear on holy relics," Harold said. "That is why we have come here, is it not?"

"What is wrong with that? Is there some uneasiness in you that you cannot stand before God and say, 'I, Harold Godwinson, Earl of Wessex, acknowledge William to be Duke of Normandy and swear never to try to usurp what is his by lawful inheritance'? Does something in you prevent that?"

"I do not see the necessity. Everyone knows you are Duke of Normandy. What do you need an oath from me for?"

"Let us be frank; King Edward is a dying man. He could be called to God at any moment. When he is, his heir can claim not only England but certain properties here in Normandy belonging to the king's late mother. Isn't that so?"

"Those claims have not been enforced in decades," Harold said. He sounded exasperated but also wary.

"Yet they still exist and they could be renewed at any time. Who knows, they might even be considered an excuse to invade my duchy and settle the matter by force of arms."

"That is ridiculous! Whoever is heir to Edward will have all he can do to keep England at peace. He won't need to go seeking foreign adventure."

"Yet such adventure can often be the route to quieting a restive kingdom. Men will unite behind a war leader as they will behind no other. No, my concern is justified and you should be more sympathetic to it. After all, my father, like you, neglected to marry the mother of his heir."

Silence followed for several moments before Harold said more quietly, "That is a personal matter."

"Of course," William said quickly, "but you must see what I mean. Surely you would want your own sons' rights acknowledged? All I ask is the same. I just don't want there being any questions later, that's all."

When Harold did not reply, William went on. "It is such a small thing, for all its importance to me. And in return, I will gladly release Wulfnooth and the others rather than continue to keep them here and"—his voice hardened—"invite your young son to join them."

Renard stiffened. At that moment curiosity got the better of him and he looked into the hall. He could see Harold and William standing near each other, separated by a long table.

Odo was there, but so, too, was someone he hadn't expected to see, the renowned abbot of Caen, Lanfranc, who was said to possess the keenest mind in all Normandy. He stood, somber and aloof, as though he found what was happening distasteful but necessary.

The four men clearly believed themselves to be alone, even the guards had been banished from the hall. But Renard could see what they could not. Toward the back, almost directly opposite where he stood, something moved in the shadows beside a column. It was the blue-eyed boy, Harold's son, and suddenly the subject of their discussion.

"Bastard," Harold said. "Truly you were rightly named."

William stiffened. He was very sensitive on this issue, as well he might be. Very much on his dignity, he said, "That is an odd remark coming from a man who beds with a concubine rather than a wife."

"I told you," Harold said, his face taut, "that is a personal matter, but since there seems to be some confusion, let me correct it. The Lady Edythe is my wife under the old Viking law of handfast marriage. The sons of her body are entirely my heirs."

"By pagan law," William said, "not Christian. The Church will have something to say about that if you ever aspire to be more than an earl, but never mind. The question is simple. Will you acknowledge my legitimacy as duke and swear never to raise arms against what is lawfully mine or will you not?"

Harold fell silent. Clearly he was angered by the proceedings and wanted to refuse. But just as obviously he realized he would be the loser if he did so. William would still be duke, nothing would change that.

He had left England knowing that he could bear to return without Wulfnooth if he had to, for that was an old wound long scarred over. But he had never bargained on having to go back without one of his own children.

"All right," he said slowly, "it will be as you wish."

Instantly William's whole demeanor changed. He smiled broadly and gestured to Odo, who stepped forward immediately, holding a small shrine sheathed in gold.

"The knucklebones of St. Peter," the bishop said in tones of awe.

Harold did not comment. He placed a hand on the shrine and looked at William. Without expression, he said, "I, Harold, Earl of Wessex, acknowledge William to be Duke of Normandy and swear that I will never attempt by force of arms to deprive him of his lawful inheritance." He removed his hand. "Is that what you wanted?"

William exhaled deeply. He nodded. "Exactly, I thank you."

"And the others?"

"Will return with you just as you wish. Now there need be no misunderstandings between us, don't you agree?"

Whatever Harold said, Renard did not hear it. Caution bade him withdraw. He returned to the kitchen. The water was boiling. He threw the dried leaves in and sat down to wait while it steeped.

What had been the point of all that? Why had William cared so much that Harold acknowledge him as lawful heir to Normandy and promise not to take arms against him? Was it really possible that the Englishman might have been considering a challenge to the duke at some future date, once Harold was King of England?

No answer presented itself. He drank the tea and went back to the bed. When he awoke the next morning, the English were already gone.

12

"*It was you,*" *Renard said.* He stared down into Aveline's white face. His hands were hard on her shoulders. When she tried to twist away, he tightened his grip yet further until she suddenly cried out.

Abruptly she was free. The sudden release caused her to fall back onto the bed. She lay there, red-gold hair tumbling around her shoulders, and stared at him.

"You," Renard repeated. His gaze was implacable, there was no relenting and no mercy in it. "It was you with the English at Rouen and Bayeux. You were the boy in Harold's train, the one we thought was his son. No wonder he was so frantic to keep you hidden."

"You are mad," Aveline said. If possible, she paled even more. Her body shook as though seized by a great wind.

"Am I?" Renard demanded. "You forget, I was there, and although it's taken me a while, I do finally remember." He bent, one knee on the bed, with his arms braced on either side of her, close enough to look her hard in the eye.

She tried to draw back, but there was nowhere to go. His arms were like hewn oak caging her.

"I saw you," he said, "first in Rouen when you came with your father and the others, then on the march into Brittany, and the last time in the hall at Bayeux where Harold swore the oath."

"You weren't there! You're lying!"

His mouth curved in a lethal smile. "The only way you could possibly be sure of that is if you were there, and you're still wrong. I was hidden near the door to the kitchens. You were standing behind a pillar on the opposite side of the hall. William said he would keep you as hostage unless Harold agreed to recognize his legitimate authority."

Her lips parted. She stared at him in horror. "Oh, my God . . ."

"I was there," he went on relentlessly, "and so were you. You are Harold Godwinson's daughter. I should have realized it sooner. You practically told me yourself."

"I did not! This is insane! You've taken something out of your own imagination and tried to twist it into—"

"You said your parents were both dead in the conquest," he interjected, "and that your mother had been your father's handfast wife. That fits perfectly. Give it up, Aveline, or whatever your real name is. You can't hide anymore."

Perhaps not, but she could make a final, desperate effort to escape. Without a second's warning, she slid from underneath him, scrambled to her feet, and lunged for the door.

Renard was after her in a flash, but terror lent her speed. She reached the door, yanked it open, and fled into the corridor beyond.

Renard was an arm's length behind her when she

reached the steps. They were tucked into a corner of the hall, set in a tight spiral, but there was an opening between them and the floor to allow heavy objects to be winched up. The opening ran the full height of the building, including the basement. At its bottom was a thick stone floor.

Aveline stood, panting, directly beside the opening. She stared down into it, her knuckles white against the narrow wood railing that was all that separated her from eternity.

"Aveline," Renard cried hoarsely, "no!"

She turned, looking at him over her shoulder. Her eyes were deep pools of pain and fear. She took a step closer to the opening.

"No!" He reached out a hand and noticed as though from a great distance that it was shaking badly. "Don't! Do you think this is what your father would want? He was a warrior and a leader. He fled from nothing. Would he expect less of you?"

Her eyes locked on his. If she died, his face would be the last thing she saw. "You said . . . you said you would force me . . . tell you . . . Oath Bearer . . ."

Desperately he tried to gauge the distance between them and how quickly he could close it. If he moved, would he be able to grab her in time or would she slip from his grasp to crush out her life on the stones below? He should take the risk, his loyalty to William demanded it.

But his love for this beautiful, astounding woman—God help him, for that was what it was—made it impossible.

A deep sigh escaped him. Without taking his eyes from her, he stepped back. His hand, still stretched out to her, steadied. "All right, come away and I swear I will not force you to tell me anything about Oath Bearer."

Still, she hesitated. Her voice shook. "Your word?"

He nodded. "My word. I swear."

Aveline sagged against the railing, all the strength gone from her. Renard seized her. He wanted to berate her, to demand how she could have done such a horrible thing to them both, but he said nothing, only held her tight against him until the worst of his terror eased. She was alive, she was safe, and for better or worse, she would not escape him again.

His face was grim as he looked past her into the startled eyes of his Saxon monk.

"My lord," Burgess said, "this woman—"

"Come with me," Renard said. He carried Aveline back down the passage to his quarters and laid her gently on the bed. She was still deathly pale, her eyes closed and her breathing shallow. Exhaustion had claimed her. He laid a thin coverlet over her and touched her hair gently before forcing himself to give his attention to Burgess.

"How much did you see out there?" he demanded.

The monk looked torn between shock and disapproval. Slowly he said, "The woman . . . she seemed to be trying to flee . . . I thought, that is, she looked almost as though she might . . . jump."

"She might have," Renard said. "She was that desperate." The admission was a knife in him. He had brought her to that, this proud and beautiful daughter of a valiant king.

Never again, he vowed silently. Whatever differences lay between them—and they were immense—he would never let her feel so threatened again.

Burgess paled. Suicide was beyond his comprehension. "What is wrong with her that she would think to do such a thing?" he asked, trying to understand.

"She has information I need but which she doesn't want to give. She feared I would force it from her and she was willing to die to prevent that."

The monk shook his head in bewilderment. "What could a woman know that would be so important?"

Renard did not enlighten him. Instead he shrugged and said, "That doesn't matter. I have given her my word that she has nothing to fear from me, but she is still in great danger. She must be kept safe here until I can find somewhere else to hide her."

Burgess grimaced. "This is trouble, I'm sure of it. She will distract you just when you can afford it least."

"I will try to control that," Renard said dryly. "At the moment all she wants to do is sleep."

"Just as well," the monk said, still eyeing Aveline suspiciously. "Rufus wants to see you."

"What?"

"You heard me. He sent a messenger requesting—make that requiring—your immediate presence. I gather it has to do with the murders, particularly the latest one."

Renard shook his head as though to clear it. All he wanted to think about was Aveline, but that wasn't to be. "Have you been able to learn anything about that?"

Burgess looked sideways down his nose as though to say that he had been out seeing to business while Renard had been doing whatever it was he'd done to land himself with the flame-haired hussy on his bed.

"The dead man's name was Edouard de Courcy. He was deacon at the abbey of the Westminster."

"*De* Courcy? A nobleman?"

Burgess nodded. "He was the third son of the Seigneur de Courcy."

"Damn! That's not good."

"Indeed not, and I rather suspect it's what Rufus wants to talk about with you. From the message, it didn't sound as though he was prepared to be patient."

"All right, I'll go, but you stay here."

"Here? You don't mean right . . . here? With her?"

"That's exactly what I mean. Don't let her out of your sight. She's not to go anywhere or talk to anyone. Most of all she isn't to do anything to hurt herself. Understood?"

Burgess nodded glumly. "A man works hard all his life, serving his God, trying to do the best he can in this vale of tears, and what happens? Pure though he be in mind and body, women will yet find a way to inflict themselves upon him."

"Quit complaining," Renard ordered. "She's an innocent, young Englishwoman in the clutches of a rapacious Norman—me. You should be sympathetic to her."

That at least gave Burgess pause. Renard left before he could come up with a reply, and before he himself could reconsider leaving Aveline. She would be safe, she had to be.

Meanwhile he had to soothe the nerves of Prince Rufus, who, understandably enough, was not pleased to see the stakes raised in the game of murder presently afoot in Londontown.

"A de Courcy," Rufus bellowed the moment he saw Renard approaching through the milling crowd of retainers who filled the great hall in the royal tower. "Not some merchant or scrivener, or even a clerk, but a damned de Courcy. Do you have any idea what that means?"

"It means the killer is growing bolder," Renard said bluntly. Without waiting for a response, he added, "It might be wise, sire, if we discussed this more privately."

Rufus grunted. He hoisted himself out of his seat at the high table and gestured to Renard to follow him. Behind velvet curtains at the end of the hall was a small chamber. It was hot in there and almost airless, but then so was most of the city.

Wearily the prince fell into another chair and glared at Renard. "Beastly weather," he said as though it was somehow the high sheriff's fault. "And no break in sight. I heard you gave new orders about the fires. You might have consulted me."

"Your pardon, my liege," Renard said. "I presumed you had more important matters to attend to."

As flattery went, it wasn't much, but Rufus accepted it all the same. "True, these English are a stubborn lot. They don't seem to understand when they're beaten and they don't fight honorably. Nobody can say they do when one of them's running around slitting Norman throats. What in God's name am I supposed to tell de Courcy?"

The prince shook his head in disgust. "He's been one of my father's most important supporters, going all the way back to the early days. He sent his son over here to find a place for himself. Instead he gets himself killed by some crazed Englishman who's performing pagan sacrifices. That's not going to go over very well in Normandy, let me tell you."

"I'm sure it won't," Renard murmured.

"Are you *any* closer to finding the culprit?"

Was he? He honestly didn't know. It wasn't as though he'd been free to devote all his time to the investigation. Far from it. There were certain other small matters—the drought, the danger of fire, the threat of rebellion.

And then there was Aveline. All sufficient to keep any man distracted, but he could hardly tell the prince that.

"I've been giving it a great deal of thought," he said at last.

"Thought? What good is that? I want action, man! I told you to round up hostages and press them for information. That's the only way to get through to these English. Put them to the screw and they'll tell us plenty."

"And I told you," Renard said, forgetting for the moment the deference due to royalty, "that you could find no surer path to aiding the rebellion. I will resign my office before I will agree to any such course, and I will go to Normandy myself to explain my action to His Majesty."

Rufus blanched. Clearly the thought of his father receiving such a report on his actions was enough to persuade him another course was preferable.

But Renard did not mistake the cost of that small victory. Rufus had him marked now as an enemy. The prince would find the earliest possible opportunity to make him pay.

Rufus's eyes narrowed. "Be careful, my lord d'Agounville, lest my royal father think you too soft for your high office. I suggest you put out any *illegal fires* with greater dispatch before you find yourself engulfed in them."

Renard did not mistake the warning. Rufus did not know for sure what had gone on in the raid on the house, but he had his suspicions. If he could prove that Renard had allowed Oath Bearer to escape, he would have the means to destroy them both.

As for Aveline, his stomach tightened at the thought of what Rufus would do to her if he ever discovered her identity.

"As you say, my lord," he replied, "we must all show even greater vigilance. When you write to de Courcy, please assure him on my behalf that everything is being done to find the murderer of his son."

"Make it so," Rufus ordered, "and swiftly. No Norman rests easily now in this cursed place."

That was true enough, Renard thought a short time later after he had left the tower and was riding slowly back toward his own residence. He should have gone more swiftly, and could have if he had taken the river road, but he wanted the time to think.

For all his blustering, Rufus did have a point: no Norman was resting easily. They were all aware, as were the English, that a killer was loose. Yet a fourth man had been lured to his death, a man who presumably should have known better.

How was it being done? He had wondered about that before, but now the question seemed more urgent than ever. What convinced apparently intelligent and sensible men to forsake all precautions and venture out into the streets at night?

A priest might have said they were under a spell, but Renard doubted it. He had seen a great deal in his life, but never anything that resembled what men called magic. Evil, yes, and occasionally great shining good. But never magic.

Which left . . . what?

He was no closer to an answer by the time he drew rein in front of his hall, but he was at least certain that if he could somehow solve that aspect of the mystery, he would have the killer. He would have liked to think about that some more, but circumstances prevented him. The groom who ran out to get his horse was wide-eyed and breathing hard.

"Thank the Lord you're back, sir! Inside . . . the Englishman . . ."

"What Englishman?" Renard asked, then ducked as the answer came flying out the nearest window at him. Actually what flew was a good chunk of a table that had apparently been ripped apart. An enraged bellow came from the same direction as the table. Renard sighed and followed it.

He went in through the window—why not when it

was simpler than going all the way around to the door? And he went in armed, sword drawn, ready for trouble.

He found it in the raging, red-eyed presence of Aveline's shadow. Wulfgarth turned on him in an instant, his own weapon unsheathed, and lunged at him.

Renard sidestepped the blow but only just. Even scarred as he was, Wulfgarth was a formidable adversary. Their swords clashed, each man straining for the advantage. Around them the servants scattered, screaming in their terror.

The sword battle raged out into the main hall and from there into the bailey yard. One moment Renard had the upper hand, the next it went to Wulfgarth. The burning sun beat down on them both. Sweat poured into Renard's eyes, threatening to blind him. He wiped it away and redoubled his efforts.

Rarely had he met an opponent as worthy as the Englishman, but this was hardly the time to dwell on that. He had to end the conflict and end it quickly.

He broke off suddenly and dove directly under Wulfgarth's sword arm. In confusion, the Englishman whirled. His balance gave and he stumbled slightly. Before he could recover, Renard dropped his sword, doubled his fist, and struck him a thunderous blow directly to the jaw.

It was the last thing Wulfgarth could have expected, for it defied all the laws and stratagems of war. But it worked. The Englishman blinked once, twice, again. A look of utter bafflement crept over him. Slowly he sank to the ground.

Renard joined him. He knelt on the hard-packed dirt of the bailey yard and struggled to regain his breath. God's blood, he hadn't fought like that in years. No wonder Harold had delegated this shaggy-haired giant to guard his precious daughter, for he was sure now that

Wulfgarth was the thegn who had stayed so close by her in Normandy. All this time later he was still performing the same duty and still going about it as relentlessly.

Climbing back to his feet, Renard gestured to several of his men who had watched the clash with professional interest, ready to intervene if their lord required it, but not surprised in the end to be unneeded.

"Take him below," Renard ordered. "Restrain him and put a guard on watch. When he's conscious again, send word to me."

The men hurried to obey and none too gently. Wulf-garth was hauled off down the steep stone steps to the basement, where there was a strong room that could double as a passable dungeon. That done, Renard entered his hall for the second time.

He felt bruised and battered, and was limping slightly. Damn these English! He was high sheriff, an adminis-trator, a bureaucrat, he was supposed to go around neatly solving problems or preventing them from ever happening in the first place.

But all he'd done since leaving his bed—much too early, for that matter—was deal with violence, natural, man-made, immediate, and imminent. Granted, he'd caused some of it himself, but that didn't change any-thing. He was definitely not in a charitable mood as he stomped up the steps to his quarters.

Burgess greeted him at the door. He looked his mas-ter over and shook his head in dismay. "I heard fighting. What happened?"

"Her watchdog tried to break in," Renard said with a nod toward the bed. Aveline was still asleep. She lay there looking unutterably beautiful and desirable, arousing him as no woman had ever done, and all the while blissfully unaware of the turmoil all around her.

Turmoil he had to cope with as best he could. Really, when he thought about that, it wasn't fair.

"Get out," he said to Burgess. Never mind what the monk made of that, he would have his way. "And tell them in the kitchens to bring water up. *Cold* water. I want a bath."

The monk went off, stiff-backed with disapproval, and Renard cursed under his breath. He was burning up under his chain mail. He'd never had a chance to take it off after the raid and now he had to be glad he hadn't. Without it, Wulfgarth could have killed him.

"If they'd had ten more like him at Hastings," he muttered under his breath, "it would have been a different story."

That close the battle had been, as those honest enough to admit it knew. Nowadays it was rated a great victory, but Renard knew how near it had come to being anything but. Men said that was the hand of God, but there were times when he wondered why the Deity hadn't made his wishes plainer and sooner, before so many good men had to die.

He yanked the mail off over his head and dropped it out in the passage for one of the squires to see to. The servants arrived with the water. They kept their eyes averted from the bed and scurried to fill the large, tin tub that sat in a corner of the room. When it was done, they left as hurriedly as they had come.

Renard stripped off his tunic and stepped into the cool water. He closed his eyes with blissful relief and laid his head back against the edge of the tub. For the first time in far too long, he was damn well going to relax, and woe betide anyone who got in his way while he was doing it.

"*Oh.*"

That sound, uttered in a female tone of immense surprise, came from the direction of the bed. Slowly

Renard opened first one eye and then the other. Aveline was sitting up, looking understandably confused and decidedly surprised. He smiled.

"You're awake."

"W-what? Awake? Yes, I am and you're—"

"Bathing. It's a fine old custom with which I'm sure you're well acquainted. In fact, as I recall, you seem to favor a lavender soap. I prefer something plainer. It's in the chest over there. Hand it to me, will you?"

"H-hand it . . . I . . . you . . ."

"Oh, very well, I'll get it myself." He made to rise, water sluicing off him.

"No! I'll get it, you stay there." She scrambled from the bed, seized the soap from the chest, and approached him as well she might a spawn of hell arisen directly from the underworld.

"H-here . . ."

"Sorry," he said unrepentantly, "I can't reach it. You'll have to come closer."

"I can't . . . you . . . Here." The soap landed with a *splat* directly in front of him.

He brushed the water from his eyes and looked at her sternly. "Was that necessary? Surely you've seen naked men before?"

The blush that suffused her cheeks was most satisfactory. Hastily she turned away. "Of course I have," she murmured, "but not . . . not lately. I live in an abbey, for heaven's sake. Surely, you remember that."

"Oh, yes," he said agreeably, "good St. Margaret's. I presume Mother Eldgythe knows who you are?"

Aveline bit her lower lip. He saw a thin line of red appear beneath her sharp white teeth and winced, thinking how he would like to kiss away the hurt and wondering what her reaction would be if he tried.

"Do we have to discuss this?" she asked.

His smile deepened. "No, but if you want me to stay over here, I suggest we give it a try."

"You are an insufferable man."

"Maybe so, but you don't have a lot of alternatives just now. Oath Bearer, whoever he may be, will have left the city if he has any sense at all. As for your faithful Wulfgarth, he sits below awaiting my judgment for invading my hall and trying to kill me."

Aveline swayed on her feet. There was no mistaking her dismay. "Oh, no, not Wulfgarth. Please, don't hurt him. Whatever's happened, he's not to blame."

Renard frowned. She seemed to have a strange idea about what her faithful servant was capable of doing.

"Very touching," he said, thinking that he wouldn't have minded a little of that fierce loyalty pointed in his direction, not that there was any chance of that. So far as she was concerned, they were fate-destined enemies.

He saw her glance slip toward the door and straightened up in the tub. "Don't think of it. There's nowhere you could go that I wouldn't find you."

"I wasn't—"

"Yes, you were. Look, this has been a hell of a day and it's still not over. Be a good girl and go sit down on the bed. I'm not going to hurt your Wulfgarth, if that's what you're worried about. Provided, of course, that he gives up trying to hurt me."

"I don't see how anyone could hurt you," Aveline muttered. "You're made of stone."

"What was that?"

Her flush deepened. "Nothing."

Renard glanced down at himself in the tub, at an angle she could not see, and sighed. He was the furthest thing from what she imagined, at least at the moment.

Even with the width of the room between them, all it took was a glance from her to arouse him.

As he would have to stay where he was for a bit or risk offending her maiden sensibilities, he said, "I promised not to ask you anything about Oath Bearer and I'll stick to that, but I said nothing about asking you about yourself. Mother Eldgythe must know who you were or you would have said otherwise. If you've been there eleven years, she took you in right after Hastings. Why didn't you stay with your mother and the others?"

Aveline sighed. She looked very weary. Compassion tugged at him, but he ignored it. Now wasn't the time.

"Because my mother wanted to be sure at least one of us survived. As it turned out, she was wise to send me to St. Margaret's. Ireland did none of them any good."

"I'm sorry," Renard said softly. Her proud grief demanded it. She asked for nothing, yet the strength with which she bore the great tragedy that had remade her life won his admiration, not to speak of his heart.

"Why should you be?" she asked with apparent sincerity. "It was a great victory for you Normans."

He looked away uncomfortably. "It was a long time ago. Nothing can unmake it. That's what Oath Bearer ought to know. We won at Hastings, where there were only a few thousand of us. Now we are spread thickly across this land. Do you really think we can be driven out?"

"You are still small in number compared to us," Aveline said. She sat on the bed with her eyes averted and her hands tightly clasped, looking for all the world—he thought—like a sacrifice. The idea irked him.

"That doesn't answer my question," he said relentlessly. "You will never force us to give up England, not now. If a unified revolt had been launched right after Hastings, it might have succeeded. But it's too late for that. To even try it will bring down suffering on this country such as no one has ever seen."

Her temper flared. "Because the Normans will it? Because you are arrogantly convinced that you have the right to rule here? Never mind that you claim that right with lies and treachery. Odo is the perfect example, stooping to anything to get what he wants. He seems like the worst of you, but really he only wants to please William, just as you do. You're all alike!"

"Indeed?" Renard inquired, calmly enough. Her temper sparked his own. He forgot his good intentions about not frightening her.

"You're wrong," he said. "At this particular moment I am interested in pleasing myself." And so saying, he pressed both hands on the side of the tub and rose. Water fell away down the length of his hard, burnished body. It pooled at his feet as he stepped out and walked across the room, straight toward her.

"What are you . . . ? Stop it!"

"No," he said, quite calmly even though he was feeling anything but. "Your father's line is most impressive, but let us not overlook that you are also your mother's daughter. The Lady Edythe was, by all reports, accounted the most beautiful woman in England. You do her proud."

Aveline opened her mouth to answer, but no sound came out. She did her very best to keep her gaze fastened on his face, but she didn't quite succeed. Her eyes widened as they slipped down the long length of him.

He was unusually big for a man, long of limb, broad through the chest and arms, his chest ribbed with muscle, his belly flat and his thighs honed to steel. His was a warrior's body, inured to hardship, bred for endurance, remorseless in its mastery. Yet, here and there, the effects of war were visible.

212 212 MAURA SEGER

A long white scar ran across his chest, the memento of an Anglo-Saxon ax that had come very close to ending his life at Hastings. There was a puckered welt on his left shoulder where he had taken an arrow during the siege of York. And there were others, burns, cuts, other battle wounds, the inevitable reminders of a manhood spent largely at war.

War had seared his soul until he thought it was in danger of being destroyed. Aveline changed that. With her he was alive again. He meant to stay that way.

Yet he waited, making no further move toward her. He wanted to give her every possible chance to become accustomed to him. As it was, he was fortunate that she was no swooning maiden, but a woman of strength and courage. Even so, her face flamed and her hands twisted the fabric of her robe.

"Go away," she said.

He smiled and stepped closer to the bed. "For almost twenty years, your mother bound one of the most powerful men in England to her. Even when he finally had to make a political marriage to secure his throne, he left his noble wife and returned to your mother's bed. Why do you suppose that was?"

"I have no idea and I'm not going to discuss my parents with you. Stop this!"

Relentlessly he ignored her and continued. "Haven't you ever wondered, Aveline? Holed up in that convent, listening to the good sisters chant their holy offices, don't tell me you haven't thought what your life would have been like if your father had won at Hastings? You would have been courted as a princess, wooed by the greatest men in the land. One of them would have won you, wed you, and . . ."

He put a knee on the bed and leaned over, brushing his hand along the silken line of her cheek. " . . . bedded you.

You are made for passion, Aveline, it flows in your blood. Not all the Mother Eldgythes in the world can change that."

His hand closed around the back of her head. Gently but implacably he brought her to him. "There is nothing for you in St. Margaret's except a struggle to fill the empty years. Give it up, Aveline. I will never let you go now."

She trembled against him, her hands pressing futilely against his powerful chest. His conscience twinged, but he ignored it. He would not hurt her, at least no more than he absolutely had to, and afterward she would be glad for he would cherish and protect her as no woman had ever been.

She would come to accept that, in time. It was the way of the world that men ruled women. She was foolish to resist.

"Aveline," he murmured as he lowered his head. His mouth blazed a line of fire down her slender throat. "Don't struggle, just relax, let this be. It is for the best, truly. I—"

"*No!*"

That single word, uttered in a harshly guttural tone, tore through him. He looked up, bewildered, and saw Aveline's face floating as though in the air. Her lips had not moved. Who then . . . ?

He tried to turn his head, but pain crashed through him. A whirling circle of darkness appeared at the outer reaches of his vision and moved swiftly inward. He fought it with every ounce of his strength, struggling against unconsciousness.

In the last instant he stared into her eyes and saw there compassion and something that might have been regret. That memory followed him down an endless, churning tunnel into nothingness.

13

"Come," Wulfgarth said, and lifted me from the bed. Renard's body slid away, landing with a thump on the floor. I stared at him in horror. He was still alive, I could see his breathing, but there was an ugly gash on the back of his head from which dark blood oozed rapidly.

I should be glad, considering what would have happened if Wulfgarth hadn't intervened. Yet I could think only of his pain.

"Wait," I said, reaching for him.

"There is no time," Wulfgarth said. He half carried, half dragged me to the door. I went, partly out of confusion but mainly because I knew there was no choice. To remain where we were was to court death.

The main hall below was empty. We managed to get through it and out onto the street without being seen. Once there, Wulfgarth did not hesitate. He struck out at a quick pace in the direction of Thorney cloister. I had to run to keep up with him.

"How did you get free?" I asked. So much had happened since our arrival the day before in London that I could hardly grasp it all. But I had to try, if only because it kept me from thinking too much about what had happened—or almost happened—with Renard.

"I tore the chain from the wall," Wulfgarth said. He raised the iron links that still manacled his wrist to show them to me. "The mortar was loose."

He is too modest. Properly roused to anger, Wulfgarth has the strength of ten. Considering how distracted Renard was, Wulfgarth could have killed him. I wondered why he had not even as I tried not to be too thankful for his restraint.

"This won't work," I said. "He will come looking for us."

Wulfgarth did not slacken his pace. "We will be gone from the city by then."

"We can't return to St. Margaret's."

He grunted as though that were obvious. "We will find someplace else. The important thing is that you be kept safe."

Wulfgarth is a good man—brave, loyal, utterly trustworthy. But once given an order, he will cling to it unswervingly. My mother told him to protect me. He has done so ever since and does so now, even as I have begun to wonder if that is truly what I want.

"We will go west," Wulfgarth was saying. He had no sense of my restless doubts. "There are allies still in Wessex and beyond in Wales. Oath Bearer—"

"Magnus," I said. Let the lies stop now, for truly I cannot bear them any longer.

Wulfgarth grunted again. "Magnus has many friends. They will welcome you."

My heart skipped. "He got away, then? You're sure?"

He nodded. "I guessed where you'd gone and followed, but by the time I got there, the raid had already happened. People from the street told me who had taken you and also that Oath Bearer had escaped. Praise God for that at least."

We were approaching Ludgate at the westernmost reaches of the city. Beyond lay the river bend and past that the island of Thorney. It was getting on for evening. A breeze, so welcome after the brutally hot day, blew at our backs.

A man, passing on a horse, turned slightly to look at us. I became aware then for the first time of my disheveled state. My hair fell in a riot of curls, I had managed to lose the veil that should have covered it, and my robe was crumpled from lying on Renard's bed. Altogether, I looked nothing at all like the abbess's ward I was supposed to be.

But then, I didn't feel like that either. Not anymore, at least.

Ludgate was directly ahead of us. The usual black-garbed guards were there, protecting the city from any lepers who might try to enter. I held my breath as we neared them, but they took no notice of us.

We stopped for a moment to let a wagon go ahead. Its rear wheels stuck in the rutted ground. The driver cursed and urged his oxen on, but they stood unmoving with the stolid endurance of their kind.

There was a boy on the wagon, a farmer's son by the look of him. They seemed to be a family that had come into town to sell whatever small crops they had managed to raise despite the drought. Now they were going home, or trying to. At the moment all they had succeeded in doing was blocking the gate.

Two of the guards came over and began shouting orders to the farmer, who, weary as he was, tried to obey. He was a small man with a stooped back. Wulfgarth watched him for a moment before he sighed impatiently and went to help.

"Stay here," he said.

I watched him tread his way between the people until he reached the wagon. Seeing him, everyone else retreated. Wulfgarth bent his back to the task, but the wagon was well and truly stuck. He would need several efforts, at least, before he could free it.

The crowd pressed forward to watch. I lost sight of him above the sea of heads. Tired myself, I fell back against the watchtower wall and paused to catch my breath.

It was then that I smelled it. There is no mistaking the woodsy, acrid scent of smoke. London is always filled with it, but this was something different. Smoke in a tended fire is a comforting thing, reminding us of chill nights spent safe indoors, of good fellowship and cheer. There is nothing frightening about it.

This was different. Wood was burning all right, but not tamely as it should. This was a living creature that had burst its bonds and was growing more lethal with every passing moment.

At the same time that I noticed the smell, so did several others standing near me. We all looked in the same direction, back toward the city. London rises slightly toward the east. Toward Aldgate, I could see a thick dark pillar of cloud pouring upward to the sky.

Fire.

Several of the people screamed and that drew the attention of more. Within seconds, the space in front of Ludgate was filled by a teeming mass of humanity that had but a single thought—escape.

The thought certainly went through my mind, but it was quickly followed by another. Even as I craned my neck, trying to catch sight of Wulfgarth, I knew what I had to do. I saw him finally, trying to fight his way toward me. The crowd was against him and he was making scant headway.

"Go back," I screamed over the milling heads. "Find Mother Eldgythe. Get her from the city."

He heard me, I was sure of that, but he kept trying to reach me without success. I hesitated a moment, frozen in place. If I stayed where I was, the crowd would pull me along with it toward Wulfgarth and out through Ludgate. I would be safe.

But Renard remained unconscious in the upper chamber of his residence. When his servants and men-at-arms realized there was a fire, they might think to look for him or they might not. They could simply presume he had already gone out to help fight it.

He could be left alone with no chance for escape.

A moment longer I stared into Wulfgarth's dearly familiar face. He must have seen what was in my mind, for he cried out and struggled all the harder to reach me. But the crowd was too much even for his strength. It carried him along as a ship borne on the sea until he vanished from my sight.

I turned, picked up my skirts, and ran, back into the narrow streets and winding lanes. The closer I got to the center of the city, the harder it was to go on. People were pouring from their houses, staring horror-struck at the pillar of smoke or hurrying panic-stricken to gather up what belongings they could.

I saw a woman rush by carrying a small child and another with a lamb tucked under her arm. A man was frantically loading a crippled girl into a wagon while another pulled a heavy chest out into the street.

Renard's hall was to the west of William's tower and hard on the river. On a normal day I should have been able to reach it in minutes. Much longer passed before I finally staggered into the bailey yard. I stopped for a moment, my heart pounding.

This close to the river, the smoke was lighter. For that I was grateful, but for nothing else. The yard was deserted, as was the hall. It was as I had feared. No one—not servant or man-at-arm—stopped to think that anyone as proud and indomitable as Renard might need help.

Swiftly I climbed the curving steps to the upper floor and made my way down the passage to the room from which I had so lately been rescued. Creaking open the door, I peered inside.

What I expected, I cannot say for certain. Perhaps a revived and enraged Renard more than capable of dealing with anything that came his way, be it fire or one frightened English woman. But instead he was as I had last seen him, slumped facedown on the floor.

I choked back a cry and ran to him.

"Renard, please, you must get up. There is fire in the city. We have to flee." As I spoke I tugged, trying to turn him. It was like trying to turn a finely chiseled block of granite, hopeless.

Giving up, I ran to the tub still filled with water. His discarded tunic lay nearby. Seizing it, I plunged it into the water and, when it was well wet, ran back to him. With only the briefest twinge, I wrung the cloth out directly over his face. That done, I ran back for more. Three times I showered water on Renard before at last he stirred.

"W-what . . . " he muttered as he raised a hand, trying to fend off whatever was coming at him.

"You must get up," I said again. "There is fire. We must go." I dropped the tunic, which seemed to have served its purpose, and from a nearby chest seized clean clothing. By the time I turned to him with it in my hands, he was sitting up, holding his head, and staring at me in bewilderment.

"Aveline . . . you . . . what happened?"

"Never mind about that," I said briskly. Why tire him with the details when there were more important matters to be seen to? "Here, put this on. We have to get away."

"Away from what?" he asked, making no effort to put on the clothes. Mary and all the saints forgive me, he is a beautifully made man. I tried not to look but—

Enough said. I knelt beside him and began pulling the tunic over his head. "There is a fire in the city. Already people are fleeing. We must leave here."

He blinked once, twice. When he opened his eyes again, they were clear as the silvery sky in the hour before dawn. "Fire. You're sure?"

I nodded quickly. The tunic was on. Getting an arm under him, I urged him to his feet. "East of here toward Aldgate, I think. The wind is blowing in this direction and it has picked up just in the last hour. It will spread quickly."

"My God," he said, and for the first time looked directly at me. "I must get you out of here."

"Indeed," I said, letting him have the point. It hardly mattered which of us rescued the other so long as we wasted no more time. I have a well-founded fear of fire based on what I saw it do to the city of Winchester when I was a child. It was my most ardent hope London would not suffer such destruction, but if it did, I did not want to witness it.

"Where is everyone?" Renard demanded as we came down the stairs into the hall.

"Gone."

He cursed under his breath. I followed him out into the bailey and watched as he stood, feet apart and hands on his lean hips, with his dark head thrown back. His nostrils flared. He looked like a great beast of prey sensing his foe and preparing to do combat with it.

"Can you row?" he asked suddenly.

I nodded. Magnus had taught me, but I thought it prudent not to mention that.

"Come then," he said, and drew me away with him in the direction of the river. "I keep a small skiff at the water steps. It is easy to manage. Take it and just go with the current. As soon as you're past the city, put into shore. Try to get as close to Wapping as you can. Have you money?"

I shook my head. "No, but it makes no difference. I will not—"

"Here, take this." He thrust a small pouch into my hands. "There is an inn at Wapping, the Three Crows. Tell the innkeeper—his name is Thomas—that I sent you. He'll find you a room no matter how crowded he is. Wait there until I can come for you."

He took my shoulders and turned me to him. His face was set, but not without an odd note of tenderness I had most certainly not expected. Perhaps getting hit on the head had some strange effect on him. At the least, it seemed to muddle his reason.

"Don't stray from there, Aveline. Understand? It will be very dangerous on the roads. Remain until I can come."

He actually believed I would do that. He thought he could put me in that boat, send me down the river to safety, and turn alone to face the fire himself. Truly the minds of men are beyond my poor comprehension.

"Come with me," I said. In truth, I pleaded, for the

thought of leaving him there was unbearable. Later I would try to understand why. For the moment it was enough that we not be separated.

"I cannot," he said gently. "The fire must be stopped. Go now."

When I continued to resist, standing rooted to the sere grass beside the river, he muttered under his breath and lifted me. In his arms I felt no more than a puff of wind blown on the hot night air. I protested, but he ignored that and set me firmly in the skiff.

Quickly he undid the mooring rope and tossed it into the boat at my feet. His eyes met mine and held for a long moment before he leaned over slightly and gave the skiff a strong shove. Before I could fully realize what was happening, I was drifting away from shore toward the center of the river. My gaze remained locked on Renard until the smoke-filled night swallowed him from sight.

Instinctively I grabbed for the oars and prayed that I would remember what to do. Magnus had taught me well and the years at St. Margaret's had made me stronger than women whose lives are more pampered. I was able to gain control of the skiff quickly.

How long would Renard wait? Probably not very. He was most likely already striding up the lawn back toward the hall. In another moment or two, he would be inside, gathering whatever he thought he would need.

Swiftly I bent my strength to the river's current. The skiff did handle well. Within minutes after casting off, I was back at the water steps. I secured the boat again and ran across the lawn. There was no sign of Renard, but there was only one way he could have gone, toward Aldgate.

For the second time within the space of an hour, I was drawn back into the burning city. Night had fully fallen. The sky was clear—as it has been for months—

and the moon was almost full. It cast ribbons of light over the huddled buildings with their walls of wood and thatched roofs, all perfect fodder for the flame.

The streets were full of people heading west away from the flames or south toward the river. But not all Londoners were fleeing. A large number remained, and these had organized themselves into brigades that were drawing buckets of water from the wells and passing them hand to hand up to the roofs, where they were quickly poured over the thatch. By this wetting down, they hoped to stop the spread of the fire. I prayed they would succeed, but I had seen the same effort made in Winchester, and there it had failed.

Aldgate was at the easternmost end of Cheapside, the major road through London and the one where all the markets were clustered. Among them was the lane where the charcoal burners had their shops. I wondered if the fire might have started there.

It seemed likely, for as I neared the Aldgate well, I could see a line of men with buckets sending water down toward Coaler Road. But the fire had already gained too strong a hold, and even as I watched, several nearby houses collapsed inward, eaten by the flame.

The resulting shower of burning timbers drove everyone back. The men gave up their efforts and stood, dazed and uncertain, in the center of the road near the well.

But they did not long remain so, for a figure suddenly appeared among them, so tall that he towered above them all. He stood, covered with soot and grime as we all were, his head thrown back and the light of battle in his eyes.

"To the next lane," Renard shouted above the roar of the fire. "We'll fight it there. Keep the buckets moving!"

The crowd did not hesitate but hurried to obey. They

were brave men—and women, too—and they were desperate to save what was theirs. I could not help but notice that while most were English, there were also Normans among them, fighting side by side with no thought to the hatred that has marked us for so long.

Again the line formed, but longer this time, for the distance from the well was greater. A bucket was thrust into my hands. Water sloshed over my arms. I passed it on and reached out for the next bucket. And so, on and on, through how much time I could not say. My breath came in gasps, my skin was hot to the touch, and I could hardly see for the sweat pouring into my eyes.

Yet there was no thought of stopping until, far ahead of me along the line, a shout went up. Those closest to the fire were forced to fall back as yet more buildings collapsed. Several screamed as falling chunks of wood struck them. They were hurried away; I could only hope they would be cared for.

I saw Renard again with several men gathered around him. Some were his own men-at-arms, others were merchants from the surrounding streets. They were speaking urgently. He listened, then turned and looked around at the raging inferno that with each passing moment gained yet further strength. Slowly I saw him shake his head.

He spoke, giving orders. Several of the men looked dismayed, but they did not argue. Clearly they knew him to be right.

West of where we were standing was Poultry Street. There were few houses here, only stalls. Between them and the rest of the city was an open stretch of ground still given over to farming. There Renard led us to make a final stand.

We were joined by others who had the same thought. English and Norman alike we stood, watching the fire eat its way toward us, devouring homes, shops, belongings, and—God have mercy on anyone caught within it—lives.

All of Aldgate was burning now; even the well itself was surrounded. At Renard's order, women ran among us handing out lengths of fabric, some salvaged from the cloth merchants' shops before they burned, others brought quickly from the wharves, where goods were packed in heavy burlap. As the fire neared and sparks began to fly into the fields, we ran frantically to beat them out.

All through that terrible night, as the fire hissed and roared scant feet away from us, we denied its advance. Smoke seared our lungs and the weakest among us collapsed, but the rest kept fighting. If we gave up now, the whole of the city would be lost.

Finally, toward dawn, the hell wind died and the fire, deprived of further food, began to sputter out. I sat, exhausted, my limbs turned to lead, and stared at the smoldering ruins.

So much gone, fully half the city, with the rest damaged by isolated fires that had been spread by sparks on the wind but, thanks be to God, had mostly been contained. An unknown number were dead and many more had lost their livelihoods.

So intense had the inferno been that even some of the boats docked near London Bridge had burned. I heard a man say that the bridge itself was damaged, but I took little notice. Indeed, I could hardly attend to anything, so weary was I in mind and body.

I was also filthy. My hair was singed, my clothes reeked of smoke, and anyone could have been pardoned for thinking me a creature from the netherworld.

A few monks had come out from the city's abbeys. They moved among us in their cowled robes, passing out water and bread, and doing what they could to comfort those overwhelmed by the night's events. I drank a ladleful of water but gave my bread to a woman sitting nearby with her child. Any effort to eat was beyond me.

Aside from the monks and a goodly number of men-at-arms who had rallied to Renard, there was no sign of London's government. The clerks had long since fled, the bishop had vanished, and as for Prince Rufus, he apparently had more important places to be. The city was left to itself and, truthfully, was the better for it.

Eventually it occurred to me that I ought to get up and do something. I rose shakily and began making my way toward the river with the thought that I would wash the worst of the soot from my face and hands, at least. It was then, naturally enough, that Renard saw me.

For an instant his eyes went right past, so unlike myself did I appear. But just as I thought I would be able to slip by, he looked again. The expression on his face might have been comical under other circumstances.

"You," he said, towering over me as I have noticed he has the habit of doing. His hands grasped my shoulders. People were watching us, but with only the mildest curiosity; they couldn't muster anything more.

"It is you," Renard said slowly. His voice was low and rough, filled with the residue of the smoke. My own sounded little better.

"I am glad to see you well," I said politely. Fear coiled within me, for he had every right to be angry, but I refused to show it.

He stared, dumbfounded, as though he still couldn't believe the apparition before his eyes. "I told you to go to Wapping," he said, as though reassuring himself he hadn't lost all touch with reality. "Did you have some trouble with the boat?"

"No, it was fine. As soon as I was sure you had gone, I rowed back to shore."

"Why?"

Pride drove me, remorseless goad that it is. My chin tilted. "For the same reason you did."

He shook his head, perplexed. "That makes no sense. I am high sheriff of London. It was my duty to be here and to do everything I could to help. You are—" He broke off, staring at me.

"You are—" he said again.

I met his eyes proudly. After all the years of denial, a newborn sense of freedom stirred within me. Head high, I said, "You know who I am."

A long moment more we stared at one another before, abruptly, he smiled. Teeth flashed whitely in that hard, unyielding face. For a moment years seemed to fall away from him. "A king's daughter," he said. "Truly you are that."

He bent slightly and lifted me high into his arms. I protested, of course, but not very much. I was tired, after all, and to be honest, it felt uncannily natural to be with him in this way.

"Where are we going?" I asked.

"To Wapping."

I laid my head back against his broad shoulder and let my eyes shut. Distantly I remember being lifted onto a horse, but it made very little impression. I was asleep before we left the smoking ruins of London behind us and turned eastward toward the brightening day.

14

"I presume it was Wulfgarth who struck me," Renard said. He winced as he spoke and touched the back of his head gingerly.

"He was only trying to protect me," I said. My cheeks warmed at the memory. If Wulfgarth could see us now, he would undoubtedly believe me in need of such protection once again. And he would be right, but not, this time, because of Renard. It is this other self of mine, this person I never suspected existed, who relishes being alone with him, away from all the world in a place where all things are possible.

We were in Wapping, at the inn of the man Thomas. Many refugees from the city had fled there. By the time we arrived, every room was taken. Indeed, every corner where bedding might be put down was already occupied.

Thomas was dismayed. He was English, but of the sort who knew full well which side of the bread held the butter.

"My lord," he exclaimed, bustling out to greet us, "praise the Maker that you are safe. Everyone is speaking of your great efforts to protect the city. Had it not been for you, who knows how far the flames might have spread?"

He shivered, despite his bulk and the heat of the day, no doubt envisioning his own fair wattle-and-timber inn being devoured by flame. Never mind that Wapping was well beyond the city walls with a thick greensward between it and the fire. Thomas's imagination was equal to the task.

"Alas," he said, hands twisting in the apron tied around his ample middle, "I had no way of knowing you would come. Every room is jammed to the rafters, although, of course, I can correct that. If you would be kind enough to wait but a moment—"

"No," Renard said. He glanced around. "There are women and children here. Put no one out on our behalf. But if you have any place quiet where we might rest . . ."

Thomas thought, his ruddy face creased with the effort. "There are people everywhere, even in the stable, but wait . . . there is the old stone cot down by the river. No one has used it in an age. I could give you clean straw—"

He looked at us doubtfully. More correctly he looked at Renard, for Thomas, good innkeep that he was, had made a point of not looking at me at all. I might not have existed so far as he was concerned.

"The cot will be fine," Renard assured him, which relieved Thomas no end. He waylaid a passing servant and gave sharp orders for our comfort.

So it was that scant time later we were alone in the cot, fresh straw laid over the floor, several buckets of clean water nearby, and a meal of bread and meats laid out on good-quality linen. Let fire destroy half a city, good Thomas will still be up to his job.

"Where is he now?" Renard inquired, returning my

attention to the matter of Wulfgarth. He spoke mildly enough, but I wasn't fooled. There is nothing at all mild about him.

"With Mother Eldgythe," I hope. "I sent him to Thorney with instructions to get her away from here."

"And he obeyed, leaving you on your own? I find that passing strange."

Briefly I told him about the scene at Ludgate. He heard me out in silence. When I was done, his face was grim.

"You returned to save me," he said.

I shrugged and looked away. The cot had a narrow wooden door that stood open to the sun. Through it I could see the river meandering by. It was a curiously peaceful scene after all that had gone before.

When I dared a glance at Renard, he was looking at me oddly.

"What?" I asked.

The corners of his mouth twitched. "You are a most surprising woman."

Without warning, he laughed, a young sound that I was glad to hear. "That puts it mildly. Since I first met you, I have scarcely had a quiet moment."

"That is hardly my fault," I said.

"No," he murmured, "I suppose it isn't." I could feel him staring at me, but I refused to look at him until his hand cupped the back of my head and compelled me to meet his gaze.

"I should be angry with you," he said. "You deliberately disobeyed me when I told you to leave the city."

"I am not yours to order about," I replied. Bravery has ever been my strong suit. Common sense has not. "I did what I had to."

"Indeed?" he replied. "Was it only honor that drew you back, Aveline?"

He moved closer, so that I could feel his breath warm on my cheek. "Only honor that demanded you save my life even after I tried not so long before to, shall we say, relieve you of your virtue? I am Norman, you are English. How many times have you told me that? Yet you came back at great risk to yourself. Only for honor, sweetling?"

I wanted to answer him, truly I did, but somehow the words would not come. My thoughts were all confusion. He was so very close and so strong.

We had washed the worst of the dirt from our faces and hands. I could see the clean line of his jaw, the hard bones and burnished skin, and above all, the eyes that seemed to look directly into my soul.

Impossible man.

Impossible situation.

Impossible not to—

Depart now if your sensibilities are readily offended, but pray, do not think badly of me, for when all is said and done I am my mother's daughter.

He called me that, Renard did, and he was right, as he and I both were about to discover.

How and why it happened I cannot say, but somewhere in that scant space of time when I turned to meet his gaze and felt the soft caress of his breath, something came undone within me. A huge knot of pain and grief I had barely acknowledged existed unraveled suddenly. I was left bondless, unchained, unfettered, gloriously free.

And with only one direction in which to turn.

I swayed slightly and reached out to steady myself. My head touched his chest. He covered it with his own. His head bent and I rose to meet him. His lips touched mine. Mine touched his.

Now here, my soul shouted, *is glory*. Not the filthy

furor of battle but this incandescent delight that gathered me up from this earth and flung me heavenward in a blinding instant.

His mouth . . . so strong yet tender, so gentle yet demanding. How he coaxed, persuaded until my better judgment—presuming I still possessed any—melted away like shards of ice set beneath the sun.

We fell backward into the fragrant straw. Renard kicked the door closed. Kindly darkness surrounded us, eased only by shafts of light that came through the old wooden planks.

"Aveline," he murmured huskily. His voice shook. So did my hands as I did at last what I had so long wanted to do. His chest was broad, hard as stone, and warm beneath my touch. I felt the tremors race through him and marveled that I could so move this proud, powerful man.

Again and again, we kissed. The first hot plunge of his tongue shocked me but, I cannot lie, it also thrilled. Swiftly I learned the rhythm of it and learned, too, that if I moved ever so slightly, I could feel the arching strength of his manhood pressed against my thigh. I moaned, my head falling back. His teeth raked my throat.

The layers of fabric between us were quickly becoming unbearable. He dragged me upright. I felt the sudden touch of air against my legs, my hips and breasts as he eased the robe from me. His tunic followed in an instant.

Naked, we pressed against each other, unable to get enough. Passion built, becoming unbearable. His mouth at my breasts, first one and then the other, made me cry out. Heat gathered deep within me. The straw was warm against my back.

He suckled urgently, tongue and teeth grazing my nipples until I thought I would go mad from the sensations he aroused. All the while, his hands moved, stroking and caressing me.

The intimacy was more than I had ever imagined. It frightened me and yet I could no more draw back from it than I could from life itself. Instead I drew nearer, touching him in turn until he cried out my name and came, this proud warrior, to lie between my legs.

His manhood touched me. I shivered, filled with need yet still with the last tremors of fear. Innocence, that great protection, had become a burden I could no longer tolerate. Yet I cannot say I gave it up easily.

The sense of ripening fullness was pleasant at first, but as he pressed further, pain seized me. I struggled then, resisting being so torn from girlhood. He stopped and held me gently, murmuring reassurance, until the pain eased and from somewhere deep within muscles I had not known I possessed began to flex and tighten.

He groaned and moved again, slowly at first, but then the full driving heat of passion seized him and he thrust within me, again and again. Pain vanished, replaced by pleasure so extreme that I thought I could not survive it.

All sense of myself as separate from him vanished. We were one in the sweet darkness of the cot, survivors of the fire and being born again in it. He muffled my cries with his mouth in that final moment when passion crested.

I sobbed his name, clinging to him, and felt the ancient power of my body welcome the seed for which it had so long waited.

* * *

Much later Renard stirred against me. We were still lying in the straw, our arms and legs entwined. His lips touched my cheek gently.

"Are you all right?" he asked.

I smiled. How like him to care about such things. Many would not. "Better than that." On a teasing note, I asked, "And you?"

He smiled in turn. "Dead, I think. I don't see how I could be otherwise." He didn't seem to mind.

How can I describe the pleasure that filled me? I felt so safe, so freed of all tension and worry, so at home in the arms of this man who had taken me into a realm where all the pain and regret of this world ceased to exist and there was only joy.

Yet, inevitably, the world intruded. Renard and I rose and dressed. I blushed when he insisted on helping me wash, stroking the cloth tenderly between my legs. But truth be told, I had no will to resist him in anything.

We remembered the food and at the same moment realized that we were both ravenous. With the door propped open again, we ate and watched the few boats passing on the river. It was abnormally quiet. Hardly an insect seemed to stir.

My eyes drooped. I was still weary from the previous day and the more recent events. Sleep beckoned, but before I could surrender to it, hoofbeats shattered the stillness.

I sat up abruptly as Renard stood. The man who drew rein before him carried a banner emblazoned with the insignia of William's house. He remained in the saddle but inclined his head respectfully.

"My lord," he said, "I am sent to tell you that the Prince Rufus, Bishop Odo, and all the government are transferring to Canterbury, there to remain until this drought is ended and Londontown can be rebuilt. You are bade follow them with all speed."

Renard cursed under his breath. "I am high sheriff of London. It makes no sense for me to leave now when the city is in such need."

The man's expression did not change. He wheeled his horse in a circle and said over his shoulder, "So, too, is the kingdom, says Prince Rufus, and he bids you to Canterbury, my lord, without delay."

Dust rose from his horse's hooves as he galloped off. Renard sighed. His face was grim when he returned to me. "As I feared, Rufus has some scheme in mind. He will try to use the fire to heighten fear of rebellion."

"But why call you to Canterbury?" I asked. "Surely you are no friend of his."

"The contrary, which is exactly why he wants me close at hand." He looked out over the river in the direction of London. "I suppose it's true there's little I can do here. Until the drought is over, it's foolish to even try to rebuild. People will stay in the country, if they can, or go to other towns temporarily."

I rose and went to him. My fingers curled in his hand. "Canterbury isn't so bad. Lanfranc is there and you like him."

He laughed, but not as before. This time there was tension in it. "Lanfranc, Rufus, and Odo all in the same town. The mind reels."

"Don't forget Mother Eldgythe. She's a force to reckon with."

"As I will have to," he said softly.

My eyes met his. I read the answer in them even before I spoke. "Why?"

"I meant what I said when I told you I would never give you up, and that is even truer now. Come with me to Canterbury. I will speak with Mother Eldgythe. You have never taken holy vows, there is nothing to prevent you leaving the abbey. She will have to understand that"

"No!" At his startled look, I said quickly, "I will return to Canterbury but not with you, at least not the way you mean. I must go back to St. Margaret's."

"Why? How can you even consider such a thing after what has happened between us?"

I could have told him it was only with the greatest pain that I faced what had to be, but instead I said simply, "Odo's tapestry, that's why. I must go back to finish it."

His face darkened. He is not a man to cross lightly. I fought to control the trembling that seized me as I confronted his anger.

"That is madness," he said. "Now that I know who you are, it makes less sense than ever that you should be involved with that *thing*. How can you bear it?"

"Because I must," I exclaimed. Damn, stubborn man, couldn't he see what was right before his face? "Odo is determined to create a memorial for his brother. If I don't do it, someone else will. Who's to say that they won't mock the English, ridicule us? That *thing*, as you call it, will exist for a very long time. It is how we, too, will be remembered and it must be with honor."

He frowned, and for a moment I thought he would argue with me. But instead he merely shook his head and gathered me gently into his arms.

"Sweet Aveline," he murmured, "so brave, so stalwart. All right, we will go to Canterbury and you will return to St. Margaret's. That much I will allow, but do not expect to hold me at a distance. I am a patient man, but there are limits even to what I will tolerate."

I could have argued then, for the notion that he was

patient was plainly absurd. But there was no point, for truth be told, I had no wish to keep him at any distance at all.

Despite the urgency of Rufus's summons, we could not leave the city at once. Certain matters had to be seen to first. The rich men of London had taken care to assure that their property and lands would be guarded during their absence. But the common folk had no such assurance.

Renard put his own men-at-arms, those he apparently trusted most, in charge of that. Also, he met with the monks to assure that all those injured in the fire were being well cared for, and he sent messengers out of the city to the surrounding farms to purchase whatever food they could.

For that, he sent his own coin, since none had been left in the royal mint or the treasury. Rufus and the others had seen to that.

To accomplish all this, he returned to his hall, which had fortunately been left undamaged by the fire. I went with him. A few of the servants had returned, lacking anywhere else to go and perhaps also drawn by the stories already being told about their master's courage. Renard did not rebuke them in any way for having fled, but told them all could remain and would be well cared for. He set the men to helping clear the wreckage from the ruined parts of town.

In the midst of all this, I was not idle. Times of calamity break down the ordinary reserves that exist between people. Seeing how busy Renard was, I set about helping the women to organize the food supplies. No one questioned this, least of all the women, who accepted my instructions without difficulty.

So the day fled. Late in the course of it, as the sun was slanting westward toward Thorney, I came into the main hall to find Renard talking with a young Saxon monk. The man was dirty and bedraggled, with a gash down one side of his face and the look of sheer exhaustion stamped on his features. When he saw me, he stiffened and shot me a look in which surprise and contempt mingled equally.

"My lord," he said, calling Renard's attention to my presence.

Whatever he expected by way of response, it clearly wasn't the warm smile that lit Renard's face when he saw me. Will he, nill he, I could do nothing but respond in kind. We stood there in the hall, smiling at one other until the monk's muttering recalled us to the present.

"Your pardon, sir," he said. "I did not realize the . . . lady . . . was still here."

"The Lady Aveline will be traveling with us to Canterbury," Renard said.

The monk's mouth dropped. "Lady . . . with us . . . but, sir . . ."

"That will be all, Burgess. Get some rest."

He went off, still looking dazed. Renard said, "Don't mind him. He's been up all night helping with the injured."

"He's English, isn't he?"

"Most of my servants are."

"But a monk, isn't that unusual?"

Renard looked faintly embarrassed. "I met Burgess several years ago. He had gotten in trouble with the law in Chichester, where I was then. Something about going around berating Normans in the street, calling them the spawn of the devil. The magistrate wanted him out of the town."

"And you took him?" I asked, amazed at the notion. Why would he have bothered?

"We came to an arrangement. I offered him sanctuary in my household in return for his pledge to behave himself and also to—"

"To what?"

"To teach me to read."

My eyes widened. I'd had no idea he could read. Almost no member of the nobility could. "And did he?"

Renard nodded. "Quite well, as it happens. He's doggedly persistent, not just in that but in all things. Before the fire and all the rest of it began, I sent him to learn what he could about the fourth victim. He managed to do that and now he's turned up something more."

"Wait. The *fourth* victim. What is this?"

"I forget, you wouldn't have heard. There was a fourth killing. The body was found yesterday morning. His name was Edouard de Courcy, third son of the Seigneur de Courcy. Rufus was most displeased."

"I should think," I said slowly. "A member of the nobility; this changes things. Were there . . . signs, as there were before?"

He nodded. "And more clear than ever. The body lay in a circle with pagan insignia drawn within."

My stomach clenched. Truly Renard was right to say that Rufus would try to use the killings and the fire to his own ends. How could he resist?

"What else did Burgess learn?" I asked.

Renard made a sound of disgust. "One of the monks he was working with last night started raving that the fire and the murders were all part of the vengeance of God. He went on in that vein at great length. Along the way, he happened to mention that de Courcy knew the clerk, Valerian, who was the third victim."

I was skeptical of that. "A clerk and a son of nobility? It isn't likely that they could have more than the most passing acquaintance, if that."

"De Courcy was a deacon at the Westminster. Valerian helped to keep the accounts for the abbey there.

Apparently that's how their paths crossed. They became . . . particular friends."

"What do you mean, particular?"

He looked uncomfortable. "Never mind. It probably means nothing. There is no reason to think the killer knew his victims."

I am no more inclined to disagree with a man than the next woman. It simply isn't prudent. But Renard was different. I could talk with him and he would listen. No wonder I loved—

"I'm not sure about that," I said before my thoughts could go any further. "These men all went out into the night to their deaths. After the first killing, and certainly after the second, they were well warned, but they went nonetheless. That suggests to me that they knew the person they went with and simply didn't think there was any danger."

I waited, unsure how he would react. For all his difference, he was a man and—as he had reminded me on numerous occasions—a warrior. He might resent the notion that I had thought of something he had missed. But instead he merely nodded.

"That is true. Perhaps there is a connection after all. You knew Lagounier and LeMeux, if only casually. Can you think of anything that would link them to Valerian and de Courcy?"

I shook my head. "Only that they all lived in London. Valerian and de Courcy are clearly tied to the Westminster. It's possible Lagounier and LeMeux went there from time to time. Their paths may all have crossed along with the killer's."

"When you bought cloth from Lagounier, did he ever come to Thorney with his wares?"

"Once, I think, and so did LeMeux when he wanted

to buy the drawings. But surely that is a very slight connection?"

"It's all I have at the moment."

I sympathized with him, for I, too, wanted to see the murderer caught. Much of London lay in ruins and the rest was being swiftly emptied as people fled to wait out the drought and whatever else might be coming.

It wasn't impossible that the killer was among the night's dead, or that with the disaster that had fallen on the city, the opportunity to kill would be gone. Either way the murders might well be over.

But when I said as much to Renard, he was not convinced. "I hope you are right, sweetling, but whether you are or not, Rufus will use the fear of more killings to his own ends. The only way to prevent that is to find the murderer."

He was right, of course. I should have thought of that. To be frank, I was too used to being the one who always saw things clearest, who always knew what needed to be done. Renard put me on my mettle.

We left for Canterbury before the day was done. I was so tired by then that I did not protest when Renard insisted I ride in the wagon. He lifted me into it before mounting his black destrier.

I was surprised to see he was riding the war-horse instead of a palfrey. That and the battle sword strapped around his waist told me he thought there could be trouble.

I prayed he was wrong. Sometimes when I pray, God answers.

This time he didn't.

15

"To arms!" *Renard shouted*. His men responded with the instinct of long training. Swords flashed, arrows flew. The enemy came at them from the safety of the trees that pressed thickly on each side of the narrow dirt road. There were a dozen of them, roughly dressed but well mounted, and all English so far as he could see in the first confused moments of the attack.

Four of his best men-at-arms took up positions around the wagon, as they had been instructed to in event of just such trouble. Renard led the rest in a slashing, savage assault that gave no quarter and asked for none. He heard Aveline scream his name, but he did not so much as hesitate. Had the attackers been merely robbers, they would never have dared to challenge the Normans. This was something far more. He ducked a sword thrust meant to kill him and plunged on. One of the English fell before him, wounded, and was dragged off by his comrades. Another came at him and another, but they were swiftly discouraged by the sheer savagery they met. He fought methodically, without pause or thought.

The man of peace, the seeker after justice, the lover of books was gone. In his place was the pure warrior, born and bred, virtually a human machine made for battle.

Another challenger rose before him, this one larger than the others. Beneath his peaked helmet, Renard smiled faintly. He stared into the scarred features and said, "You should have finished me when you had the chance, English."

Wulfgarth grunted. His horse's hooves pawed the air. Renard had tricked him once when they fought in the bailey yard. Clearly he did not mean for that to happen again.

Around them, the other men fell back. The battle was ebbing as Norman and English alike took the measure of one another and realized they were both without advantage in this struggle. It might be best left to their leaders.

Aveline staggered upright in the wagon, resisting the efforts of one of the men to keep her undercover. "Wulfgarth, no!" she screamed. She tried to get out of the wagon to reach them, but the man would not allow it. He thrust her back in and kept a firm hold on her despite her struggles.

Renard did not wait. He spurred the powerful warhorse to the gallop. The sound of metal striking metal echoed among the trees. The ancient forest of the Weald looked on as the men struggled, each seeking the slightest weakness, a moment's miscalculation that would provide the fatal opening.

A groan broke from the English when a broad sweep of Renard's sword knocked Wulfgarth from his horse. The Englishman regained his feet immediately, but he was now at a disadvantage. That changed a moment later when Renard slipped agilely from his own mount and came at Wulfgarth again on equal terms. The English murmured their surprise at such gallantry, and the Normans their dismay. Battle was a dirty business best ended quickly. There was no place in it for such gestures.

Wulfgarth squinted, staring at the Norman as they circled one another. He had long ago learned to compensate for the loss of his eye and was as deadly a fighter as ever, but he could not unbalance his opponent. No matter what he did, Renard was there ahead of him. He was the mightiest warrior Wulfgarth had ever faced, and for that he could not help but grudgingly admire him.

But admiration had no more place in battle than gallantry. Wulfgarth put aside whatever feelings of regret he might have, raised his battle sword, and brought it down in a brutal slash that should have rent the Norman in two.

Renard sidestepped it. Worse yet, he seized the moment and plunged his blade upward. Aveline cried out, thinking she was about to see Wulfgarth die. But the blade stopped just short with the tip pressed against Wulfgarth's throat.

"Yield," Renard said harshly.

Wulfgarth stared at him from beneath thick black brows drawn tightly together. The fight had been fair, the Norman had won, he, Wulfgarth, should be dead by now. Why was Renard giving him a chance to live?

There was only way to find out. Since he was a dead man anyway, he saw no reason not to take it. Slowly he released his grip on his sword and let it fall to the ground.

"Good," Renard said. His face was calm, pleasant even. His breathing was rapid, but aside from that, he did not look like a man who had just taken part in a life-or-death struggle.

"Now listen to me," he went on. "I want you to carry a

message to Oath Bearer. Tell him I am escorting the Lady Aveline back to St. Margaret's Abbey at her own request. But I will be very close at hand. Should any further attempt be made to seize her by force, Oath Bearer and all who follow him will die. I will personally see to it. Understand?"

"I understand, Norman," Wulfgarth growled. He looked to Aveline for confirmation of what Renard said. "Is this true? Are you returning to St. Margaret's."

"Yes," she said firmly, "and I wish to remain there. Tell that to Oath Bearer. Make sure he believes it."

Wulfgarth nodded. Gruffly he said, "You surprise me, Norman, but it will be as you say so long as the Lady Aveline is in no danger."

"Pick up your sword," Renard said. When Wulfgarth had done so and faced him once more armed, he went on. "Tell him also on my behalf that I wish to meet with him. The time and place are to be of his choosing. I will come alone and unarmed."

Around the clearing, the English glanced at each other in surprise. Why would the Norman make such an offer? Why present himself to be killed by their leader?

"Why?" Wulfgarth demanded.

"That is between Oath Bearer and me," Renard said. "Just tell him."

Wulfgarth shrugged. "As you will, but I can give you his answer now."

Renard smiled faintly. "Can you?" Softly, so that no one else could hear them, he said, "Then your memory is short. Tell him it is a matter of honor. His sister's, to be precise."

Wulfgarth started. He looked at the Norman narrowly. "You know . . . ?"

"All that I have to."

The Englishman's face darkened. His hand tightened

on the sword hilt, but he had been bested once and knew the futility of trying again. Very low he said, "If you have done what I think you have—"

"It must be put right. Tell that to Oath Bearer and bring me word of when we can meet."

Slowly Wulfgarth nodded. A moment longer he stared at Renard as though trying to decide exactly what to make of him. At length he gave up and shouted an order to his men. As one, they faded back into the forest.

When they were gone, Aveline sagged with relief. She waited until the wagon began moving again and Renard had ridden up next to her before she said, "You expected this."

"It was a reasonable thing for Oath Bearer to do."

She bit her lip. Grudgingly she said, "I thank you for sparing Wulfgarth's life."

"He is a good man."

"What were you and he talking about so that none could hear you?"

"Merely exchanging pleasantries."

Her eyes darkened. "You take me for a fool."

He laughed. "Oh, no, my lady, I do not. Were I to do so for even a moment, I would be the fool, not you."

She mulled that over as he rode away, back to the head of the column. They continued on for another hour or so until the last of the light was fading from the sky. Only then did Renard give the order to make camp.

His men went about the task with the ease of long practice. A perimeter was set up, guards posted, and a cookfire started. The men would sleep out in the open, those who would sleep at all. But for Aveline there was a small tent. She went into it gratefully. A servant brought her food along with water for washing. When she had finished with both, she lay down on the soft pallet and closed her eyes. After the tumultuous events of recent days, she should have slept instantly. But instead thoughts and images raced through her mind. All her senses felt painfully alert. No matter how she tried, she could not rest.

The last of the light vanished. Velvety darkness enveloped the camp. She heard the guards moving, but only faintly, for they were some distance away. The men talked quietly among themselves for a short time, then there was silence.

She lay listening to the beat of her own heart. Time stretched out moment by moment. It seemed to have slowed down, but that was deceptive. In a few days they would be in Canterbury. The world with all its responsibilities and conflicts would come crowding in on them again. There was so little time they could claim as their own.

She waited while an owl called somewhere in the trees high above and another answered. Outside the tent a footfall sounded softly.

She sat up and opened the flap of the tent even as she opened her heart.

The next morning they resumed their journey. The pace was deliberately slow, to ease the burden on the horses traveling in such heat. Each night they camped and Aveline's tent was set up a little apart from the rest. If anyone knew or suspected what went on in the long, sweet hours of darkness, the secret was deeply buried.

In daylight, Renard rode beside her. They talked of many things—their childhoods, the books they had read, the places they had seen. There was a great deal more they did not say—of war and politics and the terrible cost of both.

They were following the old Roman road and they

talked about that, too, about how glory fades, memory is lost, and only something as ordinary as a road remains.

One afternoon they stopped beside a small stream that meandered near the road. While the horses drank and the men rested from the steaming heat, Aveline and Renard wandered hand in hand beside the water. They found a clump of raspberry bushes and fell to picking them with a will. When they had finally gorged themselves, they sat under an ancient oak and watched a mother fox bring her young to drink. Renard fell asleep after a while with his head in Aveline's lap. She sat, stroking his dark hair, and thought that she had never known a moment as perfect. The pain of that was bittersweet. More than St. Margaret's walls had sheltered her all these years. She herself had been very careful never to love again. The loss of love hurt too much. Yet here she was, without warning, deeply in love with the last man she should have cared for.

She sighed and lifted her head to the remorseless blue sky. A dry breeze fluttered the leaves. It sounded like God laughing.

A day later they came to Canterbury.

Mother Eldgythe was waiting for them near the high stone arch that divided the wall in front of the abbey. She stood with her hands folded and hidden in the long sleeves of her habit, her face framed by a white wimple. Her expression was shuttered.

"Aveline," she said coldly, "you have been much in our thoughts. Are you well?"

"Yes, Mother, and I am glad to see that you are the same."

The abbess was silent for a moment, taking it all in. Aveline did not flinch from her scrutiny. She stood tall and proud, her manner composed, refusing to suggest by word or deed that she had done anything to be ashamed of.

At length Mother Eldgythe shifted her gaze to Renard. "Your kindness in returning my ward is appreciated, Lord d'Agounville. I am sure you are anxious to join Prince Rufus and the others, so we will not keep you."

This pointed suggestion that he should make himself scarce made Renard smile wryly. He inclined his head gravely. "I thank you for your consideration, but I won't be going far."

At her puzzled frown, he went on, "With the government in residence, Canterbury is very crowded. Accommodation is scarce. You have an excellent guest house, which, I observed as we passed, stands empty. I trust you won't mind my requisitioning it."

Mother Eldgythe did most clearly mind. That was obvious even to the most casual eye. Her cheeks flamed and her hands, beneath the decorous sleeves, twisted angrily.

"This is hardly the most convenient location for you, my lord," she said. "Wouldn't you rather be in the town proper?"

"Not really," he assured her. "It promises to be very dirty and noisy. Besides, I need to be close at hand to supervise the tapestry."

At this, both Aveline and Mother Eldgythe looked startled. It was Aveline who ventured to reply. "You said nothing of that, my lord. Indeed, you never mentioned it."

Renard appeared surprised. "Didn't I? With so much happening, it must have slipped my mind. But the bishop did ask me to oversee the work and I would be lax in my duties if I failed to do that."

He'd been awake a good part of the previous night

thinking of how he could reconcile the need to stay close to Aveline with respect for her reputation. The solution he'd come up with, if he did say so himself, was perfect. Given his authority, Mother Eldgythe could not refuse him.

Not that she didn't try.

"We are not set up for guests at the moment, my lord. Our provisions are at a low point, and with the harvest promising to be so poor, we really cannot accommodate you in the manner your rank demands."

"I would hardly expect you to do so," Renard assured her blandly. "Under the circumstances, my men and I will fend for ourselves."

"Your men? You mean, you intend for them to stay here, too?"

"But of course, where else would they go? I assure you, they will be no trouble. In such unsettled times, you may even find yourself glad of their presence."

Mother Eldgythe shut her mouth tightly, the better to restrain what would surely have been a sharp response. She turned on her heel and walked away. Aveline followed, but not without a chiding glance at Renard.

He suppressed a chuckle and gave his orders. The servants hurried to unload the baggage wagons while his men began settling in to their new surroundings. Renard left them to it. He had delayed as long as he possibly could. Taking a fresh horse, he rode into town.

Canterbury was, as he had expected, in turmoil. The arrival of the government as well as a large number of other refugees, had packed every inn and private home to the rafters. People were camping out in the sere gardens and fields that still remained within the old town walls. They had even found places for themselves in the open area surrounding Christ Church monastery and cathedral. Monks from the monastery were doing their best to portion out food and water and maintain some level of cleanliness. From what Renard could observe, the latter was a losing battle. He was breathing shallowly by the time he stepped inside the archbishop's residence.

Lanfranc greeted him in his retiring room. He looked tired but otherwise unchanged from when Renard had last seen him.

"There you are," the archbishop said. "I was beginning to worry about you. Took your time coming down from London, didn't you?"

"My men were weary from fighting the fire," Renard said smoothly. It would hardly do to tell this man of God that he had made the journey as long as he could because of Aveline. "There seemed no point in pressing them."

"Hmm, never mind, you're here and that's what counts. Rufus is chomping at the bit to see you."

"Why?" Renard asked as he took the seat Lanfranc indicated. "Do you know?"

"Officially he's concerned about Oath Bearer and these god-awful murders. But I think the real reason is that he wants to either assure himself of your loyalty or, failing that, neutralize you."

Renard frowned. "My loyalty is to the king. I have never left any doubt about that."

"He knows that. It's why he would like to have you on his side. My guess is he's going to claim that England is in real and imminent danger of catastrophe. He will cite the drought, the stirrings among the native population, the murders, and so on. He will call on the nobility—almost all Norman now, of course—to name him protector of the realm. Once he has that authority, he will be king in fact if not yet in name."

"Will the nobility go along with him?" Renard asked.

"They owe their positions to William, no one else. To betray him now—"

"Won't be easy," Lanfranc interrupted. "But men have been known to do stranger things when they believe them necessary. If Rufus succeeds, it truly will be a catastrophe. The English accepted William because they had no choice; he was king by force of arms. Most of them will accept his legitimate successor, however grudgingly, because they will want to keep the peace. But they won't accept a usurper, not even his own son. That truly will open the way to widespread rebellion. And *that,* my friend, will mean a bloodbath."

Renard nodded. He had felt this coming all along. Far in the back of his mind, he heard an endless, howling sound like all the dead of Hastings and the rest screaming out their rage. No more, he thought. No more of the stupid, horrible, futile waste of life. Especially not now when he had just discovered how truly precious it really was.

Quietly he said, "Rufus must be stopped."

"Indeed, but how? He's no fool. You won't find a man more closely guarded, and he knows who his friends are. I offered him the use of our guest quarters, but he preferred to stay with Odo on his holding outside the city. He's there now."

Renard stared out the window. In this direction he could see Northgate and beyond it the old St. John's hospital that had made Canterbury a center of healing for generations. There was so much here—learning, piety, hope. He could not bear to think it might become the center of a firestorm that would sweep across all of England, bringing ruin such as no man had ever seen.

"I will go and speak with him," he said quietly.

"Be careful," Lanfranc warned again.

"Rufus won't try to arrest me," Renard assured him.

"He knows word of that would reach the king quickly and make his father instantly suspicious of him."

The archbishop rose and walked with him to the door. "I'm not worried about arrest. Rufus will *kill* if he feels himself threatened. Don't turn your back on him. By the way," he added, "you're welcome to stay here."

"Thank you, but I have already secured accommodations." At Lanfranc's questioning look, he said, "Mother Eldgythe has been good enough to make the guest house at St. Margaret's available."

"She did that? It doesn't sound like her."

"Let's just say I was very persuasive."

The archbishop looked at him thoughtfully. "I see. . . . How is Odo's tapestry progressing?"

Renard's smile fled. "I don't know yet, but I intend to find out."

For a moment the temptation rose in him to ask Lanfranc's advice about Aveline. The archbishop was a genuinely good man and a wise one. He had never cut himself off from the world as did some self-professed holy men, neither did he wallow in the decadence of it as those like Odo did. He might well be sympathetic to Renard's situation. But the secret of Aveline's true identity was simply too explosive to risk revealing it to anyone, even Lanfranc.

He went away regretting that and made his way back across the crowded, bustling town. West of the walls, not far from the road that ran to St. Margaret's, Odo had a manor. When the bishop was in residence, his insignia flew from the high tower. But this time it was not alone. Rufus's lion looked out, claws bared, over the countryside.

Two hours later Renard left the bishop's manor and turned east along the road to St. Margaret's. He resisted the impulse to stop at the nearest spring to wash his hands. Rufus had left him feeling dirtied. This was William's son? This fearful, deceitful, venal man who lusted after power but, so far at least, lacked the courage to seize it? That could change at any moment. Riding through the sultry day, past fields lying brown in the sun, Renard had a sense of time racing away down some dark corridor. The situation was perilous. Something had to be done, and quickly, or they truly were all bound for disaster.

On such a dreary note, he came within sight of St. Margaret's. The moment he did so, his spirits lifted. Aveline was there. She was safe and near to hand. He dismounted swiftly in the courtyard and turned his horse over to a servant. The abbey bells were tolling nones. The good sisters would be at their prayers. On an impulse, he crossed the yard and entered the chapter house.

It was very still inside. Nothing moved in the shadowed coolness of the long stone corridors. He found the sewing room without difficulty, reasoning as he did that it must be where the solar would have been located in a noble house. The room was empty, as he had expected, but the signs of recent activity were everywhere.

A long, narrow strip of linen was tightly stretched on wooden frames. Racks held streams of brightly colored wool. On a nearby table, a thick roll of parchment was partially opened, revealing the drawings for the tapestry.

Renard looked at it thoughtfully. It began as he remembered with Harold's trip to Normandy and his oath to William. But now he considered that in a different light. William had pressured Harold into taking the oath. An argument could be made that such pressure made it invalid. But more than that, what exactly had Harold sworn to? Not to accept William as his liege

lord, as some Normans were claiming, but to acknowl-
ege him as Normandy's legitimate ruler by right of
inheritance. Later William stretched that to include
England after old King Edward supposedly named him
his heir on his deathbed.

Supposedly.

Ah, yes, here they were, the drawings dealing with
Edward's death. There was the Westminster, consecrated
at Christmas in 1065, with the dying king too ill to
attend. Scant days later Edward did die and Harold
seized the throne.

Except the drawings did not show that. They depicted
Harold as the legitimately anointed King of England.

Renard's fists clenched at his sides. This was exactly
what he had feared. Despite her protestations, Aveline
was not merely trying to prevent her father and his people from being ridiculed by the Normans. She was pre-
senting her own version of the events that had changed
the fate of a nation. She was rewriting history.

He seized the parchment. She could not do this, he
could not let her. For her own sake, she had to be
stopped. He would—

"What are you doing here?" Aveline's voice was
sharp. She did not wait for an answer, but strode
toward him. Her face was pale, her eyes brilliantly blue.
Angrily she said, "Give me that. You have no right to
handle it so roughly. What do you think you're doing?"

"What do I think? What are you doing?" He clenched
the parchment in his fist and glared at her. "Are you mad?
Do you honestly believe you can get away with this?" For
a moment he forgot all he felt for this woman, all the hot,
soaring passion, the tender intimacy, the thoughts she
stirred in him of a life that might be. None of that existed,
only anger and a deepening sense of betrayal.

Coldly he said, "William was Edward's heir. Harold tried to take what was his by right—despite his vow not to—and for that he died. You are twisting the truth to serve your own purposes."

"No, I am protecting the truth! William was not Edward's heir, my father was. Edward named him on his deathbed."

"How do you know that?" Renard demanded. "Were you there, too?"

She shook her head, her eyes darkening with the memory. "I was in Bosham with my mother. But my father was there. He was with Edward in the final moments of his life. There is no mistake. Edward named him as his heir."

Renard shook his head. More gently he said, "You believe that because you loved your father, but that isn't what happened. I cannot let you do this. It is the worst folly. You will tell Odo that you cannot, after all, make the tapestry. Someone else will take it over. You must see that is for the best."

"No," she said, and made to turn away from him.

Without thought, he reached out to stop her. The parchment fell to the floor between them. His hand closed on her shoulder.

She flinched and, with rage in her eyes, turned back to him. "Let go of me."

His grip tightened. "You will do as I say."

"No!" She raised a hand and, before he could see what was coming, struck him. The blow hit his jaw hard enough to sting, though nothing more. A swift kick to his shin hurt more. "Let go!" she said.

For once in his life Renard was caught off guard. Aveline managed to twist away. Free of him, she ran toward the door. He followed, his face taut with anger, and with a single lunge brought her down. She screamed as the breath went out of her. They grappled on the floor amid the stray bits of linen and wool. Aveline managed to land several more blows, but the contest could hardly have been more unequal. Within moments he had both her wrists held fast in one big hand, her arms stretched out above her head. His body bent over her, powerful and remorseless, holding her fast.

"Hellcat," he said through gritted teeth. "You will do as I say. These lies avail you nothing. William is the legitimate ruler of England. It is God's will that he rule."

"No! William killed the rightful king. He committed regicide and for that he will be damned through all eternity."

Renard stared down at her, his eyes shuttered. "You are lying."

"No, I am not." Though her breathing was ragged against him, she spoke with absolute certainty. "Listen to me. There were four people in the death chamber besides Edward—his wife, Edith, my aunt; Stigand, who was Archbishop of Canterbury then; my father; and one other, the man my father trusted above all, the one he rarely took a step without having at his side. Wulfgarth. Of them all, he is the only one left alive, the only surviving eyewitness to the truth."

A chill ran through him. This could not be. She had to be mistaken. But what if . . . ? Merciful God in heaven, could it be?

"Wulfgarth told you what happened?" he asked.

"Yes, but he wasn't the first. When it was over, when my father lay dead, my mother had a final meeting with my aunt. I was present at that. Edith told her that Harold was the lawful king. Wulfgarth said the same. There was no doubt."

She closed her eyes for a moment as what little strength she had left evaporated. Softly she said, "No Norman has ever claimed to have been in the death chamber. How then would William have known what was said? Who would have told him? Don't you see? He made it up."

Renard's mind reeled. Was she right? Was that possible? Everything rested on William's claim that he was the legitimate King of England—the dead of Hastings, York and elsewhere, the entire conquest. They had fought for William's lawful throne; only that justified what they had done. Only that.

He closed his eyes against a wave of horror so profound that his blood seemed to stop in his veins. When he opened them again, Aveline was looking at him not with anger but with compassion.

"Renard . . ." she murmured brokenly.

"Sweet heaven." All the pain and terror, all the regret were in those two simple words. His hand loosened on her wrists. When he released her arms, she wrapped them around him.

He trembled against her, this big, proud man, this warrior. William damned? Where did that leave the rest of them?

"Hush," she murmured when she saw the anguish in his eyes. Her pain mirrored his own. "Don't think of it anymore."

A groan broke from him. He bent his head and took her mouth with his. She met his passion with equal fire. Together, in the silence of that sun-drenched room, they clung to each other.

16

"Wake up," Burgess said.

Renard groaned. He was back in London, it was stifling hot, and the monk was trying to tell him there'd been another killing. But wait, this wasn't London, it was Canterbury. He was in the small private chamber on the second floor of the abbey guest house. His men were asleep in the hall below. He was alone, except for Burgess, having reluctantly left Aveline at the chapter house. After all the days of turmoil, he badly needed to rest. What reason could the monk possibly have for waking him?

"Go away," he said.

"There's been another one."

Renard opened his eyes abruptly. He stared into the tense face above him. "What in hell are you saying?"

"There's been another killing like the ones in London, only it's happened here. The body was found an hour ago. Rufus and Odo are both screaming for you. You have to get up."

"Who was it?" Renard demanded as he jumped from the bed and began dressing. His mind screamed denial of what was happening, but he ignored it. There was no time for anything except unrelenting truth.

"One of the priests at Christ Church," Burgess said. "The body was found in the scriptorium. His throat was cut, his torso pierced by arrows, and he lay within a circle of pagan signs. It couldn't be clearer."

"Indeed," Renard said. The murderer appeared to have gone out of his way to announce his presence in Canterbury. He thought fast as he buckled on his sword. They could count on only a few hours before word of the killing spread throughout the town. It wasn't difficult to imagine the panic that would result.

"Where are you going?" Burgess demanded as he followed Renard down the stairs and out of the building. Instead of turning in the direction of the stables, his master headed toward the chapter house.

"To wake the Lady Aveline," he said. "She is coming with me."

"A woman?" Burgess asked, trotting after him. "But why? What good can she possibly do?"

"I'm not sure," Renard admitted, "but I want her with me." If only, he added silently, in case there is trouble.

It required three rings of the night bell to summon the sleepy sister who was on duty. She was shocked to see a male visitor, and one girded for battle at that, standing by the great wooden door. And she balked at fetching Aveline.

"I will have to speak with Mother Eldgythe," she said stiffly. "This is most irregular."

"It is also most urgent, sister," Renard said gently. "Forgive me," he added as he lifted her out of his way. Ignoring her loud protests, he marched down the corridor toward the abbey's private quarters. There he found a row of small rooms stretching off into the distance. There were dozens of them and Aveline might be in any one. How was he to find her?

He needn't have worried. The good sister's squeals were warning enough. Doors opened, heads peered from them and were quickly withdrawn amid startled exclamations.

"Oh, my . . ."

"What is *he* doing . . . ?"

"The nerve . . ."

"How dare he . . ."

"Renard, what are you doing here?"

He grinned, looking at the disheveled figure who appeared suddenly before him. She had braided her hair before retiring, but stray wisps had come loose and worked themselves around her face. She wore only a thin lawn shift in deference to the heat. It did little to conceal her from his gaze.

"Get dressed," he ordered, remembering himself. "We have to go into town."

"Why?" she demanded.

He took her by the arm and led her toward her cell. "There's been another killing," he said, speaking too low for anyone else to hear.

She paled. Without asking anything further, she hurried into the small room. He waited. Most of the other sisters had withdrawn back into their cells, but one at least had gone scurrying for Mother Eldgythe. That worthy barreled down on him, swathed in an all-encompassing black shawl, looking like fury unchained.

"Get out," she said without preamble.

Regretfully he shook his head. "I am sorry, Mother, but I cannot. It is essential that—"

"I will not have this! You cannot come in, violating

anything you wish, ignoring even simple decency. I will not permit it!"

She raised her fists as though to strike him. Renard took a prudent step backward. Before he could say or do anything, Aveline was in front of him.

"Stop," she said with quiet firmness. "We've been through this before. If I can possibly help, I must."

"You don't understand what he's doing! You don't realize—"

"I understand full well." She stopped, her eyes holding the older woman's. Gently she said, "I want to go with him."

A sob broke from the abbess. She shook her head back and forth. "No, you don't mean that. You are safe here. This is where you belong."

"I am not one of you," Aveline said, "not really. If I were, I would have taken vows by now."

"It isn't too late for that," Mother Eldgythe insisted quickly.

Aveline looked at her with great tenderness. "Yes, it is. I will stay to finish the tapestry, but after that, I must find another place."

"Don't—" Mother Eldgythe began. She broke off as grief consumed her.

"Come," Renard said. He took Aveline's arm. There was nothing to be done for the older woman, at least not just then. She had loved Aveline and protected her, but in return she had expected to chart the course of her life. That was impossible now.

They went out into the night. Renard put Aveline up on the horse in front of him. Swiftly they rode into town. Canterbury was quiet. The guard at Westgate let them pass only because he had instructions to do so. Going carefully to avoid the huddled shapes sleeping in the streets, they made their way to Christ Church. There, too, everything looked as usual until they reached the adjacent monastery. Lights were burning on the lower floor and men stood outside with torches in their hands.

Lanfranc received them in the refectory. Rufus and Odo were with him. The King's half brother looked pale and angry. He twisted his beringed fingers as he strode up and down, shaking his head and moaning over the state of the world.

"Shocking," he said, "absolutely shocking. There are no standards at all nowadays. People think they can do anything they damn well please."

Rufus ignored him. He was regally garbed in a tunic of fine linen trimmed in gold. The sword at his waist sported a jeweled hilt. He looked fully awake and very much in command.

"I knew this would happen," he said when he saw Renard. "Didn't I tell you the English were closing in, that no place was safe? And what did you say, my fine high sheriff? What was your advice in these direst of circumstances?"

"That you communicate your worries to the king," Renard said flatly, "and let him decide what should be done." Pointedly he turned away from Rufus and addressed Lanfranc, who sat, somber and silent, in a chair at the head of the table.

"Where is the body?" Renard asked.

"In the chapel," Lanfranc said. He shifted his gaze to Aveline. "You are up late, child."

"What's this woman doing here?" Rufus demanded as though he had just noticed her. In fact, he had been raking her with his eyes since she entered the refectory. "What are you thinking to bring your paramour to such a meeting?" he went on. His eyes narrowed assessingly. "Not that she isn't a fetching piece. Who are you, girl?"

Lanfranc stirred in his chair. "She is the Lady Aveline, ward of the abbess of St. Margaret's and, I might add, a young woman for whom I have the greatest admiration."

Rufus grunted. A look of cunning passed behind his eyes. "Strange, I didn't think you had any truck with women."

"I admire her mind," Lanfranc said. "Something I don't expect you to understand."

"And what about you, d'Agounville?" the prince demanded with a sneer. "Is it her mind you admire?"

Renard fingered the hilt of his sword as he stared at Rufus. There was a deadly coldness in his eyes that gave even the prince pause. "As it happens," he said, "I do. I asked lady Aveline to come along because she has been helpful in trying to solve the previous murders."

"She has?" Lanfranc said, unable to hide his surprise. "How?"

"I knew two of the victims," Aveline said quickly, "Lagounier and LeMeux. It was little enough to go on, but we thought—Renard and I—that if some connection could be discovered among those who died, it might be possible to identify the killer."

"A reasonable hope," Lanfranc said. "Have you been able to do that?"

"Not really," she admitted. "Lagounier and LeMeux came to Thorney at least once that I know of. They had business with us. Valerian would have been there fairly often because he did the accounts for the Westminster. So, too, would de Courcy have been since he was a deacon. But it's impossible to say who all four of them knew or didn't know."

"These deaths have no connection with Thorney Isle or the Westminster," Rufus insisted. "That priest lying in the chapel right now with his throat cut open had nothing to do with either. The killer's after Normans, plain and simple. Not one of us is safe."

"I'm afraid I must agree," Odo said. "It's all too clear. The English were never really Christians, no matter what they claimed. They never fully accepted the pope's authority, never gave Rome its due. They were always pagan in their hearts. Now that evil has been released in the land and it's stalking *us*. We must act quickly before we all perish."

"Don't be a fool," Lanfranc muttered. He cast a warning look at Aveline. "That's all right, child, we know it isn't true."

"But you'll still say it, won't you?" she demanded of Odo. "And you'll use it as an excuse to do what? Kill? That's all you usually know how to do. You'll kill and kill and kill until what? There are none of us left? Would that satisfy you?"

Rufus reddened. He would have struck her, but the protective stance Renard took right beside her stopped him. Instead he waved a hand angrily. "Get her out of here and you with her. My father will hear how you failed in your duty, d'Agounville, don't think that he won't."

"It would suit me well to discuss the matter with my king," Renard said quietly. Without giving Rufus or anyone else a chance to reply, he took Aveline's arm and led her from the room.

Outside, she sagged against a wall and looked at him blankly. "What do we do now? They have everything they need to set off a panic. Lanfranc won't be able to stop them."

"No, but he can delay things. In the meantime I want to see where this latest killing happened."

"Why?" Aveline asked as they hurried along the passage. "What's the point if it's just like the others?"

"Is it? What was the priest doing in the scriptorium after dark?"

"That is odd," Aveline admitted.

"Every other victim was lured out into the street. The killing was done in a public place. This crime is different. There may have been another target besides the anonymous priest."

"Who?"

"Lanfranc. Having one of his own clergy killed directly under his own roof is hardly to his credit. It throws doubt on his ability to maintain security at a time when that is paramount."

"But why would the murderer want to do that? What would he care about Lanfranc?"

"That depends on who *he* is. Look," Renard added as he thrust open the door to the scriptorium. A candle still burned where someone had left it after the body was found. By its light, they could see the insignia drawn in the circle.

Renard crouched low to study them. They appeared the same as those found around de Courcy's body and yet—

"Look at that," he said, "the pentagram in London also had a horned moon, but it was pointed in the other direction, wasn't it?"

"That's right," Aveline said, bending nearer. They knelt on the edge of the circle, their bodies touching as she said, "That moon is waning, which makes no sense. The whole point of the circle is the gathering of power, not its loss."

"I'm not going to ask how you know that," Renard said.

"Good."

He rose and helped her to do the same. The moon outside was neither waxing nor waning. It hung swollen and full in the cloudless sky.

"Aveline," he said gravely, "I must see Oath Bearer."

She flinched and looked away from him. "That is impossible."

"Nonetheless it must be. You must take me to him."

"I don't know—"

"No more lies! Don't you understand what's happening here? This murder wasn't done by the same killer who was loose in London, it was merely contrived to look that way. Rufus intends to use it to create panic and justify his becoming protector of the realm. If Oath Bearer tries to rise against him now, he plays directly into his hands."

Her eyes were wide with shock. "Contrived? Are you sure?"

"As sure as I can be of anything. Rufus knew about the pagan signs around de Courcy. He could easily have sent someone here to kill the priest and make it look as though the pagan slayer had struck again. Certainly he would welcome any opportunity to embarrass Lanfranc, for they have long been at odds. But the murderer botched the job. Maybe he was clumsy or perhaps afraid of what he was doing. He got at least one of the signs wrong. The real killer, whoever he is, knows better than that."

"Sweet heaven," she murmured. "You could be right."

"I *am* right, Aveline, and that's why I must see Oath Bearer without delay."

She walked a little distance away from him and stood staring at the circle. For several moments her face was closed as she debated within herself.

Abruptly she looked up and met his eyes. "All right."

Renard sighed with relief. He took her hand and drew her into his arms. "You are doing what's right, sweetling."

"I hope so," she murmured against his broad chest. "Never in my life did I think I would so trust a Norman, but you—"

"Yes," he said, laughter in his voice and more, deep pleasure such as he had never before known.

"Never mind," she said briskly. "Come, we must go."

She led him from the stone building and down a narrow path to the stable where he had left his horse. As he lifted her back into the saddle she looked down at him solemnly.

"I will not ask for your word, Renard, but I will ask this—if you mean him ill, then do the same to me, for I would not wish to live knowing I had played the fool."

His face tightened. Deliberately he let his hand slip to her belly. "Don't speak so easily of dying, Aveline. You may have more than yourself to consider."

Color flamed in her cheeks. She put her hand on his. For a long moment they looked at one another.

The horse shying brought them back to themselves. He settled her on the saddle and mounted quickly behind her.

"Which way?" he asked.

"South."

They passed out of the town and took the road that led past the old Dane stronghold. Beyond that was open fields, orchards, and farther on thick wood.

"There's an old hunting trail," Aveline said. "Will you be able to find it in this light?"

He nodded and scanned the forest ahead. The ancient oaks lay bathed in silver. Looking carefully among them, he spied the slight irregularities that showed men had passed that way.

Renard guided the horse onto the trail and urged him along. The animal was nervous, as well he might be, with the woods full of all manner of beast, wolf, boar, and most dangerous of all, man.

They rode for an hour, perhaps more. Renard's sense of time diminished. He tried to keep track of their direction but he wasn't sufficiently familiar with the area to be sure which way they were going. They were deep into the woods now. The air grew cooler and fragrant with the scents of moss and leaves. Trees pressed in on all sides. Aveline trembled. He tightened his arms around her and murmured soothingly.

Far ahead, among the trees, a glimmer of light shone. Renard drew rein. He pointed ahead. "There?"

Aveline nodded. "There will be guards. Keep your hand from your sword."

Much as he disliked the idea, he did as she said. They moved on toward the light. Once or twice, he caught a sense of movement in the nearby trees, but turned his head too late to see whatever it was that watched them.

The light sharpened until it emerged as a small campfire. A dozen or so men were gathered around it. They were standing, hands on their weapons.

"You were right," Renard murmured.

Aveline nodded but said nothing. She kept her eyes straight ahead. They came to a halt in the middle of the clearing. One of the Englishman took the reins as Renard and Aveline dismounted.

The leader was a tall, well-built man with hair the same flame-hued shade as Aveline's. He was in his early twenties, simply dressed, and with an air of command about him.

"Oath Bearer," Renard said.

The man inclined his head fractionally. There was a mocking light in his eyes. "You are most persistent, Norman. Don't you believe in waiting for an invitation?"

"Not under these circumstances," Renard said. He spoke calmly, as though this conversation in a forest clearing surrounded by armed rebels was the most normal thing in the world. "My name is d'Agounville," he went on.

Oath Bearer made an impatient gesture. "I know who you are. Renard d'Agounville, high sheriff of London, boy hero of Hastings, scourge of York, right hand of the Conqueror. You have had an illustrious career."

Without waiting for a reply, he turned his attention to Aveline. His brows knit as his gaze swept over her. "It was poor judgment to bring him here."

"You must know why he has come before you can decide that," she replied unflinchingly.

Oath Bearer looked unconvinced, but he did not signal to his men. They parted to allow Renard and Aveline to approach the campfire.

"Sit," Oath Bearer directed. He took his place nearby and lifted the mug of ale he had been drinking from. A long swallow rippled down his throat before he said, "I am thinking of killing you."

Aveline gasped. Renard put out a hand to still her. He looked the red-haired man directly in the face and said, "Then you are a fool, Magnus Haroldson."

The color fled from Aveline's face. "I did not tell him," she protested, "I swear."

"That is true," Renard confirmed. "But then she did not have to. There were witnesses to the deaths of your brothers, but your death was never more than rumored." He paused before he added, "Besides, anyone looking at you would know you are brother and sister."

Magnus set the mug down with a thud. A pulse beat in his jaw. "You are dangerously well informed, Norman. Tell me again, why shouldn't I kill you?"

Quietly Renard said, "Because I am not your enemy."

Magnus laughed, a bitter sound in which disbelief and rage mingled equally. He raised his voice so that the men sitting a discreet distance away could hear him.

"D'Agounville says he is not our enemy."

They joined in the laughter. Several made a point of fingering their swords.

Tension simmered in the small clearing. Renard did not mistake his position. It would be the work of a moment to snap the thin bonds these men had on their self-control.

Aveline sensed the same. Angrily she said, "That is enough. Renard risked his life to come here. He did it for a purpose. Listen to him."

Magnus looked at her contemptuously. "How touching, sister, but then I gather you have a personal interest in keeping this particular Norman alive."

His derision stung, but she refused to give way before it. "Hear him," she insisted. "You are so anxious to lead men into battle, you should at least know what they will face."

Magnus hesitated. He was still angry, but the reminder of his responsibility compelled him to listen. "Make it quick, Norman," he ordered grudgingly.

"Have you heard of the murders in London?" Renard asked.

Magnus grimaced. "The pagan slayer? Who hasn't heard of them?"

"Then hear this. There has been another killing tonight in Canterbury."

Magnus stiffened. "Canterbury? You're sure?"

"We've just come from where it happened," Aveline said.

"Were there signs of paganism?"

"Unmistakably," Renard said. "A child couldn't have missed them. There's only one problem. They were faked."

"What are you saying?" Magnus demanded. "Who would fake a murder?"

"There was nothing fake about that, a man is dead right enough. But the killing was contrived to look like the London murders."

"By whom?"

"Rufus," Renard said succinctly. "I'm sure of it. He wants Canterbury in a panic, people thinking they escaped the fire only to have the pagan slayer on their heels, somewhere close by, ready to strike at any one of them. If you choose the same moment to rise against the throne, he will have everything he needs to seize power. No one will deny him; indeed the populace—at least the Norman part of it—will clamor for his protection. You will have played directly into his hands."

"That's what this is all about," Magnus demanded. "You come here to persuade me not to challenge William because you think his son will use that to over-throw him? Forgive me, Norman, but your reasoning is absurd. Why should I care how the Norman bastard and his whelp devour each other?"

"Because," Renard said, "in their destruction lies your own. England will be scourged. There won't be a town or village that doesn't feel the anguish of such a conflict. Or is it that you feel it would be better to see this land in ruins rather than have it ruled by anyone but you?"

Magnus stared into the fire for a long moment. Quietly he said, "You are clever, d'Agounville. I give you that. A less determined man might be swayed by you."

"Don't dismiss this," Aveline entreated. "If Rufus is capable of such a conspiracy, he is capable of anything. It was bad enough when we fought the Normans. At least then they had some concern for the country, believing it would be theirs. But if they are fighting each other, they won't care about that. They'll destroy anything that gets in their way."

He did not answer her, but looked again into the fire. Finally he said, "I have heard your views on this before, sister. You and Wulfgarth both believe we should just give up and accept Norman rule."

Renard shot her a startled look. "Do you?"

Aveline sighed. "Not completely. Wulfgarth and I are no more happy with Norman rule than most English are. All we asked Magnus to do was reconsider the wisdom of his present course. There has been so much death and for what? It has to stop sometime."

She broke off and looked away, unwilling to have them see her grief.

Renard cleared his throat. All he wanted to do was comfort Aveline, but there was still her brother to be dealt with. He stretched out his hands to the fire, feeling its heat licking at him.

"Ask yourself why you do this, Magnus Haroldson. Is it for revenge and personal glory? Or is it for the welfare of your people? Perhaps your father began seeking glory, but he died trying to protect his people. If your reason is anything less than that, you are not worthy to follow him."

Magnus's eyes, as green gold as Aveline's were blue, flashed at him. "Do not speak to me of my father, Norman. You are William's man, the usurper's, and unworthy to utter the name of Harold, King of England."

"I am my own man," Renard said quietly, and knew deep within his soul that he meant it. Loyalties, however well forged in blood and victory, did not ease his conscience. In the end he was accountable to himself and to God. All else was chaff on the wind.

Magnus made a harsh sound of disbelief. He reached again for the mug of ale.

"Leave me," he said. "I will think on what you have said, but I make no promises. We will speak again come dawn."

They walked a little distance away from the campfire. Renard spread out his cloak on the ground for Aveline. She lay down with a weary sigh. He sat beside her, his mind too active to hope for sleep. Around them, the camp quieted.

A hand reached out in the darkness, touching him gently. "What are you thinking about?" Aveline asked.

He laughed faintly. "The folly of great men."

"You can think about that for a lifetime."

He smiled and stretched out beside her. How odd it was to feel so content simply because she was near. Chaos swirled around them, coming ever closer, and yet so long as he could see her, look into her eyes, touch the silken fire of her hair, he felt that all would somehow be right.

In the night quiet, wrapped in velvet darkness, it was easier to speak of certain things that in the harshness of day would have been too painful.

"What was your father's folly?" he asked gently.

She was silent so long that he thought she would not answer, but finally she said sadly, "He waited too late to make the political marriage he needed in order to secure his throne. His wife's brothers, the Earls Morcar and Edwin, never really trusted him as a result. When he needed their help to face William, they hesitated, and in that hesitation, all was lost." Her voice was very low as she added, "William would never have made the same mistake."

"Probably not," Renard agreed. "But he made his own, and if you are right, it was far worse than anything Harold did."

"I know it is hard for you to believe that William was not the legitimate king."

"Not merely hard. It puts the lie to everything I thought I knew." He turned on his back, drawing her with him. Her brother be damned and all the rest of the English with him. Not one of them had said anything about caring for her. That was left to him to do and he was glad of it. No one had a better right. Magnus would have to realize that if he realized nothing else.

He sighed and tightened his arms around her. "I still remember so well how William was when he heard that Edward had died."

"You were with him then?"

He nodded. "At the court at Rouen. It was a bitterly cold day. The north wind had blown without rest for more than a week. We were all holed up in the main hall trying to find some amusement. I was playing draughts, as I recall. Suddenly the door burst open—" He stopped, lost in that distant scene.

"Tell me," she urged. "Tell me everything, what William said, what he did, how he looked. I want to understand."

He smiled slightly. "Not everything."

"Why not?"

"I was fifteen. Some things are private."

She raised herself on an elbow and looked at him mischievously. "What things?"

"Never mind."

"Let me guess, there was a girl."

"Not then, later at Dives-sur-mer, where the fleet was built, but in a way it started at Rouen."

"What was she like?"

"Like all girls—pretty, winning, eager."

She laughed and swatted at him. "Braggart. What was her name?"

"Eloise."

"So grand?"

"Not really; she was an ironmonger's daughter."

"And you loved her?"

He hesitated. Honestly he said, "No, but I needed her." Oh, yes, the need had been great in that spring of sudden thaw and rushing expectations when battle beckoned. England lay across the sea, kingless, they thought, but for a usurper who dared to wear the crown. And William . . . William was astride the earth, everywhere at every moment, supervising every detail of their plans. Nothing escaped his eagle eye. Nothing.

"I loved William," Renard said quietly. "In those days we all did."

Aveline took a breath. She laid her hand over his heart. "Tell me."

⊰ The King is Dead ⊱

"*Six!*" Renard said. "Pay up."

"Devil's luck," his friend Conan muttered. "You've been winning all afternoon."

"Sheer skill," Renard claimed as he scooped up the copper pence. "Again?"

"Why not? There's nothing else to do, curse this weather."

"It saves us from the training yard. I don't know about you, but I can use a rest from being battered and bruised."

"You?" Conan scoffed. "You're the terror of us all." He looked at his friend admiringly. They were both of a size, having reached their man's height of over six feet that was the legacy of their Viking forebears. But Renard was by far the more muscular. He looked, Conan had told him, like a granite wall, and when he had a sword in his hand . . . ah, that was poetry the way he moved, quicker and more smoothly than any of them. With the weapon in his hand, he seemed to float, unfettered by earthly limitations, free in his own element like the gods of old. Not bad for a second son of small-holders struggling to find a place for himself.

Renard shrugged modestly and went back to the game. Outside, the wind howled, but inside, the high stone hall was snug and warm, with fires burning in the huge twin chimneys set at either end. An interesting idea, the chimney. Renard applauded whoever had thought of it. In contrast to the smoky fires in braziers to which he was used, this way was far more comfortable and convenient.

The duke's lady, Matilda, had a way of transforming the roughest war keep into a pleasant home. The castle at Rouen was no exception. In less skilled hands, it would have been dark, drafty, and dank. Thanks to Matilda, it was anything but.

Colorful tapestries covered the walls of the main hall. Long trestle tables with benches were pushed out of the way at the moment, but later they would be brought out when supper was served. The food was uniformly excellent; Matilda saw to that, too. Her efforts were especially appreciated by growing young men whose exertions left them perpetually hungry.

Nor were they allowed to think only of fighting and filling their bellies. Matilda insisted that they spend some time with her ladies, accompanying them on the hunt or sitting in the hall listening to music performed or stories read. She felt women had a civilizing influence. Some of the men resented such a claim on their attentions, but no one was foolish enough to say so. The duke was genuinely devoted to his diminutive duchess. Whoever crossed her crossed him.

"Six again," Renard said.

Conan grimaced. "Hell's blood. I can't afford this."

"Let's find something else to do then."

"What? If I have to listen to any more lute playing, I'll go mad."

Renard smiled sympathetically. He happened to like the lute, but he understood that not everyone felt the same way. Better yet was when books were read, but that was rarer. There were only a few and they were kept under lock and key to protect them.

"Come with me to the smith," Renard suggested. "He's got a new whetstone I want to try on my sword."

"That thing's sharp enough now to cleave a man in two. What do you want to hone it further for?"

"I just want to see what the stone can do."

Conan complained, but he had no alternative to suggest. They wrapped their cloaks around them and went out into the freezing wind. Winter held the world in its grip. The dying time, the old ones called it, when little stirred that didn't have to and the earth itself seemed to slumber.

Piles of graying snow left over from the last storm dotted the bailey yard. Renard and Conan crossed it and entered the forge with relief, for here it was always warm. The smith was not there, but Renard knew him well. They had spent many hours talking about the qualities of various metals and what made the difference between a good sword and a great one. He knew the man would not mind if he used the stone.

He was doing that, with Conan crouched nearby enjoying the heat, when a page entered. He looked glad to have found them.

"There you are," the boy said. "The weather's breaking and the duke's decided to hunt. Best get yourselves ready."

Renard and Conan needed no further urging. They ran for the door and stood, looking out at the clearing sky. It was still cold, but just in the time they had been inside, the wind had died. A beam of sunlight broke through the remaining clouds and seemed to shine directly on them.

"Ha-ruh!" Conan exclaimed. "I'm alive again! Come on, let's go."

Renard followed as together they hurried toward the stables. It seemed as though everyone else was there ahead of them. Pages and esquires were busy readying their masters' horses and their own. The horses whinnied, throwing back their heads, manes dancing with excitement.

Hooves clattered on the hard-packed earth as the hunt formed. Men and women alike poured from the hall, all glad to be once again in the sun. They were gloriously dressed in colors bright as birds' plumage. Laughter rang as they passed beyond the castle gates into the narrow streets. Townspeople, alerted to the activity, watched from the windows of their homes and shops. They cheered their duke as he passed.

"He's in a good mood," Conan said, watching William.

"He's as glad as we are to have something to do," Renard said. He looked ahead to where the duke rode accompanied by his cousin and good friend William fitzOsborn. They were chatting amiably and waving to the crowd.

Once out of the town, they crossed the bridge spanning the Seine and followed the road toward Quevilly, the ducal park set aside for William's hunting privilege. Much of it had been cleared of wood that was then used in building Rouen, but there were still stately oaks and elms with their skeletal branches stretched against the sky.

Renard stirred in his saddle. The hunting was always good at Quevilly. The park abounded with stag and boar. With a bit of luck, he would get one for himself. That would be fine, he thought, to feast in hall that night on a portion of his own kill and know that his lord did the same.

He dismounted along with Conan and most of the other men. A page ran up to hold the reins. Not far away, William was stringing his hunter's bow. He always did that for himself, as any serious hunter did. Renard was lifting his own bow from the saddle, preparing to do the same, when he noticed a man coming through the crowd toward them. He stood out only because in that bright company he looked drab and weary. Yet he walked swiftly enough, his gaze fastened on the duke.

Renard stopped what he was doing and dug an elbow into Conan's side. "Who's that?"

His friend looked in the same direction and shrugged. "No idea." He turned back to what he had been doing.

But Renard did not. He stood, the bow still in his hands, and watched as the man went up to William. They exchanged a few words. The duke's face tightened. He handed his bow to a squire and walked away. The man followed.

"Something's happened," Renard said.

Conan laughed. "You worry too much. Come on, finish that. We'll be mounting soon."

Renard's gaze remained focused on the duke. He and the man were still talking, but far enough away from the crowd that they could not be overheard. Others had noticed the man's arrival. More than a few pairs of eyes were focused on them.

From the pleasant anticipation of the hunt, William's mood had changed completely. He looked filled with cold rage, and he stood, tying and untying the knot that held his mantle. At length he nodded and dismissed the man. Without a word to anyone, the duke walked away.

Conan looked up in time to see him go. "What?"

Softly Renard said, "I don't think we hunt today after all, my friend."

"Why the hell not? What's gotten into him. First chance we've had in more than week and he goes off like that?"

"Hush," Renard cautioned. He put his bow back on the saddle and mounted. "Come on, let's go."

"Where to?" Conan demanded sulkily. "If there's to be no hunt, what's the point?"

"Back into town. I want to find out what's happened."

Grumbling, Conan went along. They retraced their path to the river and across the bridge. By the time they reached the town, word was already spreading that William was back, having been rowed across, and had returned alone to his hall. Speculation was rampant, but it ended quickly enough when it met hard fact.

A cluster of men stood outside one of the taverns that fronted on the river. Renard and Conan approached them. So engrossed were they in their talk that none of the men noticed them.

"Dead," one was saying. "Five days ago at Westminster and Harold already crowned. Can you beat that?"

Renard's hands stiffened on the reins. He turned to Conan. "That's it then. Edward is dead and Harold crowned King of England."

Conan frowned. He paid little attention to such things compared with Renard, but even he knew what that meant. For months, Duke William had been telling everyone he was going to be Edward's heir, that the throne of England had been promised to him years before when he visited there, and that Harold himself had sworn an oath to respect his legitimacy.

Now it seemed that was not to be.

They continued on and reached the hall a few minutes later. Most of the hunting party had also returned.

"Let's go find a drink," Conan suggested when they had left their horses at the stable. He took Renard's arm and began urging him away.

Gently Renard disengaged his hand. "Later." He climbed the steps to the hall and went inside. It was very quiet. Despite the several dozen people gathered there, silence hung heavy. Once again all eyes were on the duke.

William sat in clear view on a bench next to one of the pillars that held up the hammer-beam roof. He was alone, no one having dared to approach him. His mantle was drawn over his face, his head resting against the pillar. He appeared deep in thought.

The courtiers stirred anxiously. A few whispered among themselves. From what he overheard, Renard gathered that the news had spread fast. A servant mounted the steps to the family quarters, undoubtedly to tell the duchess. Minutes passed and Matilda did not appear. In the face of such shattering news, not even she dared approach William.

But fitzOsborn did. He was a big, bluff man, lord of one of the greatest estates in William's gift and also seneschal of Normandy. As much as anyone could be, he was the duke's equal.

FitzOsborn strode into the hall. People made way for him as he crossed to William. The duke dropped the mantle from his face and straightened slightly.

"There's no good brooding about it," the seneschal declared. His voice rang among the pillars as he deliberately spoke loudly enough for everyone to hear. "Edward's dead, God rest him, and Harold's crowned.

The whole town knows, so the court might as well. Question is, what are you going to do about it?"

Renard stiffened, wondering if fitzOsborn hadn't been too bold even for one of his special standing. But far from appearing offended, William looked relieved that he didn't have to stand up and announce the news. Instead he could concentrate on what came next.

Slowly he said, "I grieve for my dear cousin Edward. Truly there was never a better man. And I grieve, too, for the great wrong Harold has done us."

The court stirred in response. Men were throwing off the fear they had felt when they beheld their duke's response, for in the talk of grief, they rightly heard the clang of rage.

"Angels sing the good king to his rest," fitzOsborn said, "but as for Harold—say rather the usurper—by God let us good Normans deal with him! Only say the word and your vassals will stream to you." He turned toward the assemblage, his eyes gleaming, face ruddy with emotion. His hand closed on the hilt of his sword and half drew it from the scabbard. "Vengeance for the wrong done Normandy! Blood for the insult to our race!"

A great cheer went up. In the midst of it, Renard remained silent. He felt the rising battle lust all around him, but he did not share it. Later, perhaps, he would. Just then all he could think of was the man he had seen pull the Norman soldiers from the quicksand at the risk of his own life. No coward that and no conspirer. Yet now a king without right.

Beside him, Conan was shouting with all the rest. In all the hall only two men were silent, Renard and William himself. A small smile played at the corners of the duke's mouth as he watched his people rouse themselves to war.

* * *

"And then what happened?" Aveline asked.

Renard was surprised that she was still awake, so silently had she lain in his arms as he recounted the events at Rouen.

Magnus's camp was wreathed in quiet. The fire still burned, well fed to keep animals away. Its crackling was the only sound other than their own breaths.

"Not much at first," he said. "There was a great deal of secret comings and goings, but I was not privy to that. "We hunted and trained as always. Mostly we listened to rumors."

"Where was Eloise in all this?"

"I thought you would have forgotten about her by now."

"Small chance. When did you meet her?"

"Near Eastertide, when we went to Dives for the building of the fleet."

Aveline was silent for a time. Her voice was hushed when she said, "That was when the fire came in the sky."

Renard nodded. He felt a tremor at the memory. They had all been so sure of what God's sign predicted. Had they been wrong?

He took a firm grip on himself. Such questions had no purpose. "As a matter of fact," he said, "I met her the first night the fire appeared."

"Surely an auspicious moment," Aveline said dryly.

He laughed and drew her closer. "Forget Eloise."

"No, no, I want to hear. What were you like then? What did you think about what was happening?"

Slowly Renard said, "I thought . . ."

What had been in his mind in those heady weeks as

the world was reborn and men prepared to die? Not that many thought of it that way. It was killing they were about and their own mortality was a subject they strove to forget.

Oh, yes, he remembered Eloise well and what drew him to her. And he remembered the sky fire with all its majestic portent. But with the fading of spring, the portent vanished and summer settled over the countryside. In the hot, dry days, the clang of steel was everywhere, in the hammers of the shipbuilders and in the feint and parry of young warriors readying themselves for battle. The time of waiting was almost over.

"Conan was your friend," Aveline said softly. It was deeper into the night. Far off, an owl called. The stars shone brilliantly. Renard could make out the Northern Cross high in the sky not far from where the Great Bear roamed.

"More than that," he replied. "He was almost my brother."

"Where is he now?"

"With God, I hope."

Aveline stiffened. Listening to him, she had come to feel almost as though she knew Conan. "What happened?"

"What happened to a great many men. He died at Hastings." Renard closed his eyes for a moment against the old hurt. Conan had died in the same arms that held Aveline so tenderly. "He never did get the little village and wife and family he wanted."

"I'm sorry," she murmured.

He smiled against the silken smoothness of her skin. "Even though he was Norman?"

"Even though."

"That's progress. It wasn't so long ago that you thought we were all the spawn of the devil."

"My brother still thinks so," Aveline said sadly. "He believes I've betrayed him by bringing you here."

"Don't be so sure of that," Renard murmured. "Wait until morning and hear what he has to say."

She sighed and snuggled closer against him. He stroked her hair gently. Soon she slept.

Toward dawn, Renard finally dropped off, too. He woke soon after to screams, the clash of arms, and the desperate sense that he was caught inside his worst nightmare.

17

They came at us from all sides. Renard rolled on top of me, protecting me with his body. He half stood in a crouch. Together we dashed toward the safety of the trees.

"Stay here," he ordered. Turning, he ran back into the melee. Moonlight glinted off the steel of his sword.

Men were shouting and cursing. I saw my brother in the midst of half a dozen men all attacking him at once. A scream bubbled up in my throat, but in an instant Renard was there, fighting his way toward Magnus.

The English were badly outnumbered even with Renard on their side, but they gave as good as they got. Several of the attackers fell, not to rise again. The Normans pulled back briefly, but then they redoubled their efforts.

They were all on foot and roughly dressed, like the more common sort of men. They could have been taken for bandits had they not fought with the ruthless skill of soldiers.

I had little time to think where they might have come from before the tide of battle turned again. Little by little the Normans were forced to give way. More than half the attackers lay dead and dying on the ground. The others, seeing that resistance was far greater than they had expected, began to reconsider the wisdom of the attack. They wavered, and as they did so Magnus rushed to press the advantage. He was in the forefront, broadsword swinging, when one of the Normans came at him. I saw it all even as I stood powerless, unable to change a thing. Magnus fought well, but he was caught by surprise. The Norman landed a savage blow to his head before Renard sent him to eternity.

The rest of the attackers vanished back into the forest. We hardly saw them go. All our attention was on Magnus, who had fallen to the ground. He lay, pale and unmoving. A trickle of blood slipped from a corner of his mouth.

Merciful heaven, how hard it is to write this and how unnatural I must be to want to do so. My tears stain the parchment and the quill shakes in my hand, but I cannot stop. I must record what I saw before pain makes memory fade. That, at least, I can do for my brother.

We carried him back to St. Margaret's. In the gray light of early dawn, Mother Eldgythe came to meet us at the gate. Wulfgarth was with her. She swayed when she saw us and would have fallen had he not been there to catch her.

"Christ save us," she said. Her face was pale, her eyes dark with emotion. Angrily she turned on Renard. "This is your doing, Norman! You betrayed him! And you, stupid girl," she said to me, "this is where caring for a man in so unholy a way will lead. This is your payment for the lusts of the flesh, that so good and fine a man should lie dying because of you!"

My heart shattered. This was the woman who had been as a mother to me. If she thought me so sinful, then surely I must be.

But quickly upon that came another response. I drew myself upright and, through the veil of my tears, saw the truth clearly.

"You are wrong," I said. "Renard had nothing to do with this. He never left my side on the way to Magnus's camp and there is no way he could have told anyone where we were going. He is not to blame, and for that matter, neither am I. Someone else betrayed my brother."

In the shock of that moment, for I had never before so defied her, no one remarked that the secret of my identity was out and Magnus's with it. Compared with all else that had happened, that seemed of small importance.

Mother Eldygthe looked disposed to argue further, but Renard took matters into his own hands. He pushed past her and said to Wulfgarth, "Whatever you believe, Magnus's well-being should be your first concern. We must hide him."

Wulfgarth looked at Renard deeply for a moment and then at me. I met his gaze without reluctance. Perhaps I should feel shame, but I cannot. Indeed, what I feel for Renard is as far removed from shame as it possibly can be.

Abruptly Wulfgarth nodded. "This way," he said.

Mother Eldygthe's mouth thinned, but she made no attempt to interfere further. She stood aside as my brother was carried unconscious to a small vesting room at the back of the abbey. Here visiting priests came to robe themselves before saying Mass.

"I have had word that Father Andrew, who serves

this abbey, is ill with a summer fever," Mother Eldgythe said, "and no other priest is available for the moment, owing to the great crowd of souls in Canterbury who need spiritual care."

"Then this will do well," Renard said as he glanced around. The room was windowless, but the air in it was fresh, owing to a vent cut into the stone wall. Gently he and Wulfgarth laid Magnus on the floor. Mother Eldgythe knelt beside him and examined him quickly.

"What happened?" she demanded.

Briefly Renard told her. He made nothing of his own participation in the battle, never mentioning that he had fought to protect my brother. Nor did he say, as he could have, that it was Magnus's own impulsiveness in the end that led to his wounding. The blood had dried at his mouth, but his pallor had deepened. Mother Eldgythe was frowning when she straightened.

"Aveline, fetch my chest of medicines and find clean linen to bind his head."

She seemed to have forgotten all about her outburst at me. I hurried off to obey. When I returned, she was alone with Magnus. I couldn't ask her where Renard had gone without risking her anger again. Silently I helped her clean and bandage Magnus. As I wiped the dried blood away I began to cry. The tears slipped soundlessly down my cheeks. Mother Eldgythe did not seem to notice them at first, but when she had finished everything she could do for Magnus, she laid a worn hand over mine.

"I will not berate you again," she said, "but tell me why you took the Norman to him?"

"To warn him of what Rufus was planning."

"And what is that?"

"To take advantage of the panic building among the

people to justify his taking over as protector of the realm. They are terrified already by the drought, the fire, the murders. If Magnus were to rise against the throne, Rufus would have the excuse he needs to seize power for himself."

She sighed and tightened her hand on mine. "So you knew Magnus could not win?"

I nodded sorrowfully. "Would that I thought otherwise, but the time for rebellion is passed. We must find some way to get along with the Normans." I stopped, thinking I had inadvertently opened the subject of Renard again, but she did not seem to notice.

Instead she said, "He is very much like your father."

I stiffened in surprise, for this was the first time she had ever spoken of my father to me. Cautiously I asked, "Is he?"

She nodded. "Oh, yes, they were all alike, the Godwinson men. All hotheaded, impulsive, filled with lusts and ambitions, always ready to seize what they thought should be theirs no matter what the consequences to anyone else."

She laughed bitterly. "You never knew your uncle Sweyn, and that's a pity, because knowing him, perhaps you would have understood the curse that lay on all of them. He came to Norfolk once when your mother and I were girls. I still remember him, riding golden in the sun, proud as Lucifer. Later he raped an abbess and was sent into exile. Died on pilgrimage to Jerusalem trying to erase his sins."

The look on my face must have revealed my shock, for she laughed again. "You didn't know that, did you? Once he was gone, everyone was careful not to speak of him much. But the seed that was in him was in all of them, your father not excepted."

I thought then, quite seriously, that I did not want to hear any more. Starved as I have been for information about my family, this was not what I wanted. But Mother Eldgythe was not to be dissuaded, although I tried.

"I'd rather you told me more about my mother," I said. "You and she were such good friends."

"We knew each other from earliest childhood. We grew up playing with each other, sharing everything, as close as two girls could be. Everywhere Edythe went, I went. Everything she did, I did. We had the most wonderful times together."

She sighed. Her gaze was faraway. "She was like a flame, your mother, fire-haired like you, with the most incredible white skin and hazel green eyes flecked with gold. I had never seen anything more beautiful. Everything she touched was special, golden in some way I can't really describe. I can still hear her laughter like music on the air." Her voice fell. "We laughed so much then."

"Did she ever think of taking religious vows like you?" I asked.

"Your mother wall herself up in some cloister? Of course not. She was made for the world, for life, for everything gay and wonderful. I never thought of taking vows either, not then when we were both young and nothing intruded on our friendship. But later—"

"What happened?" I should not have asked, for the subject was clearly painful, but curiosity is a curse I cannot seem to avoid.

"Your father, what else? He came to Norfolk as Sweyn had done, but he was even more golden, bigger, more confident, a great lord's son. Edythe was sixteen that spring. Every man desired her, but she had never paid the slightest attention to any of them until he came. He saw her and immediately he wanted her. She fired his blood, you could see that just to watch them. Still, it might have ended there, for he couldn't offer marriage, not in the church anyway, and her father was of sufficient position that he wouldn't see his daughter become any man's whore. But Harold was a Godwinson. He would have what he most desired, nothing would stop him. He put his mind to it, you see, and he came up with the idea of a handfast marriage, respected under the old Danelaw but apart from anything the Church would sanction."

"And my mother agreed to it?"

"Oh, yes, for she was under his spell by then. She couldn't have lifted a finger to save herself. He was all she saw in the world. Everything else was forgotten."

"Not you," I protested. "You and she remained close friends up to the very end. That was why she sent me to you."

"I stayed her friend," Mother Eldgythe acknowledged, "and she mine, but it was never the same. All the old knowing of each other, the bond that went beyond the need for words, was gone. In many ways she had become a stranger."

"She married," I said quietly, "and she had children, while you gave your life to the Church. There were bound to be differences between you."

"But I still loved her as before! Nothing changed that, at least not for me. It did for her, though. After your father, she never felt the same for me."

How could she have? I wondered. My mother's life had moved on, as it was meant to, while Mother Eldgythe's . . . Hers had remained frozen, the love of girlhood transformed into bitterness and rage directed against my father.

I backed away from the thought as though from the edge of a chasm. But now, safe for the moment in the privacy of my small chamber, I confront it again.

Mother Eldgythe loved my mother and hated my father.

My mother died in the end for love of my father, and that must have added to the hatred. But my father was also dead and the kingdom he so briefly ruled was rapidly being transformed by the Normans who had won it. Only a few outposts like St. Margaret's still cling to the old Anglo-Saxon ways and then only thanks to the strength and determination of people like Mother Eldgythe.

That is so, isn't it?

"Aveline?"

Renard stood at the door to the small chamber. His dark hair was rumpled and there were shadows under his eyes. Fatigue accentuated the hollows beneath his cheekbones. He looked at her quizzically.

"What are you doing?"

She flushed, her eyes wide, and drew a piece of cloth over the parchment in front of her.

"Nothing. I—"

He took a step further into the room. It was simply furnished with a narrow bed, a chest, and a table with a high stool where she sat.

She stood up hastily. "I am finished. What is it you want."

"Magnus is the same, still unconscious. Mother Eldgythe has gone to pray. I thought you might want to be with him." His eyes returned to the table and the covered parchment. "Who are you writing to?"

She hesitated. He could see the struggle in her and realized that she did not want to answer, but honesty finally compelled her. "To God, I think. I don't really know."

He nodded in understanding. "A book of prayers. I can see how you would find consolation in that." He smiled gently and laid a hand on her arm. "Take heart,

Aveline, we will find our way through this."

She swallowed against the lump her throat. "You shouldn't be here, you know. The cells are out of bounds for male visitors. But I am glad all the same."

"So am I," he murmured as he took her into his arms. They stood in the silence of her chamber, drawing strength from one another, until the outside world could no longer be denied.

Tired though she was, Aveline went to sit with Magnus. A small oil lamp provided the room's only illumination. By it, she could see that his head was swathed in bandages, his face almost as white as the linen. He lay motionless with only the shallow rise and fall of his breathing to show that life still remained within him.

Wulfgarth was there. He stood up when Aveline entered. His voice was rough-edged but gentle as he asked, "Are you all right?"

She nodded. "I'll be fine." Her gaze fixed on the still figure of her brother. "Would that the same were true of him."

"It is with God," Wulfgarth said gruffly. He stood aside to make a place for her beside the pallet. When she had sat down, he crouched beside her. Several moments passed in silence before he said, "I need to ask you something. You say the Norman couldn't have told anyone where you were going?"

"That's right," Aveline insisted. "He couldn't have."

"Is it possible you were followed?"

She shook her head. "It was night when we left Canterbury. Anyone tracking us would have had to keep us within sight. They couldn't have done that without being seen."

"Then someone betrayed the location of Magnus's camp to the Normans."

Aveline agreed. "Definitely. The question is who. How many people knew where he was hiding?"

"It's difficult to say. The men closest to him certainly knew, but they were all picked with the greatest care and I simply can't see any of them turning traitor. They had as much to lose as he did. You did and I did as well, since he sent word to the abbey of his whereabouts even before you returned."

"Mother Eldgythe knew," Aveline said, "and it's possible that some of the other sisters could have found out, but as with his men, I can't see any of them betraying him. It just doesn't make any sense."

Wulfgarth thought a few moments longer, trying to unknot the puzzle. Finally he gave up and stood. "We won't get it here. I'm going into town to find out whatever I can."

"Don't go," Aveline said, reaching out a hand to him. "There's been another of the pagan killings in Canterbury."

Wulfgarth's face reflected his shock. "I had not heard of this."

"It happened only yesterday evening, and so much has gone on since there's been no time to speak of it. But there will be panic in the town by now and every Englishman will be suspect. I entreat you to stay here."

He hesitated, obviously torn by his sense of duty, but finally he said, "As you will, my lady. Still, we must have information."

"If I might suggest, you should talk to Renard about that. He will know what to do."

Aveline held her breath. She thought surely that Wulfgarth would reject the very idea that he have dealings with a Norman. But he surprised her. Grudgingly he said, "I suppose it wouldn't hurt."

She sighed with relief and managed a smile. "Only try it, that's all I ask."

A short time later, when she left Magnus's side to fetch clean water, she saw Renard and Wulfgarth deep in discussion near the guest house. Against all the sorrow and worry of the day, a spurt of gladness filled her. If those two could find some common ground, there was hope for them all.

But not, it seemed, for Magnus. The days passed and his condition did not improve. In the great sewing room of the abbey, work continued on Odo's tapestry. Aveline finished her drawings and took some time to watch the progress of translating them to wool and linen. But most of her waking hours were spent at Magnus's side. She cleaned and fed him, held his hand, and talked to him, all the while praying that he might, in some slight way, respond.

Each day Renard sent men into the town to gather news. It was uniformly bad. Word of the murder had thrown the refugees and townspeople alike into a panic. English residents had been lucky to escape with their lives and were hiding in the country, finding shelter wherever they could. Rufus had issued several proclamations announcing large rewards for the delivery of the pagan slayer and for "the rebellious traitor," as he was called, "the scourge of honest men, known as Oath Bearer." He had said several times in public that he thought Oath Bearer himself might be the killer or at the very least share responsibility for the deaths. Bands of armed Normans were scouring the surrounding area, searching for him.

"Rufus has announced that he intends a public trial," Renard said one afternoon as he came into the vesting room where Aveline was keeping vigil. His arrival was a sudden blast of masculine strength and vigor into a place that had become as still as the grave.

He looked at Aveline with concern. She had lost weight she could not afford to lose and was pale and drawn. Lately she was nauseated too often to eat properly. He had thought that due to worry for her brother, but as it continued, he wondered if there might not be another cause.

Under the circumstances, he was tempted to tell her nothing more, but Aveline would have none of that. She insisted on knowing what he had learned. "The bill of indictment has been published," he said reluctantly. "The prince blames your brother for everything—the murders, the drought, the London fire, every calamity that has befallen us is laid at his door."

"So much for Norman justice," Aveline murmured. She was very tired. The room seemed to swim before her eyes. She would have liked to blame the heat, but the weather had cooled a little in recent days. Summer was slowly loosening its savage grip on the land. Soon it would be autumn, the time of falling leaves and the flight of birds. The harvests were meager, further heightening people's fear. There would be hunger for many and death for some.

In the abbey, reserves were being checked, decisions made as to how much could be dispersed to needy peasants on the abbey lands. There would be less suffering at St. Margaret's than in many other places. Mother Eldgythe was always good about that. Somehow she found the means to take care of her own.

Her thoughts strayed into a dark corner. She blinked hard and pulled them back.

"You must get some rest," Renard was saying. His arms were around her, drawing her upright. "If there is any change, I will call you."

She went reluctantly and only because the demands of

her body simply could no longer be ignored. When she was gone, Renard sat down again beside the pallet. Magnus appeared unchanged. He seemed to exist in some twilight area between life and death, unable to return to the one yet prevented from moving on to the other.

Renard fought a twinge of horror as he thought of that. As much as he had come to hate battle, there was something to be said for a quick, clean death. Magnus, too, had been a warrior. Surely he had never envisioned such a fate for himself.

In simple, human sympathy—forgetting all else—he took the other man's hand and held it gently. It would have been good, he thought, if he could pray, but the ability had long since deserted him. Perhaps he should get Aveline to show him her book of prayers. He had not seen it since that one glimpse days before.

It was peaceful in the room. He sat back with his head against the stone wall. His mind drifted to the generations of priests who had robed themselves there, preparing to consecrate the Mass for the generations of good sisters who had lived and died at St. Margaret's.

The smell of incense had long since soaked into the stone and mortar. It reminded him of his boyhood when he and Conan had occasionally been roped into helping the priests serve Mass at William's court.

Conan—

No, not Conan. Magnus. Renard woke from his half dream with a start. He stared at the man before him.

Magnus stared back. His eyes were opened the merest slit. Pallor remained strong on his cheeks and his breathing was no better, but he was conscious.

He made a faint sound. Renard leaned forward to catch it.

"D'Agounville . . ."

"That's right." And then, because it was what he would want to know under the same circumstances, he added, "You're at St. Margaret's. Your men are safe and Rufus doesn't know that you're here. We're going to do our damnedest to see it stays that way."

Magnus grappled with that for a moment. Slowly he said, "You fought—"

"For Aveline," Renard said bluntly. "Make no mistake about that. I will not have her harmed."

"Not Aveline," Magnus murmured. "Her name is Kendra."

"Not to me. For her own sake, she must always be Aveline. That is her surest safety."

Their eyes met. In Magnus's, Renard saw the growing darkness of eternity. "What safety?" the Englishman murmured. "Is there any for her . . . my sister . . . a king's daughter? This place—" He made a weak gesture that encompassed the narrow stone walls.

"Has served its purpose," Renard said. "Now it is in danger of becoming her prison. She deserves better." His hand tightened on Magnus. Looking him directly in the eye, he said, "I will cherish and protect her. With me, she will be safe. And despite all that has happened, your family's line will endure."

Magnus's mouth twitched slightly as though he was trying to smile. "You have only to convince her of that."

Renard grimaced. He was right, of course. "I am hoping you will help me."

The Englishman sighed. His face was drawn in pain. Softly he said, "Then fetch her quickly, for there is little time."

Renard got to his feet. But before he could go, Magnus stopped him. "Wait . . . one more question. Who was it who betrayed me?"

"I don't know," Renard said honestly.

Magnus sighed. "You must find out. There will be no safety for any of you until you do."

The truth of that lingered in Renard's mind even as he went to find Aveline. He was still thinking about it as he returned with her to the vesting room before discreetly withdrawing to give brother and sister a final chance to be alone. Outside in the passage, he stared into space as he went over the possibilities. Who had known where Oath Bearer was to be found? Who, of those, would tell?

He was no closer to an answer when Aveline emerged a few minutes later. Her hands shook slightly and her eyes were filled with tears. "He is gone," she said.

Renard took her into his arms. He held her safe within them as the storm of rage and pain finally broke, shattering the strict check she had kept on her emotions for so long. She wept against his broad chest, crying out against all the blood and death, the loneliness and fear, until she could weep no more.

When she raised her head, her eyes were dry and hard as crystal. "We must bury him quickly," she said.

Renard nodded. Quietly he said, "We will need a priest."

"O Lord God, Lamb of God, Son of the Father, who takest away the sins of the world, have mercy on us."

Burgess stood, an austere figure in his rough monk's robe, beside the open grave. Mother Eldgythe was also there, as was Wulfgarth. Aveline stood beside Renard. As many of the rebel English as had escaped death in the attack on the camp were also drawn up nearby. This was their last service to their lord before they dispersed and returned to their homes.

Burgess's voice was low and steady, gentled by compassion but strong in its absolute assurance.

"In the presence of the Lord, there is not sorrow nor pain nor loneliness but only joy. Go then to that joy, Magnus Haroldson, beloved son and brother, child of God. The peace of God be yours unto all eternity."

He bent over and picked up a handful of the good English dirt. Holding it out over the shrouded body in the grave, he let it trickle through his fingers. One by one the others did the same.

Only Aveline stood unmoving. Wrapped in a cloak against the evening's coolness, her flame-hued hair concealed, she watched unblinking as the grave was filled. When Magnus's men picked up shovels to finish the job, she still made no move to depart. Not until he was secure within the earth, the ground patted over and all traces of the digging removed, did she at last stir.

Looking at Burgess, she said, "Thank you."

The monk bowed his head as though to a queen. "Your servant, my lady," he murmured. She turned, and together they walked back inside the abbey.

A tall, thin figure wrapped in a gray cloak emerged from the shelter of the trees. He came to stand beside Renard. Softly he said, "She has made a conquest."

Renard turned to the archbishop. "It appears that way." He was not surprised to see Lanfranc, only glad that he had waited to reveal himself until after the service was done. "Have you been here all this time?"

The archbishop nodded. "I came with Burgess. Bright lad, that. He's spent the last week explaining to me why ambition is the worm eating at the Norman soul."

Renard winced. "I'm sorry. It was good of you to give him sanctuary."

"Don't apologize. A man ought to hear the truth

occasionally. Besides, I felt I had a duty to come. I was there the last time, you see."

"The what?"

Lanfranc nodded. "The last time one of that line was buried on English soil. I came today almost to try to make amends for that." He sighed and drew his cloak more closely around him. Glancing up at the sky, he said, "It's ending."

Renard's gaze followed the archbishop. The sky, so long remorselessly clear, was shrouded in clouds. Even as the men watched, the first few drops of rain began to fall. Renard felt them on his face like a benediction.

"Thank God," he murmured.

"Indeed," Lanfranc said. He looked again at the grave. "The king's son dies and is returned to the earth, and the cycle of nature is restored."

Renard felt a chill deep within him. "There was nothing pagan about Magnus's death."

"No, of course not. I was merely ruminating. I'm allowed to at my age."

Renard looked toward the abbey. He wanted to go after Aveline. It wasn't right to leave her at such a time. But Lanfranc seemed disposed to talk. Indeed, he appeared driven to do so.

"You were telling me about the last time," Renard said, thinking he might urge him along.

"Indeed." Lanfranc turned to him suddenly, his care-worn face taut with concern. "What has she drawn of that? The tumult of the battle, the charge and counter-charge, the false retreat and finally Harold falling, his brothers dying with him, the Normans triumphant, hardly daring to believe that we were the victors? All that certainly, but what more has she shown?"

"I don't really know," Renard admitted. "I haven't

looked at the last parts of the drawings as closely as I probably should."

Lanfranc sighed. "It doesn't matter, I suppose. God judges us, not man—or woman." He seemed to rouse himself from the darkness of his thoughts. "What do you remember of that day? Glory, honor, triumph? A young man's greatness born in an act of insurmountable courage? You saved William's life. If he had died then, that would have been the battle. Harold would have won."

"William was my liege lord," Renard said slowly. "He was owed all my loyalty and honor. When I saw him in mortal danger, I had an absolute responsibility to do as I did. Besides, it could have fallen to anyone else to save him."

"I could argue with that. The hand of God and so on, but never mind. What *do* you remember?"

"Fear," Renard said succinctly. If the archbishop was seeking relief from his own memories, he had come to the wrong person. "And pain. The friend of my youth died there on that blood-soaked field. I found him in the aftermath while life still flickered in him. He died in my arms. I dug his grave and buried him. I didn't return to the camp until much later and I don't think I paid much attention to anything until later still, for the grief was hard to bear.

"But tell me," Renard added, "what do *you* remember?"

Lanfranc's deep, farseeing eyes took on the look of long ago. His narrow, ascetic face flushed slightly. This priest, this man of God, this learned sage whose wisdom was surpassed only by his holiness, gazed into the past and said the last thing that Renard could ever have expected.

"A woman."

⚜ Long Live the King ⚜

"Drink," fitzOsborn said as he thrust the goblet into William's hand. *"By God, you have earned it."*

The duke took the cup, but made no effort to taste its contents. He sat on a small camp stool, gray with weariness, dressed in a crumpled tunic stained with the blood that had seeped through his chain mail. The mail, his helmet, and sword lay discarded beside him.

The others had similarly disarmed when they realized at last that it was safe to do so. The English, what was left of them, were in full retreat. As dusk fell over Senlac meadow the unusual heat of the October day lifted and a refreshing breeze blew from the sea some seven miles to the south.

But the men seated in front of William's tent hardly felt it. They had other matters on their minds.

"He has to be there," fitzOsborn insisted. He did not hesitate to drain his own share of the fine wine from Champagne brought along with unusual foresight. Somewhere in the midst of battle, a thoughtful servant of the duke's had seen to it that the wine was chilled in a nearby stream. The notion was eccentric—the battle waging, men screaming in their death throes, a people's fate being decided, and all the while wine cooling, on the assumption that it would be needed by the victors, whoever they might turn out to be.

William grimaced into his cup. "It could be Harold drinking this."

"He's dead," fitzOsborn said. "The shield wall was broken—we know that—when their last position was stormed. Everyone there was killed. Not a man escaped— not Harold, not his brothers, and not anyone else. He's dead."

William sighed deeply. He looked out into the gathering night. Torches flared on the battlefield as men searched among the dead and dying, some to give succor, most merely seeking plunder.

"Then where is he?" he asked.

"Out there," Sir Turold said. He stretched out his long legs with a groan of relief and drained his cup. "Somewhere amid the carnage. We'll find him in the morning."

"We'd damn well better," William muttered. For a man who had won a great victory, he was curiously disquieted, or so his companions thought.

FitzOsborn scowled. "You worry too much. It's over. For God's sake, you're King of England! Is there no joy in you for that?"

The duke stood up and walked a little distance away from them. Alone, looking out over the field, he said, "I will be king when we find Harold. Until then, nothing is finished. So long as there is any chance he survives, we will have to fight our way through every inch of this land."

He turned back and looked at them somberly. "And

we can't afford to do that. We were lucky today, but we still lost too many men. We must get to London quickly and take it before the other earls—Harold's brothers-in-law, for instance—can rise against us. Otherwise this fine victory we've won will mock us to our early graves."

In the shadow of the tent flap, Lanfranc stirred. Quietly he said, "Our liege is right. Send men to the hillock where the English made their last stand. Search among the dead until he is found. There can be no rest until then."

The others—fitzOsborn, Turold, and several more knights who had fought all day close to the vanguard—agreed, but reluctantly. Any thought that they might be thwarted at this late moment filled them with dread. More wine was poured, and quickly drunk, by those seeking release from the hideous memories, the haunting screams and death reek of the day.

Orders were given, men dispatched. A simple meal was brought out by William's servants. The duke ate a little, Lanfranc not at all, the rest rather more. Mostly they drank. There was very little talking. Later they would recall their exploits, the great moments of personal triumph when they strove with the strength of giants against the English horde, but just then they were merely men, exhausted, weary, and despite everything, still very much afraid.

An hour passed and another. It was fully dark. All efforts to pursue the remnants of the English force had ceased. Here and there, a few of the common soldiers were already bedding down for the night. They rolled themselves into cloaks, said their prayers with unusual sincerity, and laid their heads on earth that a scant few hours before had been alien, but which now, incredibly, belonged to them.

William did not stir. He remained seated in front of his tent, the others with him. "What's keeping them?" fitzOsborn demanded.

"It's dark," Turold said, "and hard going. Be patient, they'll find him."

Yet when the Normans returned a short time later, they were somber, with the shadow of doubt hanging over them.

"We searched, my lord," the knight appointed their leader said. He was a solid fellow, Herbert by name, known to the senior men. "The Earls Leofwine and Gyrth are there, brothers to the Usurper. The English prisoners we took along identified them right enough. But as to Harold himself—" He broke off, hesitating. Finally he said, "We just can't be sure, my lord."

"What do you mean," William demanded, "you can't be sure?"

Herbert glanced away for a moment, a look of unease on his broad face. "There, uh, isn't enough to go on, sir."

"Hellfire!" fitzOsborn exclaimed. "We all knew he had to be killed, but to not even leave enough to identify him . . . That's sheer stupidity."

"The heat of battle invariably causes such excesses," Turold said in an effort to calm the volatile Norman. The last thing they needed was recriminations among themselves. "Harold must be there. Seal off the hillock, lord. Let no man touch anything left upon it. When morning comes, we will know far better."

Reluctantly William agreed. He desperately wanted the matter settled before then, but it clearly wasn't going to be. He stood, weary to the bone, and went into his tent without a further word to anyone. His page was there, waiting with hot water for washing and one of the soft feather mattresses Matilda had insisted on sending along already laid out on the camp bed.

William allowed the page to help him remove the blood-soaked tunic. He looked at it with distaste. "Burn it."

He stood naked in the center of the tent and scrubbed himself thoroughly. The night air had cooled. His skin puckered in the chill. When the water in the basin ran red, he stopped. Wrapped in a fresh cloak, he sat on the edge of the bed and opened the small book of prayers Matilda, again, had pressed upon him immediately before his departure.

In the dim light of the lamp beside the bed, he could make out a few of the words. In broad daylight, he would have done little better. The effort frustrated him. He was glad when Lanfranc called from outside and asked if he might enter.

"The others have gone to rest," the prelate said. "I saw the light and thought you might be wakeful."

"Sit," William said, pressing forward a camp stool. "I should be at my prayers, giving thanks to God, but I can't seem to do that."

Lanfranc looked at him. "Tomorrow I will say a public Mass. We can all give thanks then."

William nodded, glad to agree. "That's better, isn't it, to do it all together?"

"If you're more comfortable with that," Lanfranc said noncommittally.

William sighed. He turned the small book over in his hands without really seeing it. His gaze was turned inward, away from the small tent and the quiet priest who sat waiting for him to speak.

Finally William said, "We've done well together, you and I, haven't we? You've advanced in the Church, as you deserved to, and I've managed to hold things together in Normandy as they needed to be held."

"You've done more than that, my lord," Lanfranc said slowly. "You brought peace and prosperity to a land riven by war. Your people have every reason to be grateful to you."

William nodded. His eyes were hard, the pupils dilated in the faint light. He stood up abruptly and began to pace back and forth within the small confines of the tent.

"That's true, isn't it? And I will do the same here. No more dynastic wars, no more earls vying for power, but peace and stability, order, discipline, exactly what England most needs. That's why I'm here."

"You are here," Lanfranc said quietly, "because the late King Edward, in his holiness and wisdom, named you his lawful successor."

"Right, of course. Edward—" The duke turned away. He ran a hand over his face. The strength that had propelled him a moment before seemed to fade abruptly.

His voice was low and shook slightly as he said, "I want you to do something for me."

"Of course, my lord."

"I want you to hear my confession."

Lanfranc frowned. "But, my lord, every man in the Norman host, yourself included, confessed and was absolved of all sin before the battle began. No man went to combat unshriven."

"I know that. I want you to hear it again."

"Again? Now?"

"Yes, right now. I will rest more easily, you see, to have my mind cleared."

"Of what?" Lanfranc asked. "The killings done this day? But you had right on your side. You fought for what was yours. Surely there is no reason to be uneasy in your spirit about that."

"I'm not! I was right to do what I did, I know I was. England is too important, too vital to the future. I could not let it—" He broke off suddenly and stared at Lanfranc. "Will you hear me under seal of the confession?"

Slowly the prelate straightened. He seemed weighed down suddenly but accepting of his burden. A look of great sadness flickered across his face. "If that is what you wish, my lord, I am bound to do so."

It was the hour before dawn. In the tent, William slept as did almost all the Norman host. Only a few sentries remained on duty, evidence of the hard discipline the duke maintained even in the face of victory. They saw but made no attempt to stop the priest who walked slowly across the field among the English dead.

Lanfranc stopped here and there, kneeling to say a prayer or simply to place a gentle touch where it could no longer be felt. There seemed to be some compulsion on him that forced him to stay there among the dead, to look at each and every one of them as though imprinting them forever in his memory.

But when he came at last to the line of sentries drawn up around the hillock, he made no attempt to pass them. Instead he stopped and looked from a distance at the shadowed heaps and tumbled shapes that scant hours before had been living, breathing men.

The sentries glanced at one another, made uneasy by his presence. Lanfranc sensed it and drew back a little. A rim of gray light grew in the east until it seeped up over the pale sky. Soon it would be day. He turned and glanced toward the west. A line of horses moved along the track that emerged from the trees.

"Who is that?" he asked softly of himself. No answer was forthcoming, nor would it be while he remained at the hillock. Lifting the hem of his robe, Lanfranc hurried toward the travelers.

He met them a little distance from William's camp. There were four in all—a woman of surpassing beauty, a girl of tender years whose daughter she had to be, a young boy, and another woman, slightly older than the first with a plain face and stern demeanor who wore the robes of a nun.

Two women and two children traveling alone in such perilous times shocked Lanfranc. He said the first thing that came into his mind.

"For pity's sake, have you no better sense than to be here? A battle was fought scant hours ago. You should be nowhere near."

The first woman, pale and composed with flame-hued hair showing from beneath her head covering, addressed him quietly. Her voice was soft, weary, and overwhelmed with sorrow. "Good priest, believe me, if I had a choice, I would be anywhere else." She looked at him more closely and he had the sense of being weighed in the balance.

"Who are you?" she asked.

"Lanfranc, Bishop of Rouen."

"I have heard of you. You used to be a teacher."

He winced. "Dear lady, I still endeavor to be that."

"A noble effort in a world gone mad."

"Who are you?" he asked, suddenly nervous, for they stood at that moment between night and day when the old ones said spirits still roamed. He tried not to believe in such things, but she was so unlikely an apparition, sitting pale and beautiful on her horse, wrapped in sorrow like a mantle.

"I am Edythe of Norfolk," she said quietly. A moment passed before she added, "Some men call me Edythe Swan's Neck."

Lanfranc's head jerked. Of Edythe of Norfolk, he knew nothing. But the other—

"Harold's wife," he said before he could stop himself. Hard on the words came growing horror. What was wrong with him that he could utter such a thing? She was not his wife, had never been, for the Church that Lanfranc so devotedly served recognized no such union. At best, she had been a concubine. At worst, a whore.

A slight smile played around her mouth. She looked at him almost pitingly. "Nothing is ever as simple as we would like, is it, priest?"

He thought of the moments in the tent, William kneeling beside him, the words pouring from the duke's mouth, and a sense of sickness threatened to overwhelm him.

"What do you want?" he demanded.

"To see the duke. I must speak with him."

Lanfranc stared at her. There was no doubt that she meant what she said. Out of the depths of her grief, she had come to speak with the very man responsible for all that had occurred. Marveling at such courage, he shifted his gaze to the others in her party.

The second woman had her mouth pressed thin. Her face was red and her hands on the reins of her palfrey trembled with barely suppressed rage. The boy, a handsome lad with reddish hair, looked exhausted and in shock. While the girl—there Lanfranc's eyes stopped. He gazed at her for several long moments. Her mother's daughter, indeed, heartbreakingly beautiful, proud, self-contained.

She knows, he thought all that has happened here, truly knows as her mother does, as though they had both been here themselves. Her eyes were blue, he saw, and that sent another shock through him as he realized where he had seen such eyes before. Not only her mother's daughter then but also seed of her father. She was drawn up very straight in the saddle. He could see that she was slender, finely boned, but with the strength of steel in her. Still, she was only a child.

Quietly he said, "I will take you to him alone. Send the others back."

"No!" the second woman said.

She would have gone on, but the Lady Edythe silenced her with a look. "He is right. Take them beyond the camp and wait for me."

The nun looked disposed to argue further, but Edythe gave her no chance. She turned to Lanfranc. "Let us go."

William was awake when they reached his tent. Turold was with him, reporting on the count of dead and wounded, both Norman and English. Both men broke off when they saw Lanfranc at the door.

"Come in—" William began only to stop when he realized the priest was not alone. He stood, staring at Edythe. "Who . . . ?"

"She is the handfast wife of the king," Lanfranc said quietly. He was aware of Turold staring at him as though he had lost his senses.

"King?" the knight demanded. "Are you mad? He—"

"Leave us," William ordered.

Turold hesitated, but he could not refuse. He went away muttering to himself.

When they were alone, William gestured to a camp stool. "You may sit if you like," he said to Edythe.

She shook her head. Without preamble she said, "I have come for the body of the king. In the name of Christian charity, I call upon you to yield it to me."

"I see," William said slowly. He sat down on the stool she had declined and stared at her. Not unkindly, he said, "You knew him well."

Edythe returned his look with one of her own that suggested she found that less than astute. "I was his wife more than twenty years."

With apparent sincerity, William said, "He was a fortunate man."

The compliment was out of place, as they both knew. Coldly Edythe said, "He? Can you not speak his name? The name of the man whose destruction you wrought?"

"His name was Harold Godwinson," William said quickly. He spoke a little too loudly, Lanfranc thought, as though he needed to deny the fear that still ate at him.

Sometimes absolution worked. Sometimes it did not.

"Harold Godwinson," Edythe repeated. "King of England."

William sighed. He stood up again. "We won't argue about that. You want the body?"

She inclined her head.

"Very well then," the duke went on. "You shall have it, but first there is a small problem."

"What is that?" Edythe asked.

William told her.

Lanfranc left the tent a short time later. He escorted

the Lady Edythe to the hillock and remained with her, in his capacity as a priest, while she went among the bodies. He did not presume to think he would be of any comfort to her, yet she seemed glad enough of his presence when at last they returned to William. Walking back across Senlac meadow, Edythe leaned heavily on his arm. She seemed to have aged a great deal in a short time.

William received her again within his tent. They spoke briefly. Edythe cried out in protest, loudly enough to draw the attention of several soldiers standing nearby. Then she fell silent and silent she remained as they escorted her alone from the Norman camp. Lanfranc went with them, because he could think of no legitimate reason not to.

In the woods a mile or so from the battlefield, they found the rest of her party. Seeing her alone except for the Normans, they knew without having to be told what had happened. The girl's face fell. She put her head in her hands and began to weep. The boy reached over and put his arm around her. Together they tried as best they could to comfort each other.

For Edythe, there was no comfort, but Lanfranc felt compelled to try to contrive some all the same. He drew her a little distance off and, taking both her hands in his, said, "I promise, he will be buried decently. All William cares about is that the location of his grave be secret. But I swear, it will be done as you would wish."

"I wish?" she asked, her eyes endless pools of grief. "I have no wishes, priest, not now that I have seen what you have done to him. Bury him, by all means, or what is left. Tell yourselves you are free of him, but you never will be, not while there is still memory."

She turned then and pressed her heels into her palfrey's sides. Slowly the horse moved forward. The others followed. Lanfranc stood frozen in place, watching them vanish down the long and winding track that led through the forest to some place he did not know and would never glimpse.

18

"You knew," Renard said.

Lanfranc nodded. They were still standing beside Magnus's grave. The rain had become heavier, but neither of them noticed, so absorbed were they in the past.

"A little more than three years later, I went to Canterbury as archbishop," Lanfranc went on. "I wasn't there very long before I realized that the nun I had seen with the Lady Edythe was the abbess of St. Margaret's. The girl, Harold and Edythe's daughter, had become her ward and was known as Aveline."

"What did you do?" Renard asked.

"Nothing as regards the child, she deserved to be left in peace. However, I did begin to make certain inquiries about the abbess."

He broke off and looked at Renard. "You must get Aveline away from here."

"I intend to as soon as Odo's damn tapestry is done. She won't leave before then."

"She may have to. There are other circumstances—"

The archbishop paused. He looked down at the

grave. "What I am about to tell you, you may use as you see fit and you may tell Aveline if you must. But apart from that, it should remain in confidence."

"As you will," Renard said.

Lanfranc took a deep breath. "It concerns St. Margaret's and how it has managed to prosper, an English abbey rich and intact, despite the conquest. But mostly it concerns Mother Eldgythe."

Aveline knelt in the chapel. Outside she could hear the rain falling. The long drought was over. God willing, come spring there would be flowers on Magnus's grave.

The stone beneath her legs was cold. She clasped her hands together tightly and tried to pray, but the words would not come. There was no consolation for her and no acceptance. Magnus was dead, nothing could change that, but rather than pray for his soul she could feel only pain and a terrible sense of loss.

She bent her head. The veil of red-gold hair fell before her face. The chapel receded as though down a tunnel darkly and she was back at the Westminster, kneeling before the altar where her father had been crowned. Remembering—

Two journeys to London. Four deaths. All occurring while she was there. Lagounier and LeMeux had been known to her. Valerian and de Courcy could have been for they were frequently at the Westminster. They might easily have crossed paths with—

The oak staff on Valerian's body, used by whoever had carried it, for the base held ground-in dirt, but too short for someone of Renard's height. The victims going out into the night despite what they knew to be the danger.

The quick slash of the knife, it must have been from behind, and then the arranging of the body to shock, to frighten. To mislead.

"I *am* mad." The words echoed against the walls. She heard the rain drumming against the roof of the chapel. Dear St. Margaret's, strong, enduring, unchanged despite everything. And in the graveyard outside, her brother, his father's son . . .

After your father, she never felt the same for me.

You are just like your mother, blinded by your feelings for a man.

The seed . . . in all of them . . .

"Mother Eldgythe knew."

Aveline spoke the words out loud even as she had to Wulfgarth only the day before. Of all those who could have known the location of Magnus's camp, she had given the least thought to Mother Eldgythe. She must have known, for she would not have allowed such a message to come into the abbey without being informed about it herself.

Yet that proved nothing. Any more than the coincidence of the trips to London was proof. Nothing at all.

Aveline got up and walked, not quickly but without hesitation, out of the chapel. The passageway was empty, all the good sisters being at their evening meal. The abbess's house was only a short distance from the chapel. A light shone through the cracks in the shutters that covered one of the ground-floor windows.

Mother Eldgythe should also have been at supper, but perhaps after the tragic events of recent days, she preferred to be alone. That was it undoubtedly. Aveline would speak with her for a few moments, apologize for the intrusion, and go.

She would—

"Aveline must leave and you will let her go without recriminations. She loves you, you see, and she has already been hurt far too much. You will say nothing except to wish her well."

The voice was Renard's. He spoke firmly, as though stating demands that could not be challenged.

Mother Eldgythe laughed harshly. "I will see you burn in hell before I let her go to you willingly, Norman. She is all I have left. No one will take her from me."

"She does not belong to you," Renard said. "Be sensible. Let her go with her love for you undamaged."

They were standing in the small corner chamber that Mother Eldgythe used as a receiving room. There she could find a few minutes' release from the demands of her high office, read her missal, and when necessary meet with sisters—or with guests—in private.

"What do you know of love?" she demanded. "You men are all alike—Norman, English, it makes no difference. You think only of your own lusts and dare to call it love. But Aveline is different. She belongs here, where I can keep her safe forever."

"That isn't going to happen," Renard insisted. "She is leaving with me. If you make trouble over this, if you cause her any more pain, I promise you will regret it."

"Threats?" the abbess scoffed. "You are wasting your time. There is nothing you could threaten me with that would make the least difference."

"Oh, no?" His voice dropped, becoming low and hard. "Within a few weeks after the battle of Hastings, Odo came here to Canterbury. He liked what he saw and he wasted no time seizing lands for himself. That's how he got the manor he has now. St. Margaret's was next, he intended to install a Norman abbess and claim overlordship of the abbey for himself. But before that could happen, you went to him. You offered loyalty and cooperation. In return for the names of English in the neighborhood who were likely to be rebellious—English who were then rounded up and killed—you were allowed to retain your position. You've never stopped cooperating with him since. You even went so far as to betray Magnus to him. That's how Rufus learned the location of Oath Bearer's camp. You are directly responsible for his death."

"I see," Mother Eldgythe said slowly. She stood up stiffly, smoothing her robe, and walked over to a small table set against the wall. "I've underestimated you, Norman. Perhaps we should talk, after all."

"There is little to say," Renard replied. "I told you what I want. Let Aveline go without difficulty."

"You understand that I am concerned only out of love for her? But I admit, perhaps I am too narrow in my thinking. You are an unusual man and she does seem to care for you."

The abbess smiled. "Have a little of this good Rhenish wine with me and let us discuss it."

Renard hesitated. He wanted to be done and gone so that he could look for for Aveline. Burgess said he had left her in the chapel. She shouldn't be alone. But Mother Eldgythe had sheltered and protected the woman he loved. He could at least spare a few minutes to listen to her.

"Oh, dear," she said, "I've misplaced the cups. Would you mind checking there in the cabinet?"

He turned to do as she asked. His back was to her. The evening air was cool through the thin tunic he wore. He heard or rather felt a movement—

"*No!*"

Renard whirled. The cups fell and shattered on the

flagstone floor. Mother Eldgythe was directly behind him, a knife held clenched in her hand. But she was not alone. Aveline had hold of her and was trying desperately to wrestle the knife away.

Renard raised his right arm, bent at the elbow, in a quick, chopping motion that knocked the knife from Mother Eldgythe's hand. At the same time he pushed Aveline to the side and wrapped both his arms around the struggling woman, subduing her.

When she lay panting on the floor, he demanded, "Why would she do this?"

Fighting for breath, Aveline said, "It's because of Odo, it's got to be. You found out that she betrayed the English. She hated my father and blamed him for everything that happened to my mother. To betray his people, even his son, must not have seemed wrong to her."

Renard bent slowly, his eyes on Mother Eldgythe. Her eyes were closed, her skin pale; she appeared to be in a swoon. He lifted the knife and studied it carefully.

"This is a killing blade." He ran a finger over it before setting it aside. "Honed to razor sharpness. Why would she have such a thing?"

"I don't know," Aveline said. "But I am afraid—" She stopped and knelt down beside the abbess. Her hands shook as gently she smoothed the iron-gray hair exposed where the veil had fallen away.

"Tell me you didn't," she pleaded. "The trips to London, the deaths, tell me you had nothing to do with them."

Renard stiffened. He stared at Aveline in disbelief. "What are you saying?"

"All the killings happened while we were in London. The victims went out into the night with their killer even after the murders had begun and they should have been more cautious. But who wouldn't go with a woman, especially a nun?" She looked up at him, her face twisted with grief. "Don't you see? They didn't think she could be dangerous. It never occurred to them. You didn't think so either. You had your back turned to her. In another instant she would have had the blade in you."

"My God," Renard murmured. "Can this be true?" He bent down beside Aveline, not touching the abbess but staring at her intently.

Mother Eldgythe's eyes opened. The pupils were pinpoint size, hard and black. She glanced from him to Aveline and back again.

"Don't look at me like that. I had no choice." She spoke quickly, the words running together. "Lagounier found out what I was doing. He came to me, extorting money. I paid, but he would have told eventually, I knew he would. He had to die. I lured him out into the dark with some tale of an accident. He was stupid enough to believe me and he never even saw the knife coming. He died without a sound."

She drew breath, a sobbing sound in the small, quiet room. Rain continued to fall.

"It was so much easier than I'd expected, but it wasn't enough. Lagounier knew LeMeux. He could have told him, so he had to die, too. But then I remembered seeing Valerian and LeMeux talking once when we were at Thorney. They were laughing together and I thought, what if he told him? I had to kill Valerian, too, but it still wasn't enough. De Courcy was his lover, I was sure they'd talked. I couldn't leave him alive." She shook her head numbly. "Don't you see? I had no choice."

Renard made no reply, but his face said all.

"Don't hurt her," Aveline pleaded. "There is a sickness in her. She needs care."

Slowly he stood and drew Aveline with him. She clung to him, her face pressed tight against his broad chest. This woman—proud, beautiful, born of the fire—had the courage to answer even the greatest sorrow with compassion. Truly a king's daughter.

"All right," he murmured, "I understand. We'll go to Lanfranc. He'll find a place where she can be kept and live out the remainder of her years."

Mother Eldgythe made a sound deep in her throat. In the depths of her madness, she heard them. They turned to look, but it was too late. She half raised herself, scrabbling for the knife left on the table. The blade flashed in her hand in the instant before she buried it deep in her own heart.

Epilogue

Aveline straightened slowly. Her back was stiff, but she was still glad to be out in the fresh spring air. Daisies and small wild roses bloomed at her feet. She smiled as she thought what Magnus would make of them.

It was very peaceful in the graveyard behind St. Margaret's, but she had no inclination to linger. The chore of weeding done, she was returning to the guest house when she saw Renard coming toward her.

Her husband was not alone; Lanfranc was with him. The archbishop smiled as he saw Aveline.

"My lady," he said, "how fare you?"

"Probably better than I should," she said. Her hand rested on her swollen belly. "The babe kicks mightily."

Renard gave her a fond look as he said, "Are you surprised?"

She met his gaze with such unabashed love, mirroring his own, that discretion required Lanfranc to look away.

The archbishop cleared his throat. "I hope you don't mind my coming by?"

"Not at all," Aveline said sincerely, "we are always glad to see you." Lanfranc had married them shortly after Mother Eldgythe's death. He had never referred to the murders or the abbess's betrayal of her fellow English. But he took a special interest in Aveline's well-being and, for that matter, in Renard's.

"I've just come from seeing Rufus off," Lanfranc said as together they walked to the guest house where Renard and Aveline had been living since their marriage. St. Margaret's had a new abbess, a sensible Norman woman as far removed from Mother Ursuline as it was possible to imagine, who had managed to make all the sisters feel both safe and welcomed under her guidance. For that and so much more, Aveline was infinitely grateful.

"He's off to Normandy," the archbishop continued with unmistakable satisfaction. "Apparently he decided those nasty rumors that were circulating about him contemplating rebellion needed to be squashed in person. He's gone to assure his father of his undying loyalty."

Renard shook his head wryly. "Poor William."

Lanfranc laughed. "By the way, he gave me a message for you before he left. Said he was sorry for any misunderstanding that might have arisen between you two. He thinks you do an exemplary job and intends to tell his father so."

"Why would he do that?" Aveline asked.

"Because all evidence to the contrary, Rufus is no fool. Someday he'll be king, and when he is, he'll need men like Renard on his side. He won't take any further risk of upsetting that."

"Good thing," Renard murmured. He stood aside to let Aveline enter the guest house first.

"So," Lanfranc said when they were all settled on the covered porch overlooking the gardens, "what are your plans now?"

"We'll stay here until after the babe is born," Renard said. "After that, William wants me to return to London to supervise the rebuilding."

"You'll do an excellent job, I'm sure," Lanfranc said. He hesitated a moment, eyeing them both. "Speaking of excellent jobs, do you think I might see it?"

Renard and Aveline exchanged a glance. "It?" she asked innocently.

"Don't tease an old man. The tapestry, all that damn Odo talks about. He says it's ready, that you're going to be sending it off any day. Before you do, might I see it?"

"If you wish," Aveline said slowly, for she could hardly refuse him. With the men following, she led the way upstairs to the small solar on the second floor of the guest house.

"I have it here for wrapping," she explained. "The messengers will come for it tomorrow."

Lanfranc bent over the heavy scroll of linen. He unwound the first few feet and gazed at them attentively. Renard and Aveline stood back a little to give him more room as slowly he unwound the rest, foot by foot, studying every detail of it.

At length he straightened and sighed with pleasure. "Magnificent. A work to endure for eternity. I knew it would be."

"You don't find anything . . . unusual about it?" Renard asked cautiously.

"Of course I do," Lanfranc said, smiling. He looked at Aveline gently. "It's unique, a true work of art. You've done Odo proud, my dear, and don't think he won't know it. A man of his intellect and perception can't fail to appreciate what you've achieved. Why, I can hear him now, bragging to all and sundry about how he gave you the commission and look at the incredible results."

"And what about William?" Aveline asked. Her hand crept into Renard's. The risk was so great, but the truth had to be told.

"He'll say: Thank you, and no, you still can't be pope."

"And when he looks at it?" she pressed.

Lanfranc shook his head. Softly he said, "He won't look at it, child. He can't bring himself to." He touched a hand to the linen with gentle wonder. "No, it will be left to others to understand all this . . . men struggling for a great prize and the lengths they would go to win it."

"Tell me," he added as he turned away from the tapestry, "are you working on anything else?"

"A book," Renard said promptly, for he was quite proud of the notion. "She's writing a book."

Lanfranc's eyebrows rose. "Really? Extraordinary. What sort of book?"

"Prayers," Renard said helpfully. "Isn't it?"

Aveline hesitated. "Not exactly and it's only a small thing, hardly worth talking about."

"Perhaps you'll let me see it sometime."

"Perhaps," she murmured noncommittally, but in her mind was the thought that the book, too, was something for others to understand.

"The sisters baked honey cakes this morning," she said. "Why don't we go see if there are any left?"

Arm in arm with her husband, she went out into the bright day. The archbishop lingered, gazing a little longer at the scenes immortalized in meticulous, tiny stitches, the devotion of anonymous women whose own courage would never be known.

Then he remembered the honey cakes and went after them.

⸬ Afterword ⸬
The Mystery of
the Bayeux Tapestry

The masterpiece of English needlework known to history as the Bayeux Tapestry depicts in vivid detail one of the most important events in the history of Western civilization, the Norman Conquest of England.

Three sections of this book—The Journey, The Oath, and The King is Dead—include events actually shown in the tapestry in order to give the reader a sense of its scope and richness. A fourth, Long Live the King, includes events from the aftermath of the battle of Hastings that may—or may not—have originally been part of the tapestry. Time, use, and possibly other unknown forces appear to have caused the final scenes to become lost. As it exists now, the tapestry ends abruptly with the pursuit of the defeated English from the battlefield near Hastings.

Although this book presents certain explanations for the events depicted in the tapestry, it should be noted that they are the author's personal conjectures and conclusions. Debate continues about the reason for Harold's journey to Normandy (and indeed when exactly it occurred), the oath he may or may not have taken there, the disposal of the English throne following King Edward's death, and the aftermath of the battle of Hastings.

However, there is now general agreement about many important aspects of the tapestry, including that it was made by English needlewomen for whom the Conquest was a living memory. References to particular individuals who fell in and out of favor place its creation between 1076 and 1082. Further it is understood that the work was created for the Conqueror's half brother, Bishop Odo, and supervised by someone familiar with the illustrated manuscripts in the inventory of Christ Church, Canterbury, as shown here.

For centuries, the tapestry has been the source of much bewilderment and debate as efforts were made to understand the seeming errors and inconsistencies that occur throughout it. Not until recent decades have scholars come to a new, much fuller, and ultimately far more exciting understanding of what the tapestry actually represents.

Within the seventy-five scenes that now make up the tapestry, a handful of Englishwomen made a valiant attempt to set the record straight. Against overwhelming odds, they preserved for posterity a subtle but unmistakable version of the Conquest that is sharply in contrast with what the Normans wanted the world to believe. And they did it before the very eyes of their conquerors.

The question is who was the daring artist who actually drew the scenes for the tapestry and guided the needlewomen at their work? The artist who turned a monument to military victory into a testament to personal courage that nine centuries later still fascinates and inspires?

Admittedly I have taken liberties in imagining who might have been responsible. Harold Godwinson did have two daughters by his handfast wife, Edythe of the Swan's Neck. But there is no evidence that either of them was involved in the creation of the Bayeux Tapestry. Aveline is, as she rightly should be, a fictional character.

In numerous other ways, however, I have adhered with a bare minimum of poetic license to what is known of the actual events of the time. For instance, the *Anglo-Saxon Chronicles,* one of the principal sources of information about these times, tell us that the spring and summer of 1077 were unusually dry. Crops failed, wildfires were common, and finally, in August, much of London burned.

William was in Normandy fighting his eldest son, Robert Curthose, who had rebelled against him. There is no direct evidence to suggest that in his absence his other son, William Rufus (called here simply Rufus to differentiate him from his father) tried to seize power in England, but such an act would have been consistent with his unpleasant character. Whatever else can be said about him, William was not fortunate in his sons.

The Conqueror died in 1087. In the last decade of his life, he visited his great prize only twice. Events in Normandy and perhaps growing disenchantment with his stubbornly rebellious subjects kept him from England. Rufus succeeded him and ruled for thirteen years; history records him as one of the worst kings Britain has ever known. He died under mysterious circumstances in August of 1100.

There has been serious conjecture that his murder was a rite of pagan sacrifice intended to rescue the country from yet another drought, a rite to which Rufus himself agreed in advance. Such self-sacrifice seems uncharacteristic of him. But the notion of a pagan ritual being carried out at the highest levels of English government in so relatively recent a time does have a certain appeal, enough to inspire the fictional series of "pagan slayings" that terrorize the London of my imagination during the hot, dry summer of 1077.

The existence of the Bayeux Tapestry was not recorded, so far as we know, until 1476, when mention is made of it being displayed in the cathedral at Bayeux in Normandy. It was understood to be centuries old, but already many questions and misconceptions had arisen about its origins and meaning. Not until 1729 did the tapestry come to general notice, beginning the tide of studies, analyses, claims, and counterclaims that continue to swirl around it.

For those interested in such things, the tapestry consists of eight panels of linen only twenty inches high but stretching two hundred and thirty feet in length. Since the eighteenth century the linen has been attached to a second length of material apparently added as backing in order to give additional strength. The original fabric is a fine tabby weave with eighteen to nineteen threads per centimeter, not very different from linen used in needlework today. Seven principal colors can be identified—terra-cotta, blue green, gold, olive green, blue, dark blue or black, and sage green. The embroidery was done in laid and couched work using stem and outline stitches. A remarkable facet of the tapestry, at least to modern practitioners of needlework, is the familiarity of the stitches. So similar are they to what is now commonly used that sections of the tapestry can be readily reproduced by those wishing to do so.

Today the tapestry is guarded with meticulous care by the government of France. With a minimum of good fortune, it will continue to exert its unique blend of historical fact and mystery for generations to come.

COMING NEXT MONTH

MORNING COMES SOFTLY by Debbie Macomber

A sweet, heartwarming, contemporary mail-order bride story. Travis Thompson, a rough-and-tough rancher, and Mary Warner, a shy librarian, have nothing in common. But when Travis finds himself the guardian of his orphaned nephew and niece, only one solution comes to his mind—to place an ad for a wife. "I relished every word, lived every scene, and shared in the laughter and tears of the characters."—Linda Lael Miller, bestselling author of *Daniel's Bride*

ECHOES AND ILLUSIONS by Kathy Lynn Emerson

A time-travel romance to treasure. A young woman finds echoes of the past in her present life in this spellbinding story, of which *Romantic Times* says, "a heady blend of romance, suspense and drama . . . a real page turner."

PHANTOM LOVER by Millie Criswell

In the turbulent period of the Revolutionary War, beautiful Danielle Sheridan must choose between the love of two different yet brave men—her gentle husband or her elusive Phantom Lover. "A hilarious, sensual, fast-paced romp."—Elaine Barbieri, author of *More Precious Than Gold*

ANGEL OF PASSAGE by Joan Avery

A riveting and passionate romance set during the Civil War. Rebecca Cunningham, the belle of Detroit society, works for the Underground Railroad, ferrying escaped slaves across the river to Canada. Captain Bradford Taylor has been sent by the government to capture the "Angel of Passage," unaware that she is the very woman with whom he has fallen in love.

JACARANDA BEND by Charlotte Douglas

A spine-tingling historical set on a Florida plantation. A beautiful Scotswoman finds herself falling in love with a man who may be capable of murder.

HEART SOUNDS by Michele Johns

A poignant love story set in nineteenth-century America. Louisa Halloran, nearly deaf from a gunpowder explosion, marries the man of her dreams. But while he lavishes her with gifts, he withholds the one thing she treasures most—his love.

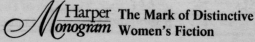 **Harper Monogram** The Mark of Distinctive Women's Fiction

ANALISE

Analise Caldwell was the reigning belle of New Orleans. Disguised as a Confederate soldier, Union major Mark Schaeffer captured the Rebel beauty's heart as part of his mission. Stunned by his deception, Analise swore never to yield to the caresses of this Yankee spy...until he delivered an ultimatum.

ROSEWOOD

Millicent Hayes had lived all her life amid the lush woodland of Emmetsville, Texas. Bound by her duty to her crippled brother, the dark-haired innocent had never known desire...until a handsome stranger moved in next door.

BONDS OF LOVE

Katherine Devereaux was a willful, defiant beauty who had yet to meet her match in any man—until the winds of war swept the Union innocent into the arms of Confederate Captain Matthew Hampton.

LIGHT AND SHADOW

The day nobleman Jason Somerville broke into her rooms and swept her away to his ancestral estate, Carolyn Mabry began living a dangerous charade. Posing as her twin sister, Jason's wife, Carolyn thought she was helping her gentle twin. Instead she found herself drawn to the man she had so seductively deceived.

CRYSTAL HEART

A seductive beauty, Lady Lettice Kenton swore never to give her heart to any man—until she met the rugged American rebel Charles Murdock. Together on a ship bound for America, they shared a perfect passion, but danger awaited them on the shores of Boston Harbor.